SHADOW RIDER

BLOOD SKY AT MORNING
— AND —
APACHE SUNDOWN

By Jory Sherman

Shadow Rider

BLOOD SKY AT MORNING
APACHE SUNDOWN
GHOST WARRIOR

THE BARON HONOR
BLOOD RIVER
THE VIGILANTE
TEXAS DUST
THE BARON WAR
THE BRAZOS
ABILENE GUN DOWN
THE SOUTH PLATTE
VISIONS OF A LOST GIRL
CHILL #1: SATAN'S SEED
CHILL #2: SEPULCHRE

SHADOW RIDER

BLOOD SKY AT MORNING

— AND —

APACHE SUNDOWN

JORY SHERMAN

𝒲𝓂

WILLIAM MORROW

An Imprint of HarperCollinsPublishers

SHADOW RIDER: BLOOD SKY AT MORNING. Copyright © 2007 by Jory Sherman.

SHADOW RIDER: APACHE SUNDOWN. Copyright © 2007 by Jory Sherman. All rights reserved. Printed in the United States of America. No part of this book may be used or reproduced in any manner whatsoever without written permission except in the case of brief quotations embodied in critical articles and reviews. For information, address HarperCollins Publishers, 195 Broadway, New York, NY 10007.

First William Morrow mass market printing: November 2018

Print Edition ISBN: 978-0-06-287891-5

Cover design by Nadine Badalaty
Cover illustration by Paul Stinson

William Morrow and HarperCollins are registered trademarks of HarperCollins Publishers in the United States of America and other countries.

18 19 20 21   QGM   10 9 8 7 6 5 4 3 2 1

CONTENTS

SHADOW RIDER

BLOOD SKY MORNING

For Arlie Weir

1

Zak Cody cut sign that morning just after he passed Dos Cabezas. The tracks were both disturbing and puzzling. There was blood, too, mixed in with the dirt and the rocks. At least six men, he figured, on unshod ponies, had lain in wait for the stagecoach. There were drag marks, and these led him to a gruesome discovery.

The bodies of two men lay spread-eagled on their backs near a clump of mesquite and cholla. Their throats were cut, gaping like hideous grins. Bluebottles and blowflies crawled over the wounds and clustered on their eyes. The men were hatless and scalped. They wore army uniforms and they had been stripped of their sidearms.

Zak stepped off his horse to examine the dead men more closely. One of them, a young lieutenant with blond fuzz still on his face, had blood on his shirt, a few inches under his armpit. He pulled the shirttail out and saw the wound. It appeared the young man had been stabbed there. The other man wore a sergeant's chevrons on his shirt. He had a dragoon moustache and there were small scars on his face that had long since healed. A fighter, from the looks of him. His nose had been broken at least once in his lifetime, which Zak judged to have been about forty years.

Moccasin tracks all around the bodies. Hard to tell the tribe. Chiricahua maybe. This was their country. The hair on both men's heads appeared to have been pulled back to take their scalps, slit their throats. A few strands around the dollar-size patch where the scalps had been lifted were sticking straight up.

At least one of the men had voided when he died. The young lieutenant, he decided, when he bent over to sniff. He smelled like a latrine. The urine smell stung his nostrils, so they hadn't been dead long. An hour, maybe less.

He set about deciphering the tracks, walking around the wagon's marks where it had stopped. Wagon or stagecoach, he couldn't tell for sure which just then. Six separate sets of horse tracks. Four horses, shod, pulling the wagon or coach. A depression where one body had fallen, close to the side. The driver, probably. On the other side, more marks, indicating a struggle, then another depression a few feet away from the wagon tracks.

Then the wagon had driven off. And it wasn't trailing any of the unshod horses. Who had been driving? Why had he or they been allowed to leave? Was the lieutenant the target? The sergeant? Both? Strange, Zak thought.

He mounted up and continued down the road in the direction the wagon had gone. The pony tracks led off on another tangent. Business finished. Where had they gone? There was no way to tell without following the tracks. And even then, he might not know why they had attacked the wagon, or coach, and why they had just let it drive off. None inside the wagon had stepped down. He had accounted for all the tracks.

Yet someone had escaped.

Why?

Zak touched a hand to his face. Two days of stubble stippled his jaw. The hairs were stiff enough to make a sound like someone scraping a match head across sandpaper. He touched spurs to his horse's flanks and left the smell of death behind.

The wind moved miniature dust devils across the land like dervishes on a giant chess board, with squares painted burnt umber and yellow ochre. Cloud shadows slipped across the rocky outcroppings and small spires like wraiths from some surreal dream, slinking and rippling over the contours of the desolate earth, making the land seem to pulse and breathe. Little lakes shimmered and vanished in the smoke of shadows, only to reappear again farther on in silver curtains that danced enticingly along the old Butterfield Stage route that wound through stone cairns and cactus like the fossilized path of an ancient serpent grown to gigantic size.

Zak Cody licked the black cracks on his lips, shifted the pebble in his mouth from one side to the other. His canteen was empty, all of the water inside him where it could oil his muscles, saturate his tendons. That was the Apache way, not the white man's, who rationed water until he died of thirst, leaving his gaunt skeleton on the desert either through ignorance or an addled mind.

He found the first object beside the trail almost

by accident. A glint of sun, something odd seen out of the corner of his eye. He rode over to see what was glittering so, thinking it a stone veined with mica or quartz. But there was a blue-green cast to it that defied immediate identification. It was small, and might have passed notice on an overcast day.

He reined in the black and dismounted. Stooping down, he picked up the dazzling object, turned it over in his fingers while he stared at it. There was gold on it, too, and he saw that it was a piece of jewelry. Woman's jewelry. The gold band was attached to the precious stone, and there was a pointed shaft through the band. A woman's earring, he determined, before he put it in his shirt pocket. A few feet away, almost hidden from view, he spotted the matching earring. He slid it into his pocket with the other one and climbed back into the saddle.

Now, what would a woman, possibly a refined woman, be doing way out in the middle of nowhere, miles from any sizable town, any town where a fine lady might wear such a fashionable accessory? Ahead, miles away still, was Apache Springs, and beyond that, Fort Bowie. He had seen the wagon tracks, knew how fresh they were, how many horses, four, were pulling it, and how fast they were going. Cody was a tracker, by both habit and training, so he always studied the ground wherever he rode his black gelding, a Missouri trotter, sixteen hands high. He called the horse Nox, knowing it was the Latin word for night.

A hawk floated over the road, dragging its rumpled shadow after it along the ground. It disappeared over a rise and a moment later he heard its shrill *scree scree.* The sound faded into the long silence of the desert, and then he heard only Nox's shod hooves striking the hard ground.

A few moments later, he figured perhaps fifteen minutes had passed, he saw something else that was out of place in such surroundings. A flash of silver light bounced off it in one short streak, almost like a falling star going in the wrong direction, from earth to the heavens. He stopped and picked it up.

A bracelet, of silver and turquoise. Probably Tasco silver, from the way it was wrought, so finely turned, turquoise beads embedded in round casings that clasped them tight. A woman's bracelet, graceful and elegant, such as a refined lady might wear.

Zak crossed and recrossed the ruts in the ground, looking for more cast-off artifacts. Ten minutes later he found a necklace made of silver and turquoise, like the bracelet. He stopped long enough to retrieve it and put it in his pocket before he rode on. He kept his gaze on the broken land, scanning both sides of the road for any sign of movement, judging the age of the tracks, holding Nox to a steady, ground-eating pace, closing the distance between him and the four-wheeled vehicle.

He spat out the pebble when Nox gave a low whicker and his ears stiffened to cones, twisted in a semiarc. Apache Springs was close, he knew, and he began to drift wide of the road, but keeping it in sight. The tracks were very fresh now, and as he topped a small rise, the springs lay below him, a wide spot in the road, deserted except for the small coach that stood off to one side. A woman sat on the seat, alone, her head facing the opposite way. He saw legs move between the horses. A man was checking the traces.

Zak rode toward the coach, his hazel eyes narrowed to thin dark slits. They flickered with little flecks of gold and light brown, specks of magenta. The man emerged from between the horse's legs, and the woman turned and stared straight at him. A hand went up to her mouth and she stiffened on the seat.

"Ho there," Zak called as he rode down to the springs, wending his way through the ocotillo and prickly pear. There was a legend painted on the side of the coach: FERGUSON'S STAGE AND FREIGHT COMPANY. Underneath, in smaller letters: HAULING, PASSENGER SERVICE. And, in still smaller letters: *Hiram Ferguson, Prop.* Zak had seen such before. Ferguson operated out of Tucson, ran lines down to Bisbee, over to Vail and up to Safford. He sometimes connected with freight out of Tucson, since he went places nobody much wanted to go in that part of the country.

The man stepped away from the horses. He was wearing a linen duster, pale yellow in color, and his hat brim was folded to a funnel that shielded his eyes.

"Howdy, stranger," the man said. "See any hostiles?"

Zak looked at the woman, then back at the man. Suspicion crept through his mind like some small night creature, sniffing, probing, twitching its whiskers. Something about the way the man was standing, the way he held his arms out, slightly bowed, away from his sides. And the woman, just in that brief glance, seemed paralyzed with fear. Fear was something Zak could almost smell, as if it gave off a scent, more subtle than sweat but as distinctive as fumes from a burning match.

"Hostiles?" Zak slowed his horse, halted it a few feet from the man, the coach, the cowering woman.

"You know. Apaches. We run into a hell of a patch back there."

The man inclined his head in the direction that the coach had come from. Zak noticed he didn't lift a hand to point a finger.

"No," Zak said. "I saw no Apaches."

"Well, they's about."

Zak reached into his pocket, fingered the bracelet. He pulled it out, dangled it like bait on a hook from his left index finger. He looked straight at the woman.

"You lose this?" he said.

The woman uttered a small breathy "Oh," and her face drained of color. She glanced quickly at the man on the ground, the man in the duster, standing at the head of the four horses.

"She didn't lose nothin'," the man said, and he glanced up at the woman. The look he gave her was so quick it might have escaped notice from the average person. But Zak caught it. He caught the warning, the puzzlement. "Well, now, she might have," the man said. "Where'd you find it?"

"I asked *her*," Zak said, his voice flat as a leaf spring.

Zak moved the bracelet up and down. Lances of bright light shot from its faceted surface as he twirled it to catch the sun.

"Or maybe you lost this," Zak said, fishing one of the earrings from the same pocket. "Or this, the other one." He held up the second earring.

The woman rubbed her wrist. It was paler than the rest of her skin, a place where a bracelet might have been worn. Then she touched her neck.

Zak put the other pieces back in his pocket, pulled out the necklace. He dangled it like some gewgaw he was hawking, his gaze taking in both the man and the woman.

"Pretty, ain't it?" he said in an exaggerated drawl, as if he were some backwoods drummer bent on a sale.

"None of them's hers," the man said, stepping away from the horses, into the open. He kept his feet apart in a belligerent stance.

"Mister, you seem to be doing all the talking. Is the lady deaf and dumb?"

The man brought his hands back, brushing the duster away from his pistol grips. He wore two guns, like some drugstore cowboy. He bent slightly into a menacing crouch.

"You take your jewelry and ride on," the man said. "The lady ain't interested."

"Here, you take it," Zak said, and tossed the necklace into the air. It made a high arc, and the man reached up to grab it.

Zak climbed down from his saddle just as the man caught the necklace. He stood facing the man.

"Think you're pretty smart, don't you?" the man said.

Zak said nothing. He stood straight and level-eyed, staring at the man.

"I think that necklace belongs to the lady," Zak said.

"I think you're full of shit, mister."

The man dropped the necklace onto the ground. His hands hovered like a pair of hunting hawks above his pistols, a pair of converted Navy Colts.

"You'll want to think about drawing those pistols," Zak said, making no move toward his own, a Walker Colt converted from percussion to center-fire.

"Why is that?"

"Because," Zak said, "I'm the quicksand under your feet."

The man's eyes widened, then flashed with anger.

His hands dove for his pistols.

Zak's right hand streaked down toward his own holster.

The man's hands grasped the butts of his pistols. He started to draw them from their holsters. He seemed fast.

An eternity winked by in a single split second and Zak's Walker cleared leather. A *snick-click* as he hammered back, the sound cracking the silence like the first rattle of a diamondback's tail.

Zak held his breath, squeezed the trigger. The Colt bucked in his hand as it exploded with orange flame, belching out golden fireflies of burnt powder and a .44 caliber lead slug that slammed into the man's chest just as the muzzles of his pistols slid free of their holsters.

A crimson flower blossomed on the man's chest. His breastbone made a crunching sound as the ball smashed into it like a thousand-pound pile driver.

He dropped to his knees. His hands went slack and the pistols slid from his grasp and hit the ground. He opened his mouth to speak, and blood enough to fill a goblet gushed from his mouth.

He never took another breath and pitched forward, dead weight succumbing to gravity.

The woman let out a short cry.

A thin tendril of gray smoke spooled from the barrel of Zak's gun, scrawling in graceful arabesques before the wind shredded it to pieces that vanished like some sleight-of-hand illusion.

Zak reached down and picked up the necklace, held it up so the woman could see it.

"This yours?" he said, his voice as soft as kid leather.

The woman's eyes rolled back in their sockets and she slumped down on the seat in a sudden swoon.

2

Zak holstered his pistol, climbed up onto the seat of the old Concord. The woman lay on her back, her eyes closed, her face drained of color, a grayish tint around her lips. She was a beautiful young woman, with coal black hair, a patrician nose, fine structure to her cheekbones and jaw. Her lips were full and lightly rouged, and her cheeks bore a faint tint of vermillion, just enough to enhance her smooth, unblemished skin.

Zak straddled her, took her chin in one hand. He leaned down and blew gently on her face, then placed his hands on her shoulders and shook her.

"Ma'am, ma'am," he said, his voice low, slightly husky.

Her eyelids fluttered, then opened, closed quickly again.

The sun splashed on her pale face. She wore no bonnet and a strand of hair drooped over her forehead like a brown tassel. She wasn't down deep, he decided. Just floating beneath the surface of wakefulness. Maybe afraid to free herself from the darkness. Afraid of what she might see, of what might happen to her if she opened her eyes and kept them open.

"Miss," he said. "You can come to, ma'am. I'm not going to hurt you."

Her eyelids quivered. It was almost like a little spasm, a trembling manifested only on that part of her anatomy. As if, somewhere down where she was, she wanted to swim up, step from the dark ocean into the blinding sun. He wasn't touching her, just straddling her, one knee on the floorboard for balance, the other leg pressing against the seat. He touched her face, smoothed his fingers down one cheek as if stroking her back to life in the gentlest way.

Her eyelids stopped quivering. Then they batted open and her blue eyes fixed on his face. He held up a hand to shield the sun from beaming down into her eyes. A shadow painted that part of her face.

"You got to wake up, ma'am," he said. "Might be time you told me what happened on this coach."

She closed her eyes, then quickly opened them again. Wider this time, as if she were alarmed, perhaps afraid. He eased away from her, scooted up on the far side of the seat. The sun struck her in the eyes and she winced, turned her head so the light no longer blinded her.

"Did you . . ."

"Did I what?"

"Kill that man. Jenkins."

"He played the card."

"Played the card?" She put one hand on the seat and pulled herself into a sitting position on the floorboards. She pulled the strand of hair away from her face, tucked it away in the folds of her hair.

"He called it. Opened the ball."

"You mean he . . ."

"It's not hard to figure out. You saw him. He had two pistols he wanted to draw on me pretty bad. It could have been me down there on the ground."

"He's dead? Jenkins?"

"Yes. If you mean that man on the ground there. I didn't know his name."

"He was driving me to Fort Bowie when we were attacked by some Apaches."

"Did you see the Apaches?"

"Yes. Of course. They were all painted. They were brutal."

"Did you see them scalp the two soldiers?"

"Yes. It was horrible. They—They cut their throats first."

"I've never known the Apaches to take scalps," he said. "Are you sure they were Apaches?"

"Mr. Jenkins said they were."

"When did he say this? When they attacked, or after they had left?"

"I—I don't recall. I think he said it when they rode up and he stopped the coach."

"Did you hear the Apaches speak?"

"Yes. A few words."

"Have you ever heard Apache speech before?"

She shook her head. "But, I did understand a word or two they said. They spoke Spanish, and I've heard Spanish before."

"Were these men Mexicans trying to look like Apaches?"

She wrinkled up her nose and squinted, as if trying to think. "They might have been. I don't know. It all happened so fast. Or seemed to."

"How come you threw your baubles off the coach?"

He reached into his pocket, drew out the items of jewelry and handed them back to her. She put them in her lap as if reluctant to put them back on her person.

"I—I was afraid of Mr. Jenkins."

"How come? He do something to you?"

"I—well, I can't be sure, of course, but when those Apaches, or Mexicans, dragged Lieutenant Coberly and Sergeant Briggs out of the coach, Mr. Jenkins was just outside. Earl and Fred resisted, of course. Jenkins made a little move. I thought he was holding a knife under his duster and it looked like he jabbed it into Earl's side. Lieutenant Coberly, I mean. It happened so quick. The Apaches shoved Jenkins away, but it looked staged."

"What do you mean?" he asked.

"They, the Indians, weren't very mean to Jenkins. The way they shoved him aside didn't look mean at all. It was just a feeling I got. And, when they didn't kill him, or me, I began to suspect that Jenkins might have known those men with their painted faces."

"Anything else made you think that?"

"Jenkins kept telling me I had to tell the soldiers at the fort what happened. He kept saying, 'those damned Apaches,' over and over. As if he wanted me to bear witness to officials at the army post."

"Why are you going to Fort Bowie?" he asked.

"My brother arranged for me to teach there."

"You're a schoolmarm?"

Customer Receipt*

1st Source Bank

Checking Deposit
Account Number   XXXXXXXXXX0017
Deposit Amount $3,800.00
09/21/2020 10:50 AM EDT
Teller# 143-15559 Seq# 0023 A
Thank you for banking with 1st Source!

"No," she said, "I'm a teacher. Music and English."

"And your brother?"

"He is posted to Fort Bowie. He's a captain in the army."

"Name?"

"Name?"

"His name," Zak said.

"Ted O'Hara. Theodore. I'm his sister. My name's Colleen."

"Can you drive this team?"

She shrank back as if terrified at such a thought.

"No. I couldn't. I wouldn't know what to do."

"Let me tie my horse to the back of the coach. I'll drive you there."

"You have business in Fort Bowie?"

"Maybe," he said. "Look, do you want to ride in the coach, or up here with me?"

She looked at him, as if trying to size him up more thoroughly before making up her mind.

"I think I'd prefer to stay up here," she said. "Why?"

"Because I'm going to pick up those dead soldiers and Jenkins there and take 'em to Fort Bowie. If you ride in the coach, I'll have to carry 'em up there with your baggage." He nodded toward the luggage rack behind him.

"Oh," she said.

Zak hopped down from the coach and tied Nox to the straps on the boot. He slipped his canteen from the saddle horn, walked to the spring, filled it. He drank, then refilled it to the brim. He stoppered it and carried it back to his horse, slung it by its strap to his saddle horn, then strolled over to Jenkins. He reached down and jerked the knife from its scabbard, examined it. There was dried blood on the blade, the color of rust. That would explain the wound he had seen in the lieutenant's side. He shoved the knife back in its scabbard, then picked up the man's pistols and slid them back into their holsters. He lifted the body and carried it to the coach. Jenkins had started to stiffen and he stank from voiding himself. Zak set him down, opened the door, then slid Jenkins's body inside, on the floor, in a sitting position, and closed the door. Then he climbed back up on the seat, picked up the reins, pulled the brake off and turned the team. Colleen never said a word, but sat there tight-lipped and wan, holding onto the side of her seat as she swayed from side to side.

The wood of the floorboards creaked and leather squeaked under the strain and motion of the coach. The wheels spun out a spool of rosy orange dust in its wake, and the wheels clanked against rocks and small stones. The sky was a pale blue, with little white cloud puffs scattered like bolls of cotton across the vast ocean of blue. They hung nearly motionless in the still air, and nothing marred the view until they saw the buzzards circling above the place where the soldiers lay dead.

He saw Colleen cringe when they came to where the coach had been stopped and attacked. He swung the rig in a half circle and brought it to a stop a few yards from the two bodies of the soldiers. Buzzards hopped around the corpses, flapping their wings. Cody set the brake and climbed down.

He walked over to the bodies, and the buzzards

lifted into the air, a half dozen of them, their pinions clawing for purchase to raise their ungainly bodies from the ground, make them airborne.

He picked up Lieutenant Coberly first, carried him to the coach. He lay him down by the door and went back for the sergeant. When he had them both there, he opened the door and placed each body inside, stacked them next to Jenkins in sitting positions. The bodies of the soldiers were stiff, their eyes plucked out, their ears and noses gouged of flesh from the beaks of the scavengers. He closed the door and walked back, studying the unshod pony tracks.

He followed the tracks for some distance, five hundred yards or so, until he was satisfied. The riders had headed off in the direction of Tucson. He couldn't be sure, of course, but it would be unlike any Apache to ride to a white man's town after killing two soldiers. When he returned to the coach, where Colleen was waiting, looking straight ahead and not at him, he climbed back up onto the seat, released the brake.

"Had the . . . had the buzzards . . ." Her voice trailed off.

"You don't want to think about that," he said.

He rippled the reins across the backs of the horses and they stepped out.

She didn't speak to him again until after they had passed Apache Springs.

"You know who I am," she said. "You know my name."

He said nothing.

"I don't know yours."

"No."

"Do you mind telling me who you are? What is your name?"

"Cody."

"Just Cody?"

"Zak Cody."

"Zachary?"

"No, just Zak."

She spelled it: "Z-A-C-H?"

"No. Z-A-K. My father couldn't spell too well."

"Cody," she said. "I've heard that name before. Somewhere. From my brother Ted, I think. Do you know him?"

"No, I don't."

"That's odd. I'm sure he's mentioned you. It'll come to me in a minute."

"It's not important," he said.

"It is to me."

"Why?"

"It might tell me who you really are. You don't talk much."

"When I have something to say, I talk."

"You're not in the army."

"No."

"But you were."

"I was."

"Ah, that's at least something."

"Is it?"

"Why, yes. It explains why you're going to Fort Bowie."

"Does it?"

"Well, I would think so."

Cody said nothing. A cloud passed below the sun, throwing a shadow over the trail. They both listened to the creak and clank of the coach as it rumbled through rough, rocky country that was almost flat and seemingly endless, with only cactus and mesquite to break the monotony.

Cody did not know why Colleen's brother might have mentioned his name, and it wasn't important. But if Ted O'Hara knew who he was, then some of his past might come out and he couldn't help that. A man carried his past with him. It followed him like a shadow.

"General Crook," she said.

"What?" Cody said.

"Were you with General Crook?"

"Yes, I was."

"I remember now. Ted said you saved Crook's life once. Is that true?"

Cody shrugged. "Who knows about such things?" he said. "I won't claim credit for such."

But she looked at him with different eyes now, as she recalled what her brother had said once, when speaking with other officers. Zak Cody, she decided, was no ordinary man. From the tone of Ted's voice, from the obvious respect and admiration implied by what he'd said, Zak Cody was almost a legend. But that was all she knew about him.

And, she wanted to know more.

Much more.

⊷ 3 ⊷

Colonel Crook did not see the Paiutes. The red man rose up off the ground, his naked body covered with earth, and crept up behind him, a war club raised over his head ready to brain the officer. Zak appeared out of nowhere, just as Crook turned and saw the Paiute. Silent as a wraith, Zak grabbed the Indian by the hair, pulled his head back and sliced his neck open with a knife, letting the lifeblood flow until the Indian went limp in his arms, his chest and legs shining red with blood. The kill was quick and merciless, and Crook felt a shiver course up his spine.

The memory of that day had come unbidden, dredged up by Colleen. Zak shook it off, but he knew it would come back. It always did.

He knew she was looking at him, trying to figure him out, perhaps trying to remember all that her brother had said about him. That's the way people were. They all wanted to know your past, as if that was the key to knowing who a man was now. He was not the same man who had fought alongside Crook in his battle with the Paiutes. A lot of water had gone under the bridge since then. But he also knew he was forever bound to General George Crook, as Crook was bound to him.

Over the beige land they rode with their grisly cargo. Low hills, studded with rocks and cactus, appeared on their flanks, looking like ancient ruins, rubble from once majestic cities that rose above the land, then crumbled to dirt and broken stone.

Zak stopped the coach at Apache Springs.

"You might want to drink," he said. "I'm going to water the horses. This is the only water hereabouts."

"Yes," she said. "I am thirsty. And I want to stretch my legs."

He unhitched the horses, leading them one by one to the crystal clear stream to drink. The others, left behind, whickered in anticipation. Colleen cupped her hands, dipped them in the water where it emerged from the rocks, and slaked her thirst. Then she walked over to the oak trees that bordered the stream and took some shade beneath the leafy branches.

Hills rose up on both sides of the long basin that sequestered the sparkling spring. It was a peaceful place, an oasis in the harsh desert where yucca bloomed like miniature minarets. There was cholla, too, beautiful, delicate, and dangerous, prickly pear that the Mexicans called *nopal*, and there, too, grew stool and agave.

"What's that I hear?" Colleen said as Zak led Nox to the stream. "Over there, in the hills."

"Probably Fort Bowie," he said.

"We're that close and you stopped to water the horses?"

"Yes'm."

"We could have watered them at the fort."

"Yeah. Now we don't have to."

She walked over to him, stood in the glaring sun. "With those men in there, you stopped, took all this time."

"They're not going anywhere, ma'am."

"No, but they—they're . . ."

"I don't want a lot of chores to do when we get to the fort."

"Just what is your business at the fort?" There was a demanding tone in her voice.

"Personal."

"I hardly think an army post is the place to conduct personal business."

Nox finished drinking and Zak started walking back to the coach, leading the horse with the reins.

"Ma'am, out here, the army serves as the eyes and ears of the public. They generally know who comes and who goes."

"So, you're looking for someone."

"I'm going to ask about someone, yes."

"I don't think it's your place to use the army for your own personal agenda, Mr. Cody. But I expect they'll tell you that at Fort Bowie."

He hitched Nox to the coach. They could hear voices from the fort. They floated on the vagrant breezes, wafting here and there, fragments of loud conversations that made no sense. A Gambel's quail, sitting atop a yucca some distance from them, piped its call, as if serving notice of its presence to any who would hear. A Mexican jay answered the call with harsh *whenks* from its throat, scolding the quail with its plumed topknot.

"Yes'm," he said, without protest.

"You're a strange man, Zak Cody," she said. "I don't know what to make of you."

"Easy decision, then."

"What?"

"You don't have to make anything of me. I'm what I am. Accept it or reject it."

"Well, so you do have a mind after all," she said.

Zak said nothing. He drew a deep breath and looked around at the ruins of the old fort. There wasn't much left. Wind and rain and neglect had pretty much wiped out all traces of the original Fort Bowie. The desert took back everything that was left to it. That's one thing he liked about the desert. It treated civilization harshly. People passed through it at their own risk.

"What are you looking at?" she asked, following his gaze.

"The fort used to be here," he said. "Do you know the story?"

"No."

"There was a big fight here, back in 'sixty-two, during the War Between the States. Chiricahua Apaches and United States troops."

"I didn't know that. What happened?"

"It was July, and Captain Tom Roberts got ambushed here. Chiricahuas. He was coming from California to fight the Confederate invasion of New Mexico. He lined up his mountain howitzers and blasted the Apaches. Scared hell out of them."

"You were here?" she said.

Zak shook his head. "No, but I heard about it."

"I think we've wasted enough time here, Mr. Cody."

He helped her onto the coach, took his seat beside her. A few minutes later they reached the fort, beyond the pass. It lay in a saddle in the mountains, east of Apache Springs. There were a lot of buildings, some made of adobe, some of stone, others, frame dwellings, made from lumber. A steam pump pulled water from a well. A flagpole stood in the center of the ramada, its banners flapping in the breeze.

"So, this is Fort Bowie," Colleen said.

"This is the second Fort Bowie. Troops have only been here since 'sixty-nine, so it's still pretty new."

He pulled the coach up in front of the corrals and stables. A corporal came out to greet them.

"Howdy, ma'am," he said, "welcome to Fort Bowie." Then he looked at Zak.

"Where's the regular driver," the young man asked. "Jenkins?"

"He's in the coach," Zak said.

"What's he doin' in the coach?" The young man's face scrunched up in genuine puzzlement.

"Nothing," Zak said.

"Huh?"

The corporal walked over to the side door and opened it. He jumped back in surprise.

"Holy shit," he said.

"Mr. Cody," Colleen said, "will you escort me to meet the post commander?"

"Sure," Cody said. He spoke to the corporal. "That black horse, rub him down and grain him, will you, soldier?"

"Wh-What about what's in the coach? Those men are dead, ain't they?"

"Yes."

"Shit, I got to report this."

Zak walked back to his horse, slid the rifle from its scabbard and lifted his saddlebags from behind the cantle. He patted Nox's withers and walked back to the stunned soldier.

"Can you point out the post commander's office, son?"

"Over yonder. Where you see the flagpole. He ain't in, though. Major Willoughby's acting in his stead. I got to report what's in that coach."

"Do it, then," Zak said.

The corporal ran off toward the guard house, legs pumping, arms flying around in all angles. Zak slung his saddlebags over his shoulder, shifted his rifle to his left hand. He crooked his arm and Colleen slipped her arm in it and they walked toward the large building beyond the parade ground. Soldiers walked here and there, not even mildly curious. Flies buzzed around their heads and the hot sun beat down. The flags flapped on the flagpole, but the air was thick and hot and the breeze brought no cool with it.

A pair of mourning doves whistled overhead, twisting and turning in the air like feathered darts. The sound of a blacksmith's hammer ringing on iron wafted across the compound. The horses hitched to the coach whickered and swatted at flies with their tails. Two soldiers crossed in front of them. Both looked longingly at Colleen, who returned their smiles and gripped Zak's arm even tighter.

Two men stood guard at the entrance to the headquarters building. Both wore sergeant's stripes.

"Miss Colleen O'Hara to see Major Willoughby," Zak said.

"She can go in," one of the men said. "You'll have to show me some papers, sir."

Zak drew out a leather wallet from his pocket, handed it, open, to the sergeant.

"Yes, sir," the man snapped, with a salute. He handed the wallet back to Zak.

They entered the building, where more men stood guard, and walked to one seated at a desk.

"What was that all about, Mr. Cody?" Colleen whispered.

"My identification."

"And you rate a salute? A civilian?"

Zak said nothing.

"Major Willoughby," Colleen said to the clerk. "I'm Colleen O'Hara and this is Mr. Zak Cody."

"Yes'm," the corporal said. "Just one minute."

He left his desk, opened one half of a double door and went inside. A moment later he returned.

"You can go right in," he said. His gaze lingered on Cody for a long moment. Colleen noticed it and frowned.

"Who are you?" she whispered.

"Just who I said I am, Miss O'Hara."

Major Willoughby was a short, fastidious man, who rose up from behind a desk so neat and polished there was but a single paper atop it. There was a map of the territory on the wall behind the desk and a window that sparkled with sunlight, giving a view of the hills and part of the compound. The desk was flanked by an American flag and one bearing the insignia of the Second Cavalry. A man stood in a far corner, his back turned to the room.

"May I see your papers, Mr. Cody?" Willoughby said. "And good afternoon to you, Miss O'Hara. We've been expecting you."

"Thank you, Major," she said.

"Please sit down," Willoughby said to her as he took Zak's wallet and opened it. Zak stood there, looking at the man whose back was turned to him.

"You've got some pay here at the post, Colonel," Willoughby said. "I think Lieutenant John Welch is the paymaster this month. Check with the quartermaster."

"I've got two of your men outside in the coach," Zak said. "They were with Miss O'Hara."

"That would be Sergeant Briggs and Lieutenant Coberly," the major said. "They were her escorts from Tucson. I wonder why they didn't report with you, Colonel."

"Because they're both dead," Colleen said. She shot an odd look at Cody. "Mr. Cody killed the driver, a man named Jenkins."

"What happened?" Willoughby's face had drained of color. It looked as if he'd swallowed a jar of paste and it had oozed out through his pores.

Colleen looked at Zak, but he said nothing.

"We—We were attacked," she said. "I think by Apaches. But Mr. Cody doesn't think they were Apaches."

"Why did you kill Jenkins?" the major asked.

"Because he was going to kill me," Zak said. "Those soldiers were scalped, sir. I don't think Apaches take scalps."

The man in the corner turned around.

"You're right, Cody. They don't. Cochise doesn't anyway, and he's the main thorn in our sides at the moment."

"Colonel Cody," Willoughby said, "shake hands with Tom Jeffords. He's the authority on Apaches in this neck of the woods."

The two men shook hands.

"I've heard of you, Jeffords," Zak said. "General Crook thinks very highly of you."

"I've heard of you, too, Cody, and the same holds for what Crook thinks of you."

"I'd like to see my brother now," Colleen said.

Willoughby froze. His eyes turned to flint.

Jeffords looked at Colleen, his face softening with an expression of concern. "I'm afraid that's not possible, Miss O'Hara," Jeffords said. "That's why I'm here with Major Willoughby. Your brother is missing."

Zak caught her on the way down as Colleen fell into a deep swoon, her legs collapsing beneath her.

"Damn," Willoughby said, his voice a raspy whisper. "If it weren't for the bad news, we wouldn't have any news at all out here."

Zak carried Colleen to a chair, looked at Willoughby.

"I'll get some water," Jeffords said, and left the room.

"Major," Zak said. "Don't call me Colonel. I'm not in the army anymore. You better read those papers in my wallet more carefully."

"But you carry the rank."

"Compliments of President Grant and General Crook, sir. But to you, I'm just an ordinary civilian."

Willoughby gulped and began to read the papers while Zak fanned Colleen's face. It was the second time she had fainted that day. He wondered that the woman could still go on, and how much more she could take before she'd have to be put in the post infirmary.

4

Major Willoughby read the short note attached to the back of Zak's identity card, which listed him as Colonel Zak Cody, U.S. Army, retired.

To Whom It May Concern:

Colonel Zak Cody is hereby detached from the U.S. Army, insofar as his military duties are concerned. He is hereby attached to my office and is under my direct command and the command of General George Crook. He is to be given every courtesy by the U.S. Military. His connection to the President and to General Crook are considered Top Secret and shall not be revealed to any civilian or military personnel who do not need to know his rank and special assignments. Any breach of confidence regarding Colonel Cody shall be dealt with severely, and any military person who divulges the content of this letter will be subject to court-martial.

The letterhead bore the seal of the President of the United States and was signed by Ulysses S. Grant.

Willoughby walked around his desk and handed the wallet to Zak.

"I understand, sir. I'm sorry."

"That's all right, Major. You didn't know. Now you do."

"There are stories about you, you know."

"I know. I ignore them. You should do the same."

"Yes, sir," Willoughby said.

Jeffords returned with a glass of water and a pitcher. He set the pitcher on the desk and handed Zak the water. Together, he and Zak propped Colleen up in the chair. Zak held the glass to her lips and poured a small amount into her mouth.

She swallowed and her eyelids batted twice. She choked on a few drops, spluttered and opened her eyes wide. Sitting up straight, she reached out for Zak. It was a reflexive motion, much like a drowning person deploys toward a rescuer. Her fingers squeezed Zak's arms as she gulped in air.

"I—I'm sorry," she said. "I—I must have fainted."

She saw Jeffords kneeling there before her and her gaze locked on his.

"My brother. Ted. You said . . ."

"He's missing, Miss O'Hara. I'm sorry. I just found out this morning. I came here to report this to Major Willoughby."

"How? Why?"

Jeffords stood up and stepped aside. He gestured to Willoughby, who cleared his throat and walked over to stand in front of her.

"Ted rode out with a patrol early yesterday morning," Willoughby said. "We had reason to believe some Apaches were banding together on the San Simon. The patrol encountered no hostiles, but last night, apparently, your brother turned up missing. Tom ran into the patrol early this morning. They were tracking a small band of Apaches."

"They think Ted was grabbed during the night," Jeffords said. "We don't know why. They took his horse, too, so we know he's still alive."

"The patrol is still out?" Zak asked.

Willoughby nodded.

"They must find him," Colleen said. "Do you think they will, Mr. Jeffords?"

"There's a chance," he said.

Colleen opened her mouth to say something, but decided against it.

Just then a young lieutenant knocked on the door.

"Enter," Willoughby said.

"Sir, you'd better take a look at what we've got out there. It's pretty grim."

"All right, Neighbors. I'll be right there."

"It's in front of the livery, sir."

The young man saluted and left the room.

"Can I stay in Ted's quarters?" Colleen asked.

"No, it's not private," Willoughby said. "We have a billet for you, though."

"I'd at least like to see Ted's room. And my carpetbag's still inside the coach. My suitcase is on top."

"We'll see that you're accommodated, Miss O'Hara. Just let me sort all this out."

"You're right. You have more important things to worry about right now. I'll go with you and get my things."

"I'll see to it that you're shown to your quarters and someone carries your luggage for you."

Willoughby swept past her. Jeffords followed. Zak took her arm and led her outside.

A crowd had gathered in front of the livery. All four coach doors stood wide open. Zak was surprised to see several white women in the crowd. The women all turned to look at Colleen, and some of them smiled at her.

Willoughby and Jeffords looked inside the coach. When the major finished his inspection, his complexion had turned ashen. He looked as if he had been kicked in the stomach. Jeffords took longer. When he turned around, he looked at Zak, shook his head.

"You might want to introduce yourself to the women, Colleen," Zak said. "I'll get your carpetbag and suitcase for you."

"Thank you," she said.

Zak walked over to Jeffords.

"Those men weren't scalped by Apaches," Tom said.

"No. I didn't figure such."

"Let's have a talk, Cody. I know you've got business with Major Willoughby you haven't even mentioned yet, but I want to fill you in on some things."

The two men walked over to the stables, stepped inside where it was cool. Willoughby was issuing orders to the post surgeon and assigning men to burial detail. It was plain to Zak that Willoughby was rattled by what he had seen. Obviously, there was a reason he'd been left in charge of the post. He was probably good at organization, but did not handle himself well under fire. It was something Zak noted when dealing with people, and it often gave him an advantage over men he did not personally know well.

Nox was tied up at the far end of the stables, his bridle replaced by a rope halter. He chomped on corn and oats set before him in a small trough. Other horses stood looking out of stalls, or rubbed up against the walls and posts. There was the sound of switching tails and low whickers as others fed or drank. Flies buzzed in an insistent monotonous drone. The smell of urine and manure, thick and pungent, mixed with the musty scent of straw.

Jeffords slid his hat toward the back of his head, cocking the brim up to show his face, the salt and pepper sideburns. He was a lean, wiry man, with weathered lines in his face, clear blue eyes set wide on either side of his chiseled nose.

"Cody, I'll be straight with you. I'm probably the only one on this post who will. There's a whole lot of war going on in this part of Arizona, and it's not just with the Apaches."

"What are you driving at, Jeffords?"

"That business with the coach, for one. Those soldiers weren't scalped by any Apache."

"I figured that."

"The whites around here want the Apaches wiped out, shipped out, buried, gone. I think this latest incident proves that the situation is coming to a head."

"The army know this?"

"It does and it doesn't. The army is dealing with some marauding Apaches. But the Apaches are being goaded, too, by whites who want the army chasing them clear out of the territory. I'm trying to make peace, but right now it looks pretty hopeless. The Apaches don't know one white man from another, and right now they think the whole world is against them."

"You have a line on who attacked the coach?" Zak asked.

"Your guess is as good as mine, but the owner of the line, Ferguson, is in this up to his armpits. And the word is that he and other businessmen have hired some outside help."

The hackles bristled on the back of Cody's neck.

"Outside help? Maybe from Taos?"

Jeffords's eyebrows arched. His eyes widened in surprise.

"There was some talk about Ferguson bringing in a gang of hired guns from Taos. I was trying to get a line on that news when I got word about Ted O'Hara being sent out on patrol. By that damned Willoughby. That was against my recommendation and directly against Captain Bernard's specific orders."

"Bernard. Reuben Bernard? Isn't he the commanding officer of Fort Bowie?"

"Yeah, he is. Then some idiot sent Major Willoughby down here and put him in charge. Reuben is putting out fires all over the territory, chasing Apaches with a vengeance, attacking their villages, burning their homes. It's an ugly situation. I can't prove it, but someone leaked information about Ted O'Hara, who never should have left this post with a damned patrol."

"Why?"

"Ted has been working with me, under orders from high up, Crook, in fact. He has information about Cochise and other Apache leaders I've been talking to. It's not just chance that he was picked out from that night camp and taken hostage. Someone wants the information he has in that Irish head of his."

"Will O'Hara tell what he knows?"

"Not unless he's tortured beyond endurance. And even then, I think he'd die before he divulged what he knows. He's trying as much as I to bring the Apaches to the peace tent."

"What exactly does O'Hara know?" Zak asked.

"He knows where all the secret camps of the Apache are. He's been to them. With me."

"Did Willoughby know this when he sent O'Hara out on patrol?"

"I think so. He had to know."

"So, do you think Willoughby deliberately sent O'Hara out so that he could be kidnapped?"

There was a silence between the two men. Jeffords squared his hat again. He looked off toward the horseless coach and let out a deep expulsion of breath.

"I hate to think that," he said. "But Willoughby, on his way out here from Tucson, spent time in Vail and Tucson, meeting with the townspeople. They could have gotten to him, persuaded him toward their point of view."

"And what is that?" Zak asked.

"That the Apaches do not want peace and that they can't be trusted. That the U.S. Army should wipe them out like they would a bunch of rattlesnakes. Bernard holds to that view as well, I fear."

"Have you heard talk of a man named Ben Trask?" Zak said.

"Trask. From Taos?"

"Yeah."

"Wait a minute. There was a man killed in Taos, in 'sixty-nine, I think. His name was Cody. Related?"

"My father. Russell Cody. Trask murdered him. And it was 'sixty-eight. I've been tracking him for a good three years."

"Cochise spoke of this man," Jeffords said.

"He did? When?"

"At least a year ago. Cochise's band was accused of wiping out several families, murdering them, burning down their houses. Cochise said a man named Trask was responsible."

"So, Trask has been out here for some time."

"You might learn more in Tucson, or Vail. Cochise tracked him to those two towns after coming across those depredations he was accused of."

Zak's mind filled with thoughts of his father and how he had died at the hand of Ben Trask. Russell Cody had come to Taos to live out his remaining years. When the beaver gave out and the fur trade collapsed, he took his money and bought a ranch in South Dakota, raised cattle and wheat. He drove cattle up from Texas, sold them for good prices, saved his profits. He sold his ranch, moved to Taos, and made even more money as a trader, selling silver in the East and hauling back goods to sell in Santa Fe and Taos.

Cody's father had been trading for gold, as well. He had not trusted the banks, so kept his hoard hidden. Trask had tortured Russell to learn the hiding place, then, after getting the gold, he killed Russell in a most brutal way, mutilating his body, leaving him for the wolves, the coyotes, and the buzzards. Zak envisioned a similar fate for Ted O'Hara if Trask was behind his kidnapping.

"So, I guess I can't trust Willoughby," Zak said.

"If I were you, Cody, I wouldn't trust anybody on this post. Or anywhere else, for that matter."

"Thanks, Tom. You've been a big help to me."

"What are you going to do, Cody? You can't go after these men all alone. They're dead serious and determined to achieve their goals at any cost."

"Desperate men make mistakes," Zak said. "I'll ride to Tucson, see what I can find out. If nothing, I'll go to Vail."

"Dangerous places for someone seeking information about the men behind this scheme to wipe out the Apache."

"Then that's where I have to go. What about you?"

"Right now I'm the only white man who can talk with the Apaches, try to bring peace to this region. I'll talk to that patrol when they come in, see what I can find out about Ted's disappearance."

"If I find out anything, I'll get word to you, here at Bowie."

"Fair enough."

The two men shook hands and walked back to the coach. Willoughby had been staring at them, a scowl on his face. He turned away when they both looked at him.

Zak walked over to Colleen, who had been talking to some of the women.

"I'm going to try and find your brother, Colleen. Just don't tell anyone about it."

"Why?"

"Maybe I'll tell you someday. You take care. Hold on to hope."

"Do you know where Ted is?"

"I'm going to find out. Take care."

He turned and walked up to a soldier.

"Can you direct me to the paymaster's office?" Zak asked.

The soldier pointed to a building.

A half hour later Zak rode out of Fort Bowie, into the setting sun. He felt a great weight lift from his shoulders. He was glad to be away from Willoughby.

But he kept a wary eye on his backtrail, and he bypassed Apache Springs. He took to open country and felt right at home.

5

The tracks were still fresh, clearly visible even in the hazy light of dusk, when Zak's shadow stretched long across the land. It was a place to start. Perhaps this trail would lead him to where he wanted to go, and perhaps it would cross other trails of interest to him.

The clouds in the western sky, long thin loaves, were bronzed, and rays of gossamer light shone like sprayed columns from beneath the horizon. A roadrunner dashed across the unshod pony tracks, legs working like high-speed darning needles. It disappeared among red and golden rocks that were turning to ash on the eastern side. Zak followed the tracks on a northwesterly course, studying them as he rode, wondering about the riders until, after a mile or two, he determined that his hunch had been correct. They were not Apaches.

He found cigarette stubs tossed to one side, barely visible in the fading light. These were hand-rolled. Later, he reined up when he spotted a crumpled piece of paper on the ground. He dismounted, picked it up, and smoothed it out. It was a label from a package of pipe tobacco. The name stamped on the paper was PIEDMONT PIPE TOBACCO.

"Careless," he said to himself. "Or sloppy." He tucked the paper into his pocket and climbed back into the saddle. He did not know who he was following, but he knew damned well the riders were not Apaches.

When it grew too dark to see clearly, he began looking for a place to throw down his bedroll and spend the night. He found a spot partially hidden by stool, chaparral, mesquite, and yucca, rimmed by prickly pear. There was grain in his saddlebags for Nox, and he would chew on jerky and hardtack and make no fire.

He dismounted, hobbled Nox, fed him half a hatful of grain. As he walked around, his spurs went *jing jing,* and he took them off, preserving the silence of evening, allowing him to hear any sounds foreign to that place. He ate and watched the sky turn to ash in the west, felt the cool breeze on his face, sniffed the aroma of the desert's faint perfume as if it were a living, breathing thing that sighed like a pleasured woman.

It was full dark when Zak lay down on his bedroll, unholstered pistol by his side, within easy reach. Bats plied the air, scooping up flying insects, their wings whispering as they passed overhead. A multitude of stars glistened and winked like the lights of a distant town, their sparkles made more brilliant by the inky backdrop of deep space. The moon had not yet risen when he closed his eyes and thought about his father and how he had met his gruesome death.

Ben Trask had used a fireplace poker to burn

Russell's flesh. He had stripped off his prisoner's shirt and pants, applied the red hot iron to his arms and chest. Then he had touched the poker to his father's testicles, as his men looked on and laughed at Russell's screams. When he had found out what he wanted to know, Trask made sure that Russell died a slow death.

He cut open his belly with a surgeon's precision until his father's intestines spilled out in blue-gray coils. Trask and his men had watched his father die, heard him beg for a bullet to his brain. They watched the elder Cody die slowly, his great strength drained from him, his tortured breathing descending to a rasp in his throat before it turned into a final death rattle.

Zak knew all this because a Mexican boy, Jorge Vargas, living next door, had watched it all through his father's window, powerless to help, his family gone to market that morning when the men rode up and entered Russell's adobe home.

From Jorge's description, he knew the man who had killed his father. Their paths had crossed before, in a Pueblo cantina when he and his father had come down from the mountains, following Fountain Creek. Ben Trask had a reputation even then. A hardcase. A gunny who preyed on prospectors and miners, a merciless killer without a trace of conscience.

All in the past, he thought, and no more grieving for his father. Instead, a vow he had made when he found his father's body and learned the story of his death. If there was such a thing as justice in the world, then Russell's death demanded it. An eye for an eye. A life for a life.

Zak folded into sleep, descended to that great ocean of dream where the events of the day were transformed into an odd journey through bewildering mazes inside massive canyons, where guns turned into unworkable mechanisms and people's faces were ever-shifting masks that concealed their true identities, and horses galloped across dreamscapes like shadowy wraiths and every shining stream turned to quicksand beneath the dreamer's awkward and clumsy feet.

It turned cold during the night, and Zak had to pull the wool blanket over him. He awoke before dawn, built a quick fire and boiled coffee. He never looked at the flames and stayed well away from the glow, scanning the horizon, listening for any alien sound. He relieved himself some distance away in a small gully and covered up his sign. He was sipping coffee as a rent appeared in the eastern sky, pouring cream over the horizon until the land glowed with a soft peach light that grew rosy by the time he had finished and put on his spurs. He checked his single cinch and gave Nox a few handfuls of grain, then let him drink water from his canteen, which he poured into his cupped left hand. He checked his rifle and pistol, rolled up his bed and secured it inside his slicker behind the cantle. He did not eat, a habit he had formed long ago. When he went hunting, it was always on an empty stomach.

Gently rolling country now, bleak, desolate, quiet, as the sun rose above the horizon, casting the earth and its rocks and flora into stark relief. The rocks seemed to glow with pulsating color, and the green leaves of the yucca, the pale blossoms, took on a vibrancy that Zak could almost feel. It was the best time of day in the desert, still cool, yet warm with the promise of diurnal life returning to a gray black hulk of territory glazed pewter by the moon, now only a pale ghost in a sky turning blue as cobalt.

He rode over a rise, following the pony tracks, and there it was, nestled in the crotch of a long wide gully that fell away, then rose again several hundred yards from its beginning. An old adobe hut, still in shadow, stood on a high hump of ground, nestled against a flimsy jacal that joined it on one crumbling side. A mesquite pole corral bristled on a flat table some two hundred yards away. Zak counted eight horses in the corral, some with noses buried in a rusty trough, another one or two drinking out of half a fifty-gallon drum, next to a pump outside the corral.

Six of the horses were small, unshod, pinto ponies, actually, while the remaining two were at least fifteen hands high and were shod. They were rangy animals, looked as if they hadn't seen a curry comb or brush, and he could almost count their ribs. None of the horses looked up at him, and Nox didn't acknowledge them with a welcome whinny, either.

A thin scrawl of smoke rose from the rusted tin chimney set in the adobe part of the dwelling. It hung in the motionless air below the gully's rim. It appeared to be coming from an untended fire, possibly one that had been banked the night before. There was no sign of life in either the adobe or the jacal, but Zak knew someone had to be inside. He debated with himself for a moment whether to ride up to the door or walk up and hail the occupant.

It took him only a moment to decide. A man on foot was not of much use in such country. Whoever lived there could be off at a well or hunting jackrabbits for all he knew, and could return at any moment. If he was off his horse, he would be caught flat-footed and might lose Nox. There could be a number of men inside the hut, and more out roaming around.

He rode up to the door without being challenged.

He loosened the Walker Colt in its holster, slid the Henry rifle out of its scabbard a half inch.

"Hello the house," Zak called.

He waited, listening.

Nox's ears stiffened and fixed on the door as they both heard sounds from inside. The sun cleared the lower rim of the gully and shone on the sod roof of the adobe like spilled liquid gold.

"*Quien es?*" a voice called out.

"*Un viajero,*" Zak replied. "*Quiero comprar un caballo.*"

There was a series of shuffling noises from inside the adobe. Then he heard the sound of a latch bar scraping against wood. A moment later the door swung open on creaky leather hinges. An unshaven, unkempt man wearing dirty baggy trousers, huarache sandals, suspenders over a grimy white undershirt, stood in the doorway, his brown eyes blinking in the glare of the sun. He wore a pistol on a worn ammunition belt. The pistol was a Navy Colt converted from cap and ball to percussion. The bullets looked to be .36 caliber. Deadly enough, Zak thought. He wore his holster low, just above his right knee.

"*Caballo? Tu quieres comprar un caballo? Tienes dinero?*"

"I have money," Zak replied in English, "in my pocket. *Habla ingles?*"

"Yes, I speak English. You are a traveler, you say. Where are you going? You do not look like you need a horse. You are sitting on a fine one."

"I need a packhorse. Maybe one of those ponies you have out there in the corral."

The man's eyes shifted in their sockets. "Ah, the pony, eh? You would buy a pony to use for a packhorse?"

"I'm a prospector," Zak lied. "I need to carry some ore to Tucson. That is where I am going."

"Ah, to Tucson? To the assay office? You have found gold?"

"I do not know what I have found."

"Where did you find this?"

Zak cocked a thumb and gestured over his shoulder. The man looked off in that direction, a look of disbelief on his face.

"There is no gold there," the man said, and took a half step backward. His face fell back into shadow. "There is an army fort. Maybe you can buy a horse there. I do not wish to sell the ponies."

"Mister, you step outside where I can see you, or I'll blow your head off as sure as you're standing there."

The Mexican hesitated. His right hand sank toward the butt of his pistol. It hovered there like a frozen bird with its wings spread for a long moment.

"You would draw the pistol on me?" he asked.

"If you don't step out right now. I'll draw so fast you won't even see it."

The man laughed and raised his arms, wiggled them to show that he wasn't going to draw his pistol. He stepped down from the doorway and stood there, looking up at Zak.

"You mean to rob me, then? I have nothing. I am a poor man with only those few horses you see out there."

"Just don't move," Zak said, and swung down from the saddle. He let the reins trail as he walked up close to the man. "What do you call yourself?" he asked.

"I am called Felipe. Felipe Lopez. You will not shoot me, eh?"

"I ask the questions, Felipe."

"Ask me anything. Just do not shoot me. Take the pony. There is no need to kill me over a horse."

"I want to know who those men were. They were riding those ponies yesterday."

"Men? What men? I do not know what you are talking about."

"Don't lie to me, Felipe, or you'll hear a rattle."

"A rattle?"

"Yeah, a rattle. That'll be the rattlesnake you stepped on, and that would be me. That's all you'll hear before I blow your lamp out. I want to know who those men were, who they work for and where they went."

Felipe said nothing for several seconds, as if he were weighing his chances, or trying to think up a good lie for the gringo.

"There were some men," he said. "They rode up here and traded those ponies for six of my good horses. My best horses. They were outlaws, I think. They did not pay me. They rode off. I do not know where they went."

Zak knew the man was lying. He thought he was a pretty good liar. Likely, he'd had a lot of practice.

"That was a good story, Felipe. You ought to thank me."

"Thank you? Why?"

"For letting you stay alive a few more minutes. Now, maybe you can live even longer by telling me the truth."

"That is the truth. I swear it on my mother's honor."

"I doubt your mother has any honor, Felipe. I heard she was a whore."

Felipe's eyes narrowed to slits. The skin of his face stretched taut as his lips compressed, his teeth clenched.

"*Ten cuidado*," Felipe said, his voice a gruff whisper.

Zak looked straight into the man's flashing brown eyes.

"Be careful," Felipe had said in Spanish. And Felipe's body tensed into a coiled spring. He was like a tiger ready to pounce, Zak knew. Like a tiger cornered. He was a man without an ounce of fear. His mother's name had been besmirched by a gringo. There were few insults more scathing than calling a man's mother a whore.

Felipe was ready to fight.

To defend his mother's honor, dubious as that honor might be, Felipe was ready to die.

6

Zak knew how dangerous Felipe had become. He'd just been slapped in the face with an insult so foul and demeaning that it had cut through to the core of the man's being. Few things were more sacred to a man than the woman who had given him life, his mother. Felipe was ready to put his life on the line in defense of the woman who had birthed him.

"All you have to do, Felipe," Zak said, "is tell me the truth and I'll take back what I said about your mother."

"It is too late for that," Felipe said.

"I'll find those men anyway. I do not need to know their names. I do not need you to tell me where they went. I will find them."

Felipe drew back, cocked his head and looked more closely at Zak.

"Who are you?" he said. "What do you call yourself?"

"Cody."

Felipe spewed air through his nostrils.

"Are you the one they call *Jinete de Sombra*?"

"I am sometimes called 'Shadow Rider.'"

"Because you wear the black clothes and ride the black horse."

"No," Zak said. "Because I am like a shadow. I come upon a man with no sound. I am not seen and I am not heard until it is too late."

"Ah, I wondered. You are the Indian fighter. You are the one who rode with the general they call Crook."

"I am the one."

"Then, perhaps you come here to kill Apaches, no?"

"Maybe," Zak said.

"Then you and I, we are on the same side. I, too, would kill Apaches. And the men you seek. They, too, wish all the Apaches killed. Maybe you would like to join them."

"Maybe."

"That is why you hunt them?"

"I wish to talk to them, yes."

"I think they would like to talk to you, Cody."

"Now we are getting somewhere, Felipe. I want to know who those men were who painted themselves like Apaches, rode the ponies here. I want to know who they work for."

"You ask much, Cody. But I will tell you so that you will go and leave me alone. Perhaps I will see you again one day."

"Perhaps."

"The men you look for have gone to Tucson. You must see a man named Ferguson. He owns the freight line."

"I am looking for a man named Ben Trask," Cody said.

"Ah, you know this man?"

"Yes, I know him."

"You are friends, no?"

Cody didn't answer. He let the question hang and watched Felipe squirm inside his skin. He could almost see the man's mind working, the way his forehead wrinkled up and his nose crinkled, making his eyes squint.

"This one, Trask, he is there. He works for Ferguson."

That was all Zak wanted to hear.

Trask was just the kind of man to stir up trouble with the Apaches, but he'd bet money that he had something else on his mind, as well. Trask might be working for Ferguson, but he was also working for himself, perhaps looking for an opportunity to make some illegal money.

"All right, Felipe. I'm leaving now."

"You do not want another horse?"

"No. You keep them."

Zak looked around at the ground, the maze of wagon tracks. The adobe with its adjoining jacal was some kind of way station, he was sure. Someone had to haul in fodder for the horses, food and supplies for Felipe. He wondered how many such stations were scattered over the territory. Someone had gone to a great amount of trouble to stir up hatred against the Apaches.

"What have you got inside that adobe?" Zak asked suddenly.

"Nothing."

"I want to take a look."

"No. This is not permitted."

"Are you hiding something in there?"

"No. I hide nothing."

"I think you are, Felipe. Step aside. I'm going to take a look."

Felipe hesitated. Zak took a step toward him, his right hand dropping to the butt of his pistol. It was a menacing move, deliberate, and Felipe got the message.

"Go inside, then."

"You first," Zak said.

Felipe shrugged. He turned and stepped inside, Cody right behind him. The hovel smelled of wood smoke and stale whiskey. A potbelly stove stood near the back wall, its fire gone out, but still leaking smoke from around its door and at a loose place on the pipe. A pot of coffee stood atop it, still steaming. Several bottles of whiskey lay on the floor, and half-empty bottles sat on a grimy table in the center of the room. The bunk in a corner reeked of sweat. On a sideboard he found several small cans of paint and brushes that had not yet been cleaned with the linseed oil standing nearby, next to a grimy wooden bowl.

Something caught Zak's eye in another corner. He walked over, his stomach swirling with a sensation like winged insects.

"What's this?" he said as Felipe stood there, his face waxen.

"I do not know. Those were there when I came here."

"Bullshit," Zak said as he picked up an army canteen. A blue officer's uniform lay in a heap. Silver lieutenant's bars gleamed from the shoulders of the tunic. A pair of cavalryman's boots, shiny, with a patina of dust on them, spurs still attached, stood against the wall behind the pile of clothes.

"I do not know who left those clothes," Felipe said.

"Do you know the name of the man who owns them?"

"No."

"Maybe you know Lieutenant Ted O'Hara."

"I do not know him," Felipe said.

Zak had seen enough. He was sure that Ted O'Hara had been brought to this place. They had stripped him of his uniform, put civilian clothes on him, perhaps. Then they had taken him someplace else. A hostage, maybe? A bargaining chip? Or maybe to torture him for information about the location of Apache camps, knowledge they somehow knew he possessed.

"You want some advice, Felipe?"

"What advice?"

"When I tell the army about this place, they're going to swarm all over you like a nest of hornets. If you're smart, you'll get on one of those horses out there and clear out."

"I have done nothing."

"I think you have. You're lucky I'm in a hurry or I'd pack you off to Fort Bowie trussed up like a Thanksgiving turkey."

Felipe, wisely, said nothing. He held his breath and walked outside with Zak.

"You leave now?" Felipe said.

"I might be back. In any case, someone will. You'd better find another place to hang your hat, Felipe."

Felipe stood in front of the door, speechless.

Zak knew his encounter with the man wasn't over. He had given Felipe fair warning. The next move was up to him. Felipe could either let him ride off or he could try to stop him.

Either way, the writing had already been painted on the wall.

Zak started to walk back to his horse when he heard a sound, the whisper of metal sliding out of leather. He knew what it was. Felipe was drawing his pistol.

Zak spun around, went into a fighting crouch. His right hand streaked to the butt of his Walker Colt. His gaze fixed on Felipe's eyes, not on his hand. But he could see, in the same range of vision, the barrel of Felipe's pistol clearing leather, the snout rising like the rigid black body of a striking snake.

The Walker Colt seemed to spring into Zak's hand. His thumb pressed down on the hammer, pushing it back into full cock as he leveled the barrel at the Mexican.

Felipe fired his pistol. Too soon. The bullet plowed a furrow at Zak's feet as he squeezed the trigger of the Walker.

He looked down a long dark tunnel as the pistol exploded, gushing flame and lead, bucking in his hand. At the end of the tunnel, Felipe, in stark relief, was hammering back for a second shot. Zak's .44 caliber ball of soft lead struck him just below his rib cage with the force of a sledgehammer. Dust flew from his shirt and a black hole appeared like a quick wink that filled suddenly with blood.

The hammered bullet drove Felipe off his moorings and he staggered backward, slamming into the wall of the adobe. A crimson flower blossomed on his chest, the smell of his half-digested supper spewing from his stomach. He gasped for air and slid down the wall, his fingers turning limp, the pistol drooping, then falling from his grasp. His eyes clouded over, the spark fading like a dying ember. The pupils turned frosty as blood pumped through the hole in his chest, ran down into his lap.

Zak stepped toward Felipe, his pistol at full cock for another shot, if needed.

He heard the death gurgle in the man's throat, but Felipe was still alive, hanging onto life with labored breaths.

Smoke spooled from the barrel of Zak's pistol as he knelt down in front of the Mexican. He lifted the pistol, the action scattering the smoke to shreds.

"I won't say adios to you, Felipe," Zak said, his voice a soft rasp, just above a whisper. "God isn't going with you on this journey. He's just going to watch you fall into a deep hole. The next sound you hear will be me. Walking over your grave, you sonofabitch."

Felipe stretched out a hand toward Zak's throat. He tried to sit up. Something broke loose inside him and he coughed up blood. His eyes glazed over with the frost of death as he gave one last gasp and fell back, his lifeless body slumped against the adobe wall. His sphincter muscle relaxed and he voided himself.

Zak stood up, walked away from the sudden stench. He ejected the empty hull in the Colt's cylinder and dug a cartridge from his gun belt. He slid it into the empty cylinder and spun it, then eased the hammer down to half-cock before sliding the pistol back in his holster.

He walked down to the corral and opened the gate.

"Heya, hiya," Zak yelled, waving his hat at the horses and ponies. They all dashed through the opening and galloped off down the gully and up the slope. They disappeared over the rim and a quiet settled over the empty corral.

Zak walked back to the adobe and went inside. He picked up the tunic with the lieutenant's bars, folded it tightly, went outside and stuffed it in his saddlebag. Then he went back inside, took a lamp from a hook over the potbellied stove and dashed coal oil on everything flammable within reach.

He stepped to the door, dug out a box of matches, struck one and tossed it onto the floor. The flame sputtered for a moment, then caught. The oil flared and tongues of flame began to lick the clothing and empty boxes, the chairs and table. It spread to the jacal as Zak mounted Nox and rode off, following one of the wagon tracks that was laced with shod hoof marks. The jacal blazed bright in the morning sun and he heard bottles of whiskey explode inside the adobe. Black smoke etched a charcoal scrawl on the horizon, rising ever higher in the still air.

The horse tracks led west, beside the faint wagon wheel ruts, and he followed them, putting Nox into a canter. The wagon tracks made it easy, and the horse tracks were only a day old, with no rain nor strong wind to erase them.

Killing a man was not easy. It was never easy. There was always that dark tunnel, that unknown blackness, that he saw and wondered about. Conscience? He didn't know. He knew only that death was so final, there was no second chance for those who went up against his gun. And the killing of a man always weighed heavy on his heart or his mind or, perhaps, his soul. Life was such a fleeting, fragile, troublesome journey, but to cut that journey short, for whatever reason, gave a man pause, made him reflect on his own breath, his own heartbeat, his own blood pulsing in his veins.

Felipe hadn't seen it coming. He hadn't thought that far ahead. But Zak had seen it. He could always see it in a man's eyes, that inkling of mortality, that wonder, just before death blotted out everything, just before the tunnel closed in darkness and the light that had been a man one moment plunged into final darkness the next.

There was one question Zak had meant to ask Felipe, but the Mexican had pressed it, had made that fatal decision to draw his pistol. So the question had never been asked. Had never been answered.

The question would have been: "Do you know a man named Major Willoughby?"

Zak would have read the answer in Felipe's eyes, even if he had never replied. Then he would have known who betrayed Ted O'Hara, and who told Ben Trask where O'Hara was.

Deep down inside him, though, Zak thought he knew the answer to the unasked question.

One day he would find the answer, and the proof to go along with it.

It was only a question of time.

He just hoped he would find Lieutenant Theodore O'Hara alive.

But he would find him.

That, he knew.

⇥ 7 ⇤

Zak saw the flash out of the corner of his eye. It was bright as silver, as intense as a bolt of lightning. He had descended into a shallow depression and was just emerging when the dazzling light streaked from a low hill a half mile away. He kept on, but his gaze scanned the surrounding countryside.

That's when he saw an answering flash.

He knew he was not alone.

He built his first smoke of the day, casually taking out the papers and the pouch of tobacco. He rolled a quirly, licked it, stuck it in his mouth. He struck a match, drew smoke into his mouth and lungs. He knew he was being watched. His every move.

But who was watching?

The army?

He didn't think so. Troopers could be stealthy, but they'd had time to look him over and should have announced their presence long before he lit up a cigarette.

Apaches?

Likely. They probably had army signal mirrors,

but they could use almost anything to reflect sunlight, send messages. A chunk of quartz, a piece of tin, broken glass from a bottle.

He looked at the ground, which had suddenly produced a maze of tracks. Besides the wagon ruts and horse tracks, the horses and ponies he had chased out of the mesquite pole corral had crossed his path. The tracks headed toward a point between the places where he had seen the flashing mirrors.

He had a decision to make.

He could follow his present course, toward Tucson, or shift to the new tracks.

Curiosity killed the cat, he thought.

He stayed to his tracking but could feel the watchers tracking him. It was an uncomfortable feeling, as if someone's eyes were boring into him, right between his shoulder blades. He saw no more flashes, but didn't expect any. The watchers knew where he was, and probably had a pretty good idea where he was going.

The land was gently rolling, swells of earth that rose up and fell away like an ocean frozen in motion. As long as the rises were shallow, he could still see ahead of him when he rode into a dip, but it was at the bottom of one of the depressions that he was brought up short.

They came in from two sides and made a line on the ridge above him. A dozen braves, Chiricahuas, he figured, all carrying rifles and wearing pistols. None were painted for war, but he knew that meant nothing. Apaches could go to war with or without decorating their bodies.

Zak's knowledge of Apache was limited. He had

a smattering of Athabascan, knew a few words that amounted to very little if his life depended on much conversation. He could speak Spanish, though, and most of the Apaches had some familiarity with that language. Right now, he wondered if he would even have a chance to talk. The Indians surrounding him all had bandoleros slung over their shoulders, and the gun belts shone with brass cartridges.

He reined up, folded his hands atop one another on the saddle horn.

The Apaches looked at him for several moments.

If there was one trait that stood out among the Apaches, it was their patience. Zak figured he could match them on that score.

As he sat there, he heard the rumble of hoofbeats. More Apaches rode up, and they were driving the horses and ponies he had released from Felipe's corral. He turned and looked back at the smoke still rising in the sky.

One of the Apaches from the first bunch moved his pinto a few yards closer to where Zak sat his horse. His face was impassive, a bronze mask under straight black hair. He wore a red bandanna around his forehead, a faded blue chambray shirt, beaded white man's trousers, moccasins. He carried an old Sharps carbine that had lost most of its bluing. The stock was worn, devoid of its original finish. The pistol tucked into his sash was a cap and ball, a Remington, Zak figured, one of the New Model Army kind with a top strap.

The Apache spoke.

"*Quien eres?*" he said in Spanish.

"*Yo soy Cody.*"

"*Soldado?*"

"No, I'm not a soldier," Cody said, also in Spanish. Then he said, "*Nodeeh*," an Apache word, and touched his chest with his hand.

"*Nodeh ligai*," the Apache said. White man.

"Yes. Who are you?"

"*Anillo*," he said, and held up his left hand. Zak saw the ring on his finger, turquoise and silver. It sparkled in the sun.

"Ring," Zak said in English.

"Yes. I am called Ring. What do you do here?"

"I follow the tracks of bad white men. They made themselves to look like Apaches. They killed two soldiers."

"You gave us these horses?" Anillo said.

"Yes. I let them run from the corral."

"You burned the jacal and the adobe."

It was a statement, not a question. Zak nodded without speaking.

"Cody."

"Yes."

"The black horse is like a shadow."

"Yes. I call him *Noche*." He didn't figure Anillo would understand the Latin word for night.

"That is a good name. Cochise has spoken of you."

"I do not know Cochise. But I have heard he is a strong man. A brave man."

"He calls you *Jinete de Sombra*. Are you the Shadow Rider?"

"That is what some call me."

"Then we will not kill you, Cody."

"And I will not kill you. I make no fight with the Apache. I chase bad white men."

"Why do you do this?"

"General Crook does not like white men who cause trouble with the Apache. He wants the Apache and the white men to live in peace."

Anillo spat upon the ground. His eyes narrowed and his face turned rigid with anger.

"Do you have tobacco?" Anillo asked.

"Yes."

"Then let us smoke and talk."

Zak reached in his pocket and pulled out the makings. Anillo spoke to one of the men in the group, gestured for him to come down. He dismounted. Zak slid from his saddle.

They sat down and the Apache who Anillo had called slid from his pony's back and walked over. He was older than Anillo. There were streaks of gray in his hair, lines in his face, wrinkles in the wattles under his chin. He had a fierce face, with close-set black eyes, a pug nose, high cheekbones burnished with the vermillion of his bloodlines.

"This is Tesoro," Anillo said. Then he spoke to Tesoro in Apache and the old warrior squatted down as Anillo took out a paper and poured tobacco into it. He handed the pouch and papers to Tesoro, who made himself a cigarette. He handed the makings to Zak, who rolled one for himself. The three sat together. The two Apaches leaned forward as Zak struck a match. He touched their cigarettes and they sucked smoke into their mouths. Zak lit his own quirly, settled in a sitting position on the warm ground.

Zak looked at Tesoro, wondering how he had acquired his name. Tesoro meant "treasure" in Spanish. It was an odd sobriquet for a seasoned

Apache warrior. Tesoro looked at him with cold ebony eyes.

"Raise your shirt, Tesoro," Anillo said.

Tesoro, his cigarette dangling from his lips, lifted his worn cotton shirt, almost proudly, Zak thought.

Zak stared at Tesoro's bare chest in disbelief.

The wounds were fresh. He had seen similar scars before, on warriors who had participated in the Sun Dance on the plains of the Dakotas, rips in their skin where they had impaled hooks that tore loose as they danced around a pole, connected to it with long leather thongs.

But these wounds were different. They were not scars made from hooks or knives. They were burns, and he had seen the likes of these before, as well. On his father's body after Ben Trask had tortured him by jabbing a red hot poker into his flesh.

The burn marks were the same, and some were scabbed over. Others were pocks with new flesh growing in the depressions. Tesoro had been tortured over a period of time. These burns were not made in a single day or night, but over a period of days, or perhaps even weeks.

"What do you see?" Anillo asked, plumes of smoke jetting from his nostrils and out the corners of his mouth.

"Burns," Zak said. "Iron burns."

Tesoro nodded and let his shirt fall back into place.

Somehow, Zak knew the burns were not connected to some Apache ritual or religious ceremony. Tesoro, he was sure, had been tortured.

"A man burned him with hot iron," Zak said. "A man who wanted Tesoro to tell him something."

"*Verdad*," Anillo said. "This is true."

"A white man burned Tesoro," Zak said. "Does Tesoro know the name of this man?"

"He knows the name of the man," Anillo said. "Do you know the name of this man?"

"Is the name difficult for the Apache to say?"

"Yes. It is hard to say this name," Anillo said.

"Trask," Zak said. "Ben Trask."

A light came into Tesoro's eyes when he heard the name. That was the only sign that he recognized it. His features remained stoic.

"Terask," Anillo said. "Ben, yes."

"A bad man," Zak said. "This is one I hunt. This is a man I would kill."

"How do you know this was the man who burned Tesoro with hot iron?"

"He did the same to my father," Zak said. "And then he killed my father."

"Ah. And why did Terask do this to your father?"

"Gold. My father had gold. Trask wanted it."

"That is why this man burned Tesoro," Anillo said.

"Does Tesoro have gold?" Zak asked.

Other Apaches had drifted down to listen. They made a ring around the three men on the ground. One still stood at the top, along with those guarding the ponies. He was standing watch, his head turning in all directions. Like an antelope guarding its herd, Zak thought.

Anillo and Tesoro exchanged glances.

"It is the name of Tesoro. Terask, he think maybe Tesoro has gold."

"Treasure," Zak said in English, more to himself than to either Anillo or Tesoro.

Anillo nodded. "Yes. Tesoro. Treasure. He captured Tesoro and he burned him with the iron to make him tell where Apache hides gold."

Zak knew such rumors had abounded for years, going all the way back to the Conquistadors from Spain who believed there were cities of gold in the New World. Ben Trask would most certainly be interested in such rumors, and probably believed them to be true. There was gold in Apache country. Whether any of the tribes had accumulated some of that gold was a question that had been debated and mulled over for many years.

"Tesoro did not tell him," Zak said.

"Tesoro does not know."

"Do the Apaches have gold?" Zak asked.

Anillo's face did not change expression.

"You ask a question many white men ask."

"But you do not answer," Zak said.

"Gold makes white men mad. It is just something that is in the earth, like rock or cactus, like trees or like water. The Apache does not seek gold. If he finds it, he hides it from the white man because he knows the yellow metal makes the white man crazy."

"Trask did not kill Tesoro. Why?"

"Tesoro was like the snake in the night. He moved so quiet. The white men did not see him. He ran away. He ran for many days. Now he, too, would kill Terask if he sees him."

"Tesoro," Zak said, addressing the silent Apache, "do you hunt Trask?"

Tesoro opened his mouth. He made a croaking sound in his throat.

Zak saw that his tongue had been cut out.

"When Tesoro would not tell Terask where the Apache hides the gold, he cut out the tongue of Tesoro," Anillo said. "The white men got drunk and they laughed. They played with the tongue of Tesoro while Tesoro swallowed his own blood and became the snake that hides in the grass and crawls away in the night."

"*Quanto lamento lo que ha pasado con Tesoro*," Zak said. I'm sorry for what happened to Tesoro.

"*No hay de que*," Anillo said. It is nothing. "Tesoro is strong. One day he will cut the throat of Terask. I will piss in his mouth before that."

"How do you know the name of Trask, if Tesoro cannot speak?"

"The Mexican you killed. He say the name. Terask was here. He bring horses, supplies, men. We watch. We hear. Trask chase us. He catch Tesoro."

"Do you know where Trask is?" Zak asked.

Anillo shook his head.

"The little adobe you burned. There are more of these *casitas*." He slowly swung his raised arm in a wide sweep to take in all of the country. "They are here and they are there. Terask he goes to them, but he does not stay long. I think he goes to Tucson."

"You will not go to Tucson," Zak said.

Anillo shook his head.

"That is a town of the white man. The Apache does not go there. The Chiricahua does not go there."

"I will go there. I will find Trask. If I take him alive, I will bring him to you. But I do not know where to find you."

"You bring Terask. We will find you, Cody."

Zak finished his smoke and stood up. Anillo and Tesoro stood up, too. The three men looked at each other, wordless in their understanding of each other.

"I go now," Zak said, and turned toward his horse.

"*Vaya con Dios*," Anillo said.

Zak pulled himself up into the saddle.

He repeated the phrase to Anillo and Tesoro.

As he rode away, he muttered to himself, "I didn't know the Apache believed in God."

And he smiled as he said it.

There was a lot he did not know about the Apache.

8

Ben Trask poured two fingers of whiskey into Hiram Ferguson's glass.

"Maybe this will calm your nerves, Hiram," Trask said. "You're as jumpy as a long-tailed cat in a room full of rocking chairs."

Ferguson's hands shook as he lifted the glass to his lips. He was almost as big a man as Trask, but he was soft, flabby, with pudgy lips, jowls like a basset hound's, and at least three chins under a round moon face. Trask was all hard muscle, half a foot taller than Ferguson, with a lean, angular face, and a hooked nose that looked as if it had been carved out of hickory with a hatchet. Wind and sun had burnished his features to a rich brown tan. His pale blue eyes were almost gray, portraying no emotion, like the eyes of a dead fish.

"That's what you wanted, Hiram, wasn't it? Get the army to chase out the Chiricahua?"

"Yeah, but we wanted to make 'em mad that the Apaches were killin' civilians, burnin' down their homes, rapin' their women. I never called on you to go after soldiers. Shit almighty, Ben. You done took one giant step. In the wrong direction, to my way of thinkin'."

"Hiram, you got nowhere with them tactics. Now you got that damned Jeffords smokin' the peace pipe with Cochise and his whole gang. Then you go to the army mollycoddlin' every red nigger from the Rio Grande to Santa Fe.

"They're even talkin' about namin' a fort after them bastards," Ferguson said.

They were sitting in the Cantina Escobar, not far from Ferguson's Stage & Freight Company. Most of the men inside were as anti-Apache as Ferguson, including the six Mexicans who had dressed up like Chiricahua and killed the two soldiers.

The others were local ranchers and their hands. Most of these were standing at the long bar, quaffing beer and eating pickled sausages prepared by Antonio Escobar's wife, Lucinda, who also cooked *bistec, frijoles refritos, juevos, papas, puerco*, and anything else a hungry man might ask for. The smells from the kitchen were not overpowered by the scent of smoke and whiskey and mescal, tequila and fresh sawdust on the dirt floor hauled in from the nearby lumberyard and sawmill. The tables were small, except for one, which was used by card players and sat in the front corner to make room for all the tables. There was no music on most nights, but sometimes Lucinda's brother would bring his guitar and sing sad Mexican folksongs on holidays when the cantina was occupied largely by Mexican vaqueros. This was not one of those nights, and the crowd was equally divided between Mexicans and *norteamericanos*.

"Look, Hiram, you wanted me to bring the army

down on the Apaches. That's why I staged that attack on one of your stages to make it look like the Apaches were on the warpath. By now, that gal has told every woman in that fort about that savage Indian attack."

"Speakin' of that, where in hell is Jenkins?" Ferguson asked. "He should have been back from Bowie this afternoon."

"Who knows?" Trask said. "I'm wondering how you're doing with O'Hara. You still got him over at the freight yard?"

"So far, he won't talk."

"He knows where every Apache camp is from here to the San Simon. Maybe you ought to let me work him over. And while we're at it, what's the difference between you kidnapping a cavalry officer and my bunch putting out the lamps on a couple of soldier boys? I'd like a crack at O'Hara. I could make him talk like a damned magpie."

"No," Ferguson said. "I've seen your work, Ben. We'll get what we need out of him."

"When?"

"By tomorrow. His sis was on that stage Jenkins took out of here to Fort Bowie. He sets store by her. I'm going to tell him we'll grab her and put the boots to her if he doesn't tell us what we want to know."

"Just what are you doing to make O'Hara tell us where those Apaches are holed up?"

"The lieutenant's bobbing for apples," Ferguson said.

"Huh?"

"You wanta see? Finish up and we'll walk over to the office."

"Damned right I want to see," Trask said.

He finished his whiskey, stood up.

Ferguson swallowed the last of his drink.

"See you later, boys," Trask said to the Mexicans still drinking at the tables, their heads and shoulders bathed in lamplight and blue smoke. He laid some bills on the table, picked up the bottle, held it against the light to see how much whiskey was left. He grunted in satisfaction.

The two men walked out of the cantina and toward the freight office. Its windows sprayed orange light on the porch. A man with a scattergun stood in the shadows beneath the eaves, while another, with a rifle, paced back and forth between the corrals and the office building, his boots crunching on sand and gravel. The shotgun man worked for Ferguson. His name was Lou Grissom. The man with the rifle was one of his own, Al Deets, as hard as they came, not a soft bone in him.

"Al," Trask said. "In the dark you got to shoot low."

"Yeah, Ben," Deets said. "Low and off to one side."

Trask laughed as they clumped up the steps onto the porch. Grissom just stood there, like a mute statue. He wasn't at all friendly, Trask thought, and that was the kind of man you needed to stand guard with a Greener chocked up with buckshot.

Ted O'Hara sat in a chair in a back room, stripped of his shirt, his arms and legs bound with manila rope. He looked haggard in the sallow light from a single lantern dangling from an overhead rafter. Two men stood on either side of him, bracing him against the chair back so he wouldn't fall forward. In front of O'Hara sat a wooden tub filled with water. O'Hara's face and hair were wet, his eyes closed, his head drooping downward so that his chin almost rested on his chest.

"He asleep?" Ferguson said.

"Tryin'," one of the men, Jesse Bob Cavins, said.

"He say anything 'bout them Apache hideouts?" Ferguson asked the other man, a gaunt stringy hardcase named Willy Rawlins.

"Nope. He's just swallered a lot of water, Hiram." Rawlins had a West Texas drawl you could cut with a butcher knife if you laid it on a chunk of wood.

"Nothing?" Trask said, a scowl forming on his face.

"Nary," Rawlins said.

"Says he don't know nothin'," Cavins said, "and we near drowneded him ten minutes ago."

"He have any papers on him?" Trask asked. "Maps, stuff like that?"

"On that table over yonder," Cavins said, nodding in the direction of a table next to a rolltop desk against one wall.

Trask walked over to the table and picked up an army pouch. He opened it, spread the contents out on the tabletop. Ferguson strode up to stand beside him.

"None of that made any sense to us," Hiram said. "Army stuff."

"You ever in the army, Hiram?"

"Nope. Not as a regular. I hauled freight out of Santa Fe and Taos up to Pueblo and Denver. Warn't no war up yonder."

Trask opened a folded paper and laid it out flat.

"This here's a field map," he said. "If you know how to read 'em, you can find out where you are. Or, in this case, where our young Lieutenant O'Hara has been."

"Lot of gibberish to me," Ferguson said.

"There's numbers on it, in different places."

"Don't make no sense."

"No, not to you and me. But I'll bet O'Hara there knows what they mean. Did you show him the map? Ask him about it?"

Ferguson looked at the two men flanking O'Hara. They both shook their heads.

"Why not?" Trask asked.

"Yeah, why not?" Ferguson asked.

"We just asked him what you told us to ask him, Hiram."

"And what was that?" Trask wanted to know, a warning tic beginning to quiver along his jawline.

"Where in hell them Apaches' camps was," Rawlins said.

"We asked him about Cochise, too," Cavins said, a defensive tone to his voice.

"What did he say to those questions?" The tic in Trask's facial muscles subsided as his jaw hardened. In the silence, the men could almost hear Trask's teeth grind together.

"He said he didn't know," Rawlins said.

"He said he was on the scout, follerin' orders is all." Cavins was on the verge of becoming belligerent, and Ferguson shot him a warning glance.

Trask huffed in a breath as if he was building up steam inside him. But he remained calm. He knew men. These would be no trouble. Not Cavins nor Rawlins, not even Ferguson. Trask had observed men like these all his life, and men like O'Hara, as well. He knew the realms of darkness they all harbored. He knew their fears. Torturing men had given him insights that few other men ever even thought about. But he also knew when torture would fail, result only in silence or death.

O'Hara had been Ferguson's idea, but then he had inside information, a conduit of some kind that led straight into Fort Bowie. An inside man. A man who hated Apaches as much as he did. Hiram knew someone high up in the military, at the post, who knew what O'Hara was scouting. But Hiram didn't know how to dig that information out of a man like O'Hara, a soldier who held to higher standards than he did.

"Mind if I take a crack at soldier boy?" Trask said. "You got any coffee you can make in here?"

"Long as you don't mark him up none, Trask," Ferguson said. "Willy, you put on some Arbuckle's. Bob, get some kindlin' started in that potbelly."

Rawlins walked over to a sideboard built into the wall. Nearby was a potbellied stove with a flat round lid on top. Cavins knelt down and opened the door, picked up a stick of kindling wood and poked around in the ashes.

"Deader'n hell," he said. "Nary a coal." Then he set about making a fire.

Rawlins rattled a pot against another, set out the one that made coffee, lifted the lid. He opened an airtight of Arbuckle's coffee, releasing the aroma of cinnamon. He dipped grinds into the pot, replaced the lid.

"What do you aim to do, Ben?" Ferguson asked.

"Perk this guy up some, first off."

Trask walked over to O'Hara, the map in his hands. He knelt down in front of the lieutenant, put his hand on O'Hara's chin, tilted his head back up. O'Hara's eyelids fluttered open. His blue eyes were watery, unfocused.

"You awake, Lieutenant O'Hara? We're not going to put your face in the water no more, son. We just want to talk."

O'Hara opened his eyes wider, stared at Trask.

"Not going to tell you anything."

"That's all right. You've been through hell, and it don't make no difference no more. We found your map. It tells us what we want to know."

"Map?"

Trask held up the map. O'Hara looked down at it.

"This field map we found on you. You recognize it?"

"No," O'Hara said.

"That's fine. It's got numbers on it. Know what they mean?"

"No."

Trask smiled. "Well, take a good look, Lieutenant. Maybe you do."

O'Hara turned his head away. He struggled with his bonds, then gave up fighting it. They didn't loosen.

"Sir, you'll pay for this," he said. "Holding me prisoner. The army will probably hang you."

"Oh, I don't think so. You're not hurt, are you? You maybe swallered some water, got your hair wet, is all."

"I was kidnapped. At gunpoint."

"Not by me."

"Who are you?" O'Hara asked.

"That's not important. I came to help you. You want to go back to Fort Bowie all in one piece. Your sis is there, waiting for you."

"Colleen?"

"Yeah, I guess that's her name."

O'Hara breathed a sigh, gulped in air. His eyes began to clear. "How do you know this?"

"Why, she rode this man's stage to Fort Bowie. There were two soldiers with her. Some damned Apaches attacked the stage. Killed and scalped the two soldiers, but the driver got her away and set her down safe in Fort Bowie. Ain't that right, Hiram?"

"Sure is."

"So, you can go back there, too. I just thought you might want to help me with this map here."

"No. I can't help you. Those numbers don't mean anything to me."

Trask stood up. O'Hara followed him with his gaze, looked up at him.

Trask's manner had changed. The smile was gone, the face hard again.

"Listen to me, you sonofabitch," Trask said, his voice a husky rasp, "if you don't want to see me cut your sister's throat, right here, right in front of you, you'd better tell me what these numbers on the map mean. Are they Apache camps?"

Before O'Hara could answer, there was a commotion outside. Hoofbeats and the rumble of a wagon or coach. A moment later Lou Grissom blasted through the door as if he were on fire.

"Mr. Ferguson, Jenkins's coach just rolled in."

"Jenkins all right?"

"I don't know. He ain't drivin' it."

"Well, who the hell is?" Ferguson snapped.

"Somebody wearing a United States Army uniform, and they's an army escort pullin' up right with him."

"Shit," Ferguson said.

O'Hara opened his mouth as if to yell. Trask clamped a hand over his mouth, drew his pistol, held it like a hammer and brought it down hard on top of O'Hara's head. There was a sharp crack and O'Hara's head dropped like a sash weight as he fell unconscious.

"Just don't let the bastards in here, Hiram," Trask said. "Get out there and find out what's going on."

Ferguson needed no urging. He was out the door a second or two later, Grissom on his heels.

Trask stared after them. Cavins and Rawlins stood frozen by the stove. The coffeepot burbled, spewed steam into the air.

Trask put a finger to his lips and holstered his pistol.

There was a silence in the room as if no one was there.

9

The two men continued to argue. They had been at it ever since the wagon came through, changed horses, and left them way out in the middle of that bleak nowhere. A place that had no name. A way station between Tucson and Fort Bowie, but not on any known trail or road that either man knew of or gave a damn about. Someplace on the distant edge of a ranch, they figured, a line shack no longer used by any white man.

A dust devil swirled across the flat above the spring, and the horses in the pole corral neighed, flattened their ears at the sound, like a great whisper in a hollow room. Miles of nothingness stretched out in all directions around the homely adobe, and Larry Tolliver, yoked with two wooden pails of springwater, paused to watch the swirling dust as if that was an event to break the monotony, a rent in the fabric of sameness that dogged his days in isolation.

Danny Grubb sat outside the adobe shack, whittling on a piece of mesquite, his eyes squinted against the glare of the falling sun, a wad of plug tobacco bulging out his cheek like some hidden growth dis-

torting his lean, angular face. The *whick whick* of
the knife blade was the only sound in his mindless
mind, the blond and gray curls of the shaven wood
falling to the parched ground like locks on a barbershop floor.

Tolliver, puffing from exertion, slipped the yoke
from his shoulders and set the pails down in front
of Grubb. The water sloshed over the rims, stained
the ground for a second before it disappeared,
sucked up by the wind and sucked down by the
thirsty earth, like ink vanishing under the pressure
of a blotter.

"Go on ahead, Larry, spill ever' damn drop of
that water," Grubb said.

"While you sit on your skinny ass, Danny."

"Hell, I might make a whistle outta this stick of
mesquite and play you a tune come dark."

"You can stick that whistle square up your ass,
Danny."

"I might stick it up yours, you keep flappin' your
sorry mouth."

"You could carry this water inside, out of the
dust."

"I could, but I been cuttin' the wood. It'll be
colder'n a well-digger's ass once that sun goes
down."

The incoming wagon had brought them two
cords of firewood. Danny had been splitting sticks
of kindling for their cookstove, so he didn't see
where Tolliver had any room for complaints. He
had also fed the six horses in the corral. The wagon
had also brought grain. When it returned, with
Rawlins and Cavins, it carried their prisoner, one
Ted O'Hara, an army lieutenant wearing shabby

civilian clothes. Grissom had been with them, too, and Danny had begged him to stay at the shack and let him go back with the wagon into Tucson.

"I got my orders, Danny," Grissom had said. "Hiram says you boys got to stay another month."

"What for?"

"For thirty a month and found," Grissom had said with a vicious little laugh that still irritated Danny when he thought about it. Everything irritated him, especially Tolliver.

"Who's going to fix supper?" Danny asked.

"My turn, I reckon," Tolliver said.

"My belly hurts already."

"Look, Danny, I don't like bein' out here anymore'n you do, but we got to make the best of it. You don't like it, you can slap a saddle on one of them horses and ride on back to town."

"When I think of Rawlins and Cavins swillin' down beer and whiskey in the cantina," Danny said, "I get plumb burned. They ought to try this shit for a time."

"Hiram said we'd take turns. They might come back in a couple of weeks."

"That'll be the day," Danny said, and threw down the stick of whittled wood, closed his Barlow knife and stuck it in his pocket.

Larry Tolliver cooked supper and opened a can of peaches. After they ate and Danny washed the tin plates, the knives, forks, and spoons, they sat outside. Larry smoked and Danny chewed on a cut plug of tobacco. The sunset was as sweet as the night was depressing. The bright clouds had turned to ash and then faded to black as the sky sparkled with stars and the wind turned chill.

"You hear anything?" Danny asked after a while. He spat a plume of tobacco into the dust.

Larry watched the smoke from his cigarette twist into ghostly shapes that resembled small animals in the lantern light, snakes and mice and tiny gray birds. They unfolded in the breezeless air like paintings on parchment.

"Nope," he said. But he listened. It got spooky out there at night, and they hadn't heard the coyotes sing as they usually did. There was a quiet that made the silence seem loud.

There wasn't so much as the crunch of a boot on sand, nor the clink of an overturned rock, but there he was, standing in front of them, dressed all in black like an undertaker, his eyes shaded by his hat brim so that they couldn't see them. He wore a big Walker Colt on his hip, and the way he stood there, as if he had come out of nowhere, made both men freeze as though thunderstruck.

"Just set there easy," Zak said, and his voice carried authority. It was low-pitched and firm, vibrated in his throat with a hypnotizing hum. The voice didn't even seem to come from him, but from somewhere else, from somewhere above him.

Tolliver's throat went dry as the dirt under his feet, but he managed to squeak out a question.

"Damn, where'd you come from?"

Zak said nothing. He looked at the two men. Both were armed, but they didn't look ready to defend anything they might have inside the adobe or on their persons.

"Mister, you oughtn't walk up on a man like that," Grubb said. "You could get yourself killed for no good reason."

"I've been watching you two fellows," Zak said. "Had my eye on you since late afternoon. If ever I saw a couple of dunces, you two were they. I doubt if either of you could hit the broadside of a barn at five paces. But if words were bullets, you two would be champion shots. I haven't heard such arguing since I stayed with a married man and his wife up on the Judith."

"You been listenin' to us?" Tolliver said, gapemouthed.

"Voices carry out here," Zak said. "A long way."

"Well, what you sneakin' around for?" Grubb said. "Spyin' on people like that. Ask me, you're the one ain't got good sense."

"I'll tell you why I stopped by, mister." Zak looked at Grubb. "Danny."

Danny recoiled in shock that the stranger knew his name. "Yeah? How come?" he said.

"There was a wagon come through here with a kidnapped soldier in it. I want you boys to tell me where it's going to wind up. I'll give you five seconds, Danny, and I'm counting real fast."

"Ain't none of your business," Tolliver said.

"Three," Zak said.

"What you gonna do if we don't tell you?" Danny asked.

"One of you I'm going to blow straight to hell," Zak said.

"Which one?" Danny asked.

"One second left."

"Jesus," Tolliver said, and he wasn't praying.

Danny, rattled, spoke first.

"Ferguson," he said.

Tolliver chimed in on the heels of Danny's one word statement.

"Edge of Tucson. You find Cantina Escobar, you'll see the freight company a stone's throw away."

"Either of you know a man named Ben Trask?"

The two men looked at each other, their expressions showing their bewilderment.

"Naw," they said, like a chorus of jackdaws.

"You know the soldier's name? The one that was in the wagon?"

"They called him O'Hara," Danny said. "Young feller. Still wet behind the ears."

"Tied up," Tolliver said.

"Where's the next station?"

"Huh?" Danny said.

"Is there another one of these 'dobes where that wagon was headed?"

"Two more," Tolliver said.

"You boys are out of business," Zak said. "As of right now. I'll leave you two horses. The rest I'm running off."

"You can't do that," Tolliver said. "They hang horse thieves in this country."

"I'm not stealing them. I'm just turning them loose. You got any apples inside that 'dobe?"

"Apples?" Danny said.

"Yeah, my horse likes apples."

Both men shook their heads.

"Does this look like a damned orchard?" Tolliver said, suddenly belligerent.

"I don't see no horse," Danny said.

Zak turned his head, gave a low whistle. Then he called, "Nox."

The black horse, his coat shining like dark water, came around the corner of the adobe, reins trailing. He ambled up to Zak, who rubbed the hollows over the horse's eyes, worried his topknot with massaging knuckles.

"I ought to burn you out," Zak said. "But I'm just going to turn those horses out and ride on."

He grabbed his reins, separated them, and draped the ends over the horse's neck, just in front of the saddle.

"Mister, you ain't running none of our horses off," Tolliver said. "I'm callin' you out."

Zak turned toward Tolliver and stared him straight in the eyes. He let his right hand slide easily down his horse's neck until it was parallel to the butt of his pistol.

Tolliver sat there, blinking. Under the brim of his grease-stained hat, his eyes glittered with lantern light and shadow. He screwed up his lips as if chewing on something distasteful. Seconds ticked by as the silence deepened into a great ocean tossing with soundless seas. Grubb swallowed and his Adam's apple bobbed, a sharp pointed spearhead beneath the skin.

"If you do," Zak finally said, "it'll be the last thing you call out."

"You don't scare me none," Tolliver said.

"You're going to hear two things, Tolliver," Zak said.

"Yeah?"

"One is the sound of my Walker Colt calling out your name. The other is old Angel Gabe blowing his trumpet, calling you to Judgment Day."

Tolliver snarled, uttered an oath under his breath.

He came up into a crouch, his hand diving for his pistol. Danny sat there, trying to hold back his bowels, his face drained of color, leaving only the white stain of fear sprawling on his features.

Zak didn't take his eyes off Tolliver as his fingers grasped the butt of his pistol. Tolliver was pulling his own pistol from its holster. In that wink of eternity, it seemed as if it took hours for the barrel of the pistol to clear the sheath. In that split second, Tolliver's face mirrored his final thought: He was going to make it.

Zak's pistol seemed to leap into his hand, and when he thumbed back the hammer, the click made Danny jump inside his skin. Tolliver's barrel came clear and his thumb pressed down on the hammer to cock the single action.

Zak's Colt bellowed, spewing a bright orange flame, unburnt powder, and a .44 caliber lead projectile from its muzzle. The roar of the explosion was like a single thunderclap drowning out the sizzle of the bullet as it sped faster than the speed of sound, making a crack like a bullwhip just before it smashed into the center of Tolliver's chest with all the impact of a pile driver.

Tolliver's finger closed around the trigger, then went slack as he was slammed back against the wall of the adobe, a jet of blood spurting from his chest, a crimson fountain that drenched his belly and the crotch of his trousers. Danny put his arms up over his head and ducked as if to ward off the next shot that he was sure would come.

Tolliver slumped against the adobe. His pistol slipped from his hand and made a dull thud as it struck the dirt. He stared a thousand yards without seeing anything but a blur, an afterglow of orange light burning into his brain.

Danny swallowed his tobacco. It made him sick and he pitched forward, vomiting it back up, along with the moil of his supper and whatever else was inside his tortured stomach.

Zak walked over, picked up Tolliver's pistol, stuck it inside his belt. He then lifted Grubb's pistol from its holster as Danny went through the throes of the dry heaves.

"I'm leaving you two horses. One for yourself, one to pack out that dead man there. You tell Ferguson and Trask I'm coming for them. And I'll ask you one more time, Danny, how many more of these line shacks between here and Tucson? The ones Ferguson is using."

A watery-eyed Danny looked up at Zak, wiped vomit from his chin.

"Two more, that I know of. Hell, I don't even know who you are," he croaked.

"The name's Cody."

Zak walked inside the adobe and kicked over the stove, threw the lantern onto the coals. Then he walked out, past Danny, and climbed into the saddle. He rode down to the corral, tied Nox to a pole, went inside. He ran all but two of the horses out and closed the gate. He looked up toward the flaming adobe and saw Danny pulling Tolliver's body away from the conflagration.

Zak untied the reins, pulled himself back up into the saddle.

He rode off through a shimmering band of firelight, into the night, following the wagon tracks.

He heard the horses galloping away and the neighs of those left behind.

In the distance, across the vastness of night, the coyotes loosed their ribbons of song. And the moon rose over the horizon, bright and full, its shining face lighting his way long after he left the burning adobe behind.

And he felt as if his father were riding alongside him, speaking to him in the Ogallala tongue, the language of his mother.

≈ 10 ≈

General Grant sipped his whiskey, then signed the paper on his desk. He handed it to General Crook, who was seated on the other side, in a high-backed, upholstered chair that he was sure had come out of a medieval torture chamber. His sword jabbed him in the thigh, and the armrests were too small, too low.

"I want just you and me to know about this, George," Grant said.

"Understood, General."

Crook read the paper.

"You sign it, too," Grant said.

"Of course. Gladly."

Crook leaned over Grant's desk and lay the paper flat. Grant handed him a quill pen. George signed his name with a celeritous flourish.

"I don't want this man wearing a uniform," Grant said. "He might as well wear a red flag draped around him. No, Cody will be more useful to us if our enemies don't see a soldier walking up to them carrying a rifle and a sidearm. Give him rank, but disguise him as a civilian."

"As you wish, General," Crook said. *"I'll make Zak Cody a colonel, fair enough?"*

"Fair and appropriate, General Crook."

"This is the last thing I wanted to accomplish before I took the oath of the presidency," Grant said. *"I think Cody will prove himself out, don't you?"*

"I have no doubt, General."

That was the story Zak heard as told to him by General Crook when the general pinned the oak leaf clusters on his uniform.

"This is the last time you'll see these on your shoulders, Zak," Crook said. "Tomorrow, you'll be a civilian. I want you to see that the Indians of this country get a fair shake."

And that was how it had started. Those same thoughts recurred time and again in Cody's mind whenever he doubted himself or his mission.

Now, as he rode through the night, he wore the mantle Crook had placed on him and it was beginning to weigh heavy on him and give him an itch. He reported to no one, but he also had no guidance but his own. He hoped he was doing the right thing, but he was a tightrope walker working high above the crowd without a net.

Sometime before midnight he made a dry camp, no fire, grass for Nox, a small hill in the open, and hid his bedroll just below it. He ate for the first time that day, filling the hollow in his stomach with beef jerky, hardtack, and water. He was used to such fare, and going for long periods without food was no hardship. He had lived worse, in deep winter snows, high above the world in the Rocky

Mountains or in the Paha Sapa, the sacred Black Hills.

If his father's spirit had ridden with him that night, it was the spirit of his mother that he felt now, as he lay under a canopy of stars with the light zephyrs whispering through the cholla and the yucca. He remembered looking up through the smoke hole of the tipi at night and seeing those same stars and how, over time, they journeyed in circles, the sacred circles so revered by the Lakota.

Her name was White Rain, and she told him once how she had come to be called by that appellation. She did not speak English well, but his father had taught her a few words because he loved her dearly and his Ogallala was not the best. Zak came to know both languages, and others, for his ear was tuned early to languages and dialects.

"When I was born," his mother told him, "my skin was so pale that the old woman who drew me from the belly of my mother said that I must have been washed by a white rain as I made the journey to this world."

"Your mother, was she Hunkpapa or Ogallala?"

"No, she had skin like mine. The red clay had been washed away. She was a captive girl, taken from the white eyes, and my father, War Shield, took her as his wife, as your father took me. My mother's Lakota name was Yellow Bead by the time she had grown into woman."

His father would not tell him much about his mother, and his few memories were hazy. He had only been with her until the Black Robe came and told his father he was going to take Zak away before he turned pure Indian. Black Robe told Russell Cody that there was a white woman at Bent's Fort who could raise the boy and teach him to read and write, to converse properly in the English language. Russell had reluctantly agreed after White Rain died, when Zak was almost eleven years old.

He had never seen a man grieve so, as his father had, after his mother died. Russell worked the traplines long after the last rendezvous. The market for beaver had vanished, and most of the mountain men, the free trappers he lived and hunted with, had gone back to St. Louis or St. Joe, or died of sadness and old age.

"Pa," Zak had said, "why do you sit and stare at nothing for hours? And you cry at night. I hear you. I hear you call out her name."

"When White Rain left me, son, it felt like she took part of me with her. A big part. And I don't know how to get it back. When I look out at the world, there's a big empty spot where your ma once stood. Just an empty place wherever she walked."

"But I miss her, too, Pa."

"I know you do, Zak. You came out of her. You were a part of her. But she and me, we were just one person like. I don't know how to explain it no better'n that. She's done gone and I'm half a man."

"No, you ain't, Pa. You're the same."

"Outside, maybe. Not inside. She squeezed my heart, that woman. Squeezed it real hard whenever she smiled, whenever she put her hand on my arm, whenever she kissed me or lay by my side on the robe."

"You don't take me hunting no more, Pa, and I've had all that book learning. You sent me off with Black Robe and I wanted to be with you and

Ma. I cried every night down at the fort. For a long time."

Russell put his arm on Zak's shoulder.

"I'm sorry, son. I thought it was for the best."

"Maybe Ma don't want you to cry for her no more, Pa. Maybe she wants you to hunt with me, fish with me, 'stead of sittin' around this Sioux camp like one of the old ones with no teeth, just waiting to die."

"You got your ma's sensibility, son, I reckon. No, she wouldn't want me to be a lie-about-camp. She'd tell me to get up off my ass and make meat. But the trappin's all played out and the buffalo are as thin as the mist on the Rosebud. Ain't no life for me no more."

"Maybe I should just give up, too, then, Pa."

"Give up? I never said you should give up."

"Well, Ma's just as dead to me as she is to you. And now you might as well be dead, too. I come back and the braves are still talking about fighting the Crow and going after buffalo and making the Sun Dance. They're living in the past same as you. I learned that much when I was staying with Mrs. McKinney down at Bent's."

"I ain't give up." Stubborn old bastard. Beard stubble on his face like mold growing on rancid deer meat. Grease worried into his buckskins so deep it would never wash out, his moccasins full of sewed up holes, and half his beadwork, White Rain's beadwork, gone, the rest hanging on sinew thread, ready to fall into the dirt. His hair long and full of lice, dirty as a dog's hind leg.

"It looks like you have given up, Pa. I can't say it no plainer than that. You got old real fast, and next your teeth are going to fall out and you'll go blind staring at those empty places all the time. You got to get up off the robes and walk up the mountain with me, make the elk come to your call, the deer to your grunt. You got to hear the crack of your rifle again and see if the beaver have come back up on Lost Creek or over in the Bitterroots."

"I probably should give up."

"Pa, what's a 'squaw man'?"

"Where'd you hear that?"

"At the fort."

"That what they call me?"

Zak dipped his head and nodded.

"Well, that's from folks who just don't understand about livin' in the wilderness, son. They can call me a 'squaw man' all they like, but your ma was a special woman. And her ma, too. A white gal gets captured by an Injun and white folks don't want nothin' to do with 'em. Treat 'em like dirt. Worse than dirt, like cur dogs."

"Did you feel sorry for Ma?"

"No. I saw who she was. Where she come from. Her ma was just a child when she was took. She didn't know nothin' of white ways after a time. So she became a Sioux woman. It takes a mite of courage to change like that, give up what you was and become somethin' else."

"I think I know what you mean, Pa. I remember Curly Jack told me once that he became a mountain man because it was a better life than he had back in Tennessee. Said a man had to become an Indian if he was going to live through a winter in the mountains."

"Curly Jack said it right, Zak. We all came up

here to trade with the red man. Once we tasted their life some, we got to lookin' at things different. We saw white people for what they was, and red people for what they was. We never learned any of that in no school down on the flat."

Zak thought about his schooling and realized that, while he had learned a lot about numbers and words and foreign countries, he had also learned that the white race hated the red men and didn't think of them as being human at all. He began to realize that he and his father lived in two different worlds. It was a sobering thought and went deep with him and stayed there all this time. That was probably why he and Crook had gotten along so well. Crook was a man who could look into both worlds and see the worth in each, as well as the worst in each.

He fell asleep thinking of White Rain and how his father had begun to recover and get back to life after that talk they had. They hunted and fished together, traveled the Rockies as carefree as a couple of kids let out from school for the summer, and they had grown close. That's when he found out that his father had been collecting gold in the Paha Sapa and saving it up, not for himself, but so that he could have a life of ease someday if he chose to live in the white world.

Neither of them had realized the path Zak would take, or that the country would take, going to war over slavery and states' rights, brother killing brother, father killing son, son killing father. Neither of them could foresee the future, but both knew what they both had lost when the beaver played out and White Rain died.

Zak could look back and see that all the signs were there, like signposts on roads that wound through the Badlands. Changes. New paths. The old ones blown over by wind and weather, the new ones dangerous, treacherous, dark.

Neither had seen a man like Ben Trask come down the trail, driven by greed, bent on torture and murder. Trask had intruded on their world as surely as the white man had intruded on the world of the Plains Indians and all the tribes in the nation. Such thoughts tightened things inside Zak, turned him hard inside, like the granite peaks of the Tetons, like a fist made out of stone.

The war changed him, too.

He had seen men torn to pieces by grapeshot and shrapnel, heard their screams and cries, seen the surgeons saw off gangrenous limbs and battlefields strewn with the bodies of young men, some with peach fuzz still on their faces, taken from life long before their allotted time, and it was all horror to see young men march into clouds of smoke and die by the hundreds.

Yet he had escaped harm, somehow, with bullets and minié balls whistling past his ear, bombs bursting all around him, horses shot from under him, and stronger men falling, left crippled for life. He thought of his mother and father often during those years, appreciating them both more than he ever had, missing them in those dark hours when he heard only the moans of the dead and dying while crickets struck up their orchestras in the blood-soaked grasses of woodland havens.

Zak fell asleep thinking back through those years, and feeling just as alone now as he had when the rattle of muskets and the clank of caissons were like a horde of metal insects marching across the land, leaving destruction in their wake, those desolate and deserted burnt lands where corpses stiffened in the sun and wild animals fed on them at night.

And the first kill strong in his mind, that bleak moment when he had shot a gray-clad soldier in the eye, seen him fall and later gaze up at him with that one sightless eye, his stomach churning with a nameless grief for the life he had taken, and the hollow feeling afterward, knowing something had changed inside him, something that could not be spelled out or described or explained.

His dreams picked up strands of these thoughts and wove them into a mysterious tapestry hanging in a great empty hall where the coyotes sang songs of the dead and White Rain smiled at him, great tears in her eyes, and his father stood knee-deep in a beaver pond filled with blood, holding up a rusted trap from which dangled a water snake with a human head that bore a strong resemblance to Ben Trask.

= 11 =

Sergeant Leon Curtis bellowed down from the driver's seat.

"Who's in charge here?"

Hiram stepped off the porch. Trask stood there, eyeing the three soldiers he saw in the lantern light. Two on the seat, one on horseback. Two horses were on lead ropes behind the coach, unsaddled.

"I'm Hiram Ferguson. That's one of my coaches you've got there."

"Sergeant Curtis, sir. Returning your coach from Fort Bowie."

Curtis set the brake, wrapped the reins around the handle, picked up his carbine and started to climb down.

"Where in hell's my driver, Danny Jenkins?"

Curtis said nothing until his boots touched the ground.

"Inside the coach," Curtis said. A trooper untied his horse from the back of the coach, led it out, toward the sergeant.

"Jenkins," Ferguson called. "Danny? Come on out."

"He can't hear you no more," Curtis said.

"Huh?"

"The man in that coach is dead. Been embalmed and everything by the post surgeon."

"Dead? How? Somebody kill him?"

"Yes sir, somebody sure killed him."

"Who?" Ferguson asked.

"Man drove the coach into the fort with the lady come to teach the Injun women and children. He shot Jenkins. Said it was self-defense."

"Damn it, Sergeant, I demand to know who killed my driver."

"Man name of Cody. Zak Cody."

Ferguson shook his head. "Who in hell is this Cody? I never heard of him."

"Well, sir, we sure as hell heard of him. The man has quite a reputation. None of it proved, of course. But I wouldn't want to go up against him. Your man Jenkins had the drop on him, according to the ladies who heard the story from Miss O'Hara, and this Cody feller shot him plumb dead."

"Shit," Ferguson said. He did not look up on the porch where Trask stood. But he could feel Trask's eyes on his back, burning holes in it.

Curtis pulled a sheet of paper from his pocket, handed it to Ferguson.

"What's this?" Ferguson asked.

"A receipt, sir," Curtis answered. "For the coach. To show that I delivered it."

Ferguson held the paper up to the light as Curtis produced a pencil, held it out for him. Ferguson signed the paper and handed it back to the sergeant.

"That all?" Ferguson asked, anxious to open the coach.

"No, sir." Curtis pulled an envelope from inside his tunic, handed it to Ferguson. "From the acting commandant."

The packet was sealed with wax, oilcloth folded over. It rattled when Ferguson took it.

Curtis took the reins of his horse, mounted it stiff-necked, his back perfectly straight. He did not salute as he turned his horse, joined the other two soldiers. They rode off toward the town, vanished into the night. When the hoofbeats of their horses faded into the silence of night, Ferguson walked over to the coach and opened the door.

"Damn," he said, peering through the gloom.

It looked like a package, a bundle. Something wrapped in burlap and bound with twine. He knew what it was. He could smell the decomposing body even through the formaldehyde and the crushed mint leaves in a sack tied around the feet, dangling down from the seat.

"What is it?" Trask asked, not moving from the porch.

"It's Jenkins. Dead. Embalmed, I guess."

"Shit," Trask said as Ferguson turned away, then nodded to Grissom. "Put him somewhere, Lou. We'll bury him in the morning."

Ferguson walked back to the porch, climbed the steps. He held the oilcloth packet in his hands, unopened.

"What you got there, Hiram?" Trask asked.

"I don't know. Something from Fort Bowie, I reckon."

"Let's go inside," Trask said. "Find out what it is."

They entered the office. O'Hara sat there, staring at them.

"You want me to give him some of that coffee, Hiram?" Cavins said. "It's ready."

Ferguson looked at Trask, who nodded. Cavins turned and walked to the stove, lifted the pot and poured steaming coffee into a tin cup. He carried it back to O'Hara as Ferguson broke the seal on the packet, opened it.

He read it while O'Hara blew on the coffee to cool it as Cavins held the cup up to his mouth.

Ferguson read the letter. It was not written on official U.S. Army stationery and it was unsigned. But he knew who had written it.

"What's it say?" Trask said, eyeing Ferguson.

"Do you know a man named Cody? The one the sergeant said killed Jenkins."

Trask stiffened. His jaw hardened and a glint sparked in his narrowed eyes.

"I know him."

"He killed Danny Jenkins, all right, says here, just like the sergeant said. And Cody drove O'Hara's sis to the fort."

O'Hara's eyes widened. Trask glanced at him, then took Ferguson by the arm.

"Outside," he growled. "We got to talk."

O'Hara's face softened as he watched the two men go back outside and stand on the porch, out of earshot. He could hear only a murmur of voices, see their shadowed forms in silhouette.

"What else does it say, Hiram?"

"Read it yourself."

"Who's it from?" Trask asked as Ferguson handed him the letter.

"That's for me to know right now. Someone at the fort."

"Fine." Trask read the letter, let out a deep sigh.

"Gives you something to use on O'Hara in there," Ferguson said, licking his lips. There was still a faint taste of whiskey on them.

"Yeah. I think we'll find out what we want to know about that map we found on O'Hara." Trask paused, then handed the letter back to Ferguson. "Want to ask you something, though."

"Go ahead."

"How come you don't want me to burn the information out of O'Hara? You know we're going to have to kill him."

"I know," Ferguson said. "But it's got to look like Injuns, Apaches, done him in. If he's got burn marks on him from a hot poker, the army won't buy it. He's got to look like he was kilt by Apaches."

"My way is quicker. Surer."

"We have to play the hand my way, Ben. Trust me."

"All right. Let's see if O'Hara will tell us what we want to know."

"You going to use his sister?"

"That's what the letter says."

Ferguson nodded. He had read the words. "You can tell your prisoner that if he doesn't divulge what he knows about the enemy, that his sister will forfeit her life after being tortured by savage Indians." Carefully worded. No names. Formal, stiff. But that was the man's way, the one who had written the letter. And Ferguson knew that he meant what he said.

"Let's see what O'Hara has to say about that map," Ferguson said. "You put it to him about his sister."

Trask smiled.

The two men walked inside. Ferguson put the letter back in its packet, folded it and stuck it in a back pocket of his trousers.

"Untie O'Hara," Trask said to Cavins.

"You sure?" Cavins held the cup of coffee suspended above the prisoner.

"Yeah. He's not going anywhere and I want to talk to the lieutenant. He's going to need his hands to show me things on that map."

"I reckon," Cavins said, "if it's all right with Mr. Ferguson."

"Go ahead," Hiram said.

Trask took the cup from Cavins, watched as he untied O'Hara.

"Can you stand up?" Trask asked. He shoved the tub of water out of the way with his foot.

O'Hara, freed from his bindings, flexed his hands and arms, moved his legs. He stood up on wobbly legs.

"Good," Trask said. "Feel like talking with me now? You don't have much choice."

"I can't divulge any information pertaining to my military duties."

"Oh, I think you can, Lieutenant. If your sister's life is at stake. What's her name? Colleen? Yes, Colleen. We can see to it that some terrible things happen to her if you don't play our cards."

O'Hara's face drained of color. "You—You have my sister?"

Trask and Ferguson exchanged glances.

"Yeah, we do," Ferguson said.

Trask smiled at the smooth deception.

"All I want you to do, O'Hara," he said, "is tell

me what those numbers mean on that map. Did you draw it?"

"No, I'm not a cartographer."

"But you wrote the numbers on it?"

"I might have."

"Let's take a look," Trask said, grabbing O'Hara by the arm and leading him over to the table. He spread the map out, pointed to a spot marked with an X, west of the San Simon River.

O'Hara stared down at the map with its X's and numerals.

"That spot there, for instance," Trask said. "You write down them numbers?"

O'Hara drew in a breath, moved his head as if to clear it.

"Yes, I wrote the numbers there."

"Is that an Apache camp? One of their hidden strongholds?"

"Yes, it is," O'Hara said tightly, as if the words were being forced out of his mouth.

"What's this twenty-five mean? Right under the X, and the number under that, ten?"

O'Hara didn't answer right away.

"Means twenty-five braves. Number under it designates women and children."

"Can you find this place?' Trask said.

"Maybe."

"Well, you're damned sure going to, O'Hara," Trask said.

He turned to Ferguson.

"It's all laid out here, Hiram. All the Apache camps. We could sneak up on 'em and do what the army won't do, kill every damned one of 'em."

"I don't know if we have enough men, Ben."

"Won't take many. We pick up the men you got at those relay stations and swoop down on the camps and clean out every nest of rattlesnakes on this here map."

"Tall order."

"We have the advantage," Trask said.

"How's that?" Ferguson said.

"The Apaches won't know we're coming."

"What if we run into soldiers?"

"We tell 'em we're a hunting party. They can't cover all that ground, and they don't have the map. We do. And O'Hara here is going to lead us right to them."

"What if they recognize him?" Ferguson asked.

"I can take care of that, Hiram. His own mother wouldn't recognize him when I get through with him."

"What do you mean to do, Ben?"

Trask smiled. "Dress him up like one of my Mexicans, put a sombrero and a serape on him, sandals, dye his hair coal black."

"It might work."

Trask looked at O'Hara. He touched a finger to his blond hair.

"You're going to make one hell of a Mexican, Pedro," Trask said.

Then he laughed as O'Hara's eyes sparked with anger.

O'Hara shot out an arm, reached for the map on the table.

Trask drove a fist straight into O'Hara's temple, knocking him to the floor.

"Don't get up too quick, O'Hara," Trask said. "Or I'll give you an even bigger wallop." To Cavins he said, "Tie the bastard back up until morning. That's when we'll do the decorating and turn this soldier into a peon."

Ferguson shrank away from Trask, sucked in a breath.

He had seen violence before, but Trask really liked it. The man was like a coiled spring, ready to lash out at anyone who stood in his way. Yes, he wanted the Apaches cleared out of the country, but he began to wonder if he hadn't made a mistake in bringing Trask out from Santa Fe. The man had a thirst for blood that was insatiable.

Trask fixed Ferguson with a look.

"Don't worry, Hiram. The end always justifies the means."

And there was that smile again on Trask's face.

It sent shivers up and down Ferguson's spine.

⟞ 12 ⟝

The land shimmered under the furnace blaze of the sun. Lakes danced and disappeared, water images rose and fell like falls, evaporated as Zak approached them, emerged farther on, shrank away in shining rivulets, trickled through the rocks and cactus and flowed along flats, puddled among the hillocks and vanished like fairy lights on a desolate moor. He was sweating and Nox's black coat shone like polished ebony while his tail flicked at flies.

Zak saw the station from afar and it, too, appeared and disappeared like some mirage as the land dipped and rose like some frozen ocean of sand and rock. Wagon tracks streamed toward the dwelling for some distance, but vanished among the low rocky hills that stood between him and the dwelling. Rather than follow the tracks through the hills, he chose to climb each one to afford himself a better view of the land ahead.

And the land he had left behind.

For Zak had the distinct feeling that he was being followed. He had looked over his shoulder more than once, but saw no sign of anyone on his trail. Yet the feeling persisted, and he knew, from long experience, that such feelings were valid. A man stayed alive because he paid attention to his instincts, those gut feelings that something was not quite right. In a room full of people, you could stare at the back of a man's head for only so long. Sooner or later that man would turn around and return the stare. He had seen this too often to ignore it.

For the past few miles he had felt someone staring at the back of his head. Not literally, of course, but he had a strong hunch that even out there in all that emptiness, he was not alone.

Nox climbed the first hill, paralleling the wagon tracks. Zak fought off the compulsion to turn around when he reached the top. Instead he started down the other side until he was well past the summit. Then he turned Nox and rode back up, spurring the horse to scramble up the slope with some speed. At the top, he scanned his backtrail, his keen eyes searching every square inch of terrain for any sign of movement.

A hawk sailed low over the ground, dragging its rumpled shadow along as it searched for prey. A pair of gray doves cut across the hawk's course with whistling wings. A yucca swayed gently in the breeze. A lizard sunned itself on a nearby rock, its eyes blinking, its tail switching. He saw no other movement, but something caught his eye and he stared at it for a long time.

Shapes in the desert could fool a man. A shadow next to a yucca could resemble a man sitting next to it, or sprawled alongside. Rocks could become human heads, poking up from shallow depressions in the earth. A dark clump of rocks could appear as a horse standing still.

Zak looked for these illusions and discounted most of them in the space of a few seconds.

But just beyond a yucca and some brush, ocotillo and prickly pear, there was something, and he stared at it for a long time. It looked like the very top of a horse's head, two ears and a topknot. It did not move, but still it held his steady, piercing gaze.

Could a horse hold still for that long? Zak began counting the seconds. He counted to thirty, and still the odd shape did not move. He looked away for a moment, then slowly turned his head back once more to that same spot.

Whatever had been there was now gone.

Was he imagining things? Did he really see that shape, or was it just another illusion of light and shadow?

The image did not reappear, although Zak stared in that direction for several more seconds. Finally, he turned Nox and rode back over the hillock and down onto the flat. There was a jumble of hills all around him and he threaded his way through them before topping another. At the summit, though, he had less of a view than he'd had on the first hill and he did not linger. As he rode down the other side, movement caught his eye and he reined up, stabbed his hand toward the butt of his pistol.

"Do not shoot. I mean you no harm." The voice was oddly accented, low and timbrous.

Zak let his hand hover just above the butt of the Walker Colt.

"Show yourself," he said. He realized that he had seen the shadow of something off to his right, nothing of substance. He saw it again, the top of a yucca, torn off, sticking straight out from behind the hill. As he watched, it shook gently, then fell to the ground. A moment later a horse, a small horse, no more than fourteen hands high, emerged from behind the hillock. It was saddled and shod and carried a small, dark-skinned man dressed in old duck pants, a linsey-woolsey shirt, a blue bandanna around his neck. He wore a sidearm, and the butt of a rifle jutted from a scabbard attached to his worn Santa Fe saddle.

"You have been following me," Zak said.

"Yes, I have been following you, because I see what you are doing. What you have done."

"Who are you?" Zak asked.

"I am called Chama. Jimmy Chama."

"You are not a Mexican."

"No. I am Apache."

"Full blood?"

The man rode up close, shook his head. He wore a crumpled felt hat that had seen better days. But it kept the sun out of his eyes, which were dark brown. His hair was coal black, cut short on the sides, streamed down his neck in straight spikes in the back.

"My father was a Mexican," he said. "My mother was a Mescalero."

"You're in Chiricahua country, Jimmy."

Jimmy smiled. "I know. I have friends here. Not many, but a few."

"What brings you on my track?"

"I am on the same track. I am an army scout and interpreter. I was sent with Lieutenant O'Hara to look for Chiricahua camps along the San Simon."

"Were you with him when he was kidnapped?"

"No. I was on a scout. When I returned, he was gone. I was sent to track those who took him."

"And the army?"

"They come. I leave sign for them. But as long as it does not rain, they can follow the wagon tracks, too."

"How many troops?"

"A dozen. But a courier was sent to Fort Bowie. There will be more."

"Are you sure?" Zak asked.

Chama cocked his head and a quizzical look spread over his face. "Why do you ask this?"

Zak shrugged. "I don't know. I have the feeling that things are not quite right at Fort Bowie."

"What makes you think this?" Chama asked.

"I don't trust Major Willoughby. He's in charge, but someone inside that fort had to tell Ferguson where O'Hara was. It's a big country."

"I see," Chama said. "I wondered about that myself. Whoever took Ted knew where he would be."

"Makes you wonder, doesn't it?"

"Why do you say the name of Ferguson? Is that one of his wagons we are following?"

Zak told Chama about the two soldiers, the coach and Colleen O'Hara, his suspicion that Apaches had not killed the two soldiers. He also told him about the men he had seen at the way stations and what they had told him.

"You know," Chama said, "that there are many whites who want the Chiricahua driven from their lands. They want to kill them or drive them far away."

"I'm beginning to see all that, yes."

"Many white people think that the only good Apache is a dead Apache."

Zak had heard that talk many times before, applied to any red man. It galled him, as it galled Crook, and his blood boiled not only at the blind prejudice of the comment, but because he knew good men and bad of both races, the white and the red. And he knew that the color of a man's skin did not reflect what was inside the man.

"Fear," Zak said.

"What?"

"We fear whatever we don't know, Jimmy. The white man fears the red man because he doesn't know him. And he never will unless he shakes a red man's hand and sits down inside his lodge and takes supper with his family. Same goes for the red man, too, of course."

"I never heard a white man talk the way you do, Cody."

"Maybe that's because I'm a breed," Zak said, "same as you."

"You are of the mixed blood? Apache?"

"No. My mother was Lakota. Of the Ogallala tribe."

Chama looked cockeyed at Zak. "Your Indian blood does not show much."

"Does it matter? Blood is the same in all men. Mine is as red as yours and yours is as red as any white man's."

"That is not what the white men say."

"No, that is true."

Zak let the sadness of his words hang in the air between them. He could almost see the thoughts work through Chama's mind, see it twitch ever so slightly in the muscles on his face. He knew it must have been hard on the young man, growing up with the Mescaleros and trying to find his father's people among the Mexicans, and seeing how they, too, were treated by what the Indians called "the white man." Skin. Like the coat of a horse or a longhorn cow, it came in all colors on a human. Yet men separated themselves according to their outward coloring and believed their blood was different, when in truth it was all the same.

"My uncle," Zak said, "*Tashunka Watogala*, Talking Horse, once told me that truth could not be put into words. He said that all we see with our eyes is not true. Only the things that cannot be seen are real and important."

"Your uncle sounds like a wise man," Chama said.

"He was a wise man. He taught me much. As did my mother, although I did not realize it at the time."

"When we are young, we do not wish to learn from the old ones. But we learn anyway," Chama said. "And when an old man dies, he takes all of his wisdom with him. If we do not listen to his words when he is alive, they are lost forever."

Zak nodded, then shook off the thoughts that came rushing in, the words of Talking Horse, his mother, his own father. Good words. Not the truth, perhaps, but guideposts to the truths that lay hidden in plain sight.

"We're not going to catch that wagon," Zak said, "but I aim to put these supply stations out of business. You want to ride along?"

"But, of course. I am on the same trail as you, Cody."

"There could be gunplay."

Chama looked down at the pistol strapped to his waist.

"That is why I carry this pistol, Cody. If it is called upon, it will speak."

Zak's mouth curved in a lazy smile.

He turned his horse and set out toward the adobe he had seen in the distance. They followed the wagon tracks, then climbed another hill to survey the trail ahead. The adobe sat atop a rocky knoll, less than a mile distant. Horses milled in a pole corral some yards from the dwelling. Shimmering pools of watery light shone like fallen stars all around, dancing and disappearing with every turn of the head. The light was blinding and Zak did not look at any of the mirages directly, but scanned the adobe for movement, for any sign of life.

"See anything, Chama?"

"A white man will not bask in the sun like a lizard on such a day as this. If a man is there, he is inside, where the adobe is cool."

"He could be watching us."

"No. There is no shadow at the window."

"You have the eyes of an eagle, Chama."

Chama chuckled. "I think that you see as well as I, Cody."

They rode down the slope of the hill, the cobbles clunking under their horses' hooves, tumbling where they were dislodged, rolling a few inches before they halted and lay still once again.

They stayed to the flat, following the wagon

ruts. These were crumbling and their edges lost to the wind, but still plainly visible, days old.

"We'd better split up, Chama," Zak said. "Come at the adobe from the sides. I'll ride up in front, call the man out. You can flank me if he opens up on me. Could be more than one man, too."

"We will see," Chama said.

Chama rode off then, on a tangent, making a wide circle so he would come up on another side of the adobe. Zak rode straight toward it, his senses honed to a keen sharpness, alert for any signs of life or belligerence.

He closed to within a hundred yards of the front door, giving Nox his head. He saw his ears stiffen and twist. The horse arched his back, lifted his head high. His neck stiffened.

What was Nox seeing that was not there? Zak wondered.

The horses in the corral spotted him and one of them whickered.

Fifty yards away. No movement at the window. The door was closed tight.

Forty yards and Nox seemed to stiffen all over, step more gingerly. Zak let his right hand fall to his holster. He put a thumb on the hammer of his pistol.

The breeze blew against his face. A small sudden gust whipped him, stung his cheeks with grit.

He thought he heard a metallic sound.

Then he heard the *whump* of a rifle booming from inside the adobe. Instinctively, Zak hunched forward, his body hiding behind Nox's neck.

He heard the whoosh of a bullet, saw it kick up dust as it plowed a divot ten yards in front of them.

"You opened the ball, you sonofabitch," Zak said to himself and drew his pistol as he dug spurs into Nox's flanks and charged straight at the adobe.

He knew the rifle that the man used, from its deep-throated roar, muffled by the adobe walls. He knew just how long it would take for the man to fire that rifle again, and each second that passed seemed an eternity.

Life hung on such a slender thread, he thought, and he could feel that thread stretching, stretching, to the breaking point.

13

The Big Fifty.

The sound of the Sharps was unmistakable, and Zak knew he had only seconds to get out of the line of fire before the shooter could reload the single shot rifle. He saw the puff of white smoke cloud the window ledge in the lower left-hand corner. He rode hard to come up in front of the house before the man inside could get off a second shot.

Nox's muscles bunched up and he galloped as the energy in those muscles uncoiled. He stretched out his neck and laid his ears down, raced under the guidance of the bit in his teeth.

There was no second shot by the time Zak reached the front of the house. He took Nox around the corner to the other side, jumped out of the saddle and hunched down beneath a window on that side.

The scrape of a boot and Zak whirled, his pistol a part of him, swinging like a weather vane to come to bear on whoever was coming around the corner of the adobe.

Chama stepped into view, hunched over, pistol in hand. He tiptoed toward Zak, who waved him down even closer to the ground.

"See anything?" Chama said.

Zak shook his head. "What's out back?" he asked.

"A worn-down old wall, a boarded-up window."

The adobe bricks were crumbling, the gypsum almost all washed away, sand along the base of the very old building.

Zak pressed his ear against the wall, listened. He heard only the faint susurrance of the breeze against the eaves and the faint rustle of the nearby brush. Underneath, a silence seemed to find harbor in the adobe wall and within.

"You get hit?" Chama whispered.

Zak pulled away from the wall, shook his head.

"I think there is only one man inside," Chama whispered.

Zak nodded in agreement.

"Jimmy, can you sneak by that front door, go around to the other side, under the open window?"

"Yes, I can do that."

"I'm going to call the man out through the front door. If he doesn't come out, I'll bust in. When you hear that door crash open, you cover that window."

"You will take all the risk, Cody."

"No. It's dark inside. You won't be able to see well through that window, but if he shoots at me, you'll have a shot."

"And you?"

"He might surrender without a fight."

"That would be the smart thing to do."

The two men considered their moves for a moment. When Chama was ready, he nodded. Zak waved him on past him. Chama crawled on his hands and knees around the front of the adobe. He made no sound, took his time. Zak followed, also

on his hands and knees. He stopped on one side of
the door as Chama disappeared around the corner
of the house.

Zak waited. He put an ear to the door and listened.

He heard the soft sounds, like dream noises from
another dimension. The shuffle of a leather sandal
sole on dry earth, the faint metallic scrapings as if
someone was fiddling with a stuck brass doorknob.
Heavy breathing, anxious breathing, like someone
gripped with fear and urgency.

Something about those odd confluences of sounds
made him think that there was a child or an idiot on
the other side of the door, someone confused and in
a state of increasing panic. Someone demented and
scared, an imbecile who couldn't figure out what
to do.

Zak touched a finger to the door, pushed gently.
It moved, and the leather hinges made no sound.
He pushed with the heel of his hand and the door
opened wider, letting a shaft of sunlight pour a sallow streak onto a dirt floor that showed signs that
it had been swept flat with a broom. He craned his
neck as he brought his pistol up close to the door-
jamb, ready to push it through the opening and
squeeze the trigger if someone came toward him.

The sounds were louder now. A rustle of cloth, a
deep sigh, and that same metallic chitter sounding
like a tin grasshopper working its mandibles, or
a squirrel muttering low in its mechanical throat.
He saw movement and stretched his neck to look
inside toward the window where someone had shot
at him moments before.

A dark shape and the unmistakable straight line

of a rifle barrel silhouetted against the window's pale light. A figure hunched over, fiddling with the trigger or the trigger guard. The action on the Sharps was jammed, he figured, and the shooter had not ejected the empty hull nor jammed in another .50 caliber round.

Zak eased up through the doorway, still hunched over in a crouch, and stepped carefully onto the dirt floor. He made no sound as he tiptoed toward the figure with its back to him. He knew, from a quick glance, that there was no one else in the room. Just that bent form below the window, struggling with the Sharps, absorbed in freeing the jam, breathing hard and fast, the sucking in and out of an open mouth and nostrils.

Zak grabbed the end of the barrel as he rammed the barrel of his pistol into the back of the person's head. He thumbed the hammer back on the Walker Colt to full cock, the sound like an iron door opening in a dark cave.

"One twitch," Zak said, "and I blow your brains to powder."

He heard a startled gasp that sounded almost like a sob, and he snatched the rifle out of the squatting person's hands, tossed it to the side and behind him.

"Just stand up," Zak said. "Real slow."

He looked downward at long black hair. As the figure rose from the floor, he saw it stream down the back of her dress. He felt something tighten in his throat. A lump began to form as she slowly turned around and looked up at him. Her lips were quivering in fear and her dress rippled from her shaking legs.

"Jimmy," Zak yelled toward the window, "you can come in now."

He saw the crown of Jimmy's hat bob up in the window, then disappear. A moment later Chama entered the hut, pistol in hand.

"Lady," Zak said, "step out where I can see you. We won't hurt you."

She was young, Zak could tell that. But as she stepped toward him, he could see that her eyes were very old, and full of pain, the pain of centuries, and the pain of her present existence. Her brown eyes lay in watery tired sockets and the flesh beneath them was darker than her face, sagging from too many nights of weeping and maybe hard drinking. There was an odd smell in the room, one that he could not define, but was faintly familiar.

Chama walked over to a table and picked up a clay pipe, sniffed it.

"Opium," he said. "She's been smoking opium."

"That's what I smelled," Zak said. "The room reeks with it."

"*Quien eres?*" the woman said in Spanish.

"My name's Cody. Do you speak English?"

"Yes. I speak it."

"What is your name?"

"Her name," Chama said, "is Carmen Delgado. She is the wife of Julio Delgado."

"You know her?"

"I have seen her before," Jimmy said. "In the jail at Taos. She was bailing out her husband, Julio, who had beaten her up the night before."

"Is this true?" Zak asked Carmen.

"He did not mean it. Julio gets loco sometimes. When he drinks too much."

"Julio stole *tiswin* from a Chiricahua and killed the man he stole it from," Chama said. "I tracked him to Taos."

"You didn't arrest him?"

"I tried. Nobody would listen to me. Julio is a bad man, a killer."

Carmen's eyes flashed. "*Mentiroso*," she spat, her eyes blazing. "You liar," she said in English.

"It is true," Chama said. "The Apaches would like to see Julio hanged, or if they could get their hands on him, they would cut him into many pieces."

"Well, Carmen," Zak said, "looks like Julio run off and left you here by yourself."

"He come back," she said.

"Was he one of those who painted himself like an Apache?"

"I no tell you nothing," she said.

Chama stepped in close and glared at her.

"Answer the questions," he said. "Maybe he won't kill you." He spoke in Spanish, but Zak understood every word.

"That's good advice, Carmen," Zak said. "You want to live, don't you?"

She didn't answer.

Zak picked up the clay pipe, held it front of her.

"You want to dream again, don't you?" he said.

Her eyes flashed, burned with need, with longing. Then they returned to their dull dead state as her shoulders slumped. She seemed resigned to the hell she was probably going through, but her lips pressed together in defiance.

"Just tell me their names, Carmen," Zak said, "and you can fill your pipe."

"They are friends of Julio," she said.

"They work for Hiram Ferguson, don't they?"

Her eyes widened and flashed again. "You know they do."

"Tell me their names."

Chama put the snout of his pistol up against Carmen's temple. He thumbed the hammer back. The double click sounded like a lock opening on an iron tomb. Silence filled the room as the blood drained from Carmen's face.

"They have gone," she said. "You will not catch them."

"No matter. But I want to know their names. There were six of them. Julio was one of them."

"Yes," she spat. "Julio is their leader. He is a very strong man. If you go after him, he will kill you."

"The names," Zak said.

Chama pushed the barrel of his pistol hard against Carmen's temple. She winced and licked dry lips with a dry tongue.

"No matter to me," she said. "Hector Gonzalez and his brother, Fidel. Renaldo Valdez, Jaime Elizondo, and Manuel Diego. They ride with Julio." She paused, then said, "Give me the pipe."

Chama eased the hammer down to half cock and pulled the pistol away from Carmen's face. But it still pointed at her.

"I think you've had enough opium, Carmen," Zak said. "Now, we're going for a little ride."

"Where do we go?" she said.

"To the next one of these adobe way stations, then to Tucson. To find Julio."

"He will kill you," she said, and as Zak threw the pipe down on the dirt floor, a shadow of a sadness came into her eyes and her dry tongue laved her lower lip.

"Saddle a horse for her, Jimmy, will you? Let's get the hell out of here, out of this stink."

The adobe reeked with the stench of whiskey, opium fumes, stale bread, and moldy tortillas. But there was also the lingering scent of pipe tobacco and burnt powder from the Sharps. Zak picked up the rifle, examined it. There was a dent in the receiver's action, a dimple that kept it from ejecting unless force was used. Apparently, he thought, Carmen didn't have the strength to force the breech open. And she was not even a good shot.

"Why would Julio leave you here all by yourself?" Zak asked her after Chama had taken saddle, bridle, and blanket from a corner and lugged it outside.

"He said he would be back soon."

"What's soon?"

"Two days, he say. Maybe three."

"Do you know why he was coming back?"

"No."

"Who was here before you came? The man who was watching the place, taking care of the stock?"

"I do not know his name. He works for Hiram."

"He went back with the wagon? With the army lieutenant?"

"There was a man in the wagon. His hands and feet were tied with rope. He did not wear an army uniform."

"But you knew he was a soldier?"

Carmen nodded. "They said he was a soldier."

"Do you know where they took this soldier?"

"To Tucson. To the office of Hiram, I think."

"Did Julio ride with the wagon?"

"No. The wagon came after he left."

Zak threw the rifle down. He picked up a lamp, shook it. There was the gurgle of oil inside its base. He pulled the stopper and splashed the coal oil around the room.

"What do you do?" Carmen asked.

"Nobody's going to use this adobe again," he said.

"You burn?"

Zak ushered her to the door, turned and struck a match. He tossed it on a place where the coal oil made a dark stain. The match flared and guttered, then flared again as the heat reached the coal oil. The oil burst into a small flame that grew larger.

"My purse," Carmen said. "My boots."

"Too late," Zak said, stepping outside and closing the door.

Inside, he could hear the crackle of flames as the fire fed on dry wood and cloth. Chama had finished saddling a horse for Carmen. He waited, holding the reins of his horse and the one he had just saddled. Zak whistled and Nox trotted up to him.

Smoke billowed from the adobe as the three rode off. Carmen looked back at the burning adobe, that same flicker of sadness in her eyes that Zak had seen before. Then she turned back around and held her head high, staring straight ahead at Chama, who rode in front, following the wagon tracks.

Zak felt sorry for her. She had nothing, and she had just lost everything.

He knew the feeling.

⇥ 14 ⇤

Lieutenant Theodore Patrick O'Hara dozed on the bunk, pretending to be in a deep sleep. At least the torture was over for the time being, he thought. A small victory in the early stages of what he expected would be a long battle. Hiram Ferguson had been only a small assault force. Ted knew that he still must face the main battalion, and that was Ben Trask. Trask was the major force, and he was formidable.

Moonlight streamed through the window above Ted's bunk, splashing dappled shadows that flirted with those sprawled by the lamp upon the wooden floor. A column of gauzy light shimmered with dancing dust motes that resembled the ghostly bodies of fireflies whose own lights no longer shone.

He was strapped down to the bunk, one of several in a bunkhouse for the stage drivers. Two were asleep across the room, one of whom was snoring loudly. Watching him was Jesse Bob Cavins, his chair tilted back against the wooden wall under a lighted lamp. He was reading a dime novel, his lips moving soundlessly as he struggled with some of the words.

Ted tested his bonds for the dozenth time, the leather cutting into his wrists, too strong to break. Thoughts of his sister Colleen drifted into his mind unbidden. Guilt-laden thoughts. He never should have suggested to the post commandant, Captain Reuben Bernard, that Colleen be hired to teach the women and children of the Chiricahua tribe. Ted had argued that there would never be peace in Apache land unless the Indians assimilated the English language. Colleen had agreed to come to Fort Bowie. She saw it as a challenge and an opportunity to bring about peace between Cochise and the whites.

Certainly the army had failed, Ted knew.

Captain Bernard, under orders, had waged a fierce and brutal campaign against the Apaches when Ted first came to the fort. He rode with Bernard as he attacked Apache villages, killing eighteen warriors in one, late in 1869. Early the next year, they swarmed down on another village, killing thirteen warriors, and just this year Ted had engaged in another village attack that left nine Apaches dead.

All to no avail, because the Apache war parties increased their depredations, attacking settlements and lone settlers, killing mail carriers and travelers out on the open plain. They even attacked army patrols, as if to show both their defiance and their bravery, and when Bernard sent detachments after the culprits, the soldiers always returned to the post empty-handed and dispirited after fruitless searches over desolate and difficult terrain.

Tom Jeffords had been brought in to palaver with the Apaches, bring them to the council table, beg them to stop their bloody raids on white villages. Some progress had been made and Bernard sent Ted out under a flag of truce to locate Apache villages and strongholds without engaging any of them in battle. Jeffords had paved the way, and Ted was able to locate many Apache camps. These he marked on a map with a special code. The X's did not denote the location of the actual camps, but denoted a marked spot where Ted had written down numbers that indicated the actual location. These numbers were meaningless to anyone but army personnel.

But Trask did not know that. Not yet. And by now, Ted reasoned, the army would be looking for him. If he could lead Trask and his cohorts on a wild goose chase, sooner or later they would encounter an army patrol and he would be freed. That was his reasoning as he lay there in the dark, thinking of Colleen and his fellow troopers, sweat beading up on his forehead and soaking the skin under his arms and at the small of his back.

He worried about Colleen because now he knew that Ferguson had eyes and ears inside Fort Bowie. That was evident in their threats and their knowledge of troop movements. Ferguson, or Trask, or both, had an informant on the post, either an army man or a civilian. It was disconcerting, but he knew there were soldiers who sympathized with the civilian whites, soldiers who wanted to drive the Apaches from Arizona or tack all their hides to a barn door and set the barn afire.

The motives of such soldiers and the motives of civilians were easy for him to understand. What puzzled him now was the motive of Ben Trask. He

had discerned that Trask was in Ferguson's employ, but he also deduced that Trask was not the
following kind. He was like a coiled spring, inert
for the moment but on the verge of exploding into
something entirely different.

What did Trask want?

Ted had a hunch that he would know the answer
to that question very soon. Trask was so full of
deceit, he reeked with it, like some fakir's woven
basket that, when opened, would reveal a writhing
nest of snakes within. Trask had something else
on his mind besides wiping out Apaches. Ferguson
might be under the illusion that Trask was in his
employ, but Trask was using Ferguson to achieve
his own ends. Ted did not yet know what those
ends were, but he'd studied the man enough in the
few hours he had been observing him to know that
Trask had no ideals, no conscience, no common
purpose he shared with Ferguson. He was like a
cur, pretending to be friendly and loyal, who at the
right moment would snarl and snap and tear a person to pieces with his deadly teeth.

Trask was the man to watch. Ferguson was weak
and indecisive. Trask was strong and purposeful,
although he concealed from others what he really
wanted. He was playing along with Ferguson, but
there was no loyalty there, and the pay he got from
Ferguson was not compensation enough. And Ted
knew that Trask wanted something from him that
went beyond the location of Apache camps and
strongholds.

Still fresh in his mind was his meeting with the
wily and wise Chiricahua leader, Cochise. Tom Jef-

fords had arranged the meeting, and Ted had to travel without an army escort. It had been just him and Tom, and the ride took nearly two days through rugged country. Tom had apologized when he told him, at the last part of the trip, that he would have to go the rest of the way blindfolded. That was Cochise's wish and there was no negotiating the terms.

Wearing the blindfold, he had ridden with Jeffords up through a steep canyon. Tom told him there were Apaches in the hills watching their progress, that they all had rifles and were within easy range.

"I can't tell you much more than that, Ted, sorry. But you have a right to know what kind of country we're in. Even if you rode up here without a blindfold, you'd never find your way back."

"I guess I have to trust you, Tom. And Cochise, too."

"Cochise is a man of his word. You will come to no harm while you're with me."

Ted was thoroughly confused by the time they halted in Cochise's camp. When Tom took off his blindfold, the glare of the sun blinded him for several seconds. Then he knew he was looking into the eyes of Cochise, looking into centuries of warfare, blood and pain, and he saw mystic shadows in Cochise's eyes, a knowing that was almost beyond human comprehension.

He was a small, wiry man, with a rugged moon face lined with deep weathered fissures. He looked, Ted thought, like a wounded eagle that was still full of fight. He wore a loose-fitting muslin shirt and a colored bolt of cloth wrapped around his head, his graying hair spiking from it like weathered splinters of wood. He wore a pistol and knife. A rifle and bandoleros sat nearby, within easy reach. Ponies stood at every lean-to, hip-shot, switching their tails at flies, their eyelids drooping like leather cowls on hunting hawks.

Apache men sat under lean-to structures made of sticks and stones that stood against canyon walls. They were little more than temporary shelters, and blended into the terrain, forming no discernible pattern. There were no women or children that Ted could see, and he knew he was in a war camp. Armed Apaches stood on rocky lookouts high above them, or sat, half hidden, squatted in clumps of cactus and stones, barely visible, their rifles and bandoleros glinting in the sun. The fire rings were under latticed roofs that broke up the smoke when it rose so that no sign of their presence ever reached the sky above the hills. It smelled of cooked meat and the dung of horses and men. It smelled of sand and rock and cactus blooms.

"You sit," Cochise said in English. "We smoke."

Ted smoked with the Apache chieftain, while Apache braves sat around them in a half circle, their faces stoical as stone, their eyes glittering like polished obsidian beads. He and Cochise talked, and Cochise asked and answered questions, as he did, too.

"Did you kill Apaches when you rode with the white eyes, Captain?" Cochise asked.

"Yes."

"Did you kill women?"

"No."

"My children?"

"No," Ted answered.

Then he asked Cochise: "Have you killed white men?"

"Yes," Cochise said.

"The army does not want to keep fighting the Chiricahua. But it does not want the Chiricahua to kill any more white people. The army thinks the two tribes can live together, in peace."

"The white man wants all the land," Cochise said. "Land that the Great Spirit gave to the Chiricahua."

"No, we do not want all your land."

"It is not our land. It belongs to the Great Spirit. He lets us hunt it and live on it and wants us to defend it. The white man drives wooden stakes in the ground and writes words on paper that tell us the land belongs to him."

Ted looked at Jeffords for help.

"That is the white man's way," Jeffords said. "The army wants to protect the Chiricahua and let Cochise have his land. He will keep the white man away from Chiricahua land. That is the white chief's promise to the Chiricahua."

"Is this true?" Cochise asked O'Hara.

"Yes," Ted said.

Before he left the camp, Ted saw a strange sight and it startled him. A white man, dressed in black and riding a black horse, appeared from behind a low hill with two Chiricahua braves. He waved to Cochise, turned his horse and rode off into the hills and canyons that formed a maze around the Apache camp.

Cochise waved back to the man.

"Who was that?" Ted asked without thinking. Jeffords shot him a look of warning.

Cochise caught the look and waved a hand in the air as if to dismiss Jeffords's attempt to silence Ted.

"He is called the Shadow Rider," Cochise said. "He comes to us from the north and he brings the words of the white chief Crook with him. He speaks our tongue."

"But he's a white man," Ted blurted out, still puzzled by the man he had seen.

Cochise shrugged and some shadow of a smile flickered from his leathery face.

"Who is to know what blood runs in the Shadow Rider's veins?" Cochise said. "My people trust him. I trust him."

"Will you also trust this man?" Jeffords asked, nodding toward Ted.

"I think this man speaks with a straight tongue. We will talk about him when you have gone. We will seek wisdom from our elders and from the Great Spirit."

"That is good enough," Jeffords said.

Ted's memory of that strange meeting was still vivid in his mind. He had a great deal of respect for Cochise, and after he reported his visit to Captain Bernard, he felt that peace with the Apaches was possible. He just hoped his superiors felt the same.

He had not told Bernard about the Shadow Rider, but he had asked Jeffords if he knew the man.

"Yes."

"What's his name?"

"Zak Cody," Jeffords told him. "And he is under orders from General Crook."

"Army?"

"I don't know. Once, I think. You better just forget you ever saw him in Cochise's camp. I think he's under secret orders from Crook and from President Grant."

Ted had let out a low whistle of surprise. Though he wanted to know more about Zak Cody and his mission, he'd asked no more questions of Jeffords.

Now, Ted opened one eye and stared at Cavins, then shifted his gaze to the shaft of moonlight streaming through the window. The light seemed placid and steady, but it was swirling with dust motes and air, and when he shifted focus, he could see only the light itself. But when he refocused, the motes twirled like tiny dervishes gone mad, with no apparent pattern to their movements. In that moment before he closed his eyes, he compared the vision to Trask's incomprehensible mind. Somewhere in that brain of his, Trask was scheming and planning.

Ted vowed that he would be patient and learn that secret. He just hoped that he would live that long and beyond that discovery. Trask was a dangerous man, and cunning, as a wolf or a fox is cunning, and he knew he must be careful. Very careful.

Finally, he fell into a restless sleep, dreamless except for shadowy shapes that flitted through the darkness of his mind, indefinable, featureless as dark smoke in a darkened room.

He was awakened by the sound of boots stalking across the floor, and when he opened his eyes, he saw a man shaking one of the stage drivers.

"Time to get up, Cooper," a voice said, and the

bearded man on the bunk rose up and rubbed his eyes.

"Shit," the driver said, "it's dark as a well-digger's ass."

"And you got a run to Yuma, Dave."

Cavins had fallen asleep in his tilted chair and he blinked in the low light from the lamp over his head. His paper book had fallen to the floor and lay there like a collapsed tent, open to the page he'd been reading.

Outside, Ted heard the creak and jingle of harness, the snorting of horses, and the low, gravelly voices of men speaking both Spanish and English. The moon had set, or had drifted beyond the window over his bunk. His back was soaked with sweat and his flesh itched under the leather straps.

Trask entered the bunkhouse.

"Cavins, go get some grub," he said.

The other driver woke up, adjusted his suspenders and walked outside to visit the privy. Trask and Ted were alone in the room.

"We'll get those straps off you pretty soon, O'Hara."

Ted just glared at him.

Trask smiled.

"We're going to use your map today. You're going to take us to those places you marked."

"Apaches move around a lot," Ted said. "They could all be gone by now."

"That would be your tough luck, Lieutenant. But I want to ask you something, and it's just between you and me, okay?"

Trask picked up a chair and set it by Ted's bunk.

He sat down and leaned over so his voice would not carry.

"Go ahead, Trask. You have me where you want me."

"Patience, patience. Only a little while longer. We'll get some breakfast for you, some hot coffee and you'll be good as new."

Ted sighed, resigned to being bound awhile longer.

"What do you want to know?" he asked Trask.

"When you and your company were checking on the Apaches out there, did you find out where they keep their gold?"

Ted stiffened. "Gold?"

"Yeah. We know they been hiding it somewheres. You must know where they keep it. You tell me."

Now he knew what Trask was really after. Apache gold. There had been rumors of it at the post and in Tucson. He'd never paid much attention to the talk. But now he knew that Trask believed the rumors and he wanted what he thought the Apaches had.

He also knew that his life depended upon his answer to Trask.

He felt as if he were in a roomful of hen's eggs, and if he made a wrong step, he would break those eggs and Trask would have no further use for him. He let the answer form in his mind, take shape, harden into what had to sound like truth coming from his mouth.

Trask's breath blew against his face, hot and smelling of stale whiskey and strong tobacco.

Ted closed his eyes and opened them again.

Trask was still there, leaning close to him, waiting for his answer.

And Ted's throat was full of gravel, and his gut had tightened with fear and uncertainty.

Trask waited for his answer, a cold look in his pale, steely eyes.

⇥ 15 ⇤

Cloud shadows grazed across the land like the lingering and bewildered shades of sheep. Buttes and mesas stood like the hulks of rusting ships lost on a long ago sea, and the sun blazed down on it all with an unrelenting fire that would bake a lizard's blood. Carmen's face sweated under the brim of her straw hat and no amount of fanning with her hands would push cool air through her mouth and nostrils.

The wagon tracks were dim now, but still visible on the baked sand, like snake tracks turned to fossilized impressions by centuries of sun compacted into a single searing moment. Chama sniffed the air as if seeking a vagrant breeze that might cool his face, dry the sweat soaking from his hairline into his eyes and staining his shirt under his armpits.

Zak worried a small pebble in his mouth, spat it out as he rode up alongside Carmen, who was riding between the two men, Jimmy in the lead, Zak following in the rear.

"You've been to the next station," he said to her. "Know who's there?"

"Why should I tell you anything, gringo?"

"Because I asked you with politeness, Carmen."

"Phaa," she spit, but she could not produce a drop of saliva. "You take me prisoner, make me ride in the hot sun, and you say you are polite? You are *ladrón*, a thief. My husband will kill you as he would kill a cockroach."

"So much killing," he said, half to himself.

"Yes. You. You kill. *Cabrón*."

"*Verdad*," he said. "True."

"And so, you too will die. By the gun."

"I knew a man," Zak said, "who taught me much. He was a Lakota. An Ogallala."

"I do not know what that is. *Indio*?"

"Yes. He was an Indian. His name was Two Hawks. We were watching the dances. He told me that when the people danced, they held hands. They formed a circle. He said that was to show that all people are connected to one another. That we are all the same, in spirit."

"We are not all the same. I am Mexican. You are gringo, *norteamericano*," she spat as if the very words left a bad taste in her mouth.

Zak looked at her and felt pity.

In her eyes, and in the lines on her face, he saw centuries of suffering and pain. He saw the Yaqui blood beneath the skin on her cheekbones, the faint glow of vermillion smeared across the high planes, the ancient bronze of Moorish ancestors in the cast of her jaw, and the black coals of Spanish mothers so sad and haunting in her eyes.

He thought that she must have been pretty once, as a girl is pretty. With a sweet, smiling face, good white teeth, soft locks of shiny black hair. Now, the years had taken their toll. She was no longer a pretty young girl. But she was a beautiful woman, in the way that old, polished wood is beautiful, in the way a gnarled, wind-blasted tree on the sea-coast is beautiful.

"You have the Indian blood in you?" she said after a while. "You do not look it."

"Yes."

"Your mother?"

"Yes."

"But not full blood?"

"No, not full blood," he said.

"That is why you do not show the Indian face of your mother," she said, and he wondered what she was thinking, through that labyrinth her reasoning took her from, that simple black and white place she had come from long ago and journeyed through over so many years.

"Do we ever know who we truly are?" Zak said. "Do we know our fathers and mothers? Can we trace their bloodlines in ourselves? Or do we forge ourselves in their molds so that we look and act the same? If so, that is very sad, and it makes the world a sad place to live."

"The world is a sad place to live," she said, so softly he had to strain to hear it.

"Someday, maybe, if the world keeps growing as it is, as people mingle and marry and leave children to grow, we will all have the same bloodlines. As it was in the beginning."

"The beginning?" she asked querulously, as if she was lost in the fabric of that world he was weaving with his words.

"Adam and Eve."

"The first man and woman," she said.

"Yes. We all sprung from that same seed. Or so the Bible says."

"I do not believe that. We are not all from the same seed. That seed did not carry the blood of blacks and red men and Chinese."

"Skin colors do not matter. A man bleeds the same red blood, no matter the color of his skin."

"Inside, you mean? We are all the same?"

"Yes. Maybe."

"It does not matter to me. I do not think of such things. I know who I am. I know where I came from."

"But do you know where you are going?" he asked, and the question went unanswered as Carmen drew back into herself and wended her way through that labyrinth of reasoning, that maze of bewilderment that faced each person who tried to plumb the depths of life's true meaning.

"You could save some lives if you tell me how many men are at the next station and, maybe, what kind of men they are. We could spare their lives if they have wives and children and just want to ride on instead of fighting us."

"I might tell you who is there," she said, sounding almost like a pouting child.

"I wish you would. Before we get there. Otherwise, we have to assume they will not ride away and we will have to kill them."

"They are just men. They work for Ferguson, too." She paused. "Like my husband."

"Do you know these men?"

"I know their names. They are—"

She broke off and he wondered what she had

been going to say. He could see that she was troubled by his questions, by her thoughts about the
two men manning the line shack, the way station.
Perhaps, he thought, she was worried about her
husband as well.

"Are you Catholic?" she asked.

"No."

"I am Catholic. So is my husband. The two men
at the little post house are, how do you call them,
heathens?"

"They do not believe in God?"

"They believe in money. They bring death with
them. That is why they work for Ferguson."

Her words were laden with a sudden bitterness.
He sensed that she wished things were different.
That her husband did not work for Ferguson, that
he did not mingle with such as those two he would
soon have to face.

"You do not like Ferguson?" he asked.

She spat. "Filth. Greed. That is what he is. I do
not like him."

Zak let out a breath. "These men . . . they are
gunmen?"

"Yes. They carry guns. I have heard my husband
speak of them. They are robbers. Murderers. These
are the kinds of men Ferguson hired to drive away
the Chiricahuas. Bad men."

"You do not want this?"

"I do not care," she said. "Nor does my husband. He does not care about Indians, and neither
do I."

But she did care. He knew that. Her voice qua
vered when she spoke of them, and he sensed that
she was a dam about to break. She had been alone

for a while. With only her thoughts. Now, she had someone to talk to about things she held inside. But he would not draw them out. It would be like lighting a fuse on a stick of dynamite.

"How far to the line shack?" he asked, more to change the subject than to garner information.

She looked around. For landmarks, he thought. Then she looked at the wagon tracks, what was left of an old stage road, as if trying to recall memorable features.

"I know there is more distance between the next one than between all the others. My husband told me this. We will not reach it while the sun is still shining. It will be dark by the time we get to it."

"How do you know this?"

"Because when we left that station, it was dark when we arrived at the other, where Julio left me."

"Then it will be dark," he said. "And maybe that is a good thing."

"You will sneak up on them," she said.

"I will talk to them. If you will tell me their names."

"You want to know who you kill."

Stubborn, she was. Honing in on his words like some bird of prey, pouncing on them with a sharp beak, trying to rip them to shreds.

"So I can call them out. Reason with them."

"To do what?"

"To leave that place without shedding blood."

She uttered a wry laugh, a mirthless laugh that was like the crackle of dried corn husks.

"They are called Lester Cunningham, he is the oldest, and Dave Newton. Dave has the hot head, how you say it, and Lester, he is the quiet mean one, who is always thinking, who always undresses me with his eyes to make me naked in his mind. Julio does not like him. He does not trust him."

"And this David, your husband trusts him?"

"No, but Julio says he is like the cocked pistol with the hair trigger. *Muy peligroso.*"

"Very dangerous, yes."

They rode on as the sun fell away in the sky, burning into their eyes, and they had cold tamales she had made when they stopped at a small spring just off the wagon path. Zak complimented Carmen on her cooking, even though the meat was old and tough, the cornmeal too salty.

Jimmy Chama had been quiet during the meal, but now, as he sat in the shade of his horse's belly, he spoke to Zak.

"I heard you talking with Carmen," he said. "We will reach the way station after dark."

"Yes."

"What will you do?"

"I will talk to the two men there, tell them to go back to Tucson or die."

"You want me to back you, then. And who will watch Carmen?"

"No, you watch Carmen. And wait. I will talk to them. See if they listen to reason."

Carmen laughed that dry toneless laugh of hers, that scoffing laugh that was at once a sign of wisdom and disbelief.

An old wooden stock tank, the tar in its seams badly shrunk and deteriorated, sat on decaying four-by-four whipsawed beams, the water inside, at the bottom, scummed over with green algae. A lizard lay along the top board, blinking its eyes, wondering if it should venture down into the tank. Zak watched it, knowing that the creature would probably drown if it ventured down to the stagnant water. Flies buzzed around the tank in aimless patterns, rejecting the lizard as a source of food.

"That Lester," she said, "he is always looking. He will see you, or hear you, and then his gun will talk to you. His gun does not reason."

"She's probably right," Chama said. "You will go up against two men. If one doesn't get you, the other one will."

"Yes," Carmen said, her breath hissing over the sibilant like a prowling serpent.

Zak drew a breath.

"I will have the night," he said. "Before the moon is up. I will be only another shadow in the darkness. They'll hear my voice, but they won't see me."

"Ah," Chama said. "You will be the shadow, eh. Is that why you are called *Jinete de Sombra*, the Shadow Rider?"

Zak did not answer.

Carmen looked at Zak, shaken by Chama's question. As if she knew. As if she had heard the appellation before, somewhere. She ate the last of her tamale and washed it down with water, her throat suddenly dry and clogged with meat and masa flour.

Zak looked up at the sky and the puffs of clouds. The sun had coursed lower on the horizon and would soon set, drawing the long shadows of afternoon into a solid mass, like a burial shroud.

Then the night would come, and he would find out if words would work better than bullets.

— 16 —

Colleen fanned herself as she faced the class of Chiricahua children and their mothers. She had a large chalkboard to work with, and some children were forced to share their slates with those who had none. It was cooler in the adobe room than outside but still unbearably hot, and she felt the uncomfortable seep of perspiration under her armpits, on the inside of her legs, and beneath her breasts.

She used pictographs to illustrate the English words while she voiced the equivalent in their language, Apache.

"*Ndeen,*'" she said. Man. The children laughed at her stick figures, and sometimes the women did, too.

She taught them to count to five in English, using her fingers.

"*Dalaa, naki, taagi,*'" she would say. One, two, three.

Some of the words were difficult to say, and the children would correct her. Or if they were not sure, one of the mothers would speak up in a loud, gravelly voice and correct her pronunciation.

Colleen had an interpreter, a small, moon-faced woman named *Tu Litsog,* or Yellow Water. She relied on Yellow Water to convey her teachings.

"The key to language," she said, "is writing. If you make the marks on paper, others can read it. You can send this paper, or carry it, over long distances so that others will know your words."

The children and the women all had pieces of paper and pencils. They all seemed fascinated with the process, and though some made drawings or just meaningless scrawls, by the second day Colleen had them writing down the letters of simple words, like dog, cat, and bird. She was delighted at the response.

"I may be going away, Yellow Water, so do you think you can teach your people to read and write with the materials I will leave with you?"

"I do not know," Yellow Water said.

"They all want to learn."

"I know. They respect the white lady. To them, I am a . . . a turn cloth."

"A turncoat? A traitor?"

"Yes, that is the word. A turncoat, a turn face, I think."

"You must not let that matter. You must teach these children and their mothers. I will return."

"Where do you go?"

"I must find my brother," Colleen said.

There was always a soldier guarding the door, usually a private or a corporal, but a grizzled old sergeant often stopped by to check on the trooper and Colleen. She noticed him and liked him. He seemed to like her as well.

His name was Francis Xavier Toole, and he had been in the army for almost thirty years.

"Francis," she said to him after they had become friends, "why is it necessary to put a guard on these children and women?"

"Oh, ma'am, the guard is not here to watch over the squaws and kiddies, oh no. Major Willoughby has the lads keepin' an eye on yourself."

"On me? Why?"

Toole shrugged, but she knew it was not because he didn't know.

"Be honest with me, Francis," she said. "Why does Major Willoughby think that I need an armed soldier watching me teach children to read and write English?"

"Well, mum, it's not for me to say." He shifted his feet and looked down at them, much like a truant boy might behave when speaking to an inquisitive teacher.

Something was wrong at Fort Bowie—she had known it from the very first day—and when news of her brother's abduction became known to her, and Willoughby or anyone else would not tell her anything, she began to feel shut out. Now, after four days of talking with Toole and asking questions of him, she knew he was struggling with his obligation to the military and his friendship with her. But she was determined to persist.

"Francis, I know you're bound by duty, but I must find out what's happened to my brother. And, somehow, I think Major Willoughby knows more than he's telling. This fort seems to be divided and without a real leader."

"Yes'm," Toole said, shuffling his feet and staring down at them, feeling awkward, and perhaps, she thought, a little ashamed.

"Are you agreeing with me, Francis? Or just being polite?"

"Both, maybe. Major Willoughby is temporary commander of the post, ma'am."

"Until when?"

"I don't know, ma'am."

"But you know he's doing things he should not be doing."

"Ma'am, I'm not privileged to read the major's mind."

"Is he doing anything about finding my brother, Lieutenant Ted O'Hara?"

"I don't know, ma'am."

"Will you please call me Colleen and don't be so stiff and formal with me, Francis."

"Yes'm."

"There you go," she said. "Being polite and proper. And you, with so much wisdom, so much information inside you. Information I may need. As a friend."

She was pressing Francis, she knew. Her face glowed in the wash of the afternoon sunlight, her cheeks painted in soft pastels with the complexion of peaches, her eyes narrowed to block the glare of the sun. Francis looked at her, his lips quivering as if he were boiling over to speak, to divulge what he knew, what he suspected.

"There's only so much I can say, Colleen. Only so much I really know."

"Anything might help," she said. "In either category."

"You mean you want me to speculate?"

"That would be a welcome change from the silence, Francis."

"You push real hard, Colleen. I've seen mules less stubborn. Not to compare you to a mule, mind you . . ."

"Let's not just chat with one another, Francis."

"Well, um, they's some soldiers what want the Apaches done in with. Rubbed out. Same as in town, over to Tucson. Your brother was sent out to locate hostiles, er, I mean, Apaches, and report back to Major Willoughby. I reckon I can speculate that the major might have a reason to do this."

"Yes. I can follow you."

"The major can't do this right out in the open. We're supposed to keep the peace, protect the citizenry of the territory, and help Mr. Jeffords bring Cochise and all the Chiricahuas to the peace table."

"But Willoughby doesn't want this to happen?" she said.

"I don't rightly know."

"Yes, you do. What about my brother? Why was he kidnapped and where was he taken?"

"I figure that faction in Tucson, them men, er, ah, those men, don't want Cochise to get off scot-free. They want him and all the other Apaches made into good Apaches."

"What does that mean?"

"It means dead, Colleen. A good Apache, they say, is a dead Apache."

"And my brother? Was he taken away so that the people in Tucson could kill Cochise? Could murder Apaches?"

"Maybe."

"And who was behind his kidnapping?"

"Same outfit that brung you—I mean brought you—here to Fort Bowie," he said.

"Hiram Ferguson?"

"Yes'm. I reckon."

"You know, you mean."

"My best guess," he said.

"I'm going there," she said.

"Going where?"

"To Hiram Ferguson's. I want to ask him what he did with Ted."

"That could be dangerous, Miss Colleen. Ferguson is one of them drum beaters what wants to wipe out the whole Apache nation. He's got him almost a regular army, I hear tell."

"I'm not afraid of him." But her dimples twittered silently like little bird mouths, quivering at the edge of her nervous, brave smile.

"You can't do nothing, even if Ferguson is behind your brother's kidnap. I mean he won't tell you nothin'. And them layabouts he hires on would just as soon kill you as look at you."

"Will you help me, Francis?"

"Help you? How?"

"I want a horse and a pistol and food to carry me to Tucson. I want to leave tonight. I can't do it without your assistance."

"Ma'am—I mean Colleen—you're askin' a lot. I could stand before a court-martial if I gave you an army horse, let alone a firearm."

"But you'll do it, won't you, Francis?"

Her smile this time was full and warm, a knowing siren's smile, as old as time, a smile that made

creases in her dimples, made them wink like con-
spiratorial smiles.

"Well, you can't go to Tucson all by yourself,
you know."

"Oh, Francis, I can do anything I set my mind to."

"Yes'm, I reckon you can. Matter of fact, a couple of the boys got leave coming and they're riding
into Tucson town tonight. Good boys. They could
escort you, I reckon."

She smiled again. "Yes, I reckon they could.
That would be quite nice, Francis."

"Can you handle a gun? I mean a big old pistol
with a kick like a mule?"

"You bet I can, Francis. Ted taught me to shoot,
and I can take a pistol apart and clean it and load a
cap and ball with nothing more than powder, ball,
and spit."

Francis laughed. "All right. You got to be sneaky,
though. I'll tell the boys to meet you behind the
livery after dark. They won't like waitin' that long
to get off to Tucson, but they'll mind what I tell
'em. You'll have a horse waiting there and grub in
your saddlebags, a canteen hanging from the horn.
Those boys are privates, but they're seasoned. Lik-
able. One of 'em's named Delbert Scofield, the
other'n is called Hugo Rivers. They know the way,
even in the dark, and they'll give a good account of
themselves if you should run into trouble."

"And a big pistol? Ammunition."

"Yes," he said, with a downtrodden tone of surrender. "All you need. You might want to take something else with you, though, you bein' Irish and all
like me."

"What's that, Francis?"

"A four-leaf clover and a St. Chris medal."

"Why, Francis," she said, "I didn't know you cared."

He smiled wanly, then left her standing in the doorway of her schoolhouse.

Colleen watched him walk across the compound, into the sunlight, and she brushed back a strand of copper hair that had fallen over her eyes.

"I'm coming, Ted," she breathed. "I'll find you."

And her voice carried the petulance of a prayer. She hoped she would find Ted alive.

She was prepared to face Ferguson and find out the truth about her brother's kidnapping, where he was.

She would not hesitate to shoot Ferguson or anybody else who got in her way.

And she would shoot to kill.

17

In the distance, across the eerie nightscape of the desert, the yellow light flickered like a winking firefly as they rode through and over small rocky hillocks dotted with the twisted forms of ocotillo and prickly pear. In the darkness, distances were deceiving, but Zak had learned to gauge them through long experience of riding at night in country more deceptive than this.

He left Chama and Carmen behind a low hill above the adobe cabin, out of harm's way, after whispering to Carmen to be quiet. She was skittery, and he had a hunch she might try to warn the two men in the hut. He also told Chama to keep a close eye on her.

"Brain her if you have to, Jimmy," Zak said.

In the darkness, he could see Chama nod.

He circled the lighted shack, a slow process because he didn't want Nox's iron shoes ringing on stone or cracking brush. Through a side window he saw shadows moving inside. The horses in the corral were feeding, so he judged that one of the men, or both, had recently set out hay or grain for them. He patted Nox's withers to calm him, keep him quiet as he neared the end of his wide circle.

Zak dismounted, looped the reins through the saddle rings so they wouldn't dangle, leaving Nox to roam free. The horse would not roam, he knew, but stay within a few feet of where he would leave him, waiting patiently for his master to return. He patted Nox on the neck and walked toward the adobe, his boots making no sound on the hard ground.

He crept up to the edge of the light from one window to the side of the front door. The feeble glow from the lamp puddled on the ground outside, its beam awash with winged gnats flying aimless circuits like demented swimmers. A faint aroma drifted from the window and the cracks around the weathered door that had shrunk with age. Zak sniffed, smelling the distinct aroma of Arbuckle's Best, with its faint scent of cinnamon. He listened, heard the burbling of what he imagined must be a coffeepot on a stove. His stomach swirled and his mouth filled with the seep of saliva.

He loosened his pistol in its holster, stepped up to the door and gave a soft knock.

"Who the hell is it?" growled a voice inside.

"I smell coffee," Zak said. "Lost my horse."

Whispers from inside the adobe. A scuffling of feet, scrape of chairs.

Zak left himself room to step aside if anyone came at him with a gun or a knife.

"Hold on," another voice called out.

The door opened.

Two men stood there, back-lighted, and Zak couldn't see their faces well. They wore grimy work clothes and their boots had no shine, dust-covered as they were.

"You what?" the taller man in front growled.

"Lost my horse. Well, he broke his leg in a gopher hole and I had to put him down. Been walking for a couple of hours. Saw your light. Smelled that Arbuckle's when I came up."

"Who the hell are you?"

"Name's Jake," Zak said, the lie coming easily to his lips. "Jake Baldwin." A name out of the past, one of the mountain men who had trapped the Rockies with his father. Jake wouldn't mind. He was long dead, his scalp hanging in a Crow lodge up in Montana Territory.

"Let him in, Lester. Jesus."

"Yeah," Lester said. "Come on in. Coffee's just made."

Zak noticed that Lester's dangling right hand was never very far from the butt of his pistol, a Colt Dragoon, from the looks of it. Well worn, too. There was the smell of rotten flesh and decayed fat in the room, mixed with the scent of candle wax and whiskey fumes.

"I'm Dave Newton," the second man said. "We don't get many folks passin' this way, stranger."

"Jake," Zak said, stepping inside where the musty smell of an old dwelling mingled with the scent of the coffee. "Pleased to meet you."

"That's Lester Cunningham," Newton said. "My partner."

"Set down," Cunningham said, his gravelly voice so distinctive that Zak looked at his throat, saw the heavy braid of a scar there, dissecting his Adam's apple. He was a tall, rangy man with long hair the color of steel that hung down past his shirt collar. His complexion was almost as gray, pasty, as if he had been in a prison cell for a good long while.

Newton was a stringy, unkempt man with a sallow complexion, bad teeth, and a strong smell that emanated from his mouth. His scraggly hair stuck out in spikes under his hat, which, like him, had seen better days. His eyes appeared to be crossed, they were so close-set, straddling a thin, bent nose that furthered the illusion. His face and wrists were marbled with pale liver spots, and Zak could see the blue veins in his nose, just under the skin.

As Lester took the coffeepot off the small square woodstove with its rusty chimney, Zak glanced around the room. There were coyote skins drying on withes, others, stiff and stacked, tied into bundles with twine, and, in a small oblong box resembling a cage, a jackrabbit hunched, its eyes glittering with fear. Some potato peelings littered its cage.

Newton saw Zak looking at the rabbit and let out a small chuckle.

"That's Bertie," he said. "Me 'n' Lester pass the time huntin' coyotes at night. We take Bertie out there in the dark and twist his ears till he squeals like a little gal. Them coyotes come slinkin' up for a meal and we pop 'em with our pistols. For sport. But we can sell them hides to the Mexicans in Tucson for two bits or so. Drinkin' money."

Zak saw that both men wore skinning knives on their belts. Newton packed an old Navy Colt, converted from percussion to handle cartridges. The brass on it was as mottled as his skin.

Lester poured coffee into three grimy cups. He

handed one to Zak, who took it in his left hand, the steam curling up from its surface like tiny wisps of fog.

"What's this about your horse?" Cunningham asked. "You say it stepped in a gopher hole? I ain't seen no gophers 'round here."

"It was a hole," Zak said. "I thought it was a gopher hole. Maybe a prairie dog hole."

He held the cup up to his lips, blew on it, but he didn't drink.

"Ain't seen no prairie dogs 'round here neither," Cunningham said. "Where'd you say you was from?"

"I didn't say," Zak said.

"Les, you don't need to be so unsociable," Newton said. "Let the man drink his coffee."

"He ain't drinkin' none," Cunningham said. "You left-handed, mister?"

"I'm ambidextrous," Zak said.

"Huh?" Newton said.

"Yeah, what's that?" Cunningham said. "Some kind of disease? That abmi—whatever."

"Ambidextrous. Means I'm good with either hand, Lester," Zak said, an amiable tone in his voice. "From the Latin. 'Ambi' means both. 'Dextrous' means right."

Both men worried over Zak's explanation. Newton was the first to figure it out.

"That means you got two right hands?"

"Something like that," Zak said. "Means I can write or play with my pecker using either hand."

Newton laughed. Cunningham scowled.

"Mister, seems to me you got a smart mouth," Cunningham said. "Something wrong with the coffee?"

"No, why?" Zak said.

"You ain't drinkin' it."

"Too hot."

"How come you're holding that cup with your left hand?" Cunningham said.

"Oh, it was the handiest, I reckon," Zak said with a disingenuous smile.

"Or maybe you mean to draw that Walker and rob us," Cunningham said.

"You got something to rob?"

Newton chuckled. "He's got you there, Les," he said.

"I don't like the bastard," Cunningham said. "We don't know where he come from. We don't know what he wants. He asks for coffee, then don't drink it. Shit, he's got something up his damned sleeve besides an arm."

"Aw, Les, you go on too much about nothin'," Newton said. "Coffee's real hot. He don't want to burn his lips."

Zak looked at the two men. Newton was oblivious to the threat voiced by Cunningham, or was unaware of the tension between the two men. But he wasn't. Cunningham's eyes were narrowed to slits and he looked like a puma ready to pounce. He decided he had played with them long enough.

He set his coffee cup down on the floor. Cunningham's gaze followed it and he stiffened. Newton looked like an idiot that had just seen a parlor trick he didn't understand.

But Zak noticed that Newton was wearing a swivel holster. He wouldn't even have to draw his pistol, just reach down, cock it as he brought the holster up on the swivel, then fire. Of the two men in the adobe, Zak figured Newton was the more dangerous one, even though he showed no signs of being belligerent.

It was the quiet ones you had to watch, he thought.

"I don't know," Zak said softly, shaking his head, "he must have scraped the bottom of the barrel."

"What's that?" Cunningham said. "Who you talkin' about?"

"Old Hiram," Zak said.

"Hiram?" Newton came out of his seeming stupor at the mention of the name.

"Ferguson?" Cunningham said. "You talkin' 'bout Hiram Ferguson?"

"Yeah, that's the man," Zak said.

"You work for him?" Newton asked, an idiotic expression on his face.

"Nope," Zak said.

"What's that about scrapin' the bottom of the barrel?" Cunningham said, pressing the issue.

"When he hired you two on," Zak said.

"What the hell . . ." Newton said, setting his cup down on a small table.

"You got somethin' in your craw, mister, you spit it out." Cunningham's right hand drifted closer to the butt of his pistol.

Zak sensed that both men were ready to open the ball. But he wanted to give them a chance, at least.

"Your other way stations up the line are all shut down," Zak said. "The men manning them are either lighting a shuck for Tucson or wolf meat. You two boys got yourself a choice."

"Yeah, what's that?" Cunningham said, his right hand opening, dropping lower still.

"You can either walk out of here, saddle up and ride back to Tucson, or . . ."

Zak reached down, casually, and picked up his coffee cup. It was still steaming.

"Or what?" Newton said, a menacing tone in his voice that was like a razor scraping on a leather strop.

"Or you'll both be corpses lying here when I burn this shack down," Zak said.

That's when Cunningham made his move. His hand dropped to the butt of his Dragoon. Zak tossed the hot coffee at him. Cunningham screamed and clawed at his face. Then Zak hurled the empty cup straight at Newton and stood up, crouching as his hand streaked for the Walker at his side.

Newton dodged the cup and tilted his holster up, hammering back with pressure from his thumb. Too late. Zak had already jerked his pistol free, cocking on the rise, and squeezed the trigger when the barrel came level with Newton's gut. The pistol roared and bucked in his hand, spewing lead and sparks and flame from its snout like some angry dragon.

Cunningham rose to his feet and drew the big Dragoon from its holster, his eyes blinking at the sting of hot coffee.

Zak swung his pistol and made it bark with another squeeze of the trigger. The bullet smashed into Cunningham's belly and he doubled over with the shock of the impact.

"You drop that pistol, Lester," Zak said, "or the next one goes right between your eyes."

Newton groaned and started to lift his pistol to fire at Zak.

"Don't you get it, Newton?" Zak said. "You just stepped on a rattlesnake."

"Huh?" Newton said, his voice almost a squeak as the pain started to spread through his bowels.

"I'm the rattler," Zak said, and shot again, drilling Newton square in the chest, cracking his breastplate and tearing out a chunk of his heart. There was a gush of blood and Newton dropped like a sack of stones.

Cunningham let his pistol fall and rolled on the floor, his back in the dirt. He stared up at Zak, his eyes glassy from the pain that seeped through him like a slow brushfire.

"Who in the hell are you, mister?" Cunningham managed to say. "We ain't done you no harm."

"It's the Apache you're hurting, Cunningham. I gave you a choice. Go or die. You chose the wrong one."

"How—How many of you are there?" Cunningham said. "You got men outside?"

"There's a nation outside, Lester. A whole nation of Apaches."

"I don't get it," Cunningham said, his voice fading as his eyes began to glaze over with the frost of death.

He shuddered and there was a crackle in his throat. He let out a long sigh and couldn't get any breath back in his lungs. He closed his eyes and went limp.

Zak looked at the two men. Both were dead and there was a silence in the room that was both blessed and cursed.

Zak walked to the cage. He took the cage outside, set it on the ground. He lifted the door, and

Bertie hopped out. Zak made a sound to scare the rabbit off, then returned to the shack.

"And you won't kill any more coyotes, either," Zak said as he picked up the oil lamp and hurled it against the wall, hitting it just above the bundle of hides. Tongues of flames leaped in all directions and began licking at the dried fur, anything that would burn.

Zak stepped outside into the clean dry air. He opened the gate to the Colt and started ejecting spent hulls. He stuffed new cartridges into the pistol as he walked slowly toward the place where he had left Nox. Before he mounted up, he could smell the sickly aroma of burning human flesh.

⊶ 18 ⊷

Ben Trask cursed the rising sun. He jerked the cinch strap tight, drove a fist into his horse's belly. The horse flinched and drew up its sagging belly, giving Trask another notch on the cinch. He buckled it and turned to the others in the stable.

"Jesse Bob, you and Willy about finished yonder?"

"Just about, Ben," Cavins said, but he was still trying to load his saddle over the blanket. His horse was sidestepping every attempt.

"I got to finish curryin' mine," Rawlins said. "He wallowed in shit durin' the night."

The eastern horizon was a blaze of red, as if billions of sumacs had exploded and dripped crimson leaves in the sky. There was a majesty and an ominous hush across the desert as the sun spread molten copper over the rocks and plants.

"It's goin' to be hotter'n a two-dollar pistol out there today," Trask grumbled. "We should have been gone long before sunrise."

"Nobody woke us up," Cavins complained. "Hell, we even hit the kip with our clothes on last night."

"It's that damned Ferguson," Rawlins said. "He said he'd have somebody wake us up before dawn."

"Where in hell is Ferguson?" Trask said, a nasty snarl in his voice. "It looks like we got a bunch of barn rats in here and no sign of Hiram."

"He said he had business to take care of," Cavins said. "He'll be along directly."

"There's only one business this day. Damn his stage line anyway."

The Mexicans were almost finished saddling their horses and were leading them out of the stables. Ferguson waded through them into the barn and started yelling at Lou Grissom.

"You got my horse saddled yet, Lou?"

"Yes, sir. He's still in his stall, though."

"Shit, you could have brought him out. Ben, this is a hell of a day for whatever you got planned," Ferguson said as he approached Trask.

"Climb down off your high horse, Hiram," Trask said. "You know the stakes."

"No, I don't know the damned stakes. I got one plan, you got another."

"O'Hara's map's gonna lead us right to the head honcho Apache hisself. We can wipe 'em out in one blow. With my men and yours, them what's in those line shacks, we'll have a small army. Just make sure everybody's got plenty of cartridges, and it wouldn't hurt to take along a few sticks of dynamite."

"Christ, Ben, what makes you think you can trust that soldier boy?"

"Did you hear that horse come in early this morning, runnin' like a bat out of hell?"

"Nope. I slept like a dadgummed log all night."

"That was a rider from Fort Bowie. Wore out saddle leather and his horse to bring me a message from Willoughby."

"Yeah?"

"Yeah. O'Hara's baby sister left the fort night before last, headin' straight for your place. I told O'Hara if this didn't pan out, she'd be the first to die, and he could watch her bleed."

"He swallered that?"

"Shivered like a dog shittin' peach seeds," Trask said.

Hiram found that hard to believe. O'Hara hadn't impressed him as a man who was much afraid of anything. But, of course, he would have strong feelings for his sister and might fear that harm would come to her if he didn't cooperate. And he had to admit, Trask was a bear of a man who could easily make most men think twice before bucking him.

"Well, just watch out he don't trick you, Ben. O'Hara looks to me like a man who puts a card or two up his sleeve when he's at the table."

"He won't double-cross us, Hiram. If he does, he's a dead man."

They finished saddling their horses and gathered outside the stables. Cavins brought O'Hara from the office. He was dressed in civilian clothing and he was no longer bound. But Cavins had his pistol out of its holster and leveled on him.

"Ready to ride, Lieutenant?" Trask said, patting his shirt where the map stuck out so O'Hara could see it.

"Yes," O'Hara said. "Under protest."

Trask laughed. "Duly noted," he said in a mocking tone. "Climb aboard that steel-dust gray over

there. You'll stand out like a sore thumb." With
a wave of his arm, Trask indicated all the other
horses, which were sorrels and bays.

"Mount up," Trask ordered the others as O'Hara
climbed into the saddle, with Cavins watching his
every move. O'Hara was the only one unarmed,
and he sighed as he looked at the small army of
men surrounding him. He knew that he did not
have a friend among them, but his philosophy had
always been, "Where there's life, there's hope." He
just didn't want to put Colleen in jeopardy. By now
he had figured out that Ferguson and Trask both
had ties to Fort Bowie. Although they had never
mentioned any names, he knew that their influ-
ence, or their connections, must reach fairly high.

He didn't know much about Willoughby, hadn't
seen that much of the major. But he knew, or suspected, that Willoughby's sympathies might lie
with the Apache-haters. It was just a feeling. Nothing he could nail down on a roof of proof.

Ted looked at the bloodred sky of dawn, said to
Cavins, "Red sky at morning."

"What's that?" Cavins asked.

"Red sky at morning," Ted said, "sailor take
warning."

"Well, you ain't no sailor and we ain't anywhere
near the sea."

"Don't have to be, Cavins. That sky dominates
the earth."

"Shut up, soldier boy," Cavins said. "You so
much as twitch on this ride and I'll blow you plumb
out of the saddle."

Ted knew that Cavins wouldn't shoot him, but
he saw no reason to argue the point. He was un-

armed and outnumbered, and this was not the place to make a stand. But he also knew that the first duty of a prisoner was to make every attempt to escape. It had been drilled into him at the military academy, and that thought had been uppermost in his mind ever since he was captured in the dead of night.

He looked around. All of the men were looking at the dawn sky. Ted had never seen a more vivid sunrise. The color was extravagant, plush bulges of the reddest red, the color of blood, fresh spilled, after a hot breeze had stiffened it. Yes, it would be hot that day, but he knew that in another day or two all hell would break loose as the sky filled with black bulging clouds and the wind blew dust and sand into their eyes just before the torrential rains hit with a force strong enough to blow a man out of his saddle. He had seen such storms before, blown down out of the mountains and onto the desert. He had seen cattle and men washed away by flash floods and rivers appear in dry creek beds that brought walls of water rushing headlong at better than six or seven feet high and then some.

That sky told Ted that within twenty-four hours they'd be caught up in a gully washer that would have these men scrambling for high ground, their eyes stung by grit and rain, blinded for a time, he hoped, unable to see more than a foot in front of their faces, if that. There would be a chance then for him to ride away from his captors, put distance between him and them as he made his way back to the fort. It was a chance. Perhaps the only chance he'd have. They couldn't make it to the first marks on his map before they would all be swept up in one hell of a frog-strangler of a storm.

Suddenly, he felt an inner surge of energy as a thought occurred to him. He began to calculate the distance in his mind, the estimated speed of travel with this group of armed killers, and he knew it was possible. Possible to outwit Trask and Ferguson, possible to escape. It was a long shot, to be sure, but he was confident there would be time. Time and opportunity. His nerves would be scraped to a fine razor edge when they reached the place he had in mind, but he could handle that.

All he had to do was wait and bide his time, he thought, as he looked at that rude dawn sky again and smiled inwardly.

"Let's get this outfit moving," Trask yelled, as the Mexicans sat their horses, their gazes still fixed on the eastern horizon. Cavins nodded to O'Hara, who turned his horse toward the main bunch of men.

"O'Hara," Trask said, "you ride with me in front. Cavins, you watch him."

"My men," Ferguson said, "you follow behind Cavins."

"Hiram, come on up. You ride with me, too. We're going to pick up those men you got on station. That should give us enough guns to do what we have to do."

"More'n enough," Hiram said. "Them are all good men. Crack shots."

There was grumbling among some of the men who had stayed too long at the cantina the night before, but Trask got the column moving, and the griping stopped once the small troop made the commitment. The sun rose above the horizon, drawing off the night dew and releasing the dry smell of the earth. The shadows evaporated and the rocks and plants stood out in stark relief, as if carved out of crystal with a razor. A horse farted and some of the men laughed.

"I want you to take us straight to where old Cochise has his gold, O'Hara, you got that?" Trask said.

"It's marked on that map in your pocket, Trask. It's a good two-day ride."

"We'll make it in a day and a half."

O'Hara suppressed a smile. That would be perfect in his estimation.

Trask set a pace that brought more grumbling from the men. The Mexicans kept up, as if to show up the gringos, and the muttering stopped once again.

A half hour later, when the smoke of Tucson was no longer visible behind them, Hiram stood up in the stirrups, peering ahead. He uttered an exclamation that there was no equivalent of in any language.

Trask followed his gaze. Small puffs of dust speared on the horizon, golden in the morning light, almost invisible against the desert hue.

"He's wearin' out saddle leather," Trask said.

"Yeah. He's in a mighty hurry, and ridin' the old trail to them ranches where I've got my men on station."

"One of yours?"

"I don't know yet. He's too far away."

"Well, we'll shorten his distance some," Trask said. "Let's keep up the pace," he called out to the men behind him.

The oncoming rider closed the distance. He loomed up, madly whipping his horse with his reins, the brim of his hat brushed back by the force of the breeze at his face.

"Damned if that ain't Danny Grubb," Hiram said. "And looky at his horse, all lathered up like a barbershop customer."

Flecks of foam flew off Grubb's horse. Hiram held up his hand as if to stop him before the animal floundered.

Grubb reined in when he was a few yards away, hauling hard on the reins to stop the horse. The horse stiffened its forelegs and pulled up a few feet away, its rubbery nostrils distended, blowing out spray and foam. It heaved its chest in an effort to breathe, then hung its head, tossing its mane.

"Danny, you 'bout to kill that horse," Hiram said. "What in hell's the all-fired rush and where the devil are you bound so early in the mornin'?"

"Boss, he done shot Tolliver. Larry's plumb dead. He didn't have a chance."

"Whoa up, Danny. Take it slow. Who shot Larry?"

"Let me get my breath," Grubb said, wheezing. The rails in his throat rattled like a stand of wind-blown cane.

"Just tell me who killed Tolliver and we'll get him," Hiram said.

"C-Cody," Grubb stammered. "Calls hisself Zak Cody. The Shadow Rider."

Trask's blood seemed to stand still in his veins, then turned cold as ice.

"Cody?" Trask said. "Are you sure?"

"Damned sure." Grubb was breathing hard, but he was more anxious to get his story off his chest than to breathe in more air. "I lit out, then circled back a ways to see where he went."

By then the other riders had crowded around Grubb and encircled him, all listening intently.

He looked over at Julio Delgado.

"He took Carmen, Julio. Seen 'em ridin' off, and there's another feller with him now, I reckon. Don't know him. But he burned down most ever' one of them 'dobes and I know he kilt Cunningham and Newton. It was dark as hell, but I seen that 'dobe burnin' and I crossed nobody's trail gettin' this far. That man Cody's a pure devil. And he's headed this way, near as I can figure."

O'Hara listened to this account and was barely breathing as he mulled it over.

He had been watching Trask the whole time and he had now found another one of the man's weaknesses. Besides a lust for gold, Trask was afraid. Afraid of one man—Zak Cody.

The Shadow Rider.

It was something to keep in mind, and Cody just might turn out to be another ace in the hole.

The eastern sky was a ruddy daub on the horizon. The sun lifted above the earth and the clouds began to fade to a soft salmon color. But the warning was still there. A storm was coming that would turn the hard desert floor to mud.

Trask turned around and looked straight at O'Hara as if he had read his thoughts.

Ted O'Hara smiled, and he saw a sudden flash of anger in Trask's eyes.

Well, Ted thought, now we know each other, don't we, Ben Trask?

Trask turned away, and the moment passed. But

now Ted felt that he had the upper hand and Trask had no control over the future. Some of the men Trask had counted on were dead. Julio's wife was a prisoner, and ahead lay a bigger unknown than the location of Cochise's rumored hoard of gold.

There was tension among the men now, and Ted knew that this was only the beginning. He was glad he was alive so he could see how it all turned out.

Red sky at night, ran silently in his mind, *sailor's delight. Red sky at morning, sailor take warning.*

"What are you smirking about?" Cavins asked when he looked at O'Hara.

"Oh, nothing. I was just thinking."

"Well, don't think, soldier boy. It might get you dead."

"If you say so," O'Hara said amiably, knowing that it was Cavins who was worried about death, not he.

19

They rode through the night and into the dawn, Zak, Carmen, and Jimmy Chama. Zak felt the weariness in his shoulders, but there was a tingling in his toes, too, as if they were not getting enough circulation. He knew they had to stop and walk around, flex all their muscles, if they were to continue on to Tucson. It was just barely light enough to see in those moments before dawn. The world was a gray-black mass that had no definition, but still, he had seen something that gave him pause.

Carmen was sagging in her saddle, dozing or deep in sleep, he didn't know which. Chama kept rubbing his eyes, and every so often his head would droop to his chest and he'd snap it back up again as if to keep from descending into that deep sea of sleep that kept tugging at him with alluring fingers.

The day before, the two had been locked in conversation, speaking Spanish to one another, their voices barely audible to Zak. He supposed it helped them pass the time and made nothing of it. Carmen was their prisoner, but she behaved well, and perhaps he had Chama to thank for that. He heard her mention her husband's name a time or two, and Chama had spoken his name more than once as well. He figured Carmen missed her husband and welcomed having someone talk to her in her native tongue.

Moments later the dark sky of night paled, then turned bloodred as the rising sun glazed the clouds gathered on the eastern horizon. Light flooded the land with a breathtaking suddenness. Zak stared at the sanguine sunrise for a long moment, caught up in its majesty. He twisted his head and craned his neck to take it all in. A vagrant thought crossed his mind that it was like being a witness to creation itself, watching that first dawn billions of years in the past. Then he turned back to face the west and his gaze scanned the ground, picking up those hoofprints that ranged in the center of the road, bisecting the twin wagon ruts, dusted over by wind and glistening with a faint, ephemeral dew.

The first thing he noticed were the hoofprints. He'd filed them away in his mind a few days ago and had expected to see them, but was surprised at their appearance. They were fresher than they should have been. The edges should have crumbled and been more blurred. No, these were only a couple of hours old, at first glance. He reined in his horse and stepped down out of the saddle to examine them more closely.

Chama halted his horse and leaned out to see what Zak was doing. Carmen also watched, as a little shiver coursed up her spine, a gift of the chill that rose up from the earth.

"Something the matter?" Chama said.

"These tracks. Belong to a horse I watched ride

off from one of the line shacks. A horse ridden by a man named Grubb."

"Slow horse?"

"Maybe. It was kicking up dirt when Grubb rode off."

"Meaning?"

"Meaning he should have been in Tucson a day or so ago."

Zak stood up. He looked at the dawn sky, the clouds beginning to redden as if splashed by barn paint.

"Light down, you two," he said. He had seen Carmen shiver. "We all need to stretch our legs."

"I am cold," Carmen said.

"You will warm up once you get out of the saddle," Zak said. He looked down at the hoofprints again, measuring them against the age of the wagon tracks. They each told a story, and he could gauge the passage of time. Thoughts flooded his mind. Why had Grubb delayed his journey to Tucson? Had he been following them, watching them from a distance? Why?

Whatever the answers were, Zak felt sure that Grubb would tell Ferguson and Trask that he was coming. He might even know that he had Carmen and Chama with him now. It was likely.

Chama walked around, leading his horse, flexing his legs. Carmen stood there, stamping first one foot, then the other, restoring circulation to her feet. She shook with the chill and flapped her arms against her body like some rain-drenched bird. The coolness rose from the ground as the sky raged in the east, a crimson tapestry so bright it seemed as if that part of the world was drenched in a fiery blood.

Zak stood up and faced the west, peering down the old road. Ahead he could see the place where it converged with the regular stage road between Tucson and Fort Bowie. He walked toward the intersection, leaving Nox standing there, reins trailing.

"I'll be back, boy," he said softly, and he caught a sharp look from Chama, who quickly looked away. Zak thought it was an odd look, and he wondered why Chama tried to conceal it. But he shook off the thought as he walked toward the convergence of the two roads.

All of the tracks led there, and he noticed that Grubb's horse had struck a different gait a few yards down the stage road. Clearly, Grubb had put the horse into a gallop, suddenly in an all-fired hurry, Zak thought.

He glanced briefly back to where Chama and Carmen were waiting. He heard Chama's voice as he spoke to her. She replied and Zak realized that they were speaking in Spanish. He caught only a word or two, but they made his skin prickle slightly. He heard *amigo,* followed quickly by its opposite, *enemigo*, then he heard Chama say, *"el gringo* Cody," which surprised him. They were talking about him, he realized, and the knowledge was disturbing. Why were they talking about him? And behind his back? He decided to wait before returning to his horse. The two had their backs turned to him, then he saw Chama step close to Carmen. He glanced over his shoulder back at Cody, then passed something to Carmen, something Zak could not see. He saw Carmen's arms move as she tucked whatever it was into the sash she wore around her waist. At least that was the way he saw it. Then Chama and Carmen turned and he could see their faces in profile. Carmen glanced his way, then averted her eyes quickly as she said something to Chama.

Her voice carried and Zak clearly heard a single question word float from her lips.

"*Cuando?*" she said.

And Zak translated instantly. *When?*

He did not hear Chama's reply, which was only a whisper, but he tried to fathom what Chama said by studying his lips. As near as he could figure, Chama had said, "*Espera.*"

"Wait."

Wait for what? Zak wondered. What had Chama given Carmen, who was their prisoner?

Zak knew they were not far from Tucson. Another two hours' ride, maybe less. But he was on his guard now. Something was going on between Chama and Carmen. And it was very puzzling at that early hour. He started walking back to his horse, and the two of them separated. Carmen walked around, stretching out first one leg, then the other. Chama ran a finger under his cinch, grabbed his saddle horn and rocked it to see if it was still on tight.

"What do you see down there?" Chama asked.

"Just where the two roads join up into a single road. Where the stage runs to the fort."

"Yes," Chama said.

"You and Carmen had words?"

"I spoke to her. She misses her husband. She is afraid."

"She will see him soon enough. Tucson's not far now."

"What will you do when you get there?"

Carmen turned and drifted closer to the two men. The sky was bloodred, sprawling over the entire eastern horizon like a burgundy banner, the red deepening to a crimson stain.

"See Ferguson. Call him to account. See if Lieutenant O'Hara is a prisoner there."

"You might be walking into something bad. Something dangerous."

"If so, I've walked that way before, Chama."

"Yes. I am certain that you have."

"You don't have to be with me."

"I, too, wish to find the lieutenant."

Zak knew Chama was lying. He spoke, but his words were empty, without conviction. Odd, he thought. Why would Chama lie about such a thing? And why now?"

"You don't know O'Hara, do you, Jimmy?"

"No, I don't know him."

"Why should you care what happens to him?"

Chama shrugged, as if to get Zak off the subject of Ted O'Hara.

"I guess I don't know you, either, Chama," Zak said. He would push Chama a little, see what he had in his craw.

"How can one man really know another?"

"Sometimes a man has to make quick judgments," Zak said.

"And how do you judge me, Zak?"

"I don't even have to think about that one. You come out of nowhere, with a story about being a half-breed, and I can either accept that at face value or carry a big suspicion around with me."

"And do you carry a big suspicion with you?"

Carmen walked over to the two men, stood some distance away from them. Zak noticed a slight bulge under the sash she wore around her waist. He couldn't tell from its outline what it was, but it looked a lot like a small pistol, a Derringer maybe, or a Lady Colt, or one of those small pistols Smith & Wesson made for women.

"I didn't," Zak said, "until you started lying about O'Hara."

"Lying?"

"It looks that way to me. I don't think you give a damn about O'Hara, and I think if you did run into him, you'd probably shoot him dead on the spot."

"What makes you think that?"

"A dog has reasons for running after something. I think you ran after me for a reason and it has nothing to do with the lieutenant or the Chiricahua."

"A man can't fight suspicion. It's like a shadow when the sun is shining. It moves, but it will not go away."

"Maybe you'd better make your intentions plain, Chama, before we go any farther down the road."

Chama stiffened as if slapped. The skin on his face tautened and a hard look came into his eyes, like a shadow drifting across the sun.

"This is as far as you go, Cody," Chama said. He cocked his right hand so it hovered just over the butt of his pistol. Zak saw Carmen jerk straight and her right hand brush against the top of her sash.

Zak looked at the two without making a move himself. Seconds ticked by, and it was so quiet, it seemed all three were holding their breaths at the same time.

"Maybe you'd better think about that for a minute, Chama," Zak said evenly. "Words like you just said can shorten a man's life real quick."

"I have thought about it, Cody. End of the line for you. Sorry."

"Any reason?"

Carmen spoke, to both men's surprise.

"You killed his brother, Cody, you bastard."

"That so?" Zak said, looking straight at Chama. "It's news to me."

"Felipe Lopez," Chama said.

"He was your brother?"

"My half brother. We had the same mother. I loved him."

"Like you, Chama, Felipe had a choice. To live or die."

"I do not know how you did it. I know I found him dead, and your tracks."

"So, you tracked me, and waited. Why now?"

"Because you will not get to Tucson alive. There is too much at stake. I want Hiram to win this one. The Apaches are our enemy."

"You are not Apache," Zak said.

Chama spat, his features crinkled in disgust.

"Filth," he said.

"You have the Indian blood."

"Not Apache. They killed my parents, held me

and Felipe prisoner until we both became men and got away from them. I have the Comanche blood."

Suddenly it all became clear. Zak understood. He had allowed himself to be duped. He had believed Chama's story. But there had been no reason to doubt it. He took a man at his word until he proved out as a liar. Now Chama had proven out.

"I guess you got cause to hate, Chama," Zak said.

"You are in the way, Cody, and you killed my brother. Now you will die."

Zak looked at Carmen, then back to Chama.

"Two against one, I reckon."

"Yes," Chama said, and gone was the sleepiness, the fatigue. Carmen had brightened up, too, was licking her lips like a hungry cat.

These two meant to kill him, for sure, gun him down like a dog and leave him for wolf meat.

Still, Zak did not move. He knew he did not have to, just yet.

The hand had been dealt. And, in death, as in life, the hand had to be played out.

He was ready.

Fate would decide who had the better hand.

Zak knew that when it came to a showdown, most men often made a fatal mistake in that moment just before a gun was drawn or a trigger pulled.

And that gave him the advantage. Always.

20

The eastern sky drained its blood, turned to ashes. Tiny mares' tails began to etch the sky with Arabic scrawls of stormy portent. Zak did not look up at the wisps, but kept his gaze fastened on Chama and Carmen. A slight breeze began to rise, its fingers tousling Carmen's hair as she stood there, her face a mask of defiance and determination.

"Tell me, Chama," Zak said, "did you have anything to do with Lieutenant O'Hara's capture? You carry yourself like a military man."

"I was there, yes. I told Ben where the patrol would be and when the best time would be to take O'Hara prisoner."

"You're a deserter, then," Zak said.

Chama shrugged. "I have done my time in the army. I was a sergeant. A good place for a spy like me, do you not think? That is finished. I go now to fight the Apache, to help Hiram and Ben wipe them out. To take their gold."

Zak caught the boastful tone in Chama's voice. Let him brag, he thought.

"The Chiricahua have no gold."

"Cochise has gold. Much gold."

Zak suppressed a laugh. This was far too serious for humor.

"That is an old wives' tale. A lie," Zak said. "Rather, it is a lie made by white men to turn the settlers against Cochise. He has no gold, beyond a few trinkets."

"That is not what Trask and Ferguson believe. And I think O'Hara knows where that gold is. He will tell us. We will find it."

"Not a good reason to die, Chama. For a pile of gold that is only a fairy tale told by white men."

"As I told you, Cody, this is as far as you go. We are two against one, Carmen and I. You can drop your gun now and I will let you walk away. We will keep your horse."

"My horse is worth more than any Apache gold," Zak said softly.

"He is not worth your life, Cody."

"Chama, let me ask you something before you draw your pistol."

"Ask," Chama said, flexing the fingers of his gun hand. "You do not have much time, gringo."

It was funny, Zak thought, how quickly people could change, how swiftly they could change their colors, like a chameleon. Chama had all these pent-up emotions inside of him that he had been carrying for many miles. Now, in the light of a new day, he had reverted to what he always was, a lying, scheming, shifty sonofabitch with murder on his mind.

"Ever stand on a high cliff and look down, wonder what it would be like to fall about a hundred feet onto the rocks below?" Zak asked.

"No, I never have done that. You ask a strange

question. Why? Do you have the fear of falling, Cody?"

"No. I was just thinking to myself about you. And me."

"There is nothing to think about," Chama said.

"Chama, I'm that tall cliff, and you're standing right on the edge of it, about to fall right off. Only in your case, you're never going to see the ground before you hit it."

The expression on Chama's face changed as he realized what Zak had said. In that moment, he knew that Zak had turned the tables on him. Zak was calling him out, not the other way around.

"All right," Chama said, and went into a crouch. As he did, his right hand stabbed downward for the butt of his pistol.

Zak was facing the sunrise, but he did not look at it. Instead, he kept his gaze focused on Chama, and in the periphery of his vision, on Carmen. He was aware of Chama's intentions with the first twitch of his hand, which echoed on his face like a tic.

Zak stood straight, his gaze locked on Chama's flickering eyes. But in one smooth motion his hand snaked down to his pistol, drew it from its holster as if it was oiled, his thumb cocking it before it cleared leather.

Carmen was slow to react, but she saw Chama grab for his pistol and she became galvanized into action. Her hand slid inside her sash, grasped the butt of the pistol Chama had given her and began to slide it upward. She appeared to be moving fast, but in that warped time frame when death dangles by a slender hair, her motion was much too slow, like an inching snail trying to escape a juggernaut.

Zak's Walker Colt roared just as Chama's barrel cleared the holster. He shot from just below his hip, the barrel at a thirty-degree angle. Just enough, Zak thought, to put Chama down.

Chama opened his mouth and yelled, "Noooooo," as Zak's pistol barked. The bullet caught him just above the belt buckle, driving into him like a twenty-pound maul, smashing through flesh as it mushroomed on its way out his back, nearly doubling the size of its soft lead point.

The air rushed out of Chama's lungs like the gush from a blacksmith's bellows and he staggered backward, blood gushing from his abdomen, a crimson fountain. He groaned and went to his knees, the pistol still clutched in his hand. He tried to raise it for a shot at Zak, then his eyes went wide as Zak took careful aim and blasted off another shot that took away Chama's scream as it ripped through his mouth and blew away three inches of his spine in a paralyzing crunch of bone.

Carmen slid her pistol from the sash and pointed it at Zak, her hand trembling, her arm swaying as she tried to aim.

"Sorry, Carmen," Zak said, "but you're standing on the edge of that same cliff."

She fired and the bullet whistled past Zak's ear. He stood there, shook his head slightly and pulled the trigger of his Colt. Carmen closed her eyes for a moment, then opened them in disbelief as the bullet spun her halfway around. Blood spurted from her shoulder, but she managed to lift her pistol again and aim it at Zak, her lips pressed together in rage and defiance. She looked like a cornered animal, her brown eyes flickering with flinty sparks. The pistol cracked and the bullet plowed a furrow in the ground between Zak's legs. He still stood straight, and now his eyes narrowed as he cocked the pistol and held it at arm's length in a straight line that pointed directly at her heart.

"Sorry, Carmen," he said as he squeezed the trigger. "But you called the tune."

The bullet smashed into Carmen's chest, slightly to the left of her breastbone. Her heart exploded under the impact as the bullet flattened and expanded after smashing through ribs. She dropped like a sash weight, a crimson stain blossoming on her chest. She lay like a broken flower in the dirt, the angry expression wiped from her face as if someone had swiped it with a towel. Her eyes glazed over with the frost of death, staring sightlessly at the sky.

The sound of the last gunshot faded into a deathly silence as Zak ejected the hulls from his pistol and slid fresh cartridges into the empty chambers. The smell of burnt gunpowder lingered in his nostrils as he gazed down at Carmen's body, shaking his head at another needless and useless death. Whatever scraps life had offered her, he had taken them all away, regretfully.

Zak saw that Chama, too, was stone dead, his bleeding stopped. He had tried to warn him, but Chama's self-confidence bordered on insane arrogance. The man had followed his own path to the end of the road. The road ended on a high cliff and Chama had taken the fall. The stench from his body, since he had voided himself, was strong, and Zak turned away.

Death was such an ugly thing, he thought. One moment a man, or a woman, was vibrant with energy, brimming with life. The next, after death, they were just carrion, all signs of life and personality gone, their bodies like cast-off rattlesnake skins. In Tibet, he knew, when a person died, the monks took his body to a place in the hills where there was a convex slab of rock. The dead body was stripped and men cut it into pieces, tossed the parts to the large waiting vultures. Their idea was to remove all traces of humanness and let the soul return to spirit form. They watched the vultures gorge themselves on human remains, then take to the sky, flying over the hills and the mountains, carrying what was left of the human corpse. The sight gave the mourners great comfort.

Zak sighed and turned away to walk toward his horse.

Nox stood there in silence, his ears still flattened, his body braced for danger.

Then the horse's ears pricked up and twisted as if to catch a distant sound.

Zak paid attention to such things. He stopped and listened, turning his head first one way, then the other. The sun was clearing the horizon, sliding up through murky logjams of clouds, spraying the land with a pale gold in its broad reach.

He heard the familiar click of a rifle cocking, and whirled to see an armed soldier pointing a Spencer repeating rifle straight at him.

"You just hold on there," the soldier said.

A moment later Zak heard the scuffle of a horse's

hooves and turned his head to see another soldier, also armed with a Spencer, bearing down on him from behind a low hill.

"Better lift them hands, mister," the first soldier said.

Zak slowly lifted his hands.

"Looks to me like we got a murder here," the second soldier said, then turned and raised a hand, beckoning to someone Zak could not see.

The two soldiers closed in on Zak, flanking him on both sides, but kept their distance, their barrels trained on him, their fingers caressing the triggers.

The Spencer had a seven-cartridge magazine, tubular, and used .56/56 rimfire cartridges. Zak knew they could shoot him to pieces at such close range.

"This wasn't murder, soldier," Zak said softly. "Self-defense."

"So you say."

"Look at the bodies. They both have pistols next to them."

"You just hold steady there."

Then Colleen O'Hara rode up. She stared at the bodies of Chama and Carmen, gasped aloud. Then she saw Zak. She stopped her horse next to the second soldier.

"Mr. Cody," she said. "Whatever happened here? Did you kill that man and that woman?"

"You know this jasper?" the first soldier asked.

"Why, yes. Slightly. Why are you pointing your guns at him?"

"It appears that Mr. Cody murdered these two people and I'm going to take him into custody."

"Mr. Scofield, Delbert, I think you may be making a big mistake," Colleen said. "I'm sure Mr. Cody has some reasonable explanation."

"Yeah, what is your explanation, Cody?" the second soldier said.

"Your name?" Cody said, looking at the soldier.

"This is Hugo," Colleen said, "Hugo Rivers. These two were escorting me to Tucson where I plan to look for my brother Ted."

"Well, Private Rivers," Zak said, "these two pulled pistols on me and were going to kill me. I beat them to the punch."

"Some story," Rivers said.

Scofield snorted. Then, he looked at Chama more closely.

"Hey, this here's Sergeant Jimmy Chama," Scofield explained. "He's a damned deserter."

River turned his head to look at Chama. "Sure as hell looks like him," he said.

"That is Chama," Zak said. "Miss O'Hara, he's the one who fixed things with Ferguson and Trask so they could kidnap your brother."

Colleen reared back in her saddle, her back stiffening.

"He is?" she said.

"That's what he told me," Zak said. "He was proud of it. He is a deserter, as these men say. Or was."

"What about that woman?" Scofield asked. "She wasn't no deserter."

"She's married to one of Ferguson's men. She was my prisoner. Chama slipped her a pistol and they both meant to kill me, to stop me from trying to free Lieutenant O'Hara."

"Well, we'll just have to sort all this out," Scofield said.

"No," Zak said, dropping his hands, "you two are now under my command. Put down those rifles. We've got a ways to ride."

"You ain't got no authority to order us to do a damned thing, mister," Rivers said.

"I think he does," Colleen said. "I learned, at the fort, that Mr. Cody is a commissioned officer in the army, working for General Crook and President Grant. You're a colonel, are you not, Mr. Cody?"

Zak nodded.

The two soldiers looked at him, their faces dumbstruck.

Before they could say anything, Colleen lifted her head and pointed to the west.

"I see a cloud of dust," she said. "Somebody's coming this way. Or, it might be the stage."

Zak walked quickly to Nox and climbed into the saddle.

"All of you," he said, "follow me to cover behind that hill over there. Until we know who that is under that dust cloud, we're all in danger."

Colleen was the first to move. Reluctantly, the two soldiers followed.

"There goes our damned leave," Rivers grumbled.

"You trust this Cody?"

"He's the onliest one who seems to know what the hell he's doin', I reckon."

Scofield stifled a curse.

The dust cloud grew closer as the four riders galloped behind the low hill well off the old wagon road.

The sun filled the sky and the blue heavens filled with mares' tails as if the gods had gone mad and scrawled their warning of impending weather for all to see.

≈ 21 ≈

Trask pulled his hat brim down to shield his eyes from the rising sun. But as he gazed at the sky ahead, he saw the first buzzard float to a point and begin circling. The bird was soon joined by two more, then, as they rode on toward the junction of the two wagon roads, several more gathered and began to circle.

"What do you make of it, Hiram?" Ben asked. "Too many buzzards for a dead jackrabbit."

"It don't look natural," Ferguson said. "Must be a big chunk of dead meat to draw that many turkeys this early of a morning."

"That's what I'm thinkin'," Trask said.

He turned in the saddle and looked at the men riding behind until he picked the face of the man he wanted.

"Deets, come on up here," Trask yelled, beckoning with his hand.

Deets rode up alongside Trask.

"Al, see them buzzards up yonder?" Trask said.

"Hell, you can't miss 'em. That's all we been lookin' at for the past five minutes."

"You ride on up under 'em and see what it is they're sniffin'."

"A dead cow, maybe."

"You check, Al. Be quick about it. You get in trouble, you fire off a shot. Got it?"

"Sure, boss," Deets said, and slapped his horse's rump with his reins. He galloped off and the men in line began talking among themselves.

Trask turned around again. "Shut up," he said, and the men fell silent.

Ferguson suppressed the urge to snort at Trask's remark. He didn't want to rile the man up any more than he already was. Trask had been in a foul mood all morning, snapping at the men, cursing the sunrise, the flies, the chill that rose from the earth earlier. He had a lot in his craw and the sight of the buzzards wasn't doing his mood any damned good.

Trask watched Deets disappear over a rise. The buzzards dipped lower, circling like slow-motion leaves caught in a slow-motion whirlwind. More buzzards had flown in to take their places on the invisible carousel, and Trask unconsciously sniffed the air for the stench of death.

Deets was taking a long time, it seemed, but when Trask looked up at the sky again, he saw that the vultures were at least a quarter mile from him, maybe more. Still, he didn't like to wait, and he put spurs to his horse's flanks. The men behind him did the same. Ferguson frowned. They had a long ride ahead of them, days of it, and Trask was already wearing out their horses.

Ted O'Hara saw the buzzards, too, and knew

that the sight of them had agitated Trask. This
gave him a twinge of pleasure. Trask was a man
who had to be in control at all times, he surmised.
When he felt that control slipping, he turned ugly
and mean. The gallop wouldn't accomplish much
over the stretch of land they had yet to cover, but
he knew Trask had sent Deets up ahead to inves-
tigate, and yet, didn't fully trust any of his men.
In fact, he probably trusted no man, and that was
almost always a fatal flaw. The loner could only
go so far in life. Then, when he began to run out
of friends, he stood completely alone, and without anyone to rely on, except himself, he was lost.
Trask wasn't at that point yet, but he was certainly
headed for it. One of his men, one day, would become fed up with him and put a bullet in his back.
And Trask would never know what hit him. He
brooked no counsel, took no advice. From anyone,
except himself.

The line of men stretched out into a ragged column as the slower riders fell behind, but nobody
complained. All of them knew where Trask was
headed, just under those circling buzzards, and
all would eventually reach it. Some of the men exchanged knowing looks, but kept their comments
to themselves.

Trask topped the rise and slowed his horse.

There was Deets, riding back and forth across the
old road. He was leaning over, scanning the ground.
He rode toward the regular stage road where it had
veered off from the old road, then back again, beyond where two saddled horses stood and there
were two dark objects on the ground that Trask
could not identify as being human or animal.

The men behind him caught up and fanned out to look at what Trask was seeing. None spoke a word, at first. They all just stared at Deets, trying to figure out what he was doing.

As if reading their thoughts, Trask said, "Studying tracks."

Julio Delgado broke the silence among the men following Trask.

"That is the horse of my wife down there," he said. "The brown one with the blaze face."

"I know the other one," Hector Gonzalez said. "Do you not recognize it, Fidel?"

"Yes, I know that horse, too," Hector's brother said.

The Mexicans all grew very excited. They slapped each other on the arms and exchanged knowing looks.

"That is the horse of Jimmy Chama," Renaldo Valdez said. "*Ay de mi.*"

"Chama, ain't he the boy what set up O'Hara for the capture?" Trask asked.

"Yep, he's the one. A sergeant in the army out at the fort. But he said he was going to desert as soon as my men got away clean with O'Hara."

"What's his horse doing there, I wonder," Grissom said. "And him not on it."

"Carmen, oh Carmencita," Julio breathed, "*'onde stas?*"

He twisted the reins in his hands as if he wanted to strangle someone.

"Let's go see what we got," Trask said, and dug spurs into his horse's flanks.

Deets rode off toward a long low hill on his left. He stopped his horse, then looked at all of the other hills, a jumble of them, rising on either side and behind. He turned his horse and rode back to where the other horses stood and where the dead bodies lay. He kept looking back over his shoulder and then he rubbed a spot behind his neck.

As he rode closer, Trask saw that the dark shapes on the ground were human. And they were dead. A man and a woman.

"Al," he said as Deets rode up.

"Found 'em like this," Deets said. "That's what brung them buzzards."

"What do you make of it?" Trask asked, looking down at the body of Chama.

"Still tryin' to sort it all out, Ben. Near as I can figger, they was three riders—Chama, that lady yonder, and one other. He might have kilt them two lyin' on the ground, or some other riders come up and they could have kilt 'em, but that don't make no sense, maybe."

"What do you mean?"

"Three riders come from over yonder like they was ridin' the stage road to Tucson. Then the tracks show four of them rode off toward them hills yonder." Deets pointed in the direction from which he had just come.

"So, we're dealing with four riders," Trask said.

"Looks thataway. Less'n there's more about."

"What the hell do you mean, Al?"

"I mean, these are the onliest tracks I seen, Ben. Maybe this was some kind of bushwhack, and four people jumped these two, then rejoined their outfit. Could be the army, I reckon."

"Shit," Trask said.

The others crowded around to listen to what

Deets had to say. Julio Delgado rode over to the body of his wife and dismounted. He bent over her and began to sob. Renaldo looked over at him and then rode his horse up close and dismounted. He patted Julio on the back. Then he, too, began to weep, so quietly the others could not hear. The other Mexicans drifted over, one by one, to console the grief-stricken Julio, who was cradling his dead wife in his arms and rocking slowly back and forth.

O'Hara suppressed a smile. This was not a military operation, but Trask was too dumb to see it.

Ferguson looked at Chama's face, then turned away, as if death were too much for him in the harsh light of day. He gulped in fresh air to keep from gagging on the smell.

Trask looked over at O'Hara. "You know that man there?" he asked.

"He was a sergeant," O'Hara said. "Rode with our patrol."

"You know anything about this?"

"Not any more than you do, Trask. Two people dead. Probably killed by gunshots."

"You're not as smart as you might think you are, O'Hara."

O'Hara said nothing. He kept his face blank, impassive as desert stone.

Trask turned back to Deets. "The tracks lead over yonder, right?"

"Right, boss. I figure they circled that long hill and either lit a shuck or are watching us right now."

Trask scanned the top of the ridge. Everything looked the same. Rocks, cactus, dirt. He saw nothing move, saw no sign of life anywhere.

"Well, if there was an army waiting up there, they could have picked us off by now. We're riding on."

"Aren't we going to bury these two?" Ferguson asked.

"I don't give a damn," Trask said. "We've already wasted enough time here." He looked up at the sky. "Them buzzards got to eat, too."

"I will bury my wife," Julio said. "And Chama, too." He crossed himself.

Trask fixed him with a look of contempt. "Do whatever you want, Delgado. We're ridin' on. You'd better catch up."

"I will catch up," Julio said, biting hard to cut back on his anger.

"I will help Julio," Renaldo said. "It will not take too long."

"I, too, will stay and help dig the graves," Manuel Diego said.

Trask headed straight up the old road, Deets, Ferguson, Cavins, and O'Hara right behind him. The others trailed after them as Julio and Renaldo drew their knives and began cutting into the hard pan of the desert. Julio's face was streaked with grimy tears and he was shaking as he dug.

"That bastard Trask," he said, in English. "*Un hijo de puta, salvaje.*"

"Calm yourself, Julio," Renaldo said in Spanish. "One day, perhaps, we will bury him."

"That would give me much satisfaction," Julio said.

He picked up the small pistol lying next to his wife, examined it and stuck it under his belt.

"I wonder where she got this pistol," he said softly.

Renaldo shrugged.

Trask turned to Ferguson when they had traveled a short distance.

"I know who killed that Chama and Carmen Delgado," he said.

"You do? How? Who?"

"Cody," Trask said. "He's in this, somewhere."

"How do you know?" Ferguson asked.

"I just know. I know it in my gut, that sonofabitch. I figure Chama made a mistake, or maybe went for his gun. The woman, she may have thrown down on Cody, too. That bastard's fast. Very fast. He sure as hell could have killed them both. And I know damned well he did."

"Who are the other riders, then?"

"I don't know. I wish I did, but I just don't know, damn it all."

He rolled a quirly and stuck it in his mouth. He lit a match and drew the smoke in. Ferguson got very quiet, but kept looking off to his left at the jumble of hills and the long ridge that seemed to be the land brooding down on them.

Over on the ridge there was just the slightest movement as Cody peered down at the old road.

He moved so slowly and held his head so still, he might have been just another rock to anyone glancing up at him. He was hatless, and his face, browned from the sun, was not much different in color than the desert itself.

⇥ 22 ⇤

Zak clamped a hand over Colleen's mouth and pushed her down, held her hard against the rocky ground. Her eyes flashed with a wild look as she struggled against him. The two soldiers looked on, uncertain about what they should do.

"Listen, Miss O'Hara," Zak said, his voice a throaty whisper, "you make one sound and we'll be captured and killed. Do you understand me?"

She calmed down, but Zak kept up the pressure on her mouth and body.

"I mean it. Those are dangerous men down there and they outnumber us."

She tried to nod her head. Her eyes flashed her response.

"You'll behave, then?" he asked.

"Umm-ummm," she replied.

"I'll let up on you," he whispered, "but if you cry out or make noise, I'll knock you cold. If you have anything to say, you whisper right into my ear as the sound won't travel. Got it?"

"Mmmm-hmmm."

Zak slowly lifted his hand from her mouth, but kept it hovering a couple of inches away. He watched her lips like a man watching a burning fuse on a stick of dynamite. He nodded and backed away so she could sit up. She beckoned to him, asking him to come close.

She put her lips right up against his ear.

"That's Ted down there. My brother," she hissed in a sizzling whisper.

"Nothing we can do about it now. But we'll get him free. I promise. Now, just keep that notion in your head and shut up."

She nodded.

Zak signed with his hands to the two soldiers, telling them he was going to crawl to the top of the ridge and that they were to stay there, out of sight, with Colleen. Both men nodded assent.

Before Zak crept to the top of the ridge, Colleen drew him close and whispered softly in his ear. She put one hand behind his head and pulled him next to her so his arm brushed against one of her breasts.

"I wish," she sighed softly, "you were still holding me down, Zak."

Zak felt the strength drain from his knees and his stomach fluttered with a thousand flying insects. The musky scent of her assailed his nostrils like coal oil thrown on an open flame. His veins sizzled with excitement and there was a twinge at his loins as the fever of her touch and the urgency of her words seared through him like wildfire.

He drew away from her, slowly, and touched a finger to his lips. She smiled at him, and he felt his insides melt as if she had poured molten honey down his throat. He turned from her and began the slow crawl to a vantage point on the ridgetop

where he could watch and listen. He mentally
shook off what had happened, needing to focus,
to concentrate.

He lay very still, his head resting on his hands
between two head-sized rocks. He saw Trask, the
man he took to be Ferguson, and the Mexicans
congregating around the body of Carmen Delgado.
And he saw Ted O'Hara, guarded by one man in
particular. O'Hara looked at ease, however, and
Zak mentally applauded his courage, his coolness.
He saw a man who was more alert than any of the
others, a prisoner who refused to allow his chains
to weigh him down. Ted O'Hara, he decided, was
a good man to ride the river with.

He saw Trask extend his arm toward the east
and start to ride up the old road, the others following in his wake. The Mexicans continued to dig a
grave for Carmen as Trask and the others moved
out of eyesight.

Zak thought for a moment. It was pretty plain
where Trask was headed. He had left the stage road
and was traveling on the old road, straight into the
heart of Apache lands. There was only one thing
Ben Trask was interested in, Zak knew—gold.
Apache gold. And if his hunch was right, he was
using O'Hara to lead him straight to an Apache
camp. O'Hara had been dealing with the Apaches
and he knew where their strongholds were. Like
Jeffords, he most likely had spoken with Cochise
and probably knew more than any other man in
the territory.

O'Hara was in a bad spot.

And so were they all, for that matter.

Zak didn't wait for the Mexicans to finish digging the grave for Carmen. Three of them stayed behind, and he knew it would take them some time to finish digging with their knives. If they buried Chama, it would take longer. The longer the better, he thought. But he knew he would have to deal with them sooner or later.

He slowly slid back off the ridgetop and descended to where Colleen and the two soldiers were still waiting. Colleen's face told him that she was anxious, while the two soldiers seemed restless and ill at ease, perhaps put out because they had been left with nothing to do.

"Have they all gone?" Colleen asked in a whisper.

"Most of them," Zak said softly. He knew his voice wouldn't carry over the hill to the other side.

"How many?" asked Scofield.

"More than you two could handle. It's not safe to leave yet. Some Mexicans are burying the dead woman. But I reckon you all are anxious to get to Tucson."

"Yes, sir," Rivers said. "I mean, we have leave, Delbert and me."

"Well, I'm certainly not going to Tucson," Colleen said, her voice pitched low. "Not while those rascals have my brother. If I have to, I'll chase them to the ends of the earth."

Zak gave her a sharp look. "I think you ought to go to Tucson, Miss O'Hara. Under the escort of Scofield and Rivers. It would be the safest thing to do."

"No. I came this far to find my brother. Well, I've found him and I'm going to . . ."

"To what?" Zak asked.

"Well, I have a gun. A pistol. I can shoot. I'm going to get Ted away from those despicable people."

"Ben Trask would shoot you dead in your tracks if you even came after him with a pair of scissors, let alone a pistol."

Colleen huffed in indignation.

Scofield stepped forward. "What you aim to do, Colonel? You can't go after all them men by yourself."

"That's my field problem," Zak said.

"It don't need to be."

"You have no stake in this. You and Rivers are on leave."

"You got any plan at all, Colonel Cody?"

Zak looked at the two men, measuring their willingness to give up their leave and help him fight a force that outnumbered them.

Buzzards floated in the sky like leaves drifting on the wind.

"Once Trask and his bunch get far enough away, I'll brace those three Mexicans," Zak said. "The sound of gunfire will draw Trask right back down on me if I shoot now."

"You're going to kill those poor Mexicans?" Colleen whispered, without any sign of enmity in her voice.

"I'll make them an offer," Zak said.

"An offer?"

"They can walk away. Go back to town."

"And will they?"

Zak cocked his head and looked at her as he would an addled child.

"One of those men is burying his wife, the woman I killed. He'll want blood for blood."

Colleen shivered. "It seems such a shame," she said. "All the killing."

"That's why you ought to go with these boys on into Tucson."

"I'm not going anywhere without my brother. Now I know where he is, I'll not give up."

"We feel the same way," Scofield said. "Lieutenant O'Hara's a mighty fine soldier."

"That's right," Rivers said. "'Sides, you can't go up against three men all by yourself. Me 'n' Delbert can even up the odds."

"Then you'll take Miss O'Hara into Tucson?" Zak said.

"I'm not going to Tucson," she hissed, her whisper loud as bacon sizzling in a fry pan.

"I'll be tracking near a dozen men, Miss O'Hara. Any one of which would shoot you dead without a second thought."

"You don't think I'd shoot back?"

"You might. But would you shoot first, before any one of them got the drop on you, Miss O'Hara?"

"Yes," she said, her voice firm and filled with conviction. "Yes, I would. My father and my brother didn't just teach me how to shoot. They taught me how to defend myself. And stop calling me Miss O'Hara like I'm some frail waif who needs coddling. And I'll call you Zak, if you don't mind."

"I think you've been out in the hot sun too long, Colleen," Zak said.

She gave a low "humph" and glared at him.

"All right," Zak said, looking at the two soldiers. "You want to mix in, I could use your help."

"We do," Scofield said. "What's your plan?"

Cody was ticking off minutes in his mind, minutes and distance, figuring Trask was keeping up a steady pace to the east. Soon, he thought, he would be out of earshot of any gunfire. Maybe. Sound carried far in the clear dry desert air.

"Rivers," Zak said, "how good are you with that Fogarty carbine?"

Rivers looked down at the rifle in his hand.

"This is a Spencer rifle," he said. "Army issue."

"Spencer sold his company to a man named Fogarty. Can you shoot it true?"

"Yes, sir, Colonel, sir. I'm the best shot in the outfit."

"He is," Scofield said. "And I'm right next to him."

"Colleen, I don't want you in this. You stay here. Scofield, you climb that ridge about two hundred yards to the east. Rivers, you climb up from here. Real slow. Soon as I round the end of this hill and you don't see me, you start your climb. Stay low and move slow. I'll ride up on those boys and tell 'em 'what for,' and you should be in position by then. Any one of them goes for his gun, you open up."

"We'll do 'er," Scofield said.

Zak walked to his horse, climbed into the saddle.

Colleen came up to him, grabbed his hand, clasped it in hers.

"Zak," she said, her whispery voice like silk sliding on silk, "be careful. I want you to come back alive."

"I will, Colleen. Just sit tight. Try to think of something pleasant."

She squeezed his hand. "I'll think about you, Zak."

He turned his horse and rode off toward the lowest point of the hill. He did not look back, but he felt three pairs of eyes burning into his back.

He slipped the Colt in and out of its holster twice, then seated it loosely in its leather sheath. In the distance he heard a quail pipe its fluting call, and above him the buzzards wheeled on air currents, so close he could see their homely heads, their jeweled eyes, sharp beaks, as they moved their heads from side to side.

To the northwest he thought he saw a blackening sky, but he couldn't be sure. The day was young and the blue sky marked only with long trailing wisps of clouds that looked like smoke from a far-away fire.

Trask should be far enough away by now, he thought. He hoped the Mexicans would take his advice and ride back to Tucson without a fight.

It was a long shot, but he'd make them the offer.

But he was ready.

For anything.

⊰ 23 ⊱

Julio Delgado heard a sound. He looked up from the shallow grave, squinted until his eyes were in focus on the rider coming toward them from the west. Renaldo Valdez saw him and turned his head, looking off in the same direction.

"Someone is coming," Julio said.

"I see him. Who is it?"

"I do not know."

Manuel Diego set down a rock he had dug up and turned to look.

"Maybe that is the man who killed your wife, Julio," he said.

"Maybe," Delgado said, his voice low and guttural.

A few of the buzzards landed some distance from the gravesite. They flexed their wings and marched to and fro like tattered generals surveying a battlefield. Their squawks scratched the air like chalk screeching on a blackboard.

"He does not ride fast," Renaldo Valdez said. "He does not hurry."

"No," Delgado said. "He is without hurry on that black horse."

"He wears black like the horse, eh?" Diego observed. "Maybe he is a messenger."

"A messenger? Who would send a messenger out here from Tucson?" Delgado wiped tears from under his eyes, squinted again.

"Maybe there is trouble at the office of Ferguson," Diego said. "Maybe it burned down."

"You have the imagination of a chicken," Valdez said.

"Why not?" Delgado said. "He has the brains of a chicken."

Valdez laughed. Diego did not laugh.

Delgado stood up. He did not dust himself off, but continued to stare at the approaching rider. Valdez and Diego got to their feet as well, slowly, knives still gripped loosely in their hands.

"You there," Delgado called to Cody, "what brings you this way?" He spoke in English.

"I have a message for you," Cody said.

"See?" Diego said. "He has a message. *El es un mensajero.*"

"You are full of the shit, Manuel," Valdez said.

"Be quiet," Delgado said.

Zak drew closer. "What message do you bring?" Delgado asked.

"I will tell you in a minute," Zak said.

"Tell me now, mister. Do not come any closer. It is very dangerous here."

Zak kept riding.

"Oh, yes, it is dangerous here," he said. "Dangerous for you. Are you Delgado?"

"Yes, I am Julio Delgado. You have news for me?"

"If you are Julio Delgado, I do have news for you. And for your companions as well."

Zak rode up to the three men and reined in Nox. He looked down at them. Delgado's knife lay on the ground, but Valdez and Diego still clutched theirs, more tightly than before.

"And what is this news that is so important that you ride out all the way from Tucson?"

"I did not ride from Tucson," Zak said. "I rode out of the night on this black horse. My message is this: If you and your companions will bury your dead and ride back to Tucson instead of catching up to Trask and Ferguson, you will live another day. Maybe many more days."

Zak's words hung there like black bunting in a funeral parlor. Delgado cleared his throat. Valdez and Diego looked at each other.

"He is loco," Valdez said in Spanish.

"He said he rides out of the night? What does he mean?" Diego asked, also in Spanish.

"Why do you want us to go back to town?" Delgado said to Zak. "Are you going to kill us if we do not do this?"

"Yes, Delgado," Zak said. "I'm going to kill you if you try and join up with Ben Trask. I am going to kill him, too."

"Who are you?"

"I am Zak Cody."

"You are the one they call the Shadow Rider?"

"Some call me that, yes."

"I am not afraid of you, Cody. Did you kill my wife? A man told me that you did."

"I killed your wife, Delgado. And I killed Chama, too."

Delgado's neck swelled up like a bull in the rut. His face purpled with rage. The blood drained from the faces of Valdez and Diego. They both looked as if someone had come up to them and kicked them in the nuts.

"*Hijo de mala leche.*" Delgado spat. Then, in English, "You bastard."

"He is only one. We are three," Valdez said in Spanish to the others.

"He might kill one of us," Diego said.

"I will kill him," Delgado said. "For what he did."

Zak understood every word.

He slid quickly from the saddle, slapped Nox on the rump and squared off to face the three men.

"What do you wish, Delgado?" Zak said in Spanish. "To bury your wife and ride to the town alive, or leave her body to the buzzards while you join her in sleep?"

"You talk very brave, gringo."

Diego and Valdez squeezed the handles of their knives. Cody was too far away. Diego let his knife slide through his fingers until he grasped only the tip.

Zak saw the move and waited.

Delgado licked his dry lips. A buzzard squawked, impatient. There was a silence after that, a silence buried deep in a soundless well.

"You are a dead man, gringo," Delgado said in English. "You do not tell me what to do."

"Delgado, it is your choice. But I will tell you this. The last sound you hear on this earth will be the voice of my Walker Colt."

Delgado's face grew livid with rage. He went into a crouch and clawed for the butt of his pistol. Diego started to draw his arm back to throw his

knife at Cody. Valdez stabbed his hand downward
to jerk his pistol free.

A single second splintered into fractions. Four
lives teetered on the fulcrum of eternity. All breathing stopped. Sweat froze. Eyes crackled and sparked
like tiny flames deep in men's souls. Time no longer existed in that place. Somewhere, out of sight,
a small door opened just a crack and there was a
darkness beyond, a limitless darkness where no
light could shine.

Cody's hand was a flash of lightning, his pistol
a thundercrack in the mute firmament. The blue
sky seemed to pale as fire belched from the barrel
of his pistol and the hornet sound of his Colt fried
the still morning air. Delgado sucked blood from
the hole in his throat and his arms flew upward,
his hands empty.

Cody sidestepped as he hammered back and his
pistol roared again. The bullet caught Diego just as
he hurled his knife and before Diego hit the ground,
Cody knocked the hammer back on the Colt with
the heel of his left hand and swung the barrel toward Valdez, who had his pistol nearly out of its
holster. His lips were pressed together as if he were
under a great strain.

"*Hijo* . . ." he breathed as Cody's pistol roared
with the exploding sound of doom. The bullet
smashed into Valdez's chest with the force of a pile
driver, cracking bone, crushing flesh and veins into
raw pulp, and his eyes clouded up as tears shot
from ducts like a salty rain.

Valdez collapsed to his knees and struggled to
draw breath into lungs that were clogged with

blood and bone. Then the feeble light in his eyes fled through that open door, into the darkness.

Zak cocked his pistol again and looked at each man sprawled on the ground, the smoke from his pistol rising like a fakir's cobra from a wicker basket, the air reeking of burnt powder.

He heard a noise then, the clattering of rocks, the crash of brush. He turned to see Hugo Rivers running headlong down the slope of the hill, his rifle held high over his head, his feet moving almost too fast for his body to follow.

"Hey," Rivers yelled, "you done it all. I didn't have a chance to help."

Zak opened the gate on the pistol and began ejecting the brass hulls. He had filled the empty cylinders with fresh cartridges by the time Rivers reached his side, out of breath and panting. In the distance, he saw Scofield running toward them at a fast lope.

"Boy, sir, I never saw nothin' like that. I mean, one minute they was three men bracin' you, and you plumb beat 'em all to the draw and dusted them off like they was flies on a buttermilk pail."

"There is an old saying about the quick and the dead, Rivers."

"Yeah, what's that, sir?"

"If you aren't quick, you're dead."

"Never heard that."

"I just made it up. You'd better get your horses and Miss O'Hara. Don't let her see any of this, though. I'll meet you on the other end of the hill, the top end."

"Yes, sir. Right away, sir. But I'm still tryin' to

figure out how you was so much faster than any of them. They wasn't slow."

"When a man goes for his gun, Rivers, he'd better not have anything else on his mind. Those men were so busy trying to figure out what to do about me, they forgot I was there."

"Well, no, sir, they knew you was there all right. That one boy, the one you shot first, well, he went for his gun long before you did."

"He might have gone for it, Rivers, but I was already there, about two seconds ahead of him."

"About a half second, I'd say."

"Well, who's counting? Now get going. We've some riding to do."

Rivers started to salute, then realized that Cody wasn't in uniform and awkwardly dropped his arm. He trotted off to climb the hill he had just come down, and ran right through a pair of buzzards that flapped and squawked as they hopped out of his way.

Scofield came up, panting for breath. He looked at the dead men in disbelief.

"Colonel Cody, sir, I never saw anything like it."

"Like what?"

"Like the shooting you did. I had a bird's eye view and saw those three men buck up against you. I thought sure you were a goner."

Zak said nothing as he holstered his pistol, then lifted it slightly to keep it loose.

"I mean, how do you do that, sir?" Scofield said.

"What?"

"Go up against three gunmen and come out without nary a scratch? I couldn't see your hand real well, but I know it was empty when that fat one went for his gun."

"It's real simple, Corporal. I knew what he was going to do. He didn't know what I was going to do."

"That simple?"

"Almost. Near enough."

"Yes, sir. Mighty fine shooting, though."

"Scofield, these men are dead. They didn't have to die. I gave them a choice. They picked the wrong one. I regret that I had to kill them. I feel sorry for the lives they gave up."

"Well, they were trying to kill you, sir."

"Yes, they were. But I walked into their world. I was the intruder, not they. Makes you wonder."

"What's that, sir?"

"Just what keeps the world in balance. A man swats at a bug, kills it with the palm of his hand. Another cuts off a snake's head, while another shoots quail out of the sky. Who keeps track of such small things? And what does it mean when the final count is tallied? Nothing? Or everything?"

"I don't follow you, sir."

"No need, Scofield. I just hate to take a life. It leaves an empty hole in the life of someone who's still living. And maybe it leaves a little hole in my life, too."

"Aw, you can't go worrying about trash like these, sir. They was rawboned killers. Probably got more blood on their hands than you got on your hankie when you was a nose-bleedin' kid."

"Let's go, Scofield," Zak said. "Rivers will bring your horse and Miss O'Hara to the high end of that hill, and we'll get on the trail of Trask and Ferguson. You want to ride double?"

"I'll walk, sir, if it's all the same to you."

Scofield looked at the dead men again and shook

his head as if he were still trying to figure it all out. The buzzards flapped, and three more landed some fifty yards away. They were ringed by the scavengers now and there were more still floating in the sky, their circles getting smaller as they slowly descended toward earth.

The smell of death lingered in Zak's nostrils a long time that day. He was glad that Colleen didn't say anything about what he'd done, although he'd bet a day's pay that Rivers told her all about it, no doubt in exaggerated terms.

"I'm sorry," she said that night when they stopped by a dry wash to rest the horses and stretch their legs.

"About what?"

"About what you had to do today. I know it was necessary."

"It wasn't necessary, Colleen. It was brutal and cruel and heartless."

"But—"

"No, that's what it was. I'm glad you weren't around to see it."

"You're awful hard on yourself, Zak."

He didn't say anything for a long time. She moved in closer to him and he could smell her scent, her soft womanly scent, like lilacs and mint growing under a cistern. Fresh and sweet. He wanted to kiss her, but Scofield and Rivers were watching them. This was not the time.

He wondered when that time would be.

24

Delbert Scofield finished smoking his cigarette, crushed it to bits between two fingers, scattered the remains on the ground. Then he scuffed up the dirt with his boot heels until there was no trace of tobacco or paper.

Hugo Rivers cleared his throat.

"When you aim to talk to Colonel Cody, Del?" he said.

Scofield looked over to where Colleen and Zak still stood.

"Directly. Soon as he gets finished sparking that schoolmarm."

"It just don't seem like he knows what for."

"He knows something, that's for sure."

"Look, we ain't follerin' the old stage road no more. We brung along all them horses what are slowin' us down. It don't seem like he's in no hurry to catch up with those outlaws we're supposed to be chasin'."

"I know. I wondered about that myself. And him goin' off by hisself ever' so often, ridin' up to the top of a hill and flashin' that little mirror."

"I ast him about that. He says it's a army helio-graph," Rivers said.

"A what?"

"A heliograph. It's got a little cross cut into it, so's he can sight the sun and make it bounce off. Says the Injuns call it a 'talkin' glass.' 'Spose he's talkin' to the Apaches?"

"I don't know what the hell he's doin', Hugo. This is gettin' to look more and more like a wild goose chase."

"Well, go ahead and ast him. We got a right to know. We're low on grub. He ain't said nothin' about beddin' down. He keeps lookin' at that sky gettin' blacker and blacker. We could get caught in a gully washer before mornin'."

"All right. Quit your bellyachin'. I'll ask him."

The horses, those that had belonged to Chama, Carmen, Julio, Manuel, and Renaldo, were all roped together, standing disconsolately a few feet away, their rumps to the north, as the sun died in the west below an ashen sky turning darker by the moment.

Bull bats knifed the air, scooping up insects, and a chill seemed to rise from the land as the shadows softened and melted together. An eerie stillness settled over the rocks and plants, the low hills.

"Time to mount up," Zak called over to Scofield and Rivers.

"Before we do, Colonel, sir, I got some questions, if that's all right."

"I have some questions of my own," Colleen said. "When you're finished asking, of course, Delbert."

"Yes'm."

"Corporal," Zak said.

"Yes, sir, well, sir, I just wanted to know why we're not trackin' them men. You left the old stage road, and they could be anywhere. Ain't nary a track out here in this open wilderness."

"I know where Trask and Ferguson are going, Scofield. I expect Miss O'Hara knows, too, don't you, Colleen?"

"Well, I know my brother makes maps. He wrote me what he was doing. He said he was marking where the Apache strongholds were, but only he can read the maps. He is probably guiding those men to one of the Apache camps, though. But I can't imagine that Ted would betray the Apaches he's made friends with. He . . . well, he said he respects them."

"I'm counting on that," Zak said.

"What about all that mirror flashing?" Scofield said. "You bringin' the Apaches down on us, maybe?"

Zak smiled. It was growing darker, but he could still see everyone's face, and they could see his.

"Tom Jeffords now knows we're coming. He'll tell Cochise, and we might be able to count on some Chiricahua help when we meet up with Trask and his bunch."

"Likely, the Apaches won't know the difference and wipe us all out," Rivers said.

"Shut up, Hugo," Scofield said. "I ain't finished with my questions yet." He paused, as if to collect his thoughts.

"Go on, Scofield," Zak said.

"Well, we got them horses what belonged to the people you killed, and they're slowin' us down. And we're about out of grub. We only brought enough to last us three until we got to Tucson."

"You'll find food in the saddlebags of those horses we brought along," Zak said. "And I have some in my own saddlebags. The horses are carrying bedrolls, water, rifles, and ammunition. They'll come in handy when we run into Trask. We're a few sleeps away from that, however."

"How long do you figure we'll be out here?"

"Oh, I expect we'll see Trask and Ferguson tomorrow. About the time that storm hits. They're riding the old stage road and I think they're going to stop at each station to see what I've done to Ferguson's operation. In fact, I'd say we're ahead of them now, and we should get a visit from Jeffords, and perhaps a few Apache braves, before dawn."

"So, you do have a plan," Scofield said.

Zak didn't answer. He turned to Colleen.

"You had some questions, Colleen?"

"I think you've answered most of them. I'm still wondering how you're—we're—going to save my brother, get him away from those awful men. I don't want him to be killed."

"I'm counting on your brother to make the right moves when we start the fight, Colleen. He's a smart man, and no doubt he's been looking for ways to escape all this time he's been in captivity. That's a bridge we'll cross when we come to it."

"Well, I worry."

"Well, don't. Worry is just something that keeps

you from thinking things through. It doesn't accomplish anything much, and it wears you down."

She gave out a small laugh.

"I see," she said.

"Look, all of you," Zak said, "I don't know what's going to happen. Trask is a dangerous man. A desperate man. I think the Chiricahua can help us. We're outgunned and outnumbered right now. But we hold some cards Trask doesn't know about. I think he's going to be surprised. I'm planning to make his hair stand on end."

There was a silence among them for several moments.

The sky blackened in the north and stars appeared to the east. The moon had not yet risen, but there were clouds blowing in over them and Zak knew they would likely see little of it during the night.

"Let's ride," Zak said. "From now on, every minute counts."

Scofield and Rivers walked to their horses. Colleen lingered. She put a hand on Zak's arm. There was a tenderness to her touch that stirred something inside him.

"I hope your plan works, Zak. For Ted's sake."

"Can you ride all night without falling off your horse, Colleen? We've a ways to go."

"Zak, I would ride anywhere with you. I want you to know that."

She squeezed his arm and moved closer to him. She tilted her head and he gazed down at her face. He could barely see it, but it seemed to him that her lips puckered slightly. He leaned down and brushed his lips against hers. She fell against him and he felt her trembling.

"I think I'm . . ."

He broke away, put a finger on her lips.

"Don't say it, Colleen. Not yet. Wait."

"Yes," she breathed, and he watched her walk away toward her horse.

He climbed onto Nox and took the lead, the others following close behind.

In the distance he heard the murmur of thunder, and when he looked back over his shoulder, he could see flashes of lightning in the black clouds. He rode into the darkness, thinking of Trask and how he had murdered his father. There would be a day of reckoning, he knew, for Trask and for him.

Then there was that blood sky of that morning. It carried a portent of much more than a storm. He took it as an omen, and he knew that was the Indian in him. Superstition. It could guide a man or defeat him. But the sky always spoke with a straight tongue.

There would be blood spilled on the morrow.

And the rain would wash it all back into the earth.

A coyote broke the stillness with its querulous call, its voice rising up and down the scale in a melodious and lonesome chant that was almost as old as the earth itself.

Nox whickered, and Zak patted him on the neck.

He felt his blood quicken and run hot.

"Trask," he whispered to himself, "I'm coming for you, you bastard."

Zak and his horse were shadows moving across

the dark land. Shadows as true and ominous as the bloody sunrise of that very morning.

Again the coyote called, but it was different this time.

The call came from a human throat.

An Apache throat.

SHADOW RIDER

APACHE SUNDOWN

For Steve and Cindy Weir

1

So many men killed now, fallen to his gun.

But none of them the man he wanted to kill: Ben Trask.

The last three men hadn't needed to die. He'd given them a chance and a choice. Maybe it was something in the outlaw way of thinking. Three against one was fair odds. Maybe they thought they were better than he. Well, they had found out and now they were cold dead meat. Fair odds, fair warning, he thought.

Ben Trask had brutally murdered Zak Cody's father years before. Now, Trask and several other men were headed east on the old stage road, and Zak meant to stop him in his tracks. He had tracked Ben Trask ever since Russell Cody had been murdered, whenever his undercover military duty allowed him the privilege.

When he'd last spotted Ben Trask and the outlaws, the circumstances were not right to make his move. He knew they would stop at the line shack before long, and figured his opportunity would come after they left the shack.

Cody looked over at Colleen O'Hara, situated

with the soldiers in a vale not far from the hill where he had stationed himself. She had been hired as a teacher at Fort Bowie, upon her brother's recommendation. But Lieutenant Ted O'Hara had been kidnapped by Trask and his men before she even arrived at the fort. She had been riding to Tucson, accompanied by two soldiers. When their path crossed that of Zak Cody and the two soldiers in their search for Ben Trask, Colleen had insisted on accompanying them.

Now, hunkered down on the side of the hill, Zak held up a silver dollar so the sun caught it just right, and flashed signals up the old stage road. He was out of sight, the hand that held the coin not visible to anyone down below. He hoped the kidnapped lieutenant, riding among his captors, would see the signals and know that help was coming.

Cody moved the coin slightly after each flash, spelling out the words he wanted the prisoner to decipher. There wasn't much time. Soon, the column of outlaws led by Trask, the man he was hunting, would be passing the hill. Then he would lose the opportunity to send any more signals to the lieutenant.

His hand ached. Pain coursed down his arm in searing rivulets, burning into his muscles, his flesh, as he manipulated the coin. Flick, flick, flick. Flash, flash, flash.

Help soon, wait, be ready, he signaled over and over until the column of men came too close for the signal to be seen beneath the rise of the hill.

He could hear the hooves of the horses hitting the ground with dull thuds. In the west, a group of clouds appeared on the horizon like the sails of distant sailing ships, their underbellies already turning sable against a stretch of desert landscape that was taking on a sepia hue. The sky had been bloodred that morning, telling him that a storm was coming. Until now, he hadn't known from where, but the signs were all there, in the western sky.

He pulled his hand down, stuck the coin back into his pocket. He flexed his arm and fingers until the feeling returned to the tendons and muscles in his right hand. His gun hand. He drew deep breaths and listened to the unintelligible mutterings of the men, the creak of saddle leather and cinches, the plod of hooves, the crackle of iron shoes on sand.

"I hope the lieutenant got the message," he said to himself, his voice so low it wasn't even a whisper. And none near enough to hear it

He had done what he could to prepare the captured soldier for rescue. That would not be soon. He would have to wait for night, or until the black clouds on the horizon swallowed up the sun.

Lieutenant Ted O'Hara didn't know what to make of it, but there was no mistaking the clear signals he had gotten. Who could have sent them? Jeffords? Could be. Tom Jeffords knew the new Morse code and semaphore. A soldier? An Apache? No, not an Apache. Had to be a soldier. But if so, when could he hope to be rescued? The signaler had told him to wait, to expect help. No time specified. Why not now? And if not now, when? A small mirror, not like the ones the army used. Very small, like a piece of glass, or a silver coin. A quarter, or a dollar, maybe. Strange, he thought. But he took the messages to be friendly. Someone was looking out for him.

Although his hands were not tied, O'Hara knew that Jesse Bob Cavins kept a close watch on him. Still, he could make plans for his escape. He could act when the time came. He was sure of that, but meanwhile went over every move he might have to make when that time came.

Trask set a punishing pace as soon as they reached level ground. He figured that Julio Delgado and the other Mexicans would catch up with them. He had no way of knowing that they were already dead. Trask and the others kept looking back, their anxious gazes on the approaching storm, and there was much talk among the men about past storms in this dry part of the country. None of them wanted to be caught out in the open, where the danger of flash floods was great.

The wind built in some secret corner of the universe and brushed against their backs. The white thunderheads in the west had turned coal black, great bulging elephants stampeding across the heavens like some malevolent herd galloping after them, spreading wide, gobbling up blue sky and blotting out the falling sun.

The clouds seemed to be descending on the outlaw band, and although some of the thunderheads were still snow white, their underbellies had begun to darken like the others, as if they had been smudged with light soot. More and more of these clouds filled the sky as the wind built, blowing high, slowly pushing the clouds together. When they all touched, they would blot out the sun and spark lightning discharges that would open the floodgates for a drenching rain.

Trask and his men stopped at one of the line shacks, fed and watered their horses, then moved on the better part of an hour later.

"When we stop for the night, O'Hara," Cavins said to the prisoner, "you're going to be hog-tied again."

"Are we stopping for the night?"

"I don't know," Cavins replied in a sullen tone. He and the other men had begun to darken like the clouds, their faces drawn and somber, their scowls apparent. They were all tired and knew they had a long way to go.

"You aim to stop for the night, Ben?" Hiram Ferguson asked as the shadows began to lengthen and the sun dropped below the clouds in the west. "I see dark skies back there. Goin' to come a hell of a blow."

"We'll stop at the next line shack tomorrow," Trask said.

"If that storm catches us out in the open, we'll be swimmin' our horses."

"We can always go to high ground."

"And get soaked, either way."

"You got a slicker. Put it on when the rain starts."

"Yeah."

As dusk descended on the land, the riders came upon an adobe line shack. To O'Hara's surprise, every man drew his pistol. Trask made hand signs and the riders fanned out and circled the adobe, each of them wary as he motioned for them to approach.

Cavins stuck close to O'Hara.

"You just hold steady there, soldier, until we find out what's what."

"You're the boss," O'Hara said in his meekest tone.

Cavins wore a satisfied smirk on his face.

"Go on inside, Rawlins," Trask ordered, waving his pistol.

Rawlins dismounted and approached the adobe. O'Hara saw that the corral was empty. The horses whickered at the smell of hay and water in the troughs. There was an eerie quiet as Rawlins went inside the small building. He emerged a moment later, pasty-faced.

"Nobody here," he called to Trask. "Nobody alive, anyways."

"All right, men. Feed and water the horses. Let's see what we have here." Trask dismounted and handed his reins to Al Deets.

"They's a mess in there, Ben," Rawlins said. "Looks like animals drug in two men, and what they didn't eat, the worms and buzzards chewed on. Stinks of buzzard and coyote crap inside."

"Tend to your horse, Rawlins," Trask said. He walked up to the door and saw the blood outside, marks of where men had been dragged inside the adobe. He stepped inside.

It was difficult to tell if the bodies inside were human. If they hadn't had pieces of clothing still clinging to their ravaged bodies, he would have been hard put to identify the men.

"Ferguson," he called. "Come on in here."

Ferguson entered a few moments later.

"Recognize these men?" Trask asked.

"Not hardly."

"Take a good look. They yours?"

Ferguson pinched his nose with two fingers and

bent over one corpse, backed away, then waddled over to the other. He swore an oath under his breath. He stood up and walked to the door.

"Well?"

"Near as I can tell, Ben, that near one used to be Dave Newton. And, t'other one might be Lester Cunningham. Men I had here, all right. Can't tell how they died."

"Well, they didn't die of old age."

"I don't reckon."

Ferguson went outside, followed a moment later by Trask.

"That damned Cody did this," Trask said.

"I don't think a human—"

"I mean he killed those men. I know he didn't eat them, you fool."

"They was good men."

"Not good enough, apparently," Trask said, his anger boiling just below the surface.

He knew that Zak Cody had been there. He felt it in his bones.

There weren't enough curses to use on the bastard, he thought. But he used the vilest that he could summon from memory at that moment.

Trask had never wanted to kill a man as much as he wanted to kill Zak Cody. He had felt his presence in the room. Could almost smell him. The man was like a damned cur dog. He just couldn't get rid of him.

Not yet, anyway. But someday he'd get Cody in his sights and blow him straight to hell.

2

O'Hara watched Trask and Ferguson step outside the adobe shack. Ferguson looked sick, as if he might throw up. His nose bore the marks of his fingertips where he had pinched it.

Most of the men rolled smokes while their horses drank the murky water or nibbled on hay in the open corral.

O'Hara walked around, stretching his legs. Cavins, like his shadow, traipsed after him.

In the distance he could see streaks of lightning lacing the far black clouds, tracing silver spiderwebs from horizon to horizon as intricate and ephemeral as snowflakes. The sun had set, but there was still a faint greenish glow at the bottom of the sky.

Trask beckoned for all the men to gather around him.

"There's food inside that 'dobe," he said. "Fidel, you and Hector start passing out what we can use. Jaime can help you. We should have more than enough to last us until we get to the next line shack."

"We goin' to ride all night?" Al Deets asked.

"Yeah, we're going to ride all night. Keep your

eyes open. We could get jumped any time. I don't expect it, but as long as Cody is riding around somewhere, he might take a pot shot or two when we least expect it."

"You expecting some kind of ambush, boss?" Willy Rawlins asked.

"Look, Cody's just one man. But there were four sets of tracks back there this morning. We don't know who those peckerwoods are or where they went. Just ride tight and stay quick. And don't make a hell of a lot of noise. You hear anything out of the ordinary, you let me know."

Most of the men nodded.

Ted thought he detected a sprig of doubt in Trask's garnish of words. Beneath the bravado, Trask seemed worried about one man, a man named Cody. Could that have been the man who had signaled to him with the small mirror or the silver coin?

"Who in hell is this Cody, anyways?" Lou Grissom asked. "And what did he do in that shack? He kill Lester and Dave all by hisself?"

Ferguson opened his mouth, but Trask cut him off.

"Zak Cody is a cold-blooded killer, Grissom. He dry-gulched those two men. The Injuns call him the Shadow Rider. He's sneaky as a snake. You don't hear him comin' up on you and he shoots you in the back."

Ted straightened up. He had heard of the Shadow Rider. Campfire talk, barracks gossip. But he had also heard about a man named Cody, supposed to be working undercover for President Grant and General Crook. He had always taken the talk as just idle rumors, though. Was that who was out there? Zak Cody? He held some kind of army commission, he had heard, but wasn't in the regular army. That's why he had discounted most of the talk. He had never heard of such a thing.

The Mexicans whispered in Spanish among themselves, but he caught some of the words, like *jinete de sombra*. So even the Mexicans knew about Cody. Remarkable, he thought.

"That's why I'm telling you to be on your guard, you men," Trask said. "Now, get to the grub, Fidel, and the rest of you gather up your horses. We're wasting time here."

"I'd like to see that bastard sneak up on me," Deets said. "I'd give him what for."

"Aw, you brag too much, Al," Grissom said. "You ain't never seen the man. That's why you're still alive."

Grissom's comment brought a laugh, but Trask cut it short when he held up his hand.

"No more talk about Cody," he said. "Keep your mind on the road ahead. We've got a lot of miles to go."

The darkness came suddenly, and with the night, the distant rumble of thunder. Lightning flashed in the northwestern sky. An hour later they began to feel the wind at their backs and the night seemed to deepen.

It was still. No coyote called. No night birds sang.

It was as if the world had just stopped, its denizens vanished into nothingness.

And all the men, except Ted, were worried about one thing: the Shadow Rider.

Zak Cody might be out there somewhere, stalking them, waiting for the chance to shoot one of them in the back, like Trask had said.

The Shadow Rider began to loom large in their minds, and the sound of thunder grew louder as the storm came toward them, behind their backs, just like Cody might do.

3

Somewhere, far away to the west, he thought he heard the faint mutter of thunder. And there was a mechanism in his brain that was ticking like a clock. Each minute that passed meant less distance between him and his quarry.

Zak held up his hand, reined up Nox just as the dusk light began to weaken and fade. He turned and began untying the thongs in back of the cantle. He shook out a black slicker and slipped his arms inside the sleeves.

"If you have slickers, best to put them on now," he told the others. Thunder murmured louder in the distance, as if to underline his words.

Colleen O'Hara pulled a yellow slicker from her saddlebags as her horse sidled up next to Zak's.

"I wish we could have rescued Ted when we saw him," she said. "Do you think we'll find him again?"

"Don't worry. Those men won't stay long at the line shack after they discover the dead bodies. They'll ride on, and I know where they're headed."

Colleen smiled. "I won't be able to see you in that dark slicker when night comes on," she said. "Do you always wear black?"

"I'm partial to it."

Her raincoat made a sound like a heavy wet shirt on a windblown clothesline as she shook it out and began to pull it on over her clothing.

"Is that why they call you the Shadow Rider, Zak?"

"I don't know why people call me that."

"Really?"

"Indians started it. The Lakota, then the Blackfeet, the Cheyenne."

"It fits you somehow. You're quiet. You wear black. You ride a black horse."

Scofield and Rivers, the two soldiers on leave from Fort Bowie, put on their dull gray slickers, then rode up to Zak, their faces taking on shadows, their eyes bright in the dwindling light. They knew Cody carried the rank of colonel in the U.S. Army, although he was not required to be in uniform. Zak answered only to his immediate superiors, General George Crook and President U.S. Grant.

"Sir?" Scofield said. "Where are we going, if I might ask?"

Zak turned in the saddle, pointed to a small hill off to their right.

"Be full dark soon," Zak said. "I figure we've gained on Trask, stand ahead of him. I want you and Rivers to take that ridge there and just wait. The old stage road is just below it."

"What about her?" Scofield asked. "Miss O'Hara, I mean."

"She'll stand out like a lighthouse in that yellow slicker," Zak said. "Best you keep her back a little and between you."

"What do you aim to do, Colonel?" Rivers asked.

"I'm going to ride into them once the rain starts and bring Lieutenant O'Hara back to that spot. Now, I'm going to backtrack and come up behind Trask."

"That sounds mighty dangerous to me," Scofield said. "You're one man against what? A dozen or so? They'll shoot you out of the saddle first time they see you."

"We'll see what that storm does for me," Zak said. "It's heading in from the west, and that bunch won't be looking back much. If there's wind—and I expect there will be—that rain will sting their eyes like blown cactus spines."

He knew he was taking a big risk. But life itself was a big risk, he thought. When a babe was born, that child was at risk until the first breath was taken. After that, it was one risk after another. He had long ago accepted as much; something his pa had told him.

"Life don't hand you nothin', Zak," Russell Cody had said. "If they shoot at you, pick up a gun. If they chase you, run. If it's kill or be killed, you be the killer, else you'll take that last breath and be right back where you started."

Good advice, Zak thought. But General Crook was paying him to put his life on the line.

"You see something wrong, Zak, you fix it before the army's called in," the general had told him. "I'm asking a lot, I know, but no more than you've already given in the service of your country."

Trask had kidnapped a soldier serving in the United States Army. And he was out to stir up trouble among the Chiricahua, who were at peace, at least temporarily. Crook, he thought, would approve of this mission. Especially if he pulled it off and kept the army out of it.

Now they could all see the lightning and hear the muttering rumble of distant thunder. The air had changed, too, and the wind was picking up, gusting in their faces, rattling the slickers, dislodging small pebbles on the hillside.

"Zak," Colleen said as he touched a forefinger to the brim of his hat and turned Nox to the west. "Please be careful. And bring Ted back with you."

The way her face glowed in the strange dim light made her look like some statues of the Madonna he had seen. There was a radiance in her that made her skin appear soft and silky. He felt a tug in his chest as if an unseen talon had pulled gently at his heart. For a schoolteacher, he thought, she was mighty pretty, and those eyes of hers seemed to bore right through him, in a gentle, caring way. Such thoughts were uncommon to him, and he knew he could not afford to be distracted by them. He tried to shake them off and not look at her inviting lips.

"If you're shot at," Zak said to all three of them, "shoot back."

His voice was sterner than it had to be, he knew, but it was the only way he could override his growing feelings for Colleen O'Hara. She seemed to gather that faint light to her, gray light that she turned into a translucent shade of pearl.

And then he was gone. As the dusky twilight melted into night, the clouds blackened to coal and lowered, as lightning flashed silver warnings in the west. Colleen watched Zak disappear into the darkness and sighed deeply as Scofield and Rivers

turned their horses toward the dim hill that rose
above a road only Zak had known was there.

Zak knew he had to be some distance ahead of
Trask. He figured they would stop at the first line
shack, grub up, and then put their horses into a
mile-eating canter. He would not have long to
wait, he knew.

Nox was tired, and for a while he let the horse
walk in his quiet, careful way. He turned toward
the road, saw its faint outline, and rode toward a
spot where broken hills came together in a jumble.
He crossed the road and found the perfect place, a
place where he could not be seen when the outlaws
rode by.

He hoped the storm would hit before he spotted
Trask, but knew it might be tight. Still, the thunder
was growing louder and more frequent, and the
bursts of lightning gave him glimpses of the road
for a good quarter mile or so. The wind stiffened
and Nox bobbed his head at every rattle of rock,
every rustle of desert flora. The road was empty.

Fifteen minutes later, Zak felt a dash and a
sprinkle of rain. The clouds descended still lower
and the wind picked up, steady, with brisk gusts
that peppered his eyes with grit, stung the skin
on his face. He pulled his hat down tighter on his
head, slid his bandanna up from around his neck
to cover his face.

Nox lifted his head and turned toward the
westering stretch of road, his ears hardening to stiff
cones, twitching ever so slightly. Beneath the rumble of thunder, Zak thought he heard hoofbeats.
Then a streak of lightning coursed the clouds and

exploded into silvery ladders. A second later the crack of thunder told him the storm was less than a mile away.

Rain splashed his face, soaking through the bandanna, and then he was caught in a steady downpour. Lightning threaded the clouds and the thunder boomed. He could hear water starting to run down the little hills, but the ground was dry where he sat his horse. He rummaged in his saddlebag and pulled out the pistol he had taken from one of the men he had killed. He slid it behind his belt so that he could get to it easily when the time came.

The rain streamed down in thick heavy sheets, and visibility dropped to a few measly yards. The sound of hoofbeats faded as if they had never existed, but he knew Trask was coming, riding his way, perhaps more slowly now that the storm had struck.

Zak patted Nox on the neck to calm him and strained his eyes, squinting to keep the rain from stinging them as he gazed hard down the road. He slid the bandanna back down around his collar and felt the icy drip of water stream down his back. He wiped his eyebrows and eyelids with a swipe of his sleeve and dipped his head, water cascading off the brim of his hat like a small watery veil.

The road turned slick, glistened under the lightning flashes, and then began to boil mud as the water soaked into the ground.

The first rider emerged out of the rain, but Zak could not identify him. Then the others plodded into sight. The riders were strung out in a long ragged line. He was looking for one man, and when he saw him, knew what he must do.

Ted O'Hara rode with his head down, another man close behind him but losing ground. Trask had already gone by, holding one hand above his eyebrows to shield his face from the rain. The wind lashed and spattered rain in all directions as it swirled in the teeth of the storm.

Zak eased Nox out of the little box they were in, drifting onto the road so slowly that he hoped the dark shape of horse and man would not be noticed. He mentally pictured himself and Nox as a large shadow.

And that's what he and Nox were, a shadow among shadows.

4

The rain pelted down hard, as if poured from a giant bucket in the sky. The wind, funneled through rocky hills on both sides of the road, blasted horses and men with a savage ferocity.

As Zak got into line with the outlaw riders, he saw that their heads were bent down. They were looking straight down, their backs hunched like mendicants, not looking around them. He rode at their pace, but tapped Nox's flanks with his spurs, easing gradually up among them until he was riding alongside O'Hara.

Zak stretched a hand to touch Ted on the arm, and the lieutenant turned toward him, head still bowed. Zak squeezed his arm twice then withdrew his hand and gestured for him to follow. To his relief, Ted complied and began to drift toward him.

When Ted was close enough, Zak pulled the Colt from his waist and handed it across to him, and he grabbed it as a drowning man would grasp a hank of driftwood. Ted held the pistol tight against his middle, his thumb on the hammer of the single-action. He looked over at Zak quickly but could

not see his face. All he saw was a man dressed in
black riding a black horse.

Zak saw an opening in front of Ted, crossed
over and began drifting left toward the other side
of the slick, muddy road. He looked back and saw
that Ted was following him, as he'd hoped the lieutenant would.

Jesse Bob Cavins, who had been riding with head
down behind Zak, looked up just then, pointed at
Ted and yelled, "The soldier's gettin' away!"

Zak drew his pistol, cocked and aimed it in
one smooth motion, then squeezed the trigger. As
the gun roared, Cavins reared back in the saddle,
clutching his stomach. He gurgled and then his
saddle emptied as he fell to the ground.

"Come on, Ted," Zak yelled, already riding toward a gap in the low hills off to his left. He glanced
up and saw the yellow raincoat atop the next rise.

The outlaws began yelling and drawing their
pistols.

Ted turned and fired at the nearest one, Al Deets.
The orange flame from the muzzle of his pistol lit
the night and painted his face with a sudden bright
flash of orange. Rain fell thick and strong as pistols cracked and bullets whistled over Ted's head.
He followed Zak through the narrow gap between
hills.

From atop the next hill, Zak heard the sharp
reports of the Spencer carbines, and then a short
bark that sounded like a pistol; O'Hara's, he
guessed. Men screamed and the line of riders broke
up and scattered. He picked out a man turning his
horse and fired at him, squeezing the trigger of
the Walker Colt. The man jerked, then fell from

his saddle. His foot caught in one stirrup and the horse dragged his flopping body away.

More shots sounded and bullets whined off sodden rocks next to where Zak and Ted sat their horses. Ted fired at one of the Mexicans and saw him throw up his hands, then slump dead in the saddle.

"Where in hell is Trask?" Zak yelled, his eyes straining to see through the rain and the dark.

"He rode off, I think," Ted yelled across to Zak. "Who's that shooting from up on that ridge?"

"Two soldiers and your sister, Colleen."

"Colleen? She's here?"

Zak didn't answer. Another man made a dash toward them, his six-gun barking, orange flame spewing from the barrel.

"Too bad you didn't follow your boss," Zak said, then dropped him with a single shot. The man tumbled out of the saddle and landed with a splash in a puddle of water.

Zak took off again, pushing Nox up the steep hill and toward the ridge on top. He heard the faint pounding of hoofbeats as the riders fled, leaving their dead behind. He listened to the rain and the wind, then wiped his eyes. He surprised Ted when he turned around and abruptly stopped. He reached into his saddlebag, pulled out a bundle and handed it to Ted.

"Put this on when you have a chance."

Ted looked down at the bundle in his hands. It was his own shirt. The bars on the shoulders lit up with a flash of lightning. He stuffed the shirt inside his raincoat.

Zak eyed the road below, making sure that Trask's men were indeed riding away.

When he turned around, Ted had his slicker off and was removing the shirt his captors had given him. He tossed the shirt to the ground, put on his regulation shirt, then slipped back into his soogan.

"Let's go find your sister," Zak said, the wind whipping the words from his mouth.

Moments later, Ted and Zak were on top of the hill. Colleen ran up to them, slipping a pistol back into her waistband. She held out her arms and collapsed in her brother's arms when he dismounted, and he hugged her tightly as Scofield and Rivers watched.

"They run like rabbits," Rivers said, looking down at the road.

"Plumb gone, lickety-split," Scofield said, grinning.

"I wonder if either of you got a shot at Ben Trask," Zak said.

"He the one who lit out first?" Rivers said.

"I think so. He might have been."

"Lit a shuck before we could level on him," Scofield said. "But I think we might have dropped one or two apiece. It was like a turkey shoot there for a minute or two."

"We need to know who we got," Zak said. "Ted, I might need you to identify some of them."

"I know you hit Cavins with your first shot," Ted said. "I saw him go down, but I don't know if he's dead. He was still squirming around on the ground, last I saw him. You Cody?"

"Yes. Zak Cody."

The two men shook hands, their faces glistening with rain.

Colleen smiled. "I'm so grateful to you, Zak—"

"Don't mention it," Zak said before she could finish.

All he could think about just then was that Trask was getting away. As long as he was alive, Zak would not rest. He would pursue him to the ends of the earth if need be. It was army business now, of course, but it was still personal, too.

"We going down to look at the dead, Colonel?" Scofield asked.

A bolt of lightning struck nearby. The smell of it filled the air with crackling ozone.

"We'll stay up here on high ground until this storm passes," Zak said. "We go down there, we could drown."

"Maybe that Trask feller will get caught in a flash flood and drown hisself," Rivers said.

Zak didn't say anything. He looked at Colleen, who was hanging onto her brother's arm. He took in a deep breath, let the air out slow.

He might have been a bit jealous if Ted hadn't been her brother.

Maybe he was anyway.

A woman like that could get to a man.

He was sure she already had.

He turned away, put his back to the rain and listened to its dancing song, the drumming thunder in the background. There was so much he wanted to say to Colleen. But now was not the time and this was definitely not the place.

But there would be another day, and until then, time to think.

Time to think about so many things.

5

Lightning stitched latticework across the sky, scratched out trees of silver in the black clouds. The rain drove at them in slanted lances, blown by the hard wind, as they huddled on the ridge. The night was as dark as the depths of a coal mine, and the desert had turned cold.

Zak Cody shaded his eyes, peered down into the gully below and the road beyond it. With the next flash of lightning, he saw that the gully was empty, except for the bodies of two dead men awash in a muddy torrent.

The wind swept across the top of the ridge as Cody bent over, his back to the pelting rain, and reloaded his Colt pistol. The two soldiers, Delbert Scofield and Hugo Rivers, tried to shield Colleen O'Hara and her brother Ted.

"We've got to get off this ridge," Cody yelled into the teeth of the wind. "Follow me. Lieutenant, lead your horse down behind me."

"Call me Ted, will you?"

Cody didn't answer.

"What about Trask and Ferguson, that band of cutthroats?" Ted said, his mouth close to Cody's ear.

"Long gone. By now they're probably in a line shack, out of the weather. I'm more concerned about somebody else right now."

"Who?" O'Hara asked.

"Three Mexicans. Part of Trask's bunch. They stayed behind to bury a woman. They ought to be up this way about now."

"You mean . . . ?"

"I mean we've got to keep an eye on our back trail."

"Hard to do. In this storm, I'm lucky if I can see ten feet ahead."

"There are other ways to see," Zak said cryptically.

Ted looked over his shoulder. Needles of rain stung his eyes and he had to close them and turn his head out of the wind. With a sinking feeling, as if his whole body were subsiding into quicksand, he realized they were all pretty much defenseless against anyone riding up behind them.

"Let's go," Zak said, loud enough for all of them to hear.

Nox, his black horse, stood hipshot, his hindquarters blasted by wind and rain. He raised his head as Cody took the reins and started down the backside of the ridge.

"I don't think I can find my horse," Scofield said. He and Rivers had left the horses below before climbing the ridge with Colleen earlier, to give Cody cover when he'd gone after Ted O'Hara. "I hope they ain't run off."

Cody said nothing. He held onto Colleen's hand, and she held onto her brother's, as the small group inched their way down a rock-strewn slope running with rivulets of water. The footing was slippery, treacherous.

The wind wasn't as strong at the foot of the ridge, but Zak knew they'd find no relief until they got to the other side of the hump. First, though, they had to find the horses Colleen and the soldiers had left on the flat.

Lightning strikes danced across the empty desert, illuminating a desolate landscape a split second at a time. It was like living in a nightmare, Zak thought. The sound of thunder rolled across the skies as if it had come from a thousand cannons, a thousand throats of unearthly demons on a rampage.

How many men will I have to kill to get to Ben Trask? he asked himself, to drown out the sound of pealing thunder in his head. He had already killed too many, and now the storm had allowed Trask to elude him. For a time. Trask could not know that the men he had left in shacks along the old stage road would not be able to help him. They were all dead. All had fallen to the snarl and roar of his gun. They were help that Trask was never going to get. But Trask would go on. He was bent on finding the Apache gold he believed Cochise had hidden. Trask was not only a stone cold killer, he was a fool.

Zak heard the low whicker of one of the horses, and led the others to them. Sheets of rain lashed them as they climbed into their saddles.

Zak climbed onto Nox and rode over to the lieutenant.

"Ted, just follow the edge of this hill to the end. You might find some shelter on the other side, near the road."

"Where are you going?" Ted asked.

"I'm going to get the gun rig off of Cavins. You might need another sidearm. I'll join up with you in a while."

"How long's this rain going to last?"

"All night, probably. Just sit tight when you find shelter. Wait for me."

Zak turned his horse, then was gone.

"Sis," Ted said to Colleen. "Who in hell is that man?"

"Nobody knows, really," she said, her voice soft, a wistful note in it.

"Can we trust him?"

"He saved your life, didn't he?"

"Yes, but—"

"Ever hear of the Shadow Rider, Ted?"

Ted didn't say anything for a long moment. His face was wet with rain. Colleen looked like a drenched bird. The two soldiers waited, their backs bowed, their heads lowered against the wind and the whipping curtains of rain.

"Not much. The men who captured me were talking about it, and I've heard talk of such a man around the fort. Ex-army. Something to do with General Crook."

"Well, that's him. Zak Cody. He's a strange man."

"But you like him, don't you?"

"I'm not sure," she said. "He . . . He's magnetic. He's not my type, but—"

"Admit it, you like him, sis."

"Shouldn't we get out of this rain, Ted? Zak put you in charge."

"Seems to me," Ted said, "that your friend Zak's in charge."

Ted dug spurs into his horse's flanks. They moved along the base of the ridge, the wind at their backs.

"Yes," she said. "I'd say you were right, Ted. From what I hear, Zak is, or was, a colonel in the army. That's what the two army men were calling him. I don't know why he's here, but I'm glad he is."

"Well, I'm damned sure going to find out who I'm riding with. Even if he did save my life. He took a hell of a risk, now that I think of it. We both could have been shot."

Colleen said nothing. She was thinking about Zak and her feelings for him. They were all tangled up, like vines in the trellis of her mind. She could not sort them out, now that he was gone into the night and the rain, after having thought of her brother, not of himself. And he'd said there might be more men coming up the road. He could be riding straight back into danger.

She shuddered at the thought, and the vines began to straighten and line up, a string of green leaves bright with energy and promise.

⟞ 6 ⟞

Lieutenant Ted O'Hara took charge. He struck out along the base of the ridge, as Cody had instructed him, with Colleen, Scofield, and Rivers following him. It was pitch-black, raining and blowing hard. There were no other reference points along the route, no trail to follow. But he had no difficulty keeping to the left of the baseline.

His mind reeled with thoughts of Zak Cody and the fight on the old stage road. Cody had been very brave to attack as he had, in the dark, badly outnumbered. He had deployed Scofield and Rivers wisely, stationing them on the top of that ridge, and Colleen had been part of it, too, providing still another rifle. His sister was a good shot. Their father had taught them well. But he was still in the dark about all of it. Where had Cody come from, and why? Was he in the army, following orders? He didn't know. He had a lot of questions and no answers.

Ted didn't mind being out in the weather. He had been cooped up as a prisoner for so long he welcomed the good air, even if it tasted like metal as lightning etched quicksilver hieroglyphs across the elephantine sky while thunder boomed like empty barrels rolling across an attic floor. He had been out, away from the fort so long—tracking Cochise and other Apache bands, sitting with them, giving them tobacco, smoking with them, eating with them—that he had lost his relish for barracks roofs and adobe walls.

He wondered what Cochise and his tribe were doing just then. From what he knew of the Apache, they would view the storm much differently than the white man did. To them, the thunder would be the voice of God, the Great Spirit, and the lightning a demonstration of power—immense power over all things. They would see the thunderbolts as arrows and lances shot and hurled from on high, striking game or humans who were not pure, setting fires, burning rocks and sand with a force no mortal man could match. He wondered now if he had gotten too close to the Apache. Was he beginning to think like they did?

One day, when he had returned from Cochise's camp to the place where his patrol was bivouacked, his sergeant, Ronnie Casteel, asked him that same question in another way.

"Lieutenant O'Hara, sir, do you think you might be spendin' too much time palaverin' with them Apaches?"

"What do you mean, Ronnie?"

"You never stayed away all night before. We was worried."

"I was perfectly safe."

"At night, when you sleep, the men can hear you talkin' that gibberish what you talk with them Apaches."

"That gibberish is Spanish, Sergeant."

"Well, the men are just wonderin' if you are turnin' into a squaw man."

"What's a squaw man?"

"More Injun than white."

"I assure you, Ronnie, I've still got the same blood. I might add that it's no different than yours or Cochise's, for that matter. I speak Spanish with Cochise because I can't speak Apache. He speaks Spanish—Mexican, really—so we can converse. It's essential that I know what he's thinking. Our conversations help me to know what's on Cochise's mind."

"Why should you care what that old bird is thinkin'?"

"Because we're here to keep the peace with the Chiricahuas, and to calm the fears of the white settlers. That good enough for you, Ronnie?"

"Sir, I didn't mean no disrespect."

"Of course you didn't. But if you're talking about respect, it wouldn't hurt to show some to the Apaches. We're in their country, after all."

"We are? I thought we was in the United States."

"The Apaches don't have the same feelings about land that we do. We whites, I mean. They believe that land is a gift from God, the Great Spirit, and they don't abide ownership, by any man or tribe, red or white."

"That ain't practical, sir."

Ted didn't argue any further, but now, that conversation came back to him, and he thought of how he felt looking at land and the ownership of land through the eyes of the Chiricahua. When he was out there, with his men or with the Apaches, he felt unfettered, free. When he lay on his bedroll at night and looked up at the stars, looking so bright and close, he thought the heavens were surely a part of it all, part of some grand scheme bestowed on man by a higher intelligence, a God, if that be the belief, or a Great Spirit, as the Apaches believed.

No man could own a star, or a bunch of stars, or a planet, the sun, or the moon. Why should it not be the same for the land on planet Earth? Sometimes he thought the Apaches made more sense than those of his own skin color and descendents. Boundaries, he thought, kept people apart. Ownership created enemies, foes that would kill to possess an acre or a section, a township or a great metropolis. And at the heart of it all was greed, the same greed that he saw in Ferguson and Trask. Trask believed that Cochise had a great golden treasure, and he was determined to possess it. And both he and Ferguson and their men would gladly kill to get it.

Among the Apaches he had known, he had seen no signs of greed or envy, and the revelation was a puzzle to him. The white men he had known, his own kind, coveted things—land, wealth, women—and none considered the cost of acquisition, but sought and strived for things they did not possess. While the Apaches were grateful for what they had, a wealth no white man could fathom, the earth, the sky, water, and, most valuable of all, friends and family. Gifts, they said, from a spirit so strong it gave them strong hearts and invaded their dreams, opened their eyes to all the wonders of the heaven and the hidden riches of the earth: food and shelter and clothing, and vistas so wondrous they painted the horizon at sunset and dawn.

They reached the butt of the ridge and Ted turned his horse, rounding the corner. His sister and the two soldiers followed after him. He noticed a decided drop in the wind. There, in the lee of the butte, or whatever it was, the rain no longer drove into them with the force of war arrows. It was still wet and rainy, but at least they were out of the wind.

"Dismount," he ordered, "and gather the horses close, bunch 'em up. We'll squat under them and maybe not get any wetter."

"Good idea, sir," Rivers said.

A bolt of lightning speared the ground nearby, atop the next hill, and thunder roared from above a moment later. The air smelled of burnt mercury and tasted faintly of iodine or copper. Colleen ducked and shivered as she brought her horse in close to the others.

They huddled together beneath their horses, exchanging the heat of their bodies with their breaths and the pulsing of the blood in their veins. The horses' bellies, too, gave off warmth and provided shelter from the pelting rain. The wind streamed past them on both sides of the hill, but whipped back now and then to lash them, draw them closer together as if they were bound together by something like the string of a purse.

"That wind's a blue one, all right," Scofield said, his teeth clacking together like dice in a tin cup.

"What I wouldn't give to be back in the barracks," Rivers said.

"If you don't think of it so much," O'Hara said, "you won't feel it so bad. Isn't that right, Colleen?"

"I think of warm zephyrs and a fire in the hearth," she said, her voice quavering from the cold, the bone-penetrating chill.

"I c-c-can't think of nothing else but the cold with that wind howlin' like a banshee," Scofield said.

"I'm thinkin' about that Cody feller," Rivers said. "He's out in it by hisself, huntin' men like they was meat."

"Yeah," Scofield said. "He be a strange one, all right."

O'Hara thought of Cody and how he had ridden into the outlaw column, all alone, and rescued him, against all odds.

"What do you think of him, Lieutenant?" Rivers asked.

"I don't know what to make of him. He's uncommon brave. I know that."

Colleen said nothing. She was thinking of Zak Cody, too, wondering why he was not with them. Was he brave or foolhardy? What could he see in the dark and the rain? Was he protecting them, or did he just thirst for blood? She did not like to think of the latter possibility. But was she just projecting him onto her mind in a fabricated image, making him into someone she wanted him to be, denying to herself who he really was? She knew she was responding to his magnetism. She felt the pull of his gravity, and it was disturbing to her, like certain dreams she'd had that she could not fathom.

No one spoke for a few moments, each locked in

their own private thoughts of Zak Cody, perhaps wondering what he was doing out in the weather while they crouched like drenched birds beneath their horses, waterfalls cascading from their saddles, rain trickling down quivering legs, pooling up in hoofprints, sputtering under the onslaught of dancing raindrops.

They heard a sound then. The wind carried it through the liquid crystal curtains of showers, carried it, muffled it, and spewed it to their ears like a dissonant crackle escaped from a long forgotten thunder. They stiffened as if each had been larruped with the lash of a bullwhip. The sound was unmistakable, oddly disconnected from the storm, but part of it as well.

A gunshot that seemed to speak of fire and blood, the violence that sprouted from a dark wet world while the sky bristled with branches fashioned of mercury and quicksilver, as if conjured by some ancient alchemist risen from the underworld.

⇒ 7 ⇐

Ben Trask had been watching the darkening sky and knew the fierce storm was coming toward them. He and his men put their horses through a punishing pace, hoping to reach the next line shack before the rain and wind hit them.

It was already dark by the time Trask spotted the adobe. And the rain had already started to fall. He rode up to the front of the shack, whose door was ajar, and motioned for the other men to follow him.

Just then, a crack of lightning lit the scene. It was followed almost immediately by thunder, which pealed across the sky like a battery of twelve-pounders. At the same time, rain sloshed down like an engulfing tidal wave, the horses screamed terrified whinnies, and the men jerked their reins to hold them, so they wouldn't bolt out from under them.

Trask yelled into the explosive downpour, "Everybody inside. We got a gusher. Tie up your horses on high ground." The men dismounted and struggled through the wind and the rain as if they were slogging through quicksand. Some shook out lariats and led their horses out in back of the adobe. They tied their mounts to anything solid they could find as the rain continued to drench them. The wind tore at their soaked clothing, stung their faces. They put hobbles on some of the horses and tied these animals to the secured mounts and fled to the front of the shack to get in out of the rain.

Trask was the first one in the door. He couldn't see at all in the darkness. He held his arms out in front of him, as a blind man might do, feeling for anything that might be in his path. He took two steps into the room and tripped over something on the floor.

"Damn," he said, regaining his balance in time to keep from falling down. A streak of lightning lit the inside of the adobe just long enough for Trask to see what he'd stumbled over. It was a body, and he got a glimpse of another corpse on the floor a few feet away. He knew they were men who worked for Hiram Ferguson.

Trask barked at Fidel and Hector Gonzalez, "Haul them bodies outside, toss 'em on the road. Flood's going to take 'em away right soon."

The other Mexicans, followed by Ferguson, poured into the adobe and helped remove the dead bodies.

The adobe sat on high ground above the road, but Trask worried that they might not be high enough. He knew what was coming. So did Ferguson, who walked over to Trask, his wet face the color of cork. With the constant strikes of lightning, Ferguson could see the fear flickering in Trask's dilated eyes like restless shadows.

"Gonna come a flash flood, Ben, sure as shootin'."

"It's a frog strangler, all right," Trask said.

Fidel and Hector bent down to pick up one of the bodies. It had been ripped and torn by animals—coyotes, possibly—and they struggled with the feet and shoulders. They turned their heads as if to avoid the stench and stood up. Trask cleared a path for them. Rain shot through the door almost in straight lines as the two men stumbled outside.

"Get that other man out of here," Trask ordered, looking at Jaime Elizondo. "Pablo, you help him," he said to Pablo Medina.

The two men went over to the other body, which was in worse shape than the first. It was hardly recognizable as being human. One leg was completely gone, the other reduced to blood-smeared bone. The face was gnawed off and there was only a skull under the matted hair. They slid their arms under the dead man's back and hefted him up. He wasn't heavy because there wasn't much left of him. They walked outside, ducking to avoid the stinging needles of rain, and sloshed off into the darkness.

Willy Rawlins turned away from the hideous sight. He doubled over and started to retch, but clamped a hand to his mouth and held on, breathing air through his nostrils. As was typical of the adobes, there was no glass covering the windows, which were more like gaping holes than windows. He stepped close to one of them and stood up straight, gulping in fresh wet air. He swore and shook his head as if to clear it of the smells of decaying flesh, coyote dung, urine, and a dozen other scents he could not identify.

"Christ," Ferguson said.

"Get used to it," Trask said, a note of contempt in his voice. "It ain't goin' to get no better."

The adobe seemed to shudder with the next crack of thunder. Lightning flashed all around, limning the windows and the doorway with a flood of bright light. The wind blew rain through every opening.

"Rawlins, close that damned door," Trask said, and Rawlins started to close it when Hector and Fidel dashed back in, their slickers bright with rain. He closed the door, and moments later the other two men opened it and came in. The wind took the door and slammed it into the adobe. Rawlins had to step outside and fight the wind to close it again. The blasts of air and rain made the door rattle and creak, but it stayed closed, pinned shut by the wind.

"Any of you boys want to catch some shut-eye, there's a bunk yonder, or you can get your bedrolls and bring 'em in here," Trask said. "I want at least three men on watch. You can take turns, starting now."

"I'll take the first watch," Rawlins said. "Shit, I'm soakin' wet. Can we make a fire in here?"

"No," Trask said. "I don't want no light showin'."

Rawlins grumbled, but took up a position next to a front window where he would stand watch.

Ferguson pointed to Jaime Elizondo and Fidel Gonzalez. "You two stand first watch," he said. "I'll relieve you, Jaime, in three hours."

Jaime nodded and stood at another window.

Gonzalez took up a position at the back window.

"Can somebody go back out there and get our bedrolls?" Lou Grissom said. Nobody answered. "I'll go, then. Who all wants their bedrolls?"

Everyone answered in the affirmative.

"Take me two trips, likely," Grissom said. "You bunch of yellow-bellied cowards."

Some of the men laughed.

He want out into the rain and closed the door behind him without being asked.

"Too bad we lost that soldier, O'Hara," Ferguson said to Trask. "And I reckon that Cody kilt Cavins and Deets."

"Looks like," Trask said. "We don't need O'Hara. I've got the maps he marked up for us. We can find Cochise's gold without him."

"You think he marked the maps right, Ben?"

"Why not? Hiram, you worry too damned much."

"I worry that those maps might take us right into a trap."

"What makes you think that?" It was turning cold, and Trask shook with a sudden chill.

"I do not trust a soldier to tell the truth to an enemy," Hiram said. "They are trained to lie."

"Maps don't lie. We know Cochise has a camp somewhere on those maps. We will find him. We will find the damned gold."

"We have lost many men. Cavins and Deets, probably. That shooting back there. They were guarding the lieutenant and now they are not here. And two men dead in this adobe. What about the others?"

"What others?" Trask said.

"The men I had in the other old shacks up the road."

"We'll cross that bridge when we come to it. Take it easy, Hiram. Worry don't get you nowhere. It gets you a damned bellyache."

"I bet that Cody killed all my men on this old road. And we need them if we're going up against the Apache."

"We have enough," Trask said. "If I quit every time the horse bucked, I'd never get anywhere."

"You're stubborn," Ferguson said. "Stubborn as a dadgummed army mule."

"Can we smoke, boss?" Rawlins said.

"No. No lights. And no talkin' from here on."

"Hell, who's gonna hear us talk in this racket?" Rawlins said, referring to the rain slapping the adobe and the rumble of thunder, which was almost constant.

Rawlins couldn't see the glare that flared in Trask's eyes, but he could feel something burn on his cheek and knew Trask was looking at him. He shifted the weight on his feet and said nothing as he turned back to stare out the window at the slashing rain that beat at the door with an erratic, windblown tattoo.

Trask admitted to himself that he was stubborn, but he gave the trait credit for keeping him alive all these years. The West was a savage place, more dangerous than the eastern settlements with their governors and laws. The wildness suited him, though. He often wondered if there was something in the water of a mountain stream that made his blood run hot when he was chasing a man down to rob him, or a man was chasing him. Ever since he had killed Cody's father, robbed him of his gold, he knew that he was a savage man at heart, and he exulted in that knowledge, as he exulted in the savagery of the West itself. In some ways, he admired the red man because an Indian lived by his wits, often with nothing more than a war club, a bow, and arrows. He had no use for them as people but admired the hot blood that ran in their veins. He had taken his share of scalps just so he would know what it felt like, and the feeling he got from taking a life was like a drink of the strongest whiskey mixed with the blackest, hottest, strongest coffee. The feeling burned all through him at such times, and it lingered in his memory like banked coals, always there, basking, glowing, ready to take flame from breath or the wave of a hand.

Lightning danced in the dark sky, dashing their faces with phosphorous. Strikes landed close by and the air smelled of sulfur. With each whip crack of sound, the thunder boomed and the adobe seemed to shake with the fury of the storm. The rain fell faster and harder, and the wind whipped and surged with a powerful energy that blew rain through every crack. Each gust made the drops sound like lead pellets hitting the adobe clay like birdshot.

Rawlins shouted above the roar. "Listen."

They all heard it, and some of the men crowded to the window. Trask stood on tiptoes to look out, while Ferguson struggled to see through the mass of men.

The sound was eerie, far off at first, but all recognized it for what it was.

A river was roaring down the road like a locomotive on a downhill run. A mighty sound of water, a wall of water, clogged their ears and struck fear deep into their bowels.

Ferguson swore.

The rushing water muffled his oath and swallowed it up as the flood burst into view. The sound became deafening as tons of water flowed over the road and surged up the slope toward the adobe.

Maybe, Trask thought, the flash flood would catch Cody out in the open and drown him like a rat.

At the same time, he prayed that the water would not rise up to the roof and burst through the windows and door, suffocating them under a deluge of adobe mud.

⊱ 8 ⊰

Zak had to ride to the end of the small butte and around it, then head back up the road to the spot where he had rescued O'Hara. Lightning lit his way, the jagged streaks some distance away but moving closer. He counted off the seconds it took for the sound of thunder to reach him. Six miles, he judged, from the last brilliant burst of lightning until the first thunderclap resounded in his ears.

One slow second of time equaled a mile in distance that the sound traveled. Six seconds, six miles. Not much time, he thought, to encircle the butte, get a rifle and scabbard, ammunition, whatever else he could find that would help him arm O'Hara and feed them all for what promised to be a long and tiring journey.

As he rounded the end of the hill, Zak worried about the storm passing over him and breaking over hard ground that sloped down the road. A flash flood could wash over him, Colleen, O'Hara, and the two soldiers, perhaps drowning them all.

A bolt of lightning speared the ground five hundred yards ahead of him. In the brilliant dazzle, Zak saw a curtain of rain that shimmered like a silver curtain. The thunder followed a second later, and he knew the massive black clouds were going to dump gallons of rain on him before he got to his destination. He touched spurs to Nox's flanks and put the horse into a trot, hoping the animal would not step into a gopher hole and break its leg.

Just before he reached the place where he would turn and head for the road, a gust of wind nearly blew him out of the saddle. It was a straight-line wind that dashed him with gallons of water, so much that he had to hold his breath and breathe through his nose. Then the gust turned into a gale that pressed against his chest and bowed Nox's head.

He rode into the brunt of the lashing front edge of the storm. Out in the open, the wind hit him full force. The rain stung his face with a thousand sharp needles, battered the brim of his hat, spattered against his slicker like steady rounds of grapeshot. Nox fought against the wind, moving his head from side to side, his neck bowed, his eyes barely open, hooded to avoid the stings.

Zak turned the corner of the hill, and Nox wanted to turn tail and head the other way to keep the wind at his rump. He urged the horse on. They found the road, which was already awash, and turned east. Now he had the wind at his back, but there was dangerous lightning all around and Nox was a handful, fighting against instinct and common sense under the annoying dig of his spurs in both flanks. The wind howled up the road, channeled on both sides by high rocky ground.

"Come on, Nox, old boy. Stay with me, son," Zak said, leaning over the pommel, his voice carrying to the horse's ears. He patted Nox's neck to reassure him. "We both could use a good dry barn or a stable."

The darkness was deep, and only the lightning lit their way to the place where Zak had used his pistol against Trask's men. He kept looking for a loose horse, hoping at least one was still there and not galloping off to high ground seeking shelter.

Water began to wash rocks and dirt down the slopes. Zak could hear the flow of water, the clack of rocks against one another, the rushing sound the liquid made as it coursed downhill. He knew the danger. If there were any large rocks above him, they could be dislodged and start a small avalanche, or even just crash into him, smashing him and Nox to the ground, perhaps breaking their bones. He stayed to the center of the road, peering into the blackness, scanning both sides at every sizzle of light from the electrified sky.

At last he saw a dark shape off to his right. He caught just a bare glimpse of something large enough to be a horse and his heart soared in his chest.

"Almost there, Nox," Zak said, and patted his horse's withers.

Another bolt of lightning touched off more thunder and more rain, but he saw the horse, its butt to the wind, its head hanging down, unaware of his presence. Rain had slicked its hide, and when the lightning struck the hilltop off to his right, the light sorrel looked like a metal sculpture, frozen for a moment in the flash, as if some photographer had touched off a tray of flash powder.

Zak headed for the horse. He eased Nox up alongside it and grabbed the trailing reins. The horse did not shy away, but held fast. Zak saw the rifle jutting out of the scabbard on the opposite side. That was enough for him. He would lead the horse to where O'Hara, Colleen, and the two soldiers were waiting and strip the animal there. Perhaps there was grub in the saddlebags. The storm was too heavy to dawdle. All he had to do was ride up the road to the end of the hill on his left and he knew he'd find them waiting for him. He wanted to get out of that false canyon quick in case the rain caused a flash flood before he could reach the folks he had sent on ahead.

As Zak started up the road, he heard a voice on the opposite side.

"You hold on there. That's my horse."

"Who are you?" Zak asked, trying to find the source of the voice. The darkness hid the man who had called out to him.

"I'm Jesse Bob Cavins. Who are you? Al? That you? Deets, I—I got plugged."

Zak wondered if it was one of the men he had shot. Probably, he thought.

If so, he hadn't killed him. But how badly was the man wounded?

"Yeah, Jesse Bob. It's me, Al," Zak lied. "Tell me where you are."

"That really you, Deets?" Cavins said.

Zak saw him then, a shadowy hulk against the bank. Crippled, but still alive and standing on his feet. Slouching was more like it.

"Yeah," Zak said. "Put away that pistol, will you?"

"You sound funny, Al," Cavins said.

"The rain."

"Yeah, the wind, too."

Cavins moved, and Zak saw that he was holstering his pistol. He nudged spurs into Nox's flanks and the horse approached Cavins with wariness, sidestepping toward him as if ready to bolt. Zak pulled on the reins so Nox felt the bit against his tongue and mouth.

A flash of lightning illuminated Cavins. Zak saw the darker stains on his slicker, streaks that were being washed away. There was a lot of blood. He figured he must have caught Cavins in the gut or just below the ribs.

The lightning revealed Zak to Cavins as well.

"You ain't Al Deets," Cavins said, his voice a throaty rasp.

"You figured that out, did you?" Zak said.

"Damn it, who in hell are you? Trask send you back for me?"

"In a way, yeah."

"Well, help me get on my horse, then."

"I'm taking your horse, Cavins."

"You what?"

"You won't need your horse anymore. And you've seen your last sunrise."

"Damn you. You ain't with Trask."

"No, I'm not."

"Who in hell are you?"

"I'm the man who put that bullet in your gut, Cavins."

The wind whipped up the road, dashed rain like flung sand on both men. Streaks of jagged lightning etched the black clouds with silver filigree, and the ensuing thunder belched in a mighty basso profundo that reverberated across the stormy skies like some dire pronouncement from an Olympian deity.

Cavins jumped when the thunder roared. Then he started to lower his hand in a furtive movement, a slow glide toward his holstered pistol.

"You might want to think twice before you draw that pistol, Cavins," Zak said.

Cavins let his hand float a few inches above the butt of his pistol. It hovered there in midair.

"How's that?" Cavins said, his voice a fear-laden rasp.

"You're looking right up at a big old boulder perched atop a mountain."

"I don't get your meanin', mister."

"I mean you're a raindrop, Cavins. I'm just teetering, waiting for that one drop to dislodge me. Then I'm going to roll down and fall right on top of you."

"You're full of shit," Cavins said, and dropped his hand. He started to pull the pistol from its holster. He might have gotten it going an inch or so when Zak's hand flew to his Walker Colt. Cavins's eyes widened as if the wind had thrown acid into them.

Zak's hand was a blur, and Cavins heard the ominous click as Zak thumbed the hammer back to full cock.

"No," Cavins gasped.

"Yes," Zak said, aiming the pistol straight at Cavins's forehead.

He squeezed the trigger and orange-red flame belched from the muzzle of the Colt. The bullet struck Cavins square between the eyes, smashing bone and flesh to pulp, flattening slightly before it sped through his brain, smashing his head backward into the rocky slope of the hill. His arm and hand went slack and he slid down into a puddle of water, leaving a red streak that turned pink in the rain and then vanished like the bloom on a December rose.

Zak ejected the empty hull from the cylinder of his pistol, shoved a fresh cartridge in, closed the gate, and slid the weapon back in its holster.

Cavins lay sprawled on the ground like a broken doll, his mouth open, eyes fixed in a frosty stare, somehow looking alive as raindrops struck them. In the next lightning flash, Zak saw the black hole in the center of his forehead, washed clean by the rain.

It felt like a graveyard in that spot, so dark and dank and lifeless. He turned Nox away and headed up the road. Cavins's horse trotted after him, his head down, soaked to the skin beneath his hide.

Lightning danced in the skies and thunder rumbled loud and far in the darkness of the night. The wind blew the rain parallel to the earth, a billion stinging needles stabbing the horses, stinging the back of Zak's neck.

Zak hunched over and pulled the collar of his slicker up at the back.

Maybe this was how it was with Noah just after he climbed into the ark, he thought. It felt like the end of the world, and he knew it wouldn't be long before there was a flood somewhere out there on that godforsaken desert where no signs of life were to be seen.

9

Lieutenant O'Hara saw it first.

A shadow in the rain, looming out of the darkness.

He reached for his pistol with his right hand, touched Colleen's arm with the left. He felt her stiffen.

"Don't shoot," Zak said. "It's me."

The shadow moved toward the clutch of horses, the people huddled beneath them.

"It's only Zak, Ted," Colleen said.

"There's two of 'em," Rivers said.

"Naw, that other shadow's just a horse," Scofield said.

Ted crabbed out from under his horse and stood up, rain pouring over his hat and slicker.

"What you got, Cody?" he asked.

"A rifle for you. Maybe some ammunition in the saddlebags, and grub. You can either change horses or unstrap the rifle and scabbard, switch it to your saddle."

"I'll change horses. Where we going?"

"High ground," Zak said. "This gusher's going to spawn flash floods."

"Right," O'Hara said. "Come on, soldiers, mount up. Colleen, bring my horse to me once I mount the other one."

He walked to the horse Zak was leading and took the reins from him. He climbed into the saddle as the others mounted up.

Colleen led Ted's horse to him and handed him the reins.

"You lead off, Cody," O'Hara said. "This is a fair mount for a civilian horse."

The two soldiers chuckled as Zak pulled away from them on Nox.

He wanted to gain ground on Trask, but he also knew they were all in danger as long as they were on flat ground, at the mercy of the heavy rains. The wind was at their backs, at least, but in such a storm it could circle and come at them head on, slowing them down. It was so dark he could not see very far ahead, but he had been down that old wagon road and he knew there were places where they could get to higher ground. But he might have to range wide of the road to find a suitable place. And wherever they wound up, they'd be at the mercy of the weather, with no trees, no shelter at all.

Lightning ripped through the clouds, splashed light on the bleak terrain. Thunder was a constant artillery barrage, sometimes so close it was deafening, and off in the distance more thunder and more lightning.

A rattlesnake skittered out in front of Nox, slithering away from the road, its diamond-back skin illuminated briefly from a flash of lightning. It disappeared in the dark, heading, Zak thought, to safer ground, probably flooded out of its home tunnel.

"Follow the snake," he said to himself.

He turned Nox in that direction, marking the path in his mind. The snake would know where to go. Zak could only take his bearings in those brief moments when the land was lighted. He would have to keep all the information in his mind, and all of it in the proper order. The storm would not last forever, and when it was over and the sun came out, he didn't want to be lost.

He didn't know how far ahead of him Trask was, but he had a hunch that the man would be holed up in one of the old stage stops, out of the rain and the wind.

He could not tell, in the darkness, whether the land was rising, but during the next splash of lightning, he saw a low hill off to his right. Was it high enough and wide enough to keep them all safe from any flooding? He did not know, but headed for the hill, and when Nox balked, he kept the horse on course. The horse's hooves dug for purchase, dislodging small stones, sliding some on the wet ground. Zak was conscious of the others behind him, although he could not see or hear them above the roar of thunder.

Nox reached the top of the hill, and as he stepped forward, the ground beneath them leveled. The hill was larger than it had looked. The next lightning strike lit up the whole top for an instant, and Zak saw that it was high enough that they might escape all but the largest flash flood. The mound of rock and dirt was at least two hundred yards long and half as wide. Nothing grew there, and the ground was soaked and muddy. But it would do, he thought.

He reined in Nox and turned the horse, waited for the others to surround him.

"Can you all hear me?" he asked.

They all nodded, their head movements aggressive enough so he could see that they had all assented.

"We're going to wait out the storm up here," he said. "We won't bunch up like you did back there. Instead, each person will have a station that covers most of the terrain up here. Kind of like a circle. It's going to be wet and windy. Probably all night. I'll check on each of you. You can hunker down under your horses, but look for anything that moves whenever there's light enough to see. And don't shoot me when I come riding or walking up on you. Any threat will probably come from down below."

Zak paused for several seconds.

"Any questions?"

"None, Colonel," O'Hara said.

"Call me Zak, or Cody, Ted. Drop the colonel from now on. I'm not in uniform."

"Right, sir," O'Hara said. "And I'd like to talk to you privately, Zak, when you're finished assigning us all posts."

"Yes."

Zak spoke to Rivers first, told him he would guard the rear of the hill. Both men dismounted.

"I shot two men when I culled Lieutenant O'Hara from that outlaw bunch," he told the soldier. "One was still alive when I went back for that horse. Never saw the other one."

"What happened to the one you did see?" Rivers asked.

"He won't mind the rain and the flood won't drown him," Zak said.

Rivers cleared his throat and saluted.

"None of that, either. Just forget I carry rank for now."

"Yes, sir," Rivers said. He held onto his reins and hunkered down underneath his horse's belly. He faced the back end of the hill.

"You'll face the wind, so get as close to the edge of this hill as you can," Zak said.

"Yes . . . um, yeah, Cody."

Zak smiled, but Rivers couldn't see it. He left the soldier there and walked back to the others. O'Hara was stripping the saddle and rifle scabbard from Cavins's horse. He handed the blanket to Colleen.

"Give you a dry place to sit for a while, sis," he said.

"Thanks, Ted. Where do you want me, Zak?"

"You can stay with your brother or walk ten paces along this side and take up that position."

"All right," she said. Zak thought she sounded disappointed. He brushed it off. He would talk to her later.

"Scofield, you take the point," Zak said. He pointed to the opposite end of the hill. "Keep a sharp eye."

"Yes, sir," Scofield said, and started walking his mount to the far end of the hill.

"I want you on this side, nearest the road, Ted," Zak said. "Close to Rivers, in case he runs into anything."

"You expect an attack from our rear?" O'Hara said.

"You never know."

"What about you, Zak?" Colleen asked. "Where will you be?"

"I'll be right across from you on that side, close to Scofield. You holler if you see anything that doesn't seem right. A stray horse, a cow, a man walking up the hill."

"I think I can handle it," she said.

"Ted, let's talk when you're finished and then you can go to your post."

"Won't take a minute." Ted finished attaching the scabbard to his horse and slid the rifle in its sheath.

"Colleen," Zak said, "you might go through those saddlebags your brother took off that horse and see if there's any grub there. Give the rifle cartridges to your brother."

"Glad to," she said cheerily, and Zak thought she needed a good slap, or a spanking.

He walked off toward the center of the hill and waited for O'Hara. Ted led his horse over a few minutes later.

"Go ahead, Ted," Zak said. "What have you got to say?"

"I just wanted to say that I don't think you need to press too much on following Trask and Ferguson. I know where they're going."

"How do you know that?"

"Trask forced me to mark on my map where Cochise's camp was located. I marked them incorrectly. But I know where and how I marked them. I can find the spots easily, even without a map."

"That's good, Ted. Do you also know where Cochise is?"

"I know where he was, and I know the places he likes. For some reason, he trusted me."

"Cochise is a good judge of character."

"You know him, Zak?"

"We've met. Anything else?"

"Thanks for getting me away from that bunch. I have no doubt they would have killed me once they found what they were looking for."

"Or didn't find what they were looking for."

"Yes."

"All right. Take your post. I'll see you by and by."

O'Hara started to salute and caught himself in time. He grinned and walked off toward Rivers.

Zak saw Colleen sitting on the folded horse blanket under her horse's belly. He knew she was wet and cold. They all were. It could not be helped.

The wind was much stronger when he took up his position almost directly opposite where she sat like a drenched bird. He crabbed under Nox and patted the horse's chest, positioning him so his rear faced the wind from the northwest. It was all he could do on such a miserable night.

He worried about the lightning. They were all in the open and on high ground. A bolt could strike any one of them and fry their insides, boil their blood like pot coffee. And the snakes would join them. Might even see a deer or two, or a jackrabbit. It was a hellish place to be, and they would all be worn to a frazzle by morning.

He settled his rump on the cold, rocky ground and tested the looseness of his pistol in its holster. He might have to draw it fast, but wasn't expecting anyone to ride up on them during the storm. Deets might still be alive. That was the name Cavins had

mentioned. Or someone else. But if he had any
sense at all, he'd be on his own hill or somewhere
out of the rain and wind, if there was such a place.

Trask was probably warm and dry in the nearest
stage stop, the bastard.

Zak didn't want to think of him any more that
night, and he didn't.

Instead, he found himself thinking about Colleen, wishing he could hold her close and keep her
warm. Lightning ripped through black clouds off
to the south and west. The tremendous crash of
thunder wiped out even those thoughts as he and
Nox both shivered in the cold, relentless rain.

10

The men in the adobe hut could all hear the water. They braced themselves in the darkness, pressing against mud-brick walls that might be washed away under tons of water at any moment. They forgot, in that moment, the stench that permeated the dwelling, the terrible odor of rotting human flesh, fecal matter, dried blood, the pungent scent of death that clung to the walls, ceiling, and floors like cave mold.

"Can we light a lamp, Ben?" Rawlins asked. "I can't see a damned thing."

"No," Trask barked. "Hell no. You just hang on, Rawlins."

The roar of water could be heard above the thunder. It sounded like something out of hell, a terrible liquid moan gushing out of the earth's bowels, louder than a locomotive's steam engine.

Trask stood near a window, looking out. Lightning splashed a brilliant glow over the land, and he saw a wall of mud and water speeding down the road. Behind the churning mass, he saw the flood tower higher still, as if some volcanic explosion were pushing it up until it swallowed everything on land in its massive voracious maw. Instinctively, he drew back from the window and threw his arms up in a defensive gesture.

Ferguson, a few feet away, saw Trask duck his head, and his eyes widened in horror and his gut knotted up in fear as a forked lightning bolt split open the darkness. A second later the adobe seemed to shudder from the thunder booming overhead. It sounded as if something had exploded inside the hut.

"What is it, Ben?" Ferguson said, his eardrums still reverberating from the sound of the thunder-clap.

"Brace yourselves, boys," Trask said. "There's a damned river out there on the road."

Ferguson heard the water. Fear clutched his throat with cold bony fingers. It sounded so close and so loud now.

The wall of water rushed past and a torrent struck the side of the adobe. Dirty water splashed through the windows. There was a loud screech as something scraped the side of the building, a board or a tree, something wooden, Trask thought.

Rawlins grunted. The Mexicans cried out the names of Jesus and Mary, in Spanish. Ferguson cursed. One of the Mexicans crossed himself. Those standing next to windows moved away from the wall and milled with the others in the center of the room.

A huge rock struck just below one window and knocked out three or four bricks. Water gushed through the hole and spread across the dirt floor. Trask jumped back and went to the opposite wall.

"Let's get the hell out of here," Rawlins shouted.

"We're all going to be drowned like rats," Ferguson yelled as more bricks fell away and more water rushed through the opening.

"You go outside, you're a dead man, Hiram," Trask yelled. "Everybody stay put."

"We are going to die," Hector Gonzalez whimpered.

"Shut up, Hector," his brother Fidel said.

The sound grew horrendous as the water crashed into the adobe, hurling rocks and debris against the outer walls. The flood ravished the side of the adobe, widening the hole, pouring more water inside in pumping gushers. Soon the entire floor was underwater. Rawlins saw a chair fall over and make a splash as still more water rushed in through the widening aperture.

"Ben, we got to get the hell out of here," Rawlins said.

"Damn you, Rawlins. Don't go loco on me. You go outside, that water will wash you away like a damned straw."

"What if that wall goes?" Ferguson asked.

"We'll get wet," Trask said. "We'll have three walls left and that's what will keep us from drowning, you dumb sonofabitch."

"Watch what you call me, Trask," Ferguson said.

"Then shut your damned mouth, Hiram."

Jaime Elizondo started muttering a prayer in Spanish. His voice quavered with fear.

All of the Mexicans moved to the opposite wall and braced themselves against it. Trask looked at them in disgust. Rawlins splashed over and stood with them. Ferguson hesitated a moment, then joined Rawlins. Trask stood alone in the center of

the adobe, water up to his ankles and more pouring in through the hole. The bricks around the
hole were crumbling, falling into the water, making plopping sounds. Outside, the flood raged on,
growing wider and stronger, as if a dam had burst
and released a deadly river.

"That wall's a-goin'," Ferguson shouted above
the tumult.

Trask could see it. The old adobe bricks were
crumbling under the force and pressure of the water. The hole widened just above the base of the
wall, allowing more water to eat at the bricks.

"Nothing we can do about it," Trask said.

"We have to get out of here," Fidel said.

"You go outside, you'll drown," Trask said.
"That flood will pass. Don't nobody go off half-
cocked here."

But he was worried that the flood waters would
engulf them as more and more of the south wall
began to erode and turn to mud. Some water was
sloshing onto the east wall, too, but so far there
had been no breech. The wall was holding.

He had seen flash floods before, but none as
dangerous as this one. He had seen horses and men
swept away in an instant when sudden water came
out of nowhere and washed over a dry streambed.
The impression was a lasting one, and he thought
of one such flood now. This one was far worse,
and all he could think of was that something must
have held the water back long enough to build up
to such proportions.

Part of the south wall was holding, but as the
water ate its way to the door, the hole widened and
they could all see the rushing water in the sporadic

flashes of lightning. It was a truly terrifying sight, Trask thought, as water rose above his ankles and began filling his boots.

Some of the others were lifting one foot up out of the water, taking off their boots, shaking them out, then doing the same with the other foot. It was a losing proposition, and Trask just wriggled his toes inside his boots to keep his blood circulating through his cold feet.

"What about the horses?" Rawlins said. "They ain't hobbled. They're liable to run off and maybe get drownded."

"Better worry about yourself, Rawlins. Horses got more sense than you do."

Trask knew that panic was the immediate danger. He didn't have to look at the men to know that they were all scared, ready to bolt out into the storm rather than face death by drowning in an old adobe hut, trapped like rats in a rain barrel.

The best way to ride it out was to stay calm, he reasoned, and he knew that if he showed any sign of panic, some of the men would start crumbling just like those adobe bricks. He thought the horses would be all right. They were on higher ground. The flooding didn't seem to be hitting the entire east wall, but only sloshing against less than half of it on the south side. As long as that wall held, they should be all right.

There was a sudden tug at the building and a large chunk of the south wall shuddered. More bricks disintegrated, disappearing in a tidal wash of water. More water gushed in, and the level rose to Trask's knees. The thunder and lightning was still close and loud. The men jumped at every thunderclap, every stab of lightning. They had stopped emptying their boots, and through the murky darkness Trask saw them now looking upward, as if for a way to climb out of the adobe.

They weren't floating yet, but he knew they might have to start treading water if the flood rose up to their necks.

Ferguson swore under his breath, but Trask heard it. He turned toward the man and shot him a hard look. He could not see his face in the dark, but he hoped Ferguson would just shut up. It took only one voice to yell fire in a crowded room to stampede the whole bunch.

Elizondo began whining.

"*Callate*, Jaime," Hector Gonzalez said.

Then a broken timber slammed into the receding wall with great force, startling everyone. The log, or post, ripped a long gash into the bricks, crumbling them into granules that turned to mud as soon as they swirled into the water. More water gushed into the adobe, and the rest of the wall nearest the east wall began to break up, letting in gallons of water. It quickly rose above the knees of the men standing there.

Elizondo began to wail. It turned into a terrified scream, and he broke from the pack of men.

"*Ya me voy*," he yelled and started toward the door.

"*Parate*," Hector said. He stretched out a hand to try and stop Elizondo, but missed.

"Come back here," Trask said. "Jaime, don't open that door."

Elizondo, in a panic, continued to splash toward

the door. When he reached down to open it, Trask drew his pistol.

Even in the dark, Trask could see Elizondo's hulk as he raised his arm, cocking his pistol. He took aim and squeezed the trigger. The loud explosion made the men jump. The flash exposed Elizondo's back for a brief moment as the bullet smacked into his spine, shattering the cord into bits.

Elizondo stiffened as his back arched in one final spasm. He let out a gasp and tumbled head first into the muddy water, paralyzed. There was a sucking sound as his mouth took in water. The smell of burnt powder and smoke hung in the air of the adobe.

The Gonzalez brothers gasped aloud. Another Mexican sobbed.

"Damn," muttered Ferguson under his breath.

"Bastard," Trask said. He did not holster his pistol, but turned to the men huddled against the wall.

"I'll put out the lamp of any man who tries what Jaime did. You all stay put, or I'll shoot every damned one of you before you take one step toward that door."

No one spoke.

Trask slid his pistol back in its holster. "Just try me," he said, glaring at the men.

"Nobody's goin' to try that, Ben," Ferguson said.

"They better not."

"Did you have to kill him?" Rawlins said.

"He would have drowned anyway," Trask said.

The water kept rising. It was up to their crotches now, and the men squirmed. They were wet and miserable. They could see the water with each flash of lightning, and most of them trembled in fear as water kept hurtling past the adobe. The thunder came from farther away now, but the rain and wind were relentless.

The water rose slightly, but now it was from the rain more than the flood.

Trask knew that if they could hold on for another hour or so, the water would go down and they could think about drying out, getting some grub in their bellies, checking on the horses.

His right hand never strayed far from the butt of his pistol.

The Mexicans would be angry, he knew, now that he had killed one of their number. They were Ferguson's men, but they were working for him. They wanted the Apache gold as much as he did, and that would serve to hold their tempers down, perhaps, keep them in check.

Ferguson would pay for his part in all of this, Trask thought. The men in the line shacks were probably all dead, killed by Zak Cody. So he could not count on them. He needed every man he had left. But he would not hesitate to kill any one of them who questioned his authority or tried to run off.

He would even kill Ferguson if he had to. The man was no longer needed.

The men who worked for the freighter might no longer be loyal to Ferguson, but they would be loyal to Trask. Or more exactly, they would be loyal to the gun he carried on his hip.

They would be loyal, all right, or they would die.

Just like Jaime Elizondo.

11

Corporal Scofield yelled, "Something's comin'."
Zak heard it in between rumbles of thunder. He stood up and ran toward Scofield at the east end of the hill. The sound was unmistakable. He looked down but couldn't see anything because the sky was too dark.

"What is it?" Scofield asked.

"Flash flood," Zak said.

"Lordy. It sounds like all hell is breakin' loose."

"I think we're high enough so the water won't reach us, but stay on your toes."

Zak left Scofield standing next to his horse, shaking like a man in a quake. He ran to Colleen, who had crawled out from under her horse and was standing up, gripping her reins as if they were lifelines and she was on a sinking ship.

"Is that sound what I think it is?" she said to Zak.

"It should hit the road below us at any second."

Colleen cocked her head to listen. She could not exactly identify the sound, for it was like no other she had ever heard. It sounded, at first, like a giant's whisper, like air whooshing through a blacksmith's bellows. It did not sound like water. There was no watery sound. And then, as it got closer, it changed, and it sounded to her like a thousand distant hoofbeats, as if some stampeding herd of beasts were trampling the earth in a mad rush down the deserted road.

"It's such an odd sound, Zak. Isn't it?"

"You can't hear the water yet, but it's a flood. A flash flood. We're high enough here so that it shouldn't hit us."

The sound was louder now. Closer.

"You're very reassuring, Zak."

The rain blew against her back, rattling like dice in a cup as it struck her slicker. Not a soothing, steady sound, but ragged, uneven, reminding her at times of flung sand, at other times like buckets of water dumped from a great height.

He wanted to hold her close to him, protect her from the rain and the chilling wind. Instead, he put an arm around her shoulders to comfort her.

"You might get mud splashed on you, Colleen, that's all."

The two did not have to wait long. As more lightning laced the rain-heavy black clouds, they saw the huge wall of water roar down the road, its muddy waters raging, tumbling, churning, washing over the ground, eating up everything in its path.

She clung to Zak, leaning back against him, grabbing one hand in her own.

Colleen said something, but he couldn't hear her above the roar of the flood. He tightened his grip on her. It seemed that the hill trembled under the onslaught of tons of water, though he knew that was probably impossible. But he heard the terrible sound of the water as it splashed against the side of the hill, gouging out rocks and dirt, adding bulk to its dimensions.

Someone yelled, either O'Hara or Rivers, Zak thought, but he gazed down through the darkness and was mesmerized by the awesome power of the flood, the tremendous force it exerted on the road, the side of the hill, like some liquid dragon gobbling up everything in its ravishing path.

"Oh," Colleen cried out.

She was looking down, as he was, captivated by the sight of so much water traveling at such speed. The flood had a long downhill run, Zak knew, and would eventually fan out and subside. In the meantime, he wondered how so much water had built up and gathered so much strength. The rain was heavy, yes, but such a large flood was uncommon in desert country. He thought there must have been a lot of runoff to feed such a flood from higher ground.

There *was* a lot of rain. He had seen more, up in the Snake country, over in Oregon and Washington. But there were large rivers there, and here there were none. Once the ground was soaked full, the water had no place to go except overland, pushing through dry creek beds, over roads, and into gullies and washes, arroyos and gulches.

Colleen's horse spooked when it saw the water. It bolted away from the rim of the hill, and Zak reached for the reins. Colleen held on, but the reins were slipping from her grasp.

"Whoa, boy," Zak said, jerking down on the

reins, digging the bit into the back of the horse's mouth. The horse fought him, bobbing its head up and down, twisting its neck. Zak bent the horse's head as he struggled with it, until its nose was almost between its front legs. He backed the horse away from Colleen and out of sight of the flood, then patted the animal's neck while still exerting pressure on the bit.

"You take it easy, boy," Zak said, his voice low and soothing. "Steady down."

The horse stopped fighting the bit, and Zak eased up. The animal shook its head, ran its tongue under the bit. The metal clacked against its teeth.

"He'll be all right now, I think," Zak said to Colleen, who had walked back over to him. "Just keep him away from where he was. Keep a firm grip on the reins, though."

"I will," she said. "Thanks, Zak. You sure know how to handle a horse. How are you with women?"

A bold statement, he thought. And from the way she was looking at him just then, he knew she expected a frank answer.

"Not much experience," he said. He was close enough to see her eyes, and his gaze did not waver.

"So you say. Not much difference between women and spirited horses. I mean their dispositions are similar."

"I wouldn't know, Colleen."

"With a horse," she said, "sometimes you have to be firm and sometimes you have to be gentle. It's the same with a woman, isn't it?"

"No argument there. But I wouldn't know."

"Wouldn't you?" That teasing tone in her voice again. Teasing, somewhat playful, he thought.

"Maybe a woman tells a man how she wants to be treated," Zak said.

"Oh, and do you always comply with a woman's wishes?"

"No."

"Zak, you don't mean that."

"A woman, same as a man, can be mighty unreasonable sometimes."

"So, if a woman's wish is unreasonable, you treat her differently?"

"I treat a woman the way she wants to be treated. I hope I do the same for a horse or a man."

"My, you are a mystery man, aren't you? A very mysterious man."

"No more than any other," he said.

She moved closer to him, until their faces were scant inches apart.

"I also think you are an experienced man. With women."

"What do you mean by 'experienced.' That word seems to be packed with dynamite when you say it."

She laughed, and the rain made her eyes sparkle as a ragged fence of lightning streaked across the sky.

"I think you know full well how to handle women, Zak. And, I think you—"

"Don't accuse me of anything you can't prove, Colleen."

"Ah, you think I'm going to accuse you of something." It was a flat statement with a wicked curl to it. More teasing, he thought.

"I didn't say that. Look, Colleen, this talk doesn't seem to be going anywhere. We're in the middle of a big storm and there's a flash flood raging down on the road. This might not be the best place for a serious conversation."

She squeezed his hand with hers.

"You're the only real man I've spoken to in months. We schoolmarms have to take our conversations where we find them. I admire your honesty, if not your evasiveness."

"I wasn't being evasive. I truly have not had much experience with women. I've been a scout and a soldier for most of my grown life. Soldiering is about all I know. I don't go to any pie socials or afternoon teas."

"No, you don't. But I don't think you'd be out of place in a fine home with a bunch of flirting women surrounding you."

"I would be uncomfortable," he said.

She laughed again, and the sound of it was soft and pleasant to his ears. He was not uncomfortable with her, but was wary of falling completely under her spell. She was a very alluring woman, and for now, and probably for some time to come, he could not allow himself to be distracted by her charms.

The truth was, he had known a number of women, many of them almost as attractive as Colleen. Others were either too obvious, too shallow, or too brainless to attract his interest. The few good women he had known were either married or widowed, and the latter were often too eager to marry again and didn't much care who the husband might be.

"I think you could handle yourself, Zak. In almost any situation. And if you couldn't, you would say so, right out loud."

"I might," he said, and felt the powerful magnetism of her as she pressed against him, her face upturned to his, a wet face with moist eager lips and eyelashes that batted at the trickles of rain that seeped into them.

"What would you say if I told you right now, this very minute, Zak Cody, that I want you? I want you so much that I'm willing to forget my proper upbringing and fling myself shamelessly at your feet and let you take me, let you fulfill me as a woman, even though I'm a virgin and have fearlessly protected my virginity all my life. What would you say, Zak Cody? What would you do?"

He felt her arms grasp him around the waist, felt her pull herself into him, pressing so close that she aroused him. She rubbed against his manhood until it rose like an iron stalk between his legs and throbbed with engorged blood, surging against the bonds of his trousers like some ravenous beast desperate to penetrate cloth and canvas and break into her guarded portal and slake its lust on her willing body.

"I—I'd say," he croaked, "that the rain must have leaked into your skull and wet down your brain."

"No," she breathed, her breath hot against his lips, "I'm not mad or crazy. I'm burning inside with a womanly fire that I've never felt before. I want you so much I'm devoid of all shame and caution. I want you now, Zak, in the rain and the wet and wind, and I'd prostrate myself at your feet if only you would take me and quench these fires so deep inside me."

"Colleen—"

She flung her arms around his neck and pulled

herself up, kissing him hard on the lips, taking his breath away. She burrowed into him with that kiss, and he felt the fire within her, the fire within himself. Her body ground against his and he wanted her then, wanted her as badly as she wanted him. He put his arms around her and held her tight against him. He pushed against her womanhood, thought that he could feel its softness past all the material that stood between.

He closed his eyes and blotted out the storm. He no longer felt the needling rain, the bruising wind, or heard any thunder but the thunder pounding in his temples, his ears, and all through his body.

He felt her body soften and begin to fall away from him. He knew she was dragging him down to the soaked ground and the rocks, and on the edge of that cliff, he felt himself following her, stepping off into space, into a dark abyss where only lovers go, a place where all time stood still and nothing mattered but the moment, the desire, the fierce animal coupling natural to all sentient beings.

Then he heard a shot. He heard it through the thick fog in his brain, the cotton in his ears, the crush of her body on his senses.

"Halt, who goes there?" Scofield cried out, his voice carrying on the wind, like a warning klaxon.

It galvanized Zak out of Colleen's arms, out of that seductive web of hers, and jolted him back to the precipice, into the world of the living, where danger rode the lightning, charging through his veins, electrifying his warrior self into being once again, where the only law was survival of the fittest.

The only thing that mattered.

12

Scofield bellowed into the rain and the night, yelling at the top of his lungs.

"Halt, or I'll shoot."

Zak stood Colleen up straight. He squeezed her arms as if to make sure her feet were firmly planted.

"Stay here," he said to her. "Keep your horse between you and Scofield."

"Be careful," she warned as he drew his pistol and started running toward the sound of Corporal Scofield's voice.

Ted O'Hara was yanking his recently acquired rifle out of its scabbard.

"Back me up, O'Hara," Zak said as he jumped past the lieutenant. "Stay here."

O'Hara did not reply, but Zak heard the rifle click as Ted jacked a cartridge into the chamber. Scofield was standing up near his horse's rump, a pistol in his right hand.

"What have you got, Scofield?" Zak was breathing hard, but he wasn't entirely winded.

"Somebody's comin' up this side. I thought I saw a horse. He won't stop. And he's comin' mighty slow."

"Stand easy," Zak said. "I'll take a look."

"You watch it, Cody. Could be more than one."

Zak said nothing. He bent over and stalked to the edge of the hill, where he stopped, cupped his left ear and listened.

He heard what sounded like the snort of a horse. He thought he could see a dark shape near the base of the hill. The animal seemed to be well away from the raging flood waters, but unless it climbed the hill, a surge might wash it away.

A peal of thunder died away, and he heard a low moan. A man was on that horse, he thought. He held his pistol at the ready.

"H-Help me," someone said.

A man's voice. Very faint, barely audible against the constant tattoo of the rain, the blustering lash of the wind.

Zak eased down the slope, crouching, setting both feet before he took another step. He sidled toward the horse at an angle. He wanted to flank the animal and the man. He stepped like an Indian, careful not to make noise or to kick loose any dirt and rocks. Slow, short steps brought him around to the horse's left flank. He stopped to listen after every few steps.

The horse was pawing the ground, trying to get a foothold, Zak thought. The water had loosened some of the soil, and the horse didn't have sense enough to follow a switchback course. And the man was obviously too hurt to take charge and guide the horse any farther.

Zak took a few more careful steps. He was close now.

He could hear the horse wheezing. He heard,

also, the low groan of the man. As he stepped still closer, he saw that the man was slumped over the saddle, hatless, his arms hanging loose and straight down.

"Mister," Zak said, "you want help, you just stay where you are. You make a move, and I shoot you out of the saddle."

"God's sake, man. I'm hurt. Hurt bad."

"I have a gun on you. Just wait."

"Hurry," the man gasped.

Zak came up on the side of the horse, from behind. He stopped, reached over for the man's pistol. It was still in its holster. He slid it free, tucked it inside his belt. The man heard the rustle of Zak's slicker and looked over at him.

"Who—" the man said.

"Never mind. Stay on, and I'll lead your horse up to the top of the hill."

"Oh God, it hurts."

"Where are you hit?" Zak asked.

"Don't know. I hurt all over. Belly, maybe."

"I'll take a look after we get up top."

Zak grabbed the reins with his left hand and pulled the horse on a straight line, parallel to the slope.

"You all right down there?"

Scofield's voice.

"Comin' up," Zak yelled back. "Wounded man."

"Come on," Scofield said.

When he reached the top, O'Hara was there with Scofield to meet him.

"What you got here, Zak?" Ted asked.

"Wounded man. Worn-out horse. Let's get him down and see what we can do for him."

"I recognize him," O'Hara said. "That's Al Deets. One of Trask's men."

Deets was moaning. He cried out when Scofield and O'Hara lifted him off the horse. By then, Colleen had rushed up.

"Take his horse, Colleen," Zak said. "Tie him to Scofield's over there."

She took the reins and led the horse away. In a few moments she was back, looking down at the wounded man. O'Hara and Cody were squatting next to him. Scofield stood watch, the rain battering him, the wind whipping his slicker so it flapped against his legs.

"Where's the most hurt, Deets?" Zak asked.

"Side. Belly."

"This man was shot," O'Hara said. "When you rescued me, right?"

"Probably," Zak said. "Hold his arms while I look for a bullet hole. This might hurt, Deets."

Zak unbuttoned the wounded man's slicker, then worked the buttons on his shirt, exposing his side and belly. It was dark and he couldn't see well, but he thought there was a stain across the man's abdomen. He rubbed there and then tasted the tip of his finger.

"Blood," he said.

Deets winced as Zak put his fingers to work, exploring the man's stomach and side. He felt something give. Deets jumped as if electrocuted when Zak probed the soft spot with his right index finger.

"Damn," Deets said. "That hurts like hell."

His voice was weak, barely audible against the relentless drumming of the rain, the angry whooshing sound of the flood along the road.

"Just lie still," Zak said as he continued to feel around the wound. He slipped his hand underneath Deets's back. The flesh was sticky with fresh blood, crusted with blood that had already dried. He finished his examination, tapped O'Hara on the arm and stood up.

He grabbed the crook of O'Hara's elbow and guided him away from Deets. He leaned close and whispered into the lieutenant's ear. "Come with me," he said.

Zak walked for several yards, then stopped and again put his face close to O'Hara's.

"Deets was lucky," he said. "He's not badly wounded. But I don't want him to know that."

"What?"

"He's got a flesh wound, O'Hara. My bullet plowed a hole in his left side. The bullet went clean through. He's lost some blood, but no broken bones, no lead in him."

"So, what do we do with him?"

"I want Deets to think he's going to die," Zak said.

"You what?"

"If he thinks he's going to die, we may be able to get some information from him."

"That sounds pretty close to torture, Zak."

"It's not torture. He's wounded. He has a bullet hole in the fatty part of his side. When it gets light, I can find some clay to stuff inside it, plug up the hole."

"In the meantime, he suffers."

"He would have suffered anyway, if we hadn't found him. He might have bled to death if that wound tore up any more. We keep him quiet and talk to him. I think he can give us information about Trask that might help us."

"All right. I'll follow your lead, Zak. What do you want me to do?"

"Just back me up when I tell the man he doesn't have long to live."

"I can do that . . . I will do that."

"Good. Let's get started. He might pass out. I don't know how much blood he's lost, but he's weak. We have him where we want him."

The two walked back and squatted down on both sides of Deets.

"Deets," Zak said. "You awake?"

Deets moaned.

Zak bent over him. Deets's eyes were fluttering, but he was awake.

"Deets, I'll call you Al. You don't have much time left."

"Huh?"

"You've got a bullet in your gut, Al. You've lost a lot of blood. You're still bleeding."

"Damn."

"Maybe I can help you when it gets light. I might be able to get that bullet out and sew you up."

"You—You got any whiskey?"

"No. You'll have to bite on a stick."

"Shit."

"What can you tell me about Ben Trask? I want to know where he's going and what he's going to do."

"You go to hell. You the one who shot me?"

"I am. And I'm the one who can make your last minutes here on earth the worst you've ever had. I can make your last moments pure hell, Al. Is that what you want?"

"I ain't tellin' you nothin'."

"Suit yourself, Al. If I start going after that bullet, you're going to scream your head off, and if I find it, I'm going to push it in so deep, you're going to beg me to put a bullet in your brain."

"I—I don't want to die."

"Then tell me what I want to know. You've got two seconds to think it over, then I'm going to stick my finger into that bullet hole. If I can't go deep enough, I'll cut you with my knife."

"What do you want to know?"

"Tell me what Trask is after. Apache gold?"

"Th-That's part of it," Deets said.

A blast of wind washed over them, drenching them with gallons of rain. Deets squirmed in pain as Zak poked him in his side. He cried out in pain. His legs twitched in a sudden spasm.

"Just spell it out, Al, and maybe I can pull you out of this."

Deets hesitated. Zak pressed down on his wound with the heel of his hand.

Deets screamed in pain.

"Sorry," Zak said. He knew he was resorting to torture, but he wanted Trask so badly, he'd do this to get the information he wanted. In the name of expediency, he reasoned. If his shot had not been off, Deets might be dead now. A little pain wouldn't kill him. He felt O'Hara's disapproving gaze burning into him, but he didn't look at the lieutenant. Deets was close to opening up with the information he wanted.

"Don't—Don't do that no more," Deets said, his voice laced with the pain shooting through him.

"Then talk, Al."

"They—They's a group of citizens what wants the Apaches wiped out. H-Hiram Ferguson, he's behind it. But Ben Trask, he—he wants Cochise's gold. They mean to start a war with the Apaches. So's the army will wipe them out. 'Stir 'em up.' Th-That's what Ferguson said to do. And there's a big payday for all of us when the army goes on the warpath. That's what Ben Trask is after. The money and the Apache gold."

O'Hara let out a long breath.

"There's more to it than that, isn't there, Al?" Zak's voice was soft and steady, his tone coaxing, almost friendly.

"Wh-What do you mean?" Deets said.

"Fort Bowie," Zak said. "Someone there is helping Ferguson and Trask."

Deets sucked in a breath. The breath brought pain to him again. He threw an arm over his forehead and rode it out, gritting his teeth.

"Deets?" O'Hara said, eager to hear an answer to Zak's question.

Lightning scarred the skies a few miles to the east. Thunder rolled over them a few seconds later. The flood seemed to be losing force and there was only a faint whisper of rushing waters as Zak waited for Deets to tell him what he wanted to know.

The comparative silence seemed to last an eternity. Scofield shifted the weight on his feet.

Colleen held her breath.

"You don't have long to live, Al," Zak said, his hand poised above the wound in Deets's side. "Time is running out. Right along with my patience."

Deets drew his arm away from his forehead and looked up into Zak's eyes. He could not see them, but he could imagine them. They were boring into him black as the twin muzzles of a double-barreled shotgun.

He could feel death coming on.

Death, he thought, was real close.

⇥ 13 ⇤

Zak drew his pistol.

O'Hara reared back in surprise. Colleen let out an involuntary gasp.

Scofield drew in a sudden breath, held it.

Zak cocked the pistol, rammed the barrel straight into the open wound.

Deets stiffened, stifled a cry of pain.

"If you don't start talking, Al, I'm going to blow this hole so big you'll start screaming for me to put the next bullet in your miserable brain. It won't kill you right off, this bullet, but you'll stay alive long enough to pray for death a thousand times. You got that?"

"M-Major. It'sthemajor," Deets said, the words blurting out so quick they ran together.

"Willoughby?" O'Hara said in astonishment.

"Yeah—Major Willoughby." Deets started to shake as if he were passing apricot seeds. His teeth chattered, clacking together in a staccato tattoo.

Zak pulled the pistol away from the wound in Deets's side, and nudged the barrel against his temple.

"No lie, Al?" Zak said.

"No lie. Honest. Willoughby wants Cochise's scalp to hang on his belt. He—He owns land in town and round about. He wants every red Apache dead. That's what he told Ferguson and that's what he told Ben Trask."

"Shit," O'Hara said, and looked at Zak. "Can we believe him?" He asked.

"Ever hear of a deathbed confession, Lieutenant?" Zak said.

"No."

"Well, you just heard one. Deets was mighty close to death, and I think he just might want to live."

"Are you . . . goin' to fix me up?" Deets said.

Zak eased the hammer back down to half cock and holstered his pistol.

"Yeah, Al, we'll fix you up come morning. I may need you down the road."

"Need me? What for?"

"To testify against Major Willoughby when I bring the traitorous bastard up on charges."

O'Hara let out a long whistle. "Boy, you go right for the throat, don't you, Cody?"

Zak stood up. "He's your prisoner, O'Hara. You, your sister, and Corporal Scofield are going to testify, too. You were all witnesses to what this bastard told us. We've got a live snake in the woodpile at Fort Bowie."

"I can't believe it," O'Hara said. "Major Willoughby is a good soldier. Trusted."

"Those are sometimes the ones you've got to watch."

"Willoughby—"

"Don't worry too much about it. Just think about

why he sent you out to track Cochise. Ask yourself that question, O'Hara."

"He—He said it was—was to protect the Chiricahua."

"You think Cochise needs army protection?"

"I don't know. I honestly don't know."

"Ask Cochise. If you ever see him again."

Zak walked away, leaving O'Hara to search for answers. Leaving him to think about his mission and why he was kidnapped by Trask's men.

Colleen came up to her brother, took him by the arm.

"You seem troubled, Ted. I hope Zak didn't say anything to upset you."

"I am troubled."

"About Zak Cody?"

"No, he seems a straight shooter. It's just . . . well, he thinks we've got a traitor at the fort."

"Do you believe him?"

"I don't know what to think. But Zak may be right. Damn it, he goes right to the heart of a matter and lays it all out like it's gospel truth. I don't know what to make of it. I know General Crook thinks mighty highly of him. President Grant, too. But it's just hard to swallow that Major Willoughby would betray the army, would deliberately send me out so I could make it easy for him and Trask to wipe out the Chiricahua."

"'Most everybody at the fort hates Apaches," Colleen said. "The only good one is a dead one, they say."

"Yes, I've heard that. More than once. But Cochise is following orders, same as me. He doesn't want to own land or build a settlement. He just wants to be left alone. To live his life the way he always has."

"You like Cochise?" she asked.

"I respect him. I admire him in many ways. He seems a man true to his own beliefs. I've smoked the pipe with him."

"But he's a savage, Ted."

"To the whites, maybe. But in his own world, he's . . . he's like a wise and kind king. I've seen him with kids, and seen the way kids and their mothers look at him. Oh, he's a fighter, all right. And I'd hate to face him in battle. But left alone, left to roam this desolate wild country, I don't think he'd be a threat to the white settlers anymore. He knows we're here, and he knows we're going to stay."

"I think you give Cochise too much credit. Too much honor, maybe."

"Well, I sure as hell wouldn't betray him. And that's what Willoughby seems to be doing."

"I—I admit I've grown somewhat fond of the Apache children myself," she said. "I taught them in another Indian village, you know. That's why I wanted to go to Fort Bowie. Their mothers are sweet, too, ignorant as they are about our ways."

"Dumb, you mean."

"No, not dumb. Ignorant. Not knowing. But even the mothers seem eager to learn new things. And they want the best for their children. They want their children to be happy and to learn."

"Maybe the answer is to bring teachers out here on the frontier, not soldiers."

"Ted," she said, "those are the wisest words you've ever spoken."

"Colleen, get back to your post. It's still raining, and we can't solve the Apache problems between us."

"Yes, sir," she mocked. "And you're right. Who
would listen to us anyway?"

"Not the army," he said.

The rain was beginning to slacken and the wind
seemed to be backing off from its former fury. But
there were still bolts of lightning ripping silver rivers in the clouds to the east and the rumble of thunder across the black heavens.

Deets groaned.

"You goin' to help me, soldier?" he said to Scofield.

"I don't know. Sir?" Scofield said to O'Hara.

"Corporal," O'Hara said, "you got a first-aid
kit in your saddlebags?"

"Yes sir."

"Got any iodine?"

"I think so, sir."

"Pour some in this man's wound."

"Now, sir?"

"When the rain lets up."

"Yes, sir," Scofield said.

"Iodine?" Deets said. "That's what you got to
give me? Ain't you got any whiskey?"

"Any more out of you, Deets," O'Hara said,
"and I'll have Corporal Scofield pour the iodine
down your throat."

"That other'n said he was going to sew me up. I
hurt awful bad."

"I wouldn't count on Mr. Cody to make good
on that promise, Deets."

"Mr. Cody? Zak Cody? Was that Zak Cody?"

"It was," O'Hara said.

"Lord God. That's the man Ben Trask wants to kill worse'n anything."

"I think the feeling's mutual," O'Hara said.

"Huh?" Deets was a voice in the rain and the dark. He lay flat on his back, spitting out rainwater.

O'Hara looked down at him without pity. The man had been his captor and was now begging for mercy. What's more, he didn't have the brains of a pissant.

"Deets," O'Hara said, "this is all going to seem like one of the best times of your life."

"I—I don't follow you, O'Hara."

"You're going to the gallows, Deets. You and Trask, the whole bunch of you."

Deets gasped, but said nothing.

"Keep an eye on him, Scofield. And don't be in any big hurry getting that iodine."

"Yes, sir," Scofield said.

O'Hara walked back to his post, his mind mired deep in a quicksand of thought. The ordinary world he had known, the army, had suddenly changed. First, he had been kidnapped, forced to draw maps and reveal secret information. Then he had learned that his own post commander, albeit on temporary duty, was essentially a traitor. Willoughby was defying military orders, contradicting the wishes of the U.S. government itself in order to further his own aims. He had brought his sister Colleen into this quagmire, this mess, and now it appeared she was about to give herself to a man with no future, Zak Cody.

He trudged to his former position, stood there as if alone on a small island. There was no one he could turn to anymore, no man he could trust, no one he could confide in or hold in confidence in the midst of his quandary.

Colleen was a grown woman, of course. But he was her older brother. He should be able to talk to her, to advise her, to warn her. But she seemed distant and alien to him now. He wondered if she had fallen for Willoughby at the fort. Was that possible? Had she even met the man? She didn't seem to understand the Apache situation. She might bear some compassion for the Chiricahuas, the children, at least, but not for Cochise and the others of his tribe.

And what of himself? Had he allowed himself to be deceived by an Apache with a price on his head? Once, he knew, the Mexicans had placed a bounty on Apache scalps. And now the Americans were trying to stir them up so they could be eliminated from the human race.

The storm seemed to embody the turmoil he felt. The lightning, the thunder, the wind, the rain, the flash flood, and now, in his heart, one flash flood after another, all roaring through him, drowning his emotions, smothering his ideals, strangling his honor, washing away his sense of duty.

He wanted to cry out, to scream, to run back to Deets and shoot bullets into him until his pistol was empty. But he knew that would not assuage the anguish he felt at Willoughby's betrayal, nor quell his anxiety over Colleen's attentions toward Cody.

And somewhere in there, in all that turmoil, was Ben Trask, a man Cody wanted to capture and bring to justice.

Cody. He was a mystery. He was a shadow rider. He came out of nowhere and he would ride on when his job at Fort Bowie was finished. He would not take Colleen with him. He would take nothing with him but his secrets and his shadow. Wherever Cody went, he left dead men in his wake, and maybe a few broken hearts.

That would be Colleen's fate, he was sure.

But what of his own?

What would become of him and his career in the United States Army? Would the stain of Willoughby be on his forehead, on his uniform, for all to see, for the rest of his days?

Ted raised his head and exposed his face to the falling rain. He should feel cleansed, he thought, but he felt dirty and ashamed, ashamed of his thoughts, ashamed of his commander, ashamed of his fellow humans.

And ultimately, he felt ashamed of himself, of his powerlessness.

There was a great force advancing toward him, and he felt defenseless. There were things, he realized, that could not be fought with sword or gun, but only with wits and courage.

Did he have such courage? he wondered.

And then he thought of Zak Cody. Colonel Zak Cody. General Crook trusted him. So did President U.S. Grant.

Could he trust him as well?

He lowered his head and listened to the patter

of rain on his hat, the subsiding waters of the flood whispering below him in the darkness.

He wanted to sleep, to dream, to float away from a world that had suddenly turned into a hellish nightmare.

14

The roof sagged where the adobe wall had once been, held up by the part of the wall that was still standing. Water covered the dirt floor, knee high. Rats swam up to the men who stood in the shack and tried to climb up their trousers. Furniture floated amid other rubble, rags, clothing, near empty air-tights, bottles, pots, pans, cups, and a myriad of unidentifiable objects.

Ben Trask stood two paces away from the gaping fissure and stared out at the receding flood waters. Ferguson, a half foot away, saw dead animals float by, even in the dark. The heads and tails bobbed up, tumbled, disappeared: prairie dogs, quail, a coyote, and a dozen or so dead rats.

"Gone down some," Ferguson said.

Trask lifted a foot out of the water, let the boot fall back with a splash.

"Yeah, only up to our ankles in here now."

"I can get my men to sweep the water out of here. Maybe light a little fire to dry things out."

"No fire," Trask said, his voice like a steel trap snapping shut. "Have your boys sweep out that dead Mex. The water'll go away on its own."

"Christ, Ben. You don't have to be so all-fired hard. The man had a family. Worked five years for me."

"The man was a coward."

"Hell, we was all scared when that flood started rushin' in here."

"This whole deal's turning to shit, Hiram. You can't make it no better with your bawlin' over spilt milk."

"You could have let the man drown by his own self."

"Hell, that what you think?"

"Maybe."

"The whole bunch would have bolted for that door if I hadn't stopped your man."

"Maybe not."

"You're a poor judge of men, Hiram. I'm thinkin' we're not likely to find any alive at the other stage stops, damn it all."

"Aw, he couldn't have got all of 'em. That Cody feller, I mean."

"I know who the hell you mean, Hiram. And you're dead wrong. Cody probably rubbed out ever' damn one of your men. I just hope your man at Bowie comes through for us. We're goin' to be way short of guns if he don't."

"It's all set, I told you. Stop worryin', Ben."

"Just like these old stage stops were all set."

"I didn't know you had a killer doggin' your tracks, Ben."

"Well, if those other men of yours are dead, you're going to have to send one of the Mexes to the fort."

"I know. Willoughby's goin' to come through for us. He wants Cochise worse'n anybody."

"Has he got enough soldiers to do the job?"

"He says he does." Hiram paused, kicked away a rat that was trying to crawl up his leg. "I believe him."

Trask shook his head. He was weary and frustrated. Losing O'Hara had been a big setback. Now he had to rely on Ferguson and an army man he'd never met. So far, Willoughby had proven reliable. He had set up the kidnapping of O'Hara by Ferguson's men. But the entire operation hinged on Willoughby's support. Trask was a gambling man, but he wouldn't bet on this one. Not with Zak Cody dogging him at every turn.

"Hiram, maybe you'd better tell me the name of the soldier who's bringing the extra guns when we go after Cochise."

"You'll like this one, Ben. None other than the quartermaster at Bowie."

"Name?"

"He's a lieutenant, but he's plenty savvy. He's got holdings in Tucson, too, and big plans. His name is John Welch."

"And you trust this man?"

"I do. And so does Willoughby."

"Do you know how many men he'll bring?"

"No. Only Willoughby knows that. But I'm sure we'll have enough."

"Why are you sure?" Trask asked.

"Because Willoughby said there's hardly a man at the fort who doesn't want Cochise's scalp."

"I don't want any of them in the way when we get that Apache gold."

"Don't worry. The major says we can keep all we can find. He just wants to start a war with the

Chiricahua while he's in command of Fort Bowie. Satisfied?"

"I reckon," Trask said.

The water inside the line shack was going down, ever so slowly. The wind was slackening, too, Trask noticed. The stench inside was still overpowering, and now there was the cloying aroma of polluted water, dead things, maybe mold. He wanted to leave, but knew it was too soon. There could be other flash floods, and for the moment they were all safe. He had kept Ferguson's men from going into a panic, and it only cost him one man—a cowardly man, he was sure.

Ferguson directed two of his men to carry out the dead body, put it in the flowing water. The two men bent to their task in silence and did not speak when they returned. But they both glared at Trask and he made note of the hostility. He not only expected their anger, he welcomed it, because he was a man used to treachery, on both sides of the coin, and such knowledge gave him the edge he wanted. Complacency was not a condition he tolerated, either in himself or in others. The complacent man stood to lose all he held dear, including, sometimes, his life.

Ferguson walked back over to Trask and stood next to him, gazing through the gaping hole that had once been an adobe wall.

"You waiting for that flood to stop running, Ben?"

"No. I don't care about that. It's still raining and at least we've got a roof over our heads."

"How long we goin' to stay in this cesspool?"

Ferguson's questions were beginning to annoy Trask. The man was trying to get into his thoughts.

To Trask, that was an invasion of his privacy. He didn't like questions. Especially questions that asked him what he was going to do when he was still figuring everything out.

"Hiram," Trask said, "ever notice how slow time crawls by when you're in a place you don't like much?"

"I never thought about it much," Ferguson said.

"Well, think about it. We ain't been in this 'dobe shack very long, but it seems like we been here for eleventeen hours, sure as shit. But we ain't. It's still rainin' like hell outside, water ever' damned where, wind blowin' a blue norther, and you want to go back out in it. Shit, you can't light a cigar or a cigarette, you're soakin' wet clean through your clothes, colder'n a well digger's ass, no shelter, no warm fire, nothing but mud and water and black night. Bite on a goddamned stick if you can't take it no more where you're at."

"Well, Christ, Ben, you don't need to go off on me like a double-barreled Greener. I was just wonderin'."

"Hiram, I declare. Sometimes you're a pain in the ass and the neck."

"Well, all right, Ben. Shit, I just asked a damn simple question."

That's what it was, Trask thought. A simple question formed in a simple mind. But he was getting cabin fever, too, and Ferguson had touched a bare nerve. He knew they would have to leave soon. As soon as the flooding stopped, maybe. That wasn't the most pressing thing on his mind, however.

Somewhere out there, on his back trail, Zak

Cody was waiting out the storm, too. And he probably had O'Hara with him, maybe others. He knew that Cody was close. He could almost feel the man's eyes on him. The way he saw it, he had two choices. He could ride on for the rendezvous with the soldiers from the fort, hoping to outrun Cody. Or he could wait, maybe set up an ambush and kill Cody before continuing on. Neither plan offered much. A betting man would pass on both.

He listened to the pelting rain, the slush and slosh of the river running down the road. He thought he heard one of the horses whinny but couldn't be sure. He thought of wolves, but knew the horses would kick up a worse racket than a whinny if they were attacked. At least they were on high ground, well away from the flash flood. They would keep.

He looked around the room, unable to see much in the darkness. But he could make out the shapes of men against the wall, all huddled together like beggars. The water inside had dwindled to a muddy puddle, level to just above the soles of his boots, dank and stinking, muddy and choked with dead insects, rats, and other varmints.

Lou Grissom stood a foot away from the Mexicans. He looked composed. He never said much, Trask had noted, but he seemed capable. He had the look of a man who knew where he was and where he was going. Like his man, Willy Rawlins. He might be able to leave those two behind to take care of Cody, ambush him. But he wondered, would two men be enough? He did not know the Mexicans, but they also seemed a capable bunch. If he and Ferguson rode on, they could rendezvous with Welch and the soldiers under his command.

But could he spare Rawlins? And would Ferguson allow Grissom to stay behind? Might it not be better if they all stuck together and just watched their back trail, pushed the horses to lengthen the distance between him and Cody? To divide his forces now might put the entire expedition in peril.

"Hiram," Trask said, "I'm going to talk to you and the men about what we're facing after we leave here. Maybe we can figure out what our best chances are to meet up with Welch."

"You worried about that Cody feller?"

"He's out there. He'll be coming after me."

"Seems to me that's your problem, Ben."

"No, it's our problem, Hiram. Just let me have my say and we'll get the hell out of here as soon as we can."

"Just so I have a say in what we do, Ben."

"Sure, Hiram," Trask said, once again concealing his irritation with the man.

"Grissom, you and the boys come over here close," Ferguson said.

"Willy," Trask said, "come on over."

"What's in the hopper?" Rawlins said as he walked close to Trask.

Trask looked the men over before speaking.

"We got a situation here," he said. "Cody and O'Hara, maybe some others, are bound to be on our trail. I've already lost too many men, and Ferguson here has probably lost all of his boys who were holed up in these old stage stations. So, I've got to figure out what's the best thing to do. I'll give you all a vote. That all right with you?"

All of the men nodded.

"I can leave some of you here to bushwhack

Cody and O'Hara. Cody's good, though. And fast. A dead shot. O'Hara, I don't know about. They may have help. Or, we can all leave this 'dobe together and ride like hell to meet up with the soldier boys who are going to help us. Now, question is, what do you boys want to do? Split up, some stayin' here to shoot it out with Cody and O'Hara, or all ride on? Think about it."

"I think we ought to stick together," Grissom said, much to Trask's surprise.

"Why?" Trask asked.

"Anybody knows you split your forces, you weaken the whole outfit. I was in the army once't and I learnt that."

"I agree with Lou," Rawlins said. "Together, we got a good chance if that Cody feller catches up with us and wants to sling lead. The more of us there is, the more chance we have of surrounding him and puttin' out his lights."

Juan Ramirez raised his hand. "May I speak?" he said.

"Sure," Ferguson said. "Go ahead, Juan. What's on your mind?"

"Together, we are strong," Ramirez said. "We are few, but maybe we are more than this Cody. I think we should ride together. We have lost friends already who were not with us on this ride. This is what I say and this is how we all feel."

Trask held up both hands.

"All right," he said. "You've convinced me. I think you're right. As soon as we can, we'll mount up and ride like hell. It's going to be rough, what with the mud and water and all, and we'll probably have to bat our way through this rain. But we'll stick together. As for Cody, and O'Hara, keep your eyes open and shoot them on sight."

All of the men nodded in assent.

"And one more thing . . ." Trask said.

He paused, and there was a silence in the room as everyone listened for his final words.

"Shoot to kill," Trask said.

15

Deets screamed as the iodine burned through raw flesh.

Scofield clamped a hand over his prisoner's mouth.

"That ain't goin' to help none," Scofield said. "And, I got more to do. That was just to wash out the germs, feller."

"What else you goin' to do?" Deets gasped, the pain gripping him, surging through the nerve ends all around the wound.

"I got some salve here I'm goin' to pack in there, make that hole heal up faster."

"Take it easy, will you, soldier?"

"If I had a fire goin' I'd put a hot iron to it and close that hole for good. You'd likely jump about four feet off the ground."

Deets swore under his breath.

O'Hara appeared next to Scofield, pulling down on the front of his hat brim to shield his face from the rain.

"Corporal," he said, "if he yells out again, knock him cold with the butt of your sidearm."

"Yes, sir."

O'Hara walked back to his post, angry with

himself for losing his temper. But Deets was one of those men who had been his captors. He was still angry about being kidnapped and held prisoner against his will. As a soldier, he was bound to avoid capture, and if captured, to use all means at his disposal to escape. He had not escaped, not on his own. Cody had been his rescuer, much to his embarrassment. He felt he had not conducted himself well, and so he knew he was packing around a lot of guilt. And that didn't feel good, he admitted to himself. As a career soldier, he felt this was a black mark on his record.

But his anger could grow legs and venture beyond himself to Major Erskine Willoughby, acting commandant of Fort Bowie. Willoughby was behind his capture, he was sure of that now. His scheme to wipe out the Chiricahuas was diabolical and traitorous. He had to be stopped. He had to be brought to justice before a military tribunal. But first, of course, there was the matter of Ben Trask and Hiram Ferguson. They were the enemy in the field. Willoughby was safe and out of reach at Fort Bowie. "Damn it all," he growled under his breath.

Scofield stuffed a salve into Deets's wound. Deets groaned but did not cry out.

"What's that you just did?" he asked, his voice quavering as he shivered with pain.

"Some kind of medicant we use to plug leaks in our boys. Keep you from bleedin'."

"It burns like fire."

"Fire would be better. If I had a hot coal, I'd stuff it down there. It would damn sure close off that hole."

"Damn," Deets said, and shivered again as if gripped by a cold chill.

Scofield stood up. "I ain't puttin' no bandage on you. Too wet out. You just lie still and let the medicine work."

"I ain't goin' nowhere."

"No, you sure as hell ain't. Next bullet you get will give you a permanent headache." He paused. "For about a half a second."

Deets shut up then, and Scofield walked over to his horse and returned the salve and iodine to his saddlebags. Then he stood guard over Deets, who turned his head to one side to try and keep the rain from drowning him.

Distant thunder rumbled, sounding like a game of nine pins in a great hall, and distant lightning made the black clouds glow with a pale orange light. The rainfall thinned to a steady patter, with only small gusts of wind to hurl patches of it to a misty spray.

Zak hunkered down under his horse's belly, squatting between his boots, Apache style, his butt just an inch or so off the wet ground. He thought of Deets and how lucky the man was to be alive. The night played tricks on a man's eyes. He knew that, but still, he should have shot more true. No matter. He had accomplished what he meant to do, getting O'Hara away from Trask and his men. Ted seemed a capable enough soldier. Someone had betrayed him, someone in the army, or he would not have been kidnapped.

So much rain in such a dry land, he thought. But he had seen odd weather before, in the Rockies and out on the Great Plains. The mountains made their own weather. One minute the sun could be shining bright, with nary a cloud in the sky, and the next, huge white thunderheads could boil up out of some hidden valley and bring rain or snow within the space of a pair of heartbeats. He had seen dust devils turn into violent twisters, and known winds that brought blizzards down from the north to a land basking in sunshine and warmth.

But he knew the storm was moving eastward, losing its strength. He could feel the air change, and the rhythm of the wind and the rain had shifted into a lower gear. The rain was no longer slanted, he noticed, but falling straight down, the wind gone, and there was less of it. He watched as the curtain of rain thinned and left spaces in the darkness. By sunup, he figured, it would all be over. Such fierce winds had driven the storm onward, and the clouds were losing their moisture so rapidly they would be puffs of white cotton before noon.

He heard a muffled shout and put a hand to his ear.

"Colonel, sump'n over here."

It was Rivers.

"Be right there," Zak shouted, and crawled out from under his horse, waddling like a crab until he could stand up.

His clothing clung to him and his boots creaked as he traversed the short distance to where Rivers stood guard.

The soldier was leaning over the edge of the hill. He stood up straight when Zak came up alongside of him.

"What you got, Rivers?" Zak asked.

"I dunno. I heard a rattle, like some loose rocks rollin' down there, and thought I saw somethin' big come up at the bottom of the bank. I thought maybe someone snuck up on us. I just caught a glimpse when some lightning sparked off in the distance."

"Is it still down there?"

"I reckon."

"Heard any more rocks tumbling?"

"No, sir. That's what's so spooky about it. I ain't heard nothin' since that kind of thud sound and them rocks clatterin'."

"You did right, calling me over, Private. Now, step back. I'll take a look. If there's another lightning strike, I might be able to see what it is."

"Yes, sir. I got the shivers from it."

Zak peered over the side. He saw nothing but darkness. The bottom of the hill was like a black pit. The water from the flood was still running, but not as fast, nor as noisily. He heard the water gurgling as it passed the base of the hill. He stared, without straining his eyes, moving them from side to side, trying to pick up some kind of shape out of the blackness.

"You go on over and stand guard by my horse, Rivers," Zak said. "I'll take this post until we find out what it was that made that noise. You did well."

"Thank you, sir. I hope it ain't no ambusher."

"Probably a dead animal."

"A big dead animal," Rivers said.

And then he was gone, sloshing through the rain to where Nox still stood, neck bowed, tail drooping and dripping water. Zak watched until the yellow slicker Rivers wore turned from bright yellow to the color of curdled milk. He noticed that Rivers didn't crawl under Nox but stood beside him, his head shielded from the wind behind Nox's neck.

Zak squatted, leaned over the edge of the hill, peering downward. He closed his eyes for a few seconds, then opened them again. He tried to distinguish what stood out from the blackness below, a shape, anything that was darker or larger than anything else. He fixed on a spot that looked promising and waited for the faint light from any distant flash of lightning. Several seconds passed and then he got what he was waiting for, a lightning strike some five or so miles away. The bolt threw just enough light for him to make out a shape sprawled at the base of the hill. He thought he saw a pair of legs rippling in a pile of water. Human legs, attached to a torso that left no more than a quick impression on his mind.

Something, or someone, was down there, but it was no animal. It was two-legged, most probably a man. He had seen just enough to make him curious. He judged the slope, figuring he might go down and be able to climb back up. He touched the butt of his pistol, eased it just a bit from its holster, then let it fall back of its own weight into the leather.

He stood up then, turned to where Rivers stood, some yards away.

"Private Rivers," he called, "come here. Bring my horse."

He heard a muffled, "Yes, sir," and the yellow raincoat moved. He saw the soldier lead Nox toward him, and he waited, holding out a hand to gauge the amount of rain falling at that moment.

Rivers came up, held out his hand with the reins.

"No, I just want that lariat," Zak said as he reached for the coiled lariat that hung from his saddle. "You hold Nox real still."

"What are you going to do, Colonel—I mean, Mr. Cody?"

"There is something down there. A man, I think. Hurt or dead, I don't know which. I'll use the rope to climb down and check what we have there."

"Yes, sir," Rivers said.

Zak uncoiled the rope, made two loops, one on each end. He settled one loop around the saddle horn and snugged it up tight. Then he threw the rope over the edge of the hill until it lay out straight.

He patted Nox on the neck. "You hold tight, boy," he said.

He stepped over the edge onto the slope. He grabbed the rope to brace himself, then started downward, digging in the heels of his boots at each step.

"Hold my horse fast, Rivers."

"Yes, sir. He's real steady so far."

Zak reached the bottom and held onto the loop as he felt around his feet with his hands. His fingers touched something soft. He squatted as he saw a man's face. No hat. He felt the man's neck, put two fingers on the carotid artery. No pulse. The man was dead.

There was enough slack in the rope for him to slip it under the man's body, up under his arms. He pulled the loop taut and then jerked on the rope.

"Rivers. Back Nox up. Real slow."

Rivers didn't answer. But the body started to move up the slope of the hill. Zak walked alongside, tugging on one arm, holding onto the rope with his other hand, both for balance and to help him with his climb.

A few moments later the body slid over the edge of the hill. Zak, out of breath, stepped up next to it and stood, breathing hard.

"You can bring my horse close now, Rivers," he said.

"Yes, sir."

Zak leaned down, slid the loop from the dead man's body and flung it aside. The man was on his back, his eyes closed. When Zak bent down to look at his face, he saw that it was a Mexican.

Rivers stood by, still holding Nox's reins. "You got you a Mex there, sir," he said.

"Let's see how he died."

"Maybe he drowned, sir."

"Now, who in hell would try to swim in a flash flood, Private?"

"I dunno, sir."

Zak grabbed the body by the shoulder and leg, tugged at it until the Mexican lay facedown. He ran his hands over the back of the dead man's shirt.

"Uh-oh," he said, and his hand stopped moving. He bent over and saw the bullet hole, right in the middle of the man's back. "Shot in the back."

"Sir, I didn't shoot nobody," Rivers said.

"No. Maybe Ben Trask shot this man. For some reason. Flood carried him down this far. Trask probably isn't far away. Maybe in one of those old stage stations."

Rivers said nothing.

Zak stood up. He didn't know what had happened, of course. But someone had shot the Mexican in the back. And he knew he hadn't done

it. Even by accident. He could feel Ben Trask's
hands all over this one. A man like Trask wouldn't
hesitate to shoot a man in the back.

But why?

Maybe Trask had some mutinous Mexicans on
his hands, he thought. Maybe Trask had blamed
this man for the loss of O'Hara.

It didn't matter. Trask was losing men right and
left.

If this kept up, the odds would rise in his own
favor.

"What are you thinking, sir?" Rivers asked finally, after Zak had been silent for several minutes.

"I'm thinking this is one less man I have to kill
to get at Ben Trask, Private."

"Yes, sir," Rivers said, and a cold shiver slith-
ered up his spine like a wet lizard crawling up a
tree.

The rain continued to spatter them as Zak
slipped the rope off the saddle horn, untied the
loop, and began to coil it back up, just to keep his
hands busy. He wanted to grab Trask's neck and
squeeze and squeeze until the man's face turned
purple and he died of manual strangulation.

The bastard.

16

Gray-black crepe hung from the dark clouds like tattered shrouds masking the sun. The rain had stopped and the clouds overhead had turned to a puffy gray pudding over a storm-ravished land. The flood had passed on and disappeared into a porous earth, leaving behind its detritus, shreds of cactus and ocotillo, the carcasses of rats and snakes and other animals, rivulets of mud and streaks of washed sand and cobbled dirt. There was a slight breeze, a warm one, and Zak knew things would dry out pretty fast.

He saw no signs of life, nor any sign of Trask and his outlaw band. Nothing moved in the feeble light of morning. He walked to each post and told those standing guard that they could walk around and stretch their legs, shake out their soogans.

Colleen and her brother Ted talked together and munched on hardtack. Zak stopped a few feet away from them, doffed his hat to Colleen.

"We'll get moving pretty quick," he said to Ted. "I think Deets hasn't told us everything he knows."

"What makes you think that, Zak?"

"Doesn't make any difference. I'm going to see

if he won't change his mind about his loyalty to
Trask and tell me more. I have a hunch he knows
plenty."

"You're not going to torture him, are you, Zak?"
Colleen said.

"It's a nice morning, Miss Colleen. You ought to
be dried out pretty soon."

With that, Zak walked away from them and
headed toward the west end of the hill.

Colleen stared after him, her face a mask of con-
sternation, her forehead creased, her eyes slitted.
She quelled the impulse to throw a retort at Zak's
back, and instead squeezed her raincoat by the collar until her fingers turned white.

Rivers and Scofield stood over Deets. They
looked up when Zak walked up on them.

"Deets here don't seem so bad this mornin',
Mr. Cody," Scofield said. "He ain't got no fever or
nothin'."

Deets looked up at Cody, a questioning look in
his eyes. His lips were parched, his skin pale. He
was still soaking wet, but Zak saw that Scofield
had put a fresh bandage over the wound.

"On your feet," Zak told Deets.

"I can't move," Deets said. "I got pain. No feelin'
in my legs."

"Boys, get Mr. Deets here on his feet, and kick
him in the ass if you have to."

Deets swore as the two men jerked him to his
feet. He groaned and doubled over after his feet
touched the ground.

"Deets, I want you to identify a dead man.
You're going to walk to the other end of this hill or
be dragged. Suit yourself."

"I don't think I can walk that far," Deets said.

"Deets, you got more than a scratch. You're lucky to be alive. But you got some more talking to do, and you can make it real hard or real easy."

"Maybe if I leaned on one of the soldier boys, I could might walk that far," Deets said.

Both Rivers and Scofield bristled at being called "soldier boys."

Zak looked at both troopers, his eyebrows arched.

"I guess we might could do that, Mr. Cody," Scofield said.

"Deets, you straighten up and try taking a couple of steps," Zak said. "Corporal Scofield will catch you if you start to fall."

Deets straightened up. He groaned in pain, sucked in a deep breath.

Zak and the two soldiers waited.

Deets put a boot out and took a short step. Then he put his weight on that foot and moved the other. He looked shaky, but no one lifted a hand to help him. He looked at Zak.

"Try a couple more steps," Zak said.

"Hell, he can walk good as you or me," Rivers said.

Deets gingerly put another foot out, then the other. He winced each time he moved, but Zak was satisfied that he could walk.

"Keep walking," Zak said. "Should tighten up that hole in you, make you heal faster."

"Like hell," Deets said.

"Do it," Zak told him.

Rivers and Scofield walked beside Deets. The three men followed Zak. As he passed Colleen and Ted, he motioned to O'Hara.

"Ted, you should come with us. I think we're going to find out a thing or two."

"Not from me, you ain't," Deets muttered.

Zak said nothing.

"I'm coming, too," Colleen said, falling in step beside her brother. Soon, all of them were standing over the body of the dead man.

The corpse lay on its back, black eyes dark as olive pits, staring vacantly at the mouse-gray sky. Deets stared at the face for a long time, his gaze taking in the deeply etched lines around the bared teeth, the lips pulled back in rigor, giving the dead man a ghastly frozen grin, the skin taut, dark as a tobacco juice stain.

"Christ," Deets uttered, a whispery breath behind the crisp sibilant.

"You know him?" Zak asked.

Deets choked out the name from a constricted throat as if the word had hissed out of a heavy clog of foreign matter.

"That's Jaime," Deets said, "Jaime Elizondo." There was a hoarseness in his voice that had not been there before.

"He one of Trask's men?" Zak asked.

"In a way, I reckon. He worked for Hiram. Hiram Ferguson. Jesus, what kilt him? Did he drown?"

"Lead poisoning," Zak said.

"You kill him, Cody?" Deets asked.

"He wasn't shot here, Deets. Flood washed him down here. I dragged him up. He was shot in the back, if that means anything to you."

"I don't know what you mean."

"None of us shot this man. He was killed by one of your pards. Maybe Ben Trask."

Deets swallowed hard. His lower lip began to quiver and his eyes turned rheumy. Zak could see that he was thinking about Trask, mulling over the possibility that his boss had shot Jaime Elizondo.

"Might be," Deets said.

"This could have been you, Deets," Zak said.

"Naw. Ben wouldn't . . ."

After a moment of silence, Zak broke in with telling words.

"You saying Trask wouldn't shoot you in the back if you crossed him?"

"I dunno."

"You know damned well he would, Deets."

"It ain't somethin' I think about a whole lot, Cody."

"Well, maybe you should. You know where Trask and Ferguson are going, don't you?"

"Generally. Maybe."

"He doesn't have enough men to take on the Chiricahuas."

Deets said nothing.

"He's going to need help. More guns than he has now. Isn't that right?"

"If you say so."

"The Apaches would wipe him out so quick he wouldn't have time to jerk his rifle out of its scabbard, Deets."

"I dunno."

"Yeah, Deets, you do. You'd better spill what you know about Trask's plans or you'll be the first one I turn over to Cochise for an Apache sundown."

"Wh-What's an Apache sundown?" Deets asked.

Zak uttered a dry laugh.

"It's not pretty. Something the Apaches do to a white man they don't like much. Something they'll do if I ask them to."

"I—I don't know much. Honest."

"Bullshit," O'Hara said. "He knows all about Trask's plans. I know. He's one of Trask's most trusted men."

Zak turned to O'Hara. "Maybe you heard something while you were a prisoner, Lieutenant. How much do you know about Trask's plans?"

"I know he's going after Cochise and his gold. That's about it. He thinks Cochise has a huge hoard of gold hidden somewhere on the desert."

Zak suppressed a smile. He knew better. But he wasn't about to say anything in front of the two soldiers and Deets.

"Nothing about meeting up with other outlaws?"

O'Hara shook his head. "No. I got the idea he thought he had enough men. But I didn't know how many until we rode out of Ferguson's. I thought he was going to be badly outnumbered if he took on the Chiricahua."

Zak looked at Deets, who was moving both his lips to keep his emotions invisible.

"Well, Deets, are you going to tell me what Trask means to do, or do I have to beat it out you?"

Colleen gave out a low gasp.

Zak shot her a look that was meant to chastise her for daring to interfere. She lowered her head and put a hand to her mouth.

"I told you, Cody, I don't know nothin'," Deets said.

Zak stepped up close to Deets, looked him straight in the eye. Deets glared at him in defiance.

All the others held their breaths as the two men stared at each other.

"You ever have hard times when you were a little kid, Deets?" Zak asked.

"Yeah. Who didn't?"

"Lean times? When there wasn't much food to put on the table?"

"Yeah. What's the point, Cody?"

"Your mother ever say there was something at the door during those times?"

"Maybe. I don't remember."

"Think, Deets. She said you had to look out for such times, didn't she?"

"She might have. Like I said, I don't remember."

"Sure you do. She told you what was at the door, didn't she?"

"You mean, like when the wolf's at the door?" Deets was starting to squirm inside his skin.

"Yes, that's right. She told you to beware of those times when there was a wolf at your door. Probably you thought there was really a wolf at your door, didn't you?"

"I reckon. Well, us kids didn't really believe there was a real wolf at the door, but we knew what she meant. I still don't—"

Zak cut him off.

"Well, there's a wolf at your door now. That's me. I'm the wolf at your door, Deets. And, if you don't tell me what you know about Trask's plans, I'm going to open that door and start eating you alive."

"Shit," Deets said.

Zak pulled the bandage off Deets's side and pressed a finger against the wound.

Deets dropped to one knee. He groaned in pain.

Zak grabbed one arm and jerked him to his feet.

"The door's open, Deets. I'm coming in. I'm a hungry wolf."

Zak stretched out his hand, a single finger pointed at the wound in Deets's side.

"No, don't. I'll tell you what you want to know."

"Spit it out," Zak said.

"Well, I know some soldiers are going to meet up with Trask and Ferguson. In a couple of days from now, I reckon."

"Where?"

"Up at the last old stage stop on this road."

"Who's bringing the soldiers?"

"I don't know for sure. I don't think Ben knows, either."

"You ever hear the name Willoughby?"

"Yeah, I heard it. He's the soldier runnin' the fort—Fort Bowie. Ben mentioned him some. More than once."

"Is Willoughby bringing him the troops?"

"I—I know Willoughby is helping out, but just before we left Tucson, I heard Hiram—Ferguson, I mean—tell one of his men to skedaddle to Fort Bowie and see the quartermaster, tell him we were leaving."

"You hear a name?" Zak asked.

O'Hara cleared his throat.

Zak looked over at him.

"The quartermaster is John Welch," O'Hara said. "He came in with Willoughby and a bunch of other soldiers. I believe they served together."

"That's all I know," Deets said, staring down at the wet ground where his bandage lay, stained with the suppurated fluids from his wound.

"You've tortured that man enough, Zak," Colleen said.

"Miss Colleen," Zak said, "you don't know what torture is until you've seen an Apache sundown."

The words hung in the air like a warning.

Zak turned away from Deets, spoke to O'Hara.

"Saddle up," he said. "All of you. We can't let Trask meet up with those soldiers. We're outnumbered as it is."

"Zak," O'Hara said, "are you crazy? We don't stand a chance. I won't put my sister in danger, either."

Zak stopped and turned around to face him.

"Ted, I outrank you. I'm playing that card. You and the soldiers are now under my orders. We leave in five minutes." He turned to Scofield and Rivers. "You keep Deets braced between you. He makes one false move, you empty his saddle. Got that?"

"Yes, sir," Scofield said.

Rivers nodded.

"Now," Zak said, "let's burn what little daylight there is and light a shuck for that last stage stop."

Colleen glared at him, but Zak turned away.

He was a military man, but he knew he didn't stand much of a chance against Trask and Ferguson with the men he had under his command.

But that was a bridge he'd cross when he came to it.

And, he knew, he might have some help by the time they got to the last stage stop.

The old stage road led straight into Indian territory, home of the Chiricahua Apaches. And Cochise.

⊰ 17 ⊱

Trask stood in a corner, his arms folded, his eyes closed. He had dozed like that for two hours or more. Ferguson had rescued a chair and was sitting in it, leaning against the north wall of the adobe. The Mexicans had taken turns sleeping in wet bunks. One of them, Fidel Gonzalez, stood guard at a window, his eyelids at half mast as he looked out over the crumbled wall. The land was a mystery of darkness, flooded over, earthy smells hanging in the air like a nightmarish odor borne of dead animals.

"You wake me when it's daylight, Fidel," Trask had told the sentry. "Or just before first light. Savvy?"

Fidel had not replied, but nodded that he understood.

Now he approached Trask and put a hand on his elbow. Trask jerked awake, startled, wide-eyed, caught for a moment in that confusing state between sleep and wakefulness.

"Yeah?"

"*Es la madrugada*," Fidel said. "The dawn. It comes."

"All right," Trask said. He walked over and put the toe of his boot in Ferguson's shin, rousing him from his shallow reverie.

"Wh-Wha . . . ?" Ferguson said as his chair rocked away from the wall and he had to struggle to maintain his balance.

"Time to get crackin', Hiram," Trask said. "See if our horses washed away during the night."

The rest of the men came out of their collective stupor, groaning, yawning, stretching, as if they had been roused from the dead.

"Lou, you and the Gonzalez brothers go check on the horses real quick," Ferguson said as he rose to his feet, kicked the chair away.

"Willy," Trask said to Rawlins, "you check around outside."

"Yeah, boss," Rawlins said. He knew what Trask meant. The man wanted to know if Cody was anywhere to be seen. He hefted his rifle and strode out of the adobe in the wake of the Gonzalez brothers, mud sucking at his boots with every step. Lou Grissom got up off one of the bunks.

"I'll go with you, Willy," he said, grabbing his rifle and falling in behind Rawlins. "Anything to get out of this damned shithouse."

Trask walked to the opening in the wall, looked out at a bleak world overhung with gray, elephantine clouds. He adjusted his eyes to the faint light, stared at the washed-out roadway.

"At least the damned rain's stopped," Ferguson said, walking up beside him.

"It stopped an hour ago, Hiram," Trask said.

"Hell, I musta been asleep. I can still hear it, seems like."

"That's the roof leaking. Let's get the hell out of here. Lou was right. This is a shithouse."

"Men are pretty tired, Ben. Me, too."

Trask turned on Ferguson.

"You keep that to yourself, Hiram. I don't want to hear no whinin'. We lost time because of that storm. Time we got to make up, wearin' out horse-flesh. I don't want no slackers today."

"Hell, Ben, I was just—"

"I know what you were doin', Hiram. Best to keep your mouth shut about such around the men."

"I get you," Ferguson said, and started for the door.

Trask laughed and stepped over the broken wall and outside. Men were such damned sheep, he thought. If all the walls had been down and a door frame the only thing left standing, they would all walk through that empty doorway. Habit, stupidity, he didn't know which. He met a sheepish Ferguson and they walked up the rise, barely able to see the ground. The rains had washed the slope clean, pretty much, and dead vegetation was strewn everywhere. Little piles of rocks stood at the end of now barren rivulets where streams of water had rushed down to join the flood.

Trask heard the horses nickering up on the rise. Rawlins and Grissom stood a few yards up the slope, both looking to the west.

"See anything, Willy?"

"Nope," Rawlins said. "Can't see far, but it's mighty quiet."

"You keep an eye out until we all get mounted. I'll bring your horse down to you."

"Lou, you come on with me," Ferguson said. "See can we get some grain into our horses."

"Don't give 'em much," Trask said. "A handful, maybe."

"You got any heart at all, Ben?" Ferguson said as he puffed while climbing up the slope.

"I got the heart of a bull," Trask said, as if taking Ferguson seriously. "I just don't want them horses to founder. We got some ridin' to do."

"Welch will wait for us if we're not there on time." Ferguson was still short on breath, but he gamely trudged on up the slope.

"You know that for certain, Hiram?"

"We got maybe five or six days leeway. Hell, I just sent word to him yesterday. My rider probably won't reach the fort for a couple more days."

"You forget. I got Cody on my trail. Him and no tellin' how many others."

"I ain't forgettin'. You plan to outrun him? Maybe wear out our horses? We ain't got no spares."

"You can't outrun a man like Zak Cody, Hiram."

Ferguson was puffing so hard by then he could hardly muster enough breath to speak. He stopped and drew in breath through his nostrils. Trask didn't wait for him. He continued on toward the horses, counting heads as he walked.

Ferguson started walking again, but his lungs were burning.

"Too damned much gut," he said to himself, every breath a draught of fire.

"Don't give 'em too much fodder, boys," Trask said as he reached the men. "They'll have plenty of water to drink once we get goin'."

Ferguson caught up with Trask. He leaned over, hands just above his knees, struggling to quench the flames in his lungs. His belly sagged below him like an extra hundred-pound sack of oats. He wheezed like a blacksmith's bellows, and all the men looked at him with something like pity in their eyes.

"Jesus," Ferguson breathed, and stood up straight, hands on his hips.

"You better pray, Hiram," Trask said, a smear of sarcasm coating his tone. "That belly of yours is goin' to be the death of you."

"I know it," Ferguson said, still panting. "That old lady of mine feeds me too many frijole beans and beefsteak."

"It ain't the beans and beef, Hiram, it's the damn beer. You got to cut out all the B's in your grub."

The men all laughed, enjoying that moment of levity after a nightmare night and at the start of a grim gray day.

Trask looked back down at Rawlins, beckoned to him. Rawlins turned and started up the slope, Grissom following a few steps behind.

"What plan you got for gettin' rid of Cody?" Ferguson asked as he walked to his horse and patted the animal on the neck.

"I'm chewin' on it," Trask said.

"Well, when you got it all chawed, you let me know, eh?"

"Which one of your men is the best shot with a rifle?" Trask pulled the makings out of his pocket, felt the sack to see if it was still dry. It was. He fished out a packet of papers, which was also dry, took one out and began rolling a cigarette.

Ferguson looked at his men. One of them widened his eyes. Ferguson nodded.

"Pablo Medina there. He's a right good sharpshooter. Seen him take down a antelope once't at better'n five hundred yards."

Trask looked at Medina. He was young, wiry, with high cheekbones, almond eyes black as tar, a stylus-thin moustache, square-cut sideburns. His cheeks bore the faint roses of Indian blood running in his veins.

"Medina, huh? He don't look like much," Trask said. "Could have been a lucky shot."

"He takes down deer, runnin' deer, all the time at better'n two hunnert yards, Ben. The man's got a feel for a rifle, any rifle. But that's a new Winchester in his boot. He bore-sighted hisself and he shoots one- and two-inch groups on targets real regular. Sometimes, I think Pablo cut his teeth on a rifle barrel. Comes real natural to him."

"All right. I'll take your word for it," Trask said.

"Want me to call him over?"

"Not yet. What about Grissom? Can he shoot?"

"He's a fair shot, all right. But Pablo, he's the best I ever seed."

Rawlins and Grissom came up.

"Didn't see nothin', Ben," Rawlins said. "Lou didn't see ner hear nothin', either."

"All right, Willy. See to your horses, you and Lou."

In the gauzy light of a gray morning, a lone hawk soared overhead. A sign of life after a deluge, Trask thought. He watched the hawk float over a desolate land, some parts of it still invisible, for the sun had not yet risen. He heard the far-off yelp of a coyote, and the horses twisted stiffened ears to locate the sound, their rubbery nostrils sniffing the still, cool air.

Trask turned to Ferguson, who was just reaching for his saddle horn to pull himself aboard his horse.

"How far you reckon to the next old station, Hiram?"

"A long day's ride, Ben. On muddy ground, maybe longer."

"Cody will surely follow the road, same as us. If that 'dobe is still standing, maybe I'll leave that Mex sure-shot there to bushwhack Cody."

Ferguson pulled his arm down, turned toward Trask.

"You might be committing Pablo to a death sentence. Cody's got O'Hara with him. That's two against one right there. And you think this Cody ain't by hisself. Might be Pablo would have to go up against a dozen or so rifles."

"Might be. But he drops Cody, he's got a good chance to make his getaway. If he can shoot and kill as far away as you say, he'd have a good chance to outrun O'Hara or them others. A man drops in a bunch, the rest all gawk and hightail it for cover until they figure out what the hell happened."

"That's so," Ferguson said. He scratched the back of his head, tipping his hat forward. "I don't know. I'd hate to lose Medina. He's a good man. Got him a family, two little kids."

"All the more reason he'd watch after his own hide after he kills Cody."

"You make it sound real easy, Ben."

They were whispering, almost, speaking in low

tones, but the other men were looking at them. They were all on horseback, just waiting for Ben's or Hiram's orders. The horses switched their tails and tamped the ground with their forefeet, pawing dirt with their hooves.

"I'll talk to Pablo on the ride to the next station, Hiram. Feel him out, see what he thinks about the whole idea. That good enough? If he don't want to do me this favor, no hard feelings. I'll get Willy to stake out that 'dobe and put some lead in Cody. Fair enough?"

"Fair enough, I reckon. Seems to me, though, that you put a lot of your chips down on rubbing out one man. He must have really got under your hide, Ben."

"It goes back a long way," Trask said.

He walked to his horse and hauled himself into the saddle. Ferguson mounted his horse. All of the men were still wearing their slickers. Trask made a face and took off his raincoat.

"Pack them slickers away," he said to the others. "You look like a bunch of yaller flowers. Anybody trailin' us could spot you ten miles away."

The men all removed their soogans and tied them to the backs of their saddles.

"Lead the way, Hiram," Trask said. "I'll ride with Medina. Gus and Willy can take up the rear. We'll go two by two. Pick your man to side you."

Ferguson motioned to Fidel Gonzalez, who rode up alongside him. Trask beckoned to Medina.

"You ride with me, Pablo," he said. "We got some fat to chew."

"Huh?" Medina said.

"Want to talk to you. Some palaver."

"Yes. We ride together. You talk. I listen."

Trask smiled. This was going to be easier than he thought. Medina might be just the man to get Cody off his back forever.

A thin line of pale light appeared on the eastern horizon. The sun was just edging up out of the darkness, casting an eerie glow over the land, tingeing the far clouds with cream and the faintest glimmer of gold.

Ferguson set a good pace, one that the horses might keep up for a good long stretch, Trask thought.

Trask smiled and looked over at Medina.

"So," he said, "ever kill a man, Pablo?"

⇥ 18 ⇤

Al Deets was going to be a problem. He already was, Zak thought. The man was doubled over, puking onto the ground, while Rivers and Scofield stood on either side of him, averting their eyes so they didn't have to look at the vomit. They could avoid looking at the puke, but they couldn't escape its smell. Deets's face was florid, then drained of color as he finished retching. He stood up and sucked air into his lungs.

Colleen watched all this with a mingled look of compassion and disdain on her face. Zak shifted his gaze to her. She must have caught the movement of his head because she turned and looked at him from a few yards away. Her brother Ted was checking the cinches on her saddle, making sure they were snug but not too tight.

"You all finished throwing up, Deets?" Zak asked.

"I reckon." Deets wiped a sleeve across his mouth.

"Should I put another bandage on that wound, Mr. Cody?" Scofield asked.

"No, he'll be fine," Zak said. He held out his black slicker to Scofield. "Put this on him, Corporal."

"You want him to wear your slicker, Mr. Cody?"

"That's what I said."

Scofield took the slicker and helped Deets put his arms through the sleeves.

"Button it up good," Zak said, taking off his hat. He removed the hat from Deets's head and put it on his own. They were about the same size. Then he put his hat on Deets's head, squared it up, made it fit tight.

"What's all that for?" Colleen asked.

"We want him to look nice, don't we?"

Then Zak turned to the two soldiers.

"Put him up on my horse," he said. He walked to his horse and pulled his rifle out of its scabbard. The two soldiers stood there, looking puzzled.

"You want him to ride that fine black horse of yours?" Scofield said.

"And I'll ride his."

Deets looked pale, bewildered. The soldiers still stood there, as if uncertain that they had heard right. Rivers looked at Scofield, then back at Zak. Deets made some ugly sounds in his throat. Scofield stepped away from him. So did Rivers. But Deets didn't throw up again. He swallowed and his eyes watered, but he stood there, looking forlorn and lost in that black slicker and under Zak's black hat.

"Get Deets up on that horse, now," Zak told Scofield. "Then tie his hands. Loop the rope through that hole between the horn and the seat."

"Yes, sir," Scofield said. "Soon as he gets through bein' sick."

"He's through," Zak said. He stood, holding Nox's reins, avoiding Colleen's penetrating gaze.

He looked to the eastern sky, saw the horizon brim with a pale light, a light tangled up in blankets of gray clouds. Some of the clouds began to brighten, with thin rims of gold that flickered and paled to yellow rust as they drifted toward the horizon, swallowing up some of the scraps of that feeble light.

"Zak," Colleen said, striding toward him, "I want to talk to you."

"Not now," he said.

"Now, Zak."

He saw that she was determined, and she looked as if she had something in her craw, all right. He shrugged.

"Make it quick."

"Privately," she said, taking his arm and leading him away from the others.

"You got some push in you," he said. "I'll give you that."

"Maybe it's time somebody did push you, Zak Cody."

"Uh-oh. When you use both my names, I know you're mad."

"Damned right I'm mad."

He could see the flare of anger in her blue eyes. There was an ocean in her, and he knew he was seeing only a small part of its surface. He felt drawn to her by those sparkling eyes, mesmerized by the clarity he saw in them. She was like a striking serpent at that moment, and he felt impaled on an invisible thorn.

When the two were well out of earshot of the others, Colleen released her grip on his arm.

Again she skewered him with her piercing gaze.

"What's the matter with you?" he asked.

"With me? Zak Cody, I didn't take you for a cruel man. Not once, since I met you. But the way you treat that man—that Deets—is just deplorable. Now you are going to have him tied to his horse like a—a trophy—or something you've shot."

"I did shoot him. But that's not why I'm having him tied to his horse. Deets is a dangerous man."

"And you tortured him. You know the man is wounded, so you deliberately touched his wound to make him talk. That's torture."

"Ma'am, I think you missed your calling."

"My calling?"

"Yes, you ought to be a missionary, going out and saving the miscreants of this world from the likes of me."

"Don't try to make light of this, Zak Cody. You're a cruel man, after all."

"That man, Deets, had important information. Vital information. His boss, a man named Ben Trask, is joining up with a military detachment to stir up a war with the Chiricahua Apaches. Now that's cruel, little lady. Not what I did to Deets. I just touched him on a sore spot."

"Don't you call me 'little lady,' you—you scalawag. Oh, what an arrogant, self-righteous man you are. I could . . ."

"Could what?"

"I . . . I don't know. Scratch your eyes out, maybe."

Zak laughed, but it was a mirthless and wry laugh that was not without a touch of scorn.

"Now, scratching a man's eyes out," he said, "that would be cruelty. To a high degree."

"You know what I mean," she said, miffed by his logic.

"This is war, Colleen. I needed information from Deets. I got it. You could call it torture if I got the information and then kept hurting him. I gave him a nudge. He told me what I needed to know. Don't try and make something out of it that it isn't."

"I guess I just don't understand you, Zak," she said, her manner softening.

"That's another matter entirely. Something you'll have to work out for yourself."

"Oh, you are an exasperating man."

"That, too," he said, a flicker of a smile on his face.

In the distance he heard a coyote yelp. The sound only emphasized how quiet it was after the rain and the flood. In the east, he saw a glimmer of pale light, a faint trace of salmon on some of the clouds, a shimmering tinge of gold that quickly disappeared.

"I wish I knew you better," she said.

"Who can really know someone, Colleen? People are mysteries."

"Mysteries? I've never heard that before."

"You can never truly know a person, Colleen. People wear masks. People hide who they really are. If you observed a single person all your life, every day and night, you still would only see a little bit of that person."

"I've never thought of people that way," she said.

"I have."

He started walking away from her. She opened her mouth to stop him, to pursue the conversation, perhaps, but instead just shook her head and followed him.

When Zak got back to his horse, he took Deets's rifle out of the scabbard on his saddle and replaced it with his rifle. He tied Deets's rifle in back of his cantle, after wrapping it in his bedroll and retying the bundle.

"Zak, got a minute?" O'Hara said to him.

"Less than that, Ted. We need to get moving. Trask is probably gaining more ground on us."

"It's about Deets." O'Hara's voice was pitched low so the others, including their prisoner, wouldn't overhear him.

"What about Deets?" Zak asked.

"Why are you trading horses with him and why did you dress him in your slicker and hat?"

"If Trask means to pick me off when we get close, he might mistake Deets for me."

"I don't think Deets will make it very far."

"You mean Trask will shoot him instead of me?"

"He'll probably bleed to death."

"He might."

"I say we ought to leave him here. He might stand a chance, if we leave him some food and water."

"Your kindness is admirable, Ted."

"I'm not trying to be kind. Colleen and I think that man's been tortured enough. Now you want to make him a target for Trask. That's pretty damned cruel."

"It's not meant to be. Deets has a better chance of surviving his wound if he comes with us. Scofield can doctor him. As for Deets being a target instead of me, I call that simple justice."

"Not in my book."

"Maybe you ought to get another book, Ted."

"Look, I know you're a hard man, but Colleen is pretty upset. And I think she's right."

"Well, if Colleen's right and you're backing her, maybe you and she ought to go on to Tucson or make it to Fort Bowie on your own."

"If I left with Colleen, I'd take Scofield and Rivers with me."

Zak shrugged. He saw that the day was getting lighter by the moment. They had already spent too much time getting ready to pick up Trask's trail. And the outlaw would leave tracks. Tracks that had to be followed.

"Ted, that's fine with me. You can all go to Fort Bowie. I won't try and stop you."

"We'd take Deets with us."

Zak felt his anger begin to boil. He knew he could pull rank on O'Hara and order him to stay. But he didn't want to do that. What galled him was that Ted and his sister were trying to protect a man who deserved no consideration whatsoever. Deets was a killer. He was the enemy. And he was something else.

"Deets is my prisoner, Lieutenant O'Hara. You can leave if you like, but Deets stays."

"So he can be killed."

"So he can be employed in a military situation, if you want it that way."

"Splitting hairs, Cody."

"My hairs to split. Now make up your mind. You can go with me to try and stop Trask and Ferguson from meeting up with renegade soldiers, or you can tuck your tail between your legs and crawl

back to the fort. I'm sure Willoughby will welcome
you with open arms."

"You do make a point there, Zak."

"Well, which is it, Ted?"

"I'm concerned about my sister."

"Maybe you'd better take her to some safe place.
Tucson, Fort Bowie."

O'Hara sighed. "Knowing her," he said, "she
wouldn't go."

"I can't guarantee her safety, or anyone else's for
that matter. I'm after a bunch of killers and they
want to start a war. That's a lot of lives at stake,
Ted. I'm all out of argue with you, so I'm going to
do what I have to do. You follow your own path."

With that, Zak climbed up into the saddle. He
and Deets were the only ones who were mounted.
Scofield and Rivers stood on either side of Nox,
holding the horse still. Scofield held onto the reins.

"Come on, Deets," Zak said, riding up to him.
"Follow me."

"What about us?" Scofield asked.

Zak leaned down and snatched the reins out of
his hand.

"I'm turning you over to the lieutenant. He'll
give you your orders from now on."

Zak rode off then, leading Deets.

There was a silence in his wake, and then he
heard Colleen's voice.

"Ted, what is going on?" she asked her brother.

"Damn that man," Ted said.

Zak smiled to himself as he rode down off the
hill, Deets behind him.

There was more talk, more arguing, but Zak

couldn't hear the words. Five minutes later he heard the clatter of small stones. He looked back to see Ted, Colleen, Rivers, and Scofield riding down the slope in single file. He wondered if they would cut across the road and head for Fort Bowie or turn down it and head west to Tucson. He kept going.

"Hold up, Zak," O'Hara called out. "We're going with you."

"Catch up, then, Ted. I'm going on."

He heard hoofbeats as O'Hara put his horse into a gallop. A moment later he was riding alongside.

"Zak, you're hard to deal with," O'Hara said.

Zak said nothing.

"Colleen said we ought to go with you. So, I'm putting myself under your command."

"Make sure Rivers and Scofield know that, Ted. And have them ride up here and take Deets in tow. I'm going to scout ahead. Stay alert. All of you."

"Yes, sir," O'Hara said, and turned his horse to ride back to the others and issue orders.

The day brightened, illuminating the landscape ahead. He would stay off the road for a time. He knew they were not far from one of the old stage stops. There, he might learn something. For now, his gaze roved the land, looking for any movement, anything out of the ordinary. Sprays of lemony light shot through distant clouds on the horizon. He watched a hawk float overhead, wings outstretched, head turning from side to side as it hunted.

The stillness of morning made him feel good inside.

He looked back at Deets.

Deets glowered at him, and Zak nodded. The

man still had some fight in him. That would help him if he was going to pull through.

The wound wouldn't kill him.

But Trask might, he thought.

Over that possibility, Zak knew he had no control.

But Fate might.

⚔ 19 ⚔

Trask rode alongside Pablo Medina for two or three miles before he started asking him questions. He was sizing the man up, watching the way he rode, how he looked over the country. He wanted to see if Pablo had any horse sense. He also wanted to know if he was too inquisitive. He would have expected Pablo to start asking questions, but he did not; he kept his silence. To Trask, that was a point in his favor.

Pablo seemed alert. His head turned from side to side as they rode, and Trask saw that he was looking all around, his hand not far from the butt of his pistol or, for that matter, the stock of his rifle in its boot. He seemed at home in the saddle. He rode easy, but his left hand kept a firm grip on the reins.

"You got a family, Pablo?" Trask looked over at him to gauge his reaction to the question.

"I have a wife and a baby son," he said, his English only faintly accented.

"You born in Mexico?"

"Santa Fe."

"School?"

"Yes, I went to school."

"You didn't answer my first question. I asked you if you'd ever killed a man."

"I heard you ask, Mr. Trask," Pablo said, a note of respect in his voice. "I do not know how to say it."

"Yes or no. Simple."

"Not so simple. But, yes. I have killed a man before. More than one. I think you ask if I have shot a man with a rifle. I have not."

"Who did you kill?"

"My brother. And, my father."

"That's pretty close to home."

"My brother raped my wife. I caught him in the bed with her."

"And your father?"

"I see him in bed with my sister. She was screaming."

"How did you kill them?"

"I use the knife."

"You live with it. Aren't you afraid you will go to hell for killing your father and your brother?"

"If I do, I will meet them there."

Trask thought about what Pablo had said. It told him very little about the man. Medina was either simple-minded or wasn't bothered much by killing another human being. He hoped Pablo felt the same way he did about killing a man. When you took a man's life, you robbed him of everything, of all power, and thereafter, that man's power was yours to use for your benefit. That was the kind of man Trask admired and respected. No quarter, no live and let live, but rather, live and don't let live, anybody who stood in your way.

Now that the sun was up, the clouds took on a blue cast, a pale lavender to their underbellies.

And here and there, to the south and north, he saw streaks of white where the clouds were shredding up, dissipating and showing patches of faint blue that might have been sky, but he wasn't sure.

"Tell me, Pablo," he said, "how do you feel about killing a man you don't even know, a man who did you no harm, who didn't rape your sister or bed your wife?"

"I do not think of such things, Mr. Trask."

"Maybe you oughta."

"What?"

"If I asked you to kill a man, shoot him off his horse from some distance, could you do that?"

Pablo thought about that for a moment or two.

"Mr. Ferguson, he say I might have to kill somebody if I come to work for him. I say, okay. You pay me, I kill anybody. I tell him—Mr. Ferguson— you pay me to shoot you and I shoot you. He laugh and I laugh. It is a joke."

"A joke, yeah. But did you mean what you said? That you would kill anybody if he, or someone like me, asked you to do it?"

"When I was a boy, I worked on a big ranch. The boss told me when I work there, I ride for the brand. He mean—"

"I know what he meant, Pablo."

"I ride for the brand," Pablo said. "Always."

"That's good enough for me," Trask said.

"You want me to kill somebody, Mr. Trask?"

"That man who took the soldier away from us. I want you to kill him."

"Where is this man?"

"I think—I know—he's on our trail. I want you to hide out at the next stage stop and shoot him when you see him. He will probably be with the lieutenant—O'Hara—maybe some others. But you will shoot him first when you see him. He's easy to spot. He wears black clothes and he rides a black horse."

"This is the man you want me to kill?"

"On the first shot, Pablo."

"He is the one they call *jinete de sombra*, no?"

"What does that mean? I don't speak the Spanish."

"The rider of shadow."

"Shadow Rider. Yeah, they call him that. He's the one. The bastard."

"*Un carbon*," Pablo said. "That is what they say he is."

"Could you kill him?"

"If I see him, I could kill him. Yes."

"That's what I want you to do, Pablo. There's a hundred dollars for you if you do that for me."

"I will do it."

"And, if you also kill O'Hara, the army lieutenant, I will give you another fifty dollars."

"Silver or gold?"

Trask laughed. "Gold, if you want it."

"I like the gold," Medina said.

"When the time comes, I will tell you what to do, Pablo. Think about it. Think about that shot."

"When will I do this?" Pablo asked.

"Maybe tomorrow. I'll let you know."

"Good," Pablo said, and Trask touched a finger to his hat in salute and rode off to join Ferguson at the head of the column.

The blue in the sky softened and the white streaks grew larger and longer, the wind sculpting the clouds. The lavender was fading, giving way to patches of the purest blue, as if a giant ceramic bowl had been glazed in a kiln and was just emerging into the cool high reaches of the atmosphere. Trask studied the sky and thought it was going to be a good day when the sun broke through and dried the road where travel would be easier.

"You and Pablo come to an agreement?" Ferguson asked when Trask rode up alongside him.

"I think so. We'll leave him at the next stage stop while we ride on."

"You payin' him?"

"I said I would. Why?"

"Just curious. I hope it works out. This Cody feller, from all I've heard, is a pretty tough bird."

"No man can stop a bullet, Hiram."

"I just hope Pablo doesn't stop one."

The ground they traveled was witness to the previous night's storm. They rode past washouts and piles of debris, dead animals, broken plants. Late in the afternoon they turned toward the road and saw that it was washed bare of tracks. Old wagon ruts still existed, but they were shallower, their edges smoothed. They passed the place where the flash flood had originated, a confluence of gullies that bordered the road, fed water into them through several spouts and drains.

"This would have been a bad place to be last night," Ferguson said.

"I don't even want to think about it," Trask said. He raised a hand and beckoned to Willy Rawlins. "Let's take the road, Willy," he called. "You all follow us."

"Goin' to leave tracks for that Cody feller," Ferguson said.

"I know. Hell, I want him to follow us now. I think Pablo's going to take care of Zak Cody."

"I hope to hell you're right, Ben."

They spoke little as Trask set a faster pace. It was easier going on the road, and he knew he was leaving tracks. Cody would know just how many of them were ahead of him and where they were going. Well, he thought, that was just Cody's bad luck.

The clouds began to break up and drift apart. Some were shredded by high altitude winds and hung like tattered gray curtains from puffy, elongated lintels. Others looked like the foam circling a whirlpool, and these were drifting apart in clumps from the center. Clouds with smudged underbellies turned white as they passed under them, like optical illusions, or perhaps a deception brought on by the constant shift of light as it played over land and sky.

By late afternoon there were only puffs and streamers as reminders of the night before, a few scattered white clouds with little definition and an uncertain destination. The sun was boiling hot and the men were all sweating, griping about the heat. They drank from their canteens and chewed on jerky and hardtack. They smoked and kept riding, their horses striped with sweat, switching their tails at ravenous flies, snorting and wheezing under the grueling pace.

As the sun fell away in the sky, their shadows stretched out in front of them, growing longer and longer. The land itself seemed to change as the shadows pooled up, shapes shifting and reshifting as they rode. Trask kept looking at the road behind him, and every time he did, Grissom and Rawlins did the same. The Mexicans all looked ahead and to the sides, their nerves stretched taut, their horses laboring as they tired and perspired.

Just at dusk, Ferguson raised an arm and pointed ahead.

"There's the next stage stop," he said.

"I see it," Trask said. He turned and made a circling sign with his hand.

Grissom peeled off to the right, Rawlins to the left, leaving the road. They rode in a wide semicircle to flank the adobe.

"Thin out," Trask said to the others. "Don't bunch up. You see anything don't look right, you shoot it."

"Do it, boys," Ferguson said, and the Mexicans fanned out.

Trask slowed his horse. Ferguson did the same.

"Let's see if Willy or Lou run into anything," Trask said.

The sun was sinking below the western horizon now, painting the clouds silver and gold, tinting the undersides with soft orange pastels. The shadows deepened to the east, twisted into formless shapes like clay in the hands of a mad sculptor.

Willy reached the adobe first and circled it on his horse. Lou took an opposite tack on his horse, and the two met out front. Trask reined up and held his hand high to stop the others. They all waited and watched as Willy dismounted and drew his pistol. He crept up to the open door and called out, "Hello the house."

There was no answer.

Then he went inside and Trask held his breath.

He returned a few moments later, stood in the doorway and wig-wagged an arm to signal all clear.

"Let's go, Hiram," Trask said, and motioned for the others to follow.

Lou dismounted and tied his horse to a hitchrail.

"Empty?" Trask said as he rode up.

"Nobody alive in there, if that's what you mean," Willy said.

"Well, anybody dead in there?"

"Ben, it looks like the two men here were blown to bits and what was left of their skins was gnawed off. Just skeletons, mostly, a couple of skulls grinnin' and settin' apart from a lot of bones. Stinks to high heaven."

Ferguson let out a groaning sigh.

Trask looked at him.

"Hiram, you didn't expect no good news here, did you?"

"No, I reckon not. Them were both good boys. I hate to lose 'em."

"Well, you lost 'em and we're ridin' on." He stared at Grissom and Rawlins. "You boys get mounted. We're ridin' on."

"Hell, it'll be dark soon," Grissom said, looking at Ferguson for support. There was none.

"We'll get you a pet owl, Lou. He can be your eyes. We're ridin' on."

"Yeah, damn it all."

"You wouldn't want to stay here no ways, Lou," Rawlins said. "It's worsen the place we stayed in last night. The smell, I mean."

The other riders rode up. Some of them started to dismount. Ferguson put up a hand to stop them.

"We're not bunkin' here tonight, boys," he said.

"Trask says we're goin' on." Then he turned to Trask. "It's another day's ride or so to the next station, Ben."

"I know. Just sit tight while I work this out."

Trask touched spurs to his horse's flanks and guided him around the adobe. Behind it, he rode some distance, scouting the terrain. When he returned, the sun was nearly set and the faces of the men were in shadow.

"Pablo," Trask said, "come with me. The rest of you just wait. Roll a quirly, scratch your ass, stretch your legs. But stay close to your horses."

Trask and Medina rode to the back of the adobe and beyond.

"You can tie your horse to that pile of lumber yonder, Pablo. Anyone comin' up the road won't see him. Then you sit in that house and poke your gun barrel out one of the winders. If Cody rides up, he's going to be real close. He'll be wearin' black and ridin' a black horse, like I said. You might drop him at close range. There's a back door. Leave it open, and after you've killed that bastard and maybe the soldier, you hightail it for your horse and light a shuck. You got that?"

"Yes. I will wait inside the adobe for this Cody and shoot him."

"Kill him."

"Yes."

"Maybe you'll get lucky and he won't get here until tomorrow, after the sun is up."

"I have seen dust in the sky," Pablo said. "He is coming. He is near."

"How come you didn't tell me?"

"Sometimes I look and it is there. I look again

and it is gone. I think he rides fast and then rides slow. The dust was far away."

"You got good eyes, Pablo. I'm countin' on them tonight. You see good in the dark?"

"*Yo soy un tecolote*," he said.

"What's that mean?" Trask asked.

"I am the owl."

Trask laughed, reached over and patted Pablo between his shoulder blades.

"You'll do, Pablo. You'll do right fine."

When Trask and the others left, the sun had set and the temperature began dropping.

Pablo squatted by a front window, his Winchester resting on the ledge, the barrel pointing toward the road. It was quiet and dark, the sky sprinkled with diamond stars, the moon not yet risen.

He waited and fought against superstition and fear, his stomach fluttering like a child's on All Hallow's Eve, when the ghosts of the dead floated on the night air and the faintest whisper would make him shiver as if touched by the bony hand of a skeleton.

He waited and thought about the man he was going to kill. The one they called the Shadow Rider.

20

Zak had not ridden more than ten feet before Colleen caught up to him.

One look at her face and he knew she had the bit in her teeth. This was one woman no man would ever best in an argument. He braced himself for what he suspected would be another angry tirade.

"Zak Cody," she said, lighting into him like a mother hen attacking a hawk in the chicken house, "are you just going to let that dead man lie up there on that hill without a proper burial?"

"Yes, I am," he said. "There's no way to bury him proper."

"Well, you can dig a hole, or cover him with rocks, at least."

"Wouldn't do any good, Colleen. And it would hold us back. We have to move on Trask, stop him from rendezvousing with . . . well, with some renegades who are trying to start a war with the Apache nation."

"Where's your respect for the dead, Zak?"

"I don't respect the dead, I reckon. I respect the living."

"What? I've never heard such a thing. No respect for the dead?"

"No'm."

"That man needs to be buried. By you. By us. Before we leave."

"No'm, he does not."

"Why?"

Zak tried to avoid those penetrating blue eyes of hers, but they were like magnets. They drew his own gaze to them, so he could not avoid mentally plunging into their depths and being snared there like a rabbit in a trap. Her eyes were especially beautiful and magnetic when she was angry. And he was sure that Colleen was hopping mad.

"Be like burying a suit, ma'am."

"What?" Her eyes flared like twin star sapphires struck with a sudden glaring light.

"The man's dead, Colleen. Gone. Nothing more we can do for him. It would be just like burying a man's suit clothes. Senseless."

"Oh, you are really something, Zak Cody. As heartless a man as I've ever met, and I've met my share of them, all right."

"Maybe so," he said.

"Just to leave that poor dead man lying up there, out in the open, subject to the ravages of weather and vermin, all kinds of awful things."

"Yes'm. Nature takes care of such. Mother Nature cleans up the messes we human folks leave. Worms are already at work on him. Flies will get at his eyes, start drinking all the wet stuff. Buzzards will pick at him until the coyotes pick up the scent, and then they'll cart off arms and legs. Ants and bugs will get a share, until there's not much of a trace. His clothes will eventually rot, his pistol turn to rust. That's the way life works, Colleen. Dust to dust."

"Oh, you're impossible, Zak. I expected you'd show a little compassion, a little respect for—"

"Colleen, the Lakota, the Crow, the Cheyenne, maybe all Indian tribes, always thank the spirit of the creatures they kill for food. So do I. The Lakota say this: 'Thank you, brother, for feeding me and my family. One day I will die and feed the grasses so your descendants can eat and live and become strong.' That's the way life works. Everything alive feeds on something else to survive. When we pluck a fruit or a vegetable to eat, we kill it. When we slaughter a beef or shoot a deer, we are living life, the life the Great Spirit gave us."

"People are different," she said. "They deserve some reverence when they die."

"Why? People are just another animal, as far as the Great Spirit is concerned. Oh, we think we're smarter than most animals, but I've seen animals that have more good sense than a lot of men."

"That's not what I'm talking about, Zak."

"Colleen, you haven't seen all of life. Neither have I. But I've seen maybe a great deal more than you have. No death is ever pretty, but it's just a condition that all creatures must experience. The Indians believe that a man's spirit lives in his body while he is alive on this earth. After death, the spirit leaves, goes along the star path to a better place."

"Heaven, you mean."

"You can call it anything you want," he said. "The point is that we are all here on this earth for only a little while. When death takes us, we are no longer here."

"And you believe that?" Her voice had softened, grown less shrill. The light in her eyes was now filled with flitting shadows of doubt.

"Yes, Colleen, I guess I do. Now, we can talk about this later, if you like, but I have a job to do and we're moving on."

"I must say, you do give a person food for thought."

"Thinking can brighten the darkest path, sometimes."

She looked at him as if seeing him for the first time. Her eyes narrowed. Her lips pursed as if she was about to speak, but she pressed them back together and turned her horse away. He did not detect anger, but a kind of puzzlement that she couldn't unravel as long as she was in his presence. A smile flickered on his lips as he touched spurs to his mount's flanks. The horse responded with bunched muscles that suddenly released the energy in its legs and hooves.

The sky grew lighter in color and softer in texture as they rode away from the hill, along a path Zak set, parallel to the washed-out roadway, clouds still hiding the rising sun.

O'Hara caught up with Cody, rode alongside him. He didn't speak for some time and Zak didn't encourage him to talk.

Finally, the lieutenant cleared his throat.

"Prisoner seems to be doing all right," he said.

"We haven't gone far. There should be a stage stop up ahead any minute now."

"What did you say to Colleen?" O'Hara was

blunt, and Zak knew that was what he really wanted to talk about, not Al Deets.

"About what?"

"She seemed pretty upset when we left that Mexican up there on the hill."

"She wanted me to bury him."

"And you refused."

"He's not buried, is he?"

"Colleen, well, she's sensitive, I guess you'd say. Delicate, maybe, in some ways. I just didn't want her feelings hurt. Unnecessarily, I mean."

Zak said nothing. He let Ted chew on that for a while. The way he figured it, if Ted had something more to say, he would say it.

And he did, finally.

"Maybe we should have buried that dead man, Zak."

"You think so? Why?"

"A matter of decency, I guess."

"What would be decent about piling rocks on a rotting corpse?"

"Good lord, Zak, I hope you didn't say anything like that to Colleen."

"I hope I didn't, either," Zak said.

O'Hara frowned.

Zak was watching the land ahead, his gaze scanning the terrain for any sign of movement, any glint of light on a gun barrel. The sunlight had not broken through yet, but it was stronger now, the heavy purple of the far clouds to the east fading to a light lavender, while some were tinged a pale cobalt, and there were signs that the lower clouds were breaking up, swirled into spirals by the lofty winds. The sun would break through eventually, and the dank coolness that clung to the land would vanish as it bathed in scorching heat.

"You must know what you said to Colleen," O'Hara said.

"Some of it. Why?"

"I guess it might not be any of my business."

"It might not," Zak agreed.

"You're a hard man to get to know, Zak. I sure can't figure you out."

"It's not important, Ted. You ought to have more to figure out than me. Like how we're going to bring Ben Trask down and stop a bloody war with the Apaches."

"Oh, I'm thinking about that, sure. Not much we can do right now."

"No. Just make sure Trask and his men don't jump us."

"You think he might? This early in the day?"

"Trask is capable of 'most anything. My guess is that he'll look for a good place to dry-gulch us and start slinging a whole lot of lead our way."

"When?"

"I don't know. Today. Tomorrow, maybe."

Zak stood up in the stirrups. Ahead, on a low rise, he saw the adobe, just jutting up on the edge of his vision.

"There's the old stage stop," he said. "Trask probably holed up there during the storm. He might be there now. Or he might have left a couple of rifles behind to pick us off."

"Hard to see," O'Hara said, squinting. "It looks just like the land around it. Same drab color and all."

"I left two men dead in it last time I was here."

"You did? Trask's men?"

"Trask's or Ferguson's. They were left there to join up with Trask. There were two men at each old stage stop."

"You kill all of them?" There was a hollow sound to O'Hara's voice, as if he were swallowing the words as he spoke them.

"I did."

O'Hara said nothing. Zak reined his horse to a halt.

"You stay here, Ted. Spread out. I'll circle and come up from the left side of that adobe yonder. You keep your eyes on the road to your right."

"You want me to go with you? Maybe one of the men?"

"No. I can tell if there are any surprises waiting for us."

"You're in command, Colonel."

Zak shot him a sharp look, a silent reprimand.

Then he rode on, circling to the left, keeping the horse at a walk so he would not make much noise.

He found the places where Trask had hobbled the horses the night before. He dismounted and broke open the freshest horse apples. No steam arose from the balls of dung. He checked the hoofprints to gauge how old they were, and then, when he had remounted, he rode out, counting tracks, making sure that none doubled back. Then he rode back up behind the adobe and around to the other side. He saw the collapsed wall, the ruins inside. He rode back out front and waved to O'Hara, beckoning him to ride up with Colleen, Deets, and the two soldiers.

Zak dismounted then, checked the front door, looked at the disheveled interior. There was mud inside, along with standing water, debris scattered everywhere.

When Ted rode up with the others, Zak stepped outside.

"What'd you find, Zak?" Ted asked.

"Well, Trask and his bunch spent a miserable night here. They left a good hour or so ahead of us. At this point, he doesn't outnumber us much."

"How many?"

"I counted eight horse tracks, but one of them is traveling empty. Probably belonged to that dead Mexican back there."

"That doesn't sound so bad, then."

"Bad enough. They're all killers and they're riding faster than we are."

"You can tell that from the tracks?"

"I figure they'll let that riderless horse loose when they get far enough away. It will slow them down. And Trask is in a hurry."

"Now what?" Ted wanted to know.

"We follow Trask. But from here on out, he can dry-gulch us most anywhere. I figure that at some point he'll ride down to the road so he can make better time. Along here, the road looks pretty bad. Still muddy, still choked with a lot of dead animals, brush, and such."

O'Hara looked off toward the road, then at the crumbled wall.

"Rain must have damned near drowned them if they were all inside. I wonder why he killed one of his own men."

Zak looked at Deets.

"He might know," he said. "What about it,

Deets? Any idea why Trask would shoot that Mexican?"

"No tellin'," Deets said. "He might've looked at Trask crosswise."

"We may never know," Zak said. He started to walk to his horse. "Let's keep moving. There's another old stage stop about a day's ride from here. Trask might hole up there tonight."

"You think so?" O'Hara asked.

"I echo Deets there. No telling what Trask might do, but he'll go there to see if the two men they put there are still alive."

O'Hara looked at Colleen as Zak climbed back up in the saddle.

A knowing look spread across her face.

"He won't find them alive, will he, Zak?" she said.

"Not unless they've been resurrected. I only know of one such case of that."

"You're not only crass and heartless," she said, "you're also sacrilegious, Zak Cody."

"I wish you'd quit calling me by both my names," he said. "You make me think of my mother when she was mad at me."

"Well, I'm not your mother, but you do make me mad."

O'Hara opened his mouth to say something, but wisely kept silent.

"Thank God for that," Zak said with a wry smile. He turned his horse and rode up the slope to where Trask's trail began.

Behind him, Zak heard Colleen give out an indignant snort.

And he smiled again.

⟢ 21 ⟣

Zak rode well ahead of the others, following the tracks of Trask's bunch. The others stopped a few times so that Colleen, her brother, Deets, Scofield, and Rivers could heed calls to nature. Colleen, of course, took longer than the others. Zak stopped to relieve himself a few times, too. They all had to use precious water to wash their hands. Ted guarded his sister when she was occupied with those private tasks, staying at a discreet distance, his rifle at the ready.

Zak came across a saddle, saw where Trask and the others had stopped to strip it from the riderless horse. A few yards away he saw a discarded bridle. Attached to the saddle was an empty rifle scabbard, which he did not examine. He saw the tracks left by the horse the outlaws shooed away. He scanned the terrain all around but saw no sign of the abandoned horse.

A while later the tracks left the rough country and joined the road. Zak saw that all of the riders moved much faster over the washed-out road. There were clumps of mud thrown up by the horses' hooves when they rode at a gallop. He dismounted and broke open a few mud balls to gauge how old they were. Trask, he figured, was now at least two hours ahead of them, perhaps more.

When he reached the road, he stopped and waited for O'Hara and the others to join him.

"So," Ted said, "Trask is taking to the road."

"And picking up the pace. He's a good two hours ahead of us, maybe three. More like three, I'd say."

"That's a good long stretch," O'Hara said.

"We can't make it up, for sure. We have to spare our horses. Look at that sky. By mid-afternoon we'll be sweating rivers."

O'Hara looked up at the sky, saw the swirls of decimated clouds, the basking loaves floating on separate seas of blue, the grated remnants of white carpets floating in the high ether. The sun was blinding by then, coursing slow and blazing toward its noon zenith.

"No way to catch him before he meets up with Welch, I suppose," O'Hara said.

"There might be a way," Zak said.

"How?"

"If we stop less, sleep on our horses. Trask may hole up in one of those adobe line shacks for some shut-eye. If so, we gain on him."

"None of us got any sleep last night, Zak."

"I know. We've got three or four days of hard riding ahead of us. We might go three days without sleep. After that, we'll start to fall off our horses, make mistakes, maybe get all mixed up on time and directions."

"You paint a pretty grim picture," O'Hara said.

"Grim, not pretty."

O'Hara laughed at the wry observation. "I

guess we can try," he said. "I've slept in the saddle before."

"It's your sister I'm worried about, Ted."

"Colleen? She's holding up well so far. I can keep an eye on her, so she doesn't tumble out of the saddle."

"You might have Rivers or Scofield do that. I may need your eyes and your rifle before this day is done."

"I understand."

"I'm going to have Deets ride with me from now on."

"Your decoy?"

"He won't be any big loss if he takes a bullet."

"You expect that will happen?"

"I don't know what to expect. But if we are shot at—if Deets is shot at—it might give me the split second I need to shoot back."

"Sound reasoning, Zak."

Zak laughed. "I don't know how sound it is. I'm just trying to give us a chance if Trask is waiting up ahead to pick us off. We're outgunned, Ted."

"Is there anything else we can do? Maybe go to the fort and put Willoughby in irons, get together a troop to go after Trask, Ferguson, and Welch?"

"That would eat up days we don't have," Zak said.

O'Hara thought about it for a minute or so. There wasn't a hint of a breeze, and the sun was bearing down on them with molten persistence. Sweat began to trickle out from under his hat and he swiped at it with his hand.

"What would General Crook do, Zak?"

"Good question."

"Do you know the answer?"

O'Hara, Zak thought, was as persistent as a wood tick. Once he landed on live meat, he burrowed right into it.

"Crook would rest his troops before he went into battle."

"Then there's your answer."

"You're right, Ted. General Crook would also pick his own battlefield."

"Your point, Zak?"

"We can do that. We know where Trask is going. And we know where Cochise is."

"So, what's your decision?" Ted asked.

"I'll let you know at the end of the day."

"Why then?"

"Because I hope to make it to the next adobe. What I find there will tell me what to do."

"Fair enough. I hope you make the right decision."

"Every decision is the right one," Zak said. "At the time you make it. You only know if it's wrong if it turns out to be a bad decision."

They followed the tracks up the road, with Deets riding alongside Zak, the others following some hundred yards in the rear.

"I feel wet inside," Deets said to Zak sometime after noon.

"You've been drinking too much water."

"No, I mean where your bullet went through me, Cody."

"You're probably bleeding again. Put your hand on the wound and press hard. Keep it there."

"I touched it a minute ago. Burns like fire."

"Bleed to death, then, Deets."

"Damn, Cody. I'm hurtin', I tell you."

"If you feel pain, that's a good sign, Deets."

"What about the bleeding?"

"That, too, is a good sign."

"A good sign?"

Zak decided that Deets wasn't too bright. And he obviously wasn't a leader. He was a follower.

"Yeah, Deets. If you hurt and you're bleeding, that's a sign you're still alive. Give thanks to your Maker, son."

"You bastard."

"Your mouth works all right, too. Maybe tonight I'll build a fire and put some iron to that wound, seal it up. And maybe wash your mouth out with some lava soap."

"We gonna stop somewheres?"

Zak didn't answer. He studied the tracks, getting a picture of Trask's tactics from the sign. Trask and his men would walk their horses for a good stretch, three or four miles, then gallop them for nearly a mile. He was unwavering in that maneuver. But he noticed that some of the horses were starting to drag their hooves, a sure sign of fatigue.

As the day wore on, Trask no longer ran the horses, but kept to a steady, plodding pace. He seemed pretty confident, Zak thought. And Zak noticed that two horses had paired up for a time, then one went ahead, leaving the other behind. After that, the horses all stuck to their positions. When they stopped, it was only briefly, to relieve themselves, and always, two riders stood off from the others, probably to stand guard until they took their turns. The doodle bug holes marked both their passing and their activities.

Zak could see that Trask was thorough, and smart. It was what made him dangerous.

Later, he thought about Crook and something the general had told him once, when they were fighting Indians, tracking a band that had escaped a battle in rugged country.

"You have to think like your enemy, Zak," Crook had told him. "When you're on his track, you have to see ahead of him, think what he might do, what you might do if you were in his shoes, or his moccasins."

"Can you do that, General?"

"Any animal will only run so far. Then it gets tired or mad and makes a stand. But the animal always picks the place to make a stand. If you're chasing that animal, you have to think like it thinks. Where would it make its stand? How would it defend itself? In the case of these redskins, they'll find high ground with plenty of cover. And they'll have a back door, a place where they can run and escape if they fail to stop me."

"And do you know where that is?"

"No, but I will. And so will you. That's why you're my scout, Zak. You can read sign and you can read what those redskins are thinking. Am I right?"

"Yes, sir, I reckon you are."

And Zak had figured out where the Indians were going and where they would halt and make a stand. Crook acted accordingly and they killed or captured the entire band. Crook was a good general. He knew when to delegate authority and how to do it. Not a bad example to follow, Zak thought.

The sun drifted down the arch of the western sky, hovered over the horizon, then started dipping beyond it, striping the land with shadows, painting clouds gold and silver, purple and a soft orange. Zak called a halt while it was still light enough to see everyone with him and the terrain ahead.

He beckoned to O'Hara and the others to catch up to him and Deets, then waited. When they were all there, gathered around him, he spoke.

"We're not too far from the next old stage stop," he said. "I notice that Trask's horses are tired, so he and his men must be tired."

"And so are we, Mr. Cody," Colleen said, a sharp tone to her voice.

"We may not be able to see that adobe right off, especially if it's real dark, so stay alert. If Trask is holed up there, he probably won't light a fire, and he'll try and be real quiet. When I see the shack, I'll call a halt and deploy you all until I find out if the adobe is occupied. From now on you'll ride close behind me and Deets. Lieutenant O'Hara, you'll take the lead. Scofield, you and Rivers will flank Miss O'Hara. Check your rifles. Keep them at the ready."

"How far is that adobe?" Ted asked.

"Maybe less than ten miles. We've kept a pretty good pace, but the tracks tell me Trask is probably just about there, or will be shortly after sunset. So, we've got a good two hours ride, maybe longer, before we know anything."

"Lead on, Zak," O'Hara said. "The quicker we get there, the better."

"Maybe," Zak said, and turned his horse, motioned for Deets to follow him.

Three quarters of an hour later the sun set below the horizon. The afterglow lingered for another fifteen or twenty minutes, a last blaze against the western clouds as those ahead of them turned to ash, then to ebony, before they disappeared.

As they rode on, Venus winked on in an aquamarine sky and the darkness crept across the heavens, leaving more stars, like scattered diamonds, on black velvet.

Zak tried to recall the exact location of the stage stop that had been turned into a line shack before its abandonment. The darkness didn't help, although he had passed this same way a few days ago on just such a night.

Deets was making noises, groaning, muttering under his breath.

"Shut up," Zak told him in a loud whisper. "You make any more noise and I'll stuff a rag in your mouth."

Deets shut up.

Another hour passed and the darkness deepened.

The moon rose and Zak got his bearings. He pulled on the reins and halted the horse he was riding, Deets's horse. The others caught up to him.

He kept his voice low when he spoke to them.

"The old line shack's just head. Maybe five hundred yards. Keep Deets here. I'm going to dismount and proceed on foot. If you hear a shot, wait five minutes before you circle the adobe on horseback. If I don't come back in five minutes, I probably won't be back."

"Want me to go with you?" O'Hara asked.

"No, I'll go this one alone. I have a funny feeling in my stomach. And I always pay attention to funny feelings."

"What do you think?"

"I don't know. If Trask and his men are up there, we should hear some noises. Faint noises, maybe, but some sounds. Sounds of life. He may not be there. Or there might be one or a bunch up there, just waiting for anyone to come up on that adobe from this road."

"Be careful," Colleen said, and Zak felt the softness in her voice, the concern she expressed. He swung out of the saddle and drew his rifle from its sheath.

He handed the reins of the horse to Ted.

"I'll be seeing you," he said.

Then he walked a few paces and disappeared into the darkness.

══ 22 ══

Major Erskine Willoughby studied the map that lay on top of his desk. An oil lamp flickered with a yellow-orange flame, spraying a wavering light over the lines and boxes, the X's and circles, the numbers and letters. He tapped an impatient foot against one leg of his chair, creating a rhythmic tattoo that served to calm his clamorous nerves.

"Orderly," he called through the closed door, "where in hell is Lieutenant Welch?"

"He's coming, sir," a voice replied, warped by the wood barrier through which it traveled. "Corporal Hopson ran to fetch him ten minutes ago."

"As you were," Willoughby said, gaining some equilibrium with his thoughts in issuing a meaningless order. Of course the orderly would be as he was. Willoughby couldn't see him through the door, but he knew the man was standing stiff as a board, as apprehensive as he himself would be until Lieutenant Welch appeared.

Fort Bowie was on the map. The cartographer had drawn a line from the fort to the last old stage stop. The road from Tucson to all the adobes was

indicated, as well as the domain of the Chiricahua
Apaches. There were little lines drawn in circular
fashion to indicate prominent hills all through the
area designated as Apache Territory.

Willoughby had studied the map intensely, figuring distances, time of travel by horseback, the
rendezvous point with Ferguson, and possible lo-
gistical sites should there be a need to reinforce the
men or resupply them with food and ammunition,
fresh horses, and water.

He loved every minute of the planning. Willoughby not only saw himself as a great general
someday, but as a man of property, of immense
wealth. He could imagine becoming a land baron on
the largely unsettled frontier. And not only would
he be an owner of vast acreage, but he would found
a town, establish a bank and mercantile store, be
wealthy and respected by all who came to settle in
what once had been a wild and dangerous country
populated by savage Indians.

These were his dreams, and he lived them each
time he studied the map and made notations on a
separate piece of paper. Perhaps the army was content to live in peace with the Apaches, but he was
not. As long as there were Apaches in the territory,
his dreams were in danger of being shattered or
never coming to fruition.

Willoughby scratched more notes on the piece
of foolscap next to the map. He scribbled each
word with an intense focus, picturing himself as a
military genius whose strategies would one day be
studied by hordes of students attending the academy at West Point. He was so absorbed in this task
that he did not hear the discreet knock on his door

until after his orderly had rapped on the wood several times.

"Yes?" he said.

"Lieutenant Welch, sir. He has arrived."

"Send him in, Corporal Loomis."

The door opened. John Welch strode into the room, a leather map case tucked under his left arm. He saluted smartly before Loomis closed the door behind him. Willoughby, who was uncovered, did not return his salute.

"Come on over, Johnny. We'll go over this map one more time. You bring yours?"

"Yes, Erskine, of course. I made some notations on it, as you suggested."

"Spread it out here."

Willoughby slid his map and note paper to one side, leaving a space for Welch to place his map of the same terrain. When Welch was finished placing weights on the four corners, Willoughby leaned over the desk and studied it, a series of "Uh-hums" issuing from his throat. Welch glanced over at Willoughby's map to compare the two, but the major blocked most of the light so he could not tell much.

"Very good, Johnny," Willoughby said. "I've got some ideas that might help you in this campaign. How many men have you got so far, and were you able to obtain clothing for them?"

"I've got twenty-five men, eight from the stockade. The rest are family conscripts."

"Family conscripts?"

"Men whose families forced them to join the army. They fucked up at every post and were sent out here for disciplinary reasons. Ain't a one of 'em what's not thoroughly expendable."

Willoughby smiled.

"Good, good."

"All will be wearing civilian clothing, which I obtained from Ferguson. His man rode in from Tucson less than an hour ago. Ferguson and Trask left three days ago. I figure we can rendezvous with them sometime tomorrow afternoon at that last old station."

"About how we figured it, right?"

"Right on the money; right on the barrelhead, Erskine."

"Weaponry?"

"Spencer rifles, forty rounds per man, extra horses, grub for a week."

"I want this done right, Johnny."

Welch was an officious officer, prim as a martinet, stiff-backed, army regulation all the way. He stood at attention even when relaxed. The army was his life, but he was as greedy as Willoughby, and twice as dishonest. He bore a thin black moustache, flared sideburns an inch short of being overly ostentatious, and a uniform so starched and pressed it appeared brand new. But he was the quartermaster. He could get anything he wanted, from almost anywhere.

"The men don't know where they're going, and they won't until we're well away from the fort. They've been told that they will all be granted honorable discharges from the army upon completion of this expedition."

"What do they think this expedition is all about?" Willoughby asked.

Welch smiled. "They think they're going on a hunt for Apache artifacts to be sent back to a museum in Washington, D.C. They believe the expedition is at the request of our President, Ulysses S. Grant."

"Very good, Johnny. Inspired."

"Yes, sir, I thought so."

"And you'll tell them to kill Apaches."

"Once we're well into the field, sir."

"When do you leave?"

"Shortly after midnight, I'll give the orders. We should be moving before two A.M. At daylight, or shortly thereafter, I'll break the news to the troops that we're going to start a war with the Chiricahua Apaches."

Willoughby stood up. He rolled up his map, placed it atop Welch's on one edge and rolled his map inside the other one. He handed the roll to Welch, then opened the humidor on his desk. He took out two cigars, handed one to the lieutenant.

"I'll see you back here in about a week, minus a few of those miscreants who are going with you, I hope."

"Yes, sir. I'll be coming back with Ferguson and Trask. Just the two of them, sir."

"There won't be any trace of this, ah, expedition, then?"

"No, Erskine, not a goddamned trace."

Willoughby lifted the chimney on the oil lamp, thrust a taper inside until it caught fire. He lighted Welch's cigar, then his own. He blew a plume of smoke into the air, patted his flat stomach and sat down in his chair.

"Have a seat, Johnny," Willoughby said, "this might be the last good smoke we'll have together for a whole week."

Welch sat down, puffed on his cigar.

"It's going to be sweet, when it's over, Erskine," he said.

"It damned well better be. Our futures depend on this mission."

"The world will be a better place out here when we finish the job."

"You know we have to kill those two men when you bring them back here," Willoughby said.

"Sir?"

"Ferguson and Trask. They will be found guilty of murder and hanged. We can't have them sticking their fingers into our pie."

"No, sir, we can't."

"I want you to bring evidence back with you that they shot two of my soldiers. Can you do that?"

Welch didn't even have to think about it.

"I can, Erskine. You know I can."

Willoughby smiled, blew a smoke ring. It hung in the air like the ghost of a doughnut, wafted across his desk and vanished in a golden spray of lamplight.

The wood inside the room ticked like a clock in the silence.

⊰ 23 ⊱

Zak stepped into the shadows. He became a shadow. Behind him, he heard Colleen let out a tiny gasp. Then he heard someone else draw in a quick breath. Then the silence of the night enveloped him and he circled below the adobe to come up on its north side. He could see only the roof, barely visible in the starlight, the moon just beginning to rise, far to the east.

He stood still for a few moments, almost willing his eyes to adjust to the darkest regions ahead of him. He waited, listened, glad that the horses were quiet. So, too, his ears adjusted to that silence, and he thought of them as small cushions that would absorb every slight noise so he could interpret their origins. Soft, cushiony sponges, soaking up the stillness, adjusting, constantly adjusting, to every nuance of sound the night might have to offer.

He took a step, a careful step, short enough so he could keep his balance. He did not move the other foot until the first one had settled. He did not disturb the small pebbles nor dislodge the larger rocks, but sought out the open sandy spots where he might place a boot without making a sound.

He took his time, and after a while reached a place parallel to the north wall of the adobe. He approached it with careful steps, watching for anything growing, since he did not want his trouser legs to brush against leaves or bark or cactus. He reached the wall and pressed an ear against it and stood there for several long moments, listening for the scrape of a boot, the clearing of a throat, the shifting of a body in waiting.

He eased himself to the front corner, again pressed his ear to the adobe brick, holding his breath, listening with the intensity of an owl listening for the cheep of a chick or the squeak of a mouse.

He heard a slight scraping sound.

Very slight.

What was it? A rodent inside the shack? A snake slithering across something on the floor? He waited, ear hugging the wall.

Or a man?

He tried to think about what position a man inside might take if he were on guard, waiting to catch some unsuspecting riders coming up on him. He would stand or sit near a window or an open door. He would have a rifle, so he might be at a window, resting the barrel on the sill. He would be looking toward the road, ready to crack off a shot at anyone who approached.

Such a man might have been waiting inside for a long time. Many hours. He might be tired, or sleepy. He might have to change his position often to avoid fatigue. Such a man would be patient.

As Zak was patient now.

There had been no sound for several seconds. The seconds became minutes and passed. Still,

Zak stood there, listening, feeling the weight of his rifle as it rested on his forearm, feeling the weight of it grow into a leaden burden. He did not move. He brushed away the thought of that particular discomfort. He made the weight go away until there was a numbness in that spot where the barrel rested, until his hand on the stock felt no weight.

Then he heard a louder noise. A scraping sound, then a sound like metal striking wood, sharp and quick. More scraping sounds and one that was difficult to define. A light stomping sound as if a man was lifting up one foot, then the other, perhaps restoring blood circulation to deadened feet. A perfectly natural thing to do, Zak thought. If a man had been squatting or sitting for some time, perhaps several hours, he would have to stand up, stretch. If he had a rifle in his hands, that rifle might fall to the sill or on a board and make one of the sounds he had heard.

He took his ear away from the wall, rubbed it to bring the blood back into the squashed parts.

He stepped around the corner, hugging the wall. He did not need to put his ear to the wall. He saw that the window on his side was open. He heard the rustle of cloth.

Was there one man inside? Or two? Trask's whole bunch was certainly not inside. That many men would make a lot more noise than he had heard. Most likely one, he thought.

The sounds stopped then, and he knew the man was no longer lifting his boots. Instead, there was a rustle of cloth as the man turned or flexed his arms. It was a sound that was hard to detect, but unmistakable to Zak. He could picture the man standing there, perhaps at the window on the other side of the door. He stretched his neck out and saw that the door was closed.

He moved toward it, a slow, careful step at a time. When he reached it, he did not lean against it, but stood there. He craned his neck again and saw what he had expected to see.

The other window was open, also, and the dark snout of a rifle rested on the sill, ten or twelve inches poking out.

One lone man, then, as he'd thought.

Who would Trask leave behind? he wondered.

A crack shot, for one thing.

Trask would tell his man to look for a man dressed in black riding a black horse. He would probably trust this man to do the job of assassination. Well, Zak thought, perhaps trust was the wrong word. He would expect the man to carry out his assignment. Perhaps he offered bonus money. Bounty money.

He looked at the door. He traced a finger along the crack. The door was closed tightly, but if he remembered correctly, the doors on these old shacks used leather hinges. Over the years, the leather had probably started to rot or lose its toughness. There might be a latch or a bar on the other side. It might be too risky to knock down the door, crash it open, rush inside and hope he got the waiting killer with his first shot.

But they could not stay there all night. Something had to be done.

Again Zak's thoughts turned to Trask and which of his men he might have left behind. He might not leave someone he'd known for some time. Too dangerous. He might leave one of Ferguson's men, perhaps one of the Mexicans.

More likely, Trask would do that. Risk someone he did not know too well or might need for the big job ahead.

So there could be a Mexican inside.

Zak set his rifle down behind him, leaned it against the wall. It was not cocked, and if he had to cock it, that would alert the man inside the adobe, give him the advantage.

He drew his pistol, easing it up out of its holster with a practiced slowness. He thumbed the trigger back while gently squeezing the trigger so it would not click when it was fully cocked.

The locking sear might make a small sound, but nothing loud. No more than a muffled *snick*, at best.

He cocked the pistol, held it at the ready. He listened to see if the slight sound had caused any alarm to the man inside.

It was very quiet.

His next move, he knew, would be the most crucial one.

Zak leaned toward the open window and whispered.

"*¿Quien es?*" Who's there? in Spanish.

He heard a sucking of breath, the scrape of a boot.

"*¿Quien es?*" the man inside hissed in a loud whisper.

Zak thought fast. He knew now that he had been right. There was a Mexican on guard. His accent was perfect for a man who spoke Spanish. He picked a common Mexican name, hoped that would confuse the man inside. No, he thought, he would use the name of the man they had found shot in the back during the flash flood. He tried to remember his name. *"Es Jaime,"* he said.

He heard the man inside curse under his breath. He murmured the names of saints and invoked Jesus, Mary, and God, all in Spanish.

"¿Tu no eres muerto, Jaime?" Pablo Medina said.

Zak saw the rifle barrel disappear, then reappear.

"Yo soy el espirito de Jaime Elizondo. Soy muerto. Dame agua, dame pan." Give me water, give me bread.

"Jesús Cristo," Pablo exclaimed. *"Vete, vete."*

"Tira su rifle afuera," Zak said. Throw your rifle outside.

"¿Por qué?" the man inside said. Why? in Spanish.

In Spanish, Zak replied. At the same time, he kept his eye on the man's rifle, measured the number of strides it would take to reach it, snatch it out of the would-be killer's hands.

"I am the ghost of Jaime Elizondo. I am looking for the man who shot me in the back. I am going to kill that man so I can be free of this earth."

"I did not kill you. Ben Trask shot you, Jaime. Go. Go away."

That was enough for Zak.

He took two long strides, leaping past the door, pouncing downward. With his left hand, he grabbed the rifle barrel, jerked it hard. The man inside held onto it, cried out, then released his hold on it.

Zak flung the rifle away from him like a man would throw a stick to a dog, then rose to a crouch and fired his pistol through the window at point-blank range.

Orange flame spouted from the barrel. The pistol bucked in his hand.

For one terrible moment all time stood still. The deafening roar in Zak's ears blotted out all other sounds. He seemed rooted to that spot where he crouched like a leopard, frozen there for an eternity, not knowing whether his bullet had struck the man at the window or if the next shot would come from that man's pistol and blow his own heart to a bloody pulp.

For that split second of infinity, he did not know whether he would live or die.

He just did not know.

24

The man inside the adobe cried out. Zak climbed through the open window, cocking his pistol as he cleared the sill. In the flash from his pistol, he had caught just a quick glimpse of the man; not in that instant he had fired, but a second later, when the afterimage registered on his brain.

He was taking a chance, he knew, but also knew he had the advantage. He seized the moment, shoved the man backward, swung his pistol next to the man's head and squeezed the trigger. The explosion reverberated inside the adobe. The man screamed as the concussion shattered his eardrums. Zak saw him clearly in the bright orange flame that erupted from his barrel. He smashed the butt of his pistol into the man's temple, and he dropped like a twenty-pound sash weight, stunned.

Zak pounced on him, pinned him to the littered floor. He put the muzzle of his gun square at the man's temple, waited a second, then cocked the hammer back. There was a loud click, and the man beneath him stiffened in fear.

"¿Como te llamas?" Zak asked.

"M-Me llamo Pablo Medina. ¿Quien eres tu?"

"I'm the Shadow Rider," Zak said, in Spanish. "I am the man Ben Trask wanted you to kill."

Zak heard hoofbeats and voices. He remembered that he had told Ted to come looking for him if he heard a shot. Ted had heard two shots, and Zak knew he must be wondering what had happened. The voices grew louder, and he heard Colleen's voice and Scofield's. He could not decipher what they were saying to one another. In a few moments the sound of hoofbeats separated and he figured Rivers and Scofield were flanking the adobe, perhaps covering the closed door.

"Zak?" O'Hara called out.

"In here," Zak replied. "Come on in."

A moment later the door opened and the shadow of a man filled the doorway. Ted O'Hara stood there, rifle in hand. Zak heard more hoofbeats, the creaking of leather as people dismounted outside.

"Zak?"

"Down here. I've got a prisoner," Zak said. "There should be a stove or a fireplace in here. Let's have some light."

"Right," O'Hara said.

Pablo Medina struggled to free himself, rolling from side to side, pushing upward with his torso. Zak exerted more pressure on the man's face with his arm. Medina stopped struggling.

O'Hara issued orders from the doorway.

"Rivers, bring Deets in here. Scofield, you stand guard outside. Colleen, come in and help me get a fire going."

O'Hara crashed around the room, feeling his way. Zak heard a clank and a rattle of wood that sounded like loose kindling. A moment later he heard crumpling paper. Rivers and Deets came in after tying up their horses. Colleen followed right after.

"I can't see," she said.

"Just walk toward the sound of my voice, Colleen," O'Hara said. "Be careful. There's stuff on the floor."

Then more sounds as O'Hara stuffed kindling and newspapers into the potbellied stove. He struck a match, and Zak saw the outlines of Medina's face, his black eyes staring up at him in terror.

"I do not want to die," Medina said, in English.

Colleen paused and looked down at Zak's prisoner.

"Did you shoot him?" she asked Zak.

"Help your brother," he said.

She snorted and walked toward her squatting brother and the stove.

The paper caught fire and then the wood started to burn. There was enough light now for Zak to see around the room.

"There's an awful smell in here," Colleen said. "And the place is filthy."

"Find a broom," Ted said to her. "Be careful where you step. There are human remains in here, sis."

Colleen gasped.

Zak spoke to Medina. "Are you hurt?"

"No."

"I'm going to let you up, after I take your pistol from you. If you try to run, I will shoot you dead. Do you understand?"

"Yes."

Zak slipped the pistol from Medina's holster, handed it to Rivers. Then he stood up. He reached down and helped Medina to his feet.

The fire was brighter by then, and threw large shadows on the walls of the adobe. Colleen gasped when she saw the mess inside the shack. She looked around for a broom and a shovel, while Rivers took Deets over to a corner so he would be out of the way.

O'Hara walked over to Zak, who still had a gun on Medina.

"What are you going to do with this man?" he asked.

"Probably let him go," Zak said.

"Let him go?"

"First, a few questions for Pablo here."

Medina blinked both eyes. Then he looked over at Deets, who was still wearing the black slicker and Zak's black hat, then looked again at Zak.

"Yes, that's Al Deets," Zak said to Medina. "If you had seen us ride up in daylight, you'd probably have shot him instead of me, eh, Pablo?"

"It is possible," Medina said in Spanish.

"Speak English," Zak ordered. "How long ago did Trask leave here?"

"I do not know."

Zak poked the barrel of his pistol into Medina's gut, just above the belt buckle. "Drop your gun belt," he said.

Medina unbuckled his belt, let it and the empty holster fall to the floor.

"Now, answer my question, Pablo."

Medina shrugged. "An hour, maybe two."

"He left longer ago than that. Sunset? Just after sunset?"

"Maybe."

Zak lowered his pistol and placed the barrel an inch from Medina's genitals.

Medina flinched. One of his eyes flickered as the skin over his cheekbone twitched.

"I'll blow your *juevos* clean off if you don't give me a straight answer, Pablo."

"After sunset. Maybe three hours ago."

"Zak," O'Hara said, "you know damned well how long ago Trask lit out of here. You can read tracks like I can read an army map."

Zak smiled.

Understanding flickered in Medina's eyes.

"That is true, Ted. So now I know that Pablo can lie, and he knows that I do not lie. Isn't that right, Pablo?"

"Yes. Three hours go by. I wait here."

"Would you like to catch up to Ferguson? You work for him, don't you?"

"I work for Mr. Ferguson. Yes. I would like to go to him."

"Surely, you're not going to let this man go, Zak." O'Hara said. "He'll tell Trask and Ferguson how many men we have and that my sister is with us. Trask would have us at a disadvantage."

Zak watched Pablo Medina's eyes. They pulsed like gelatinous jewels.

Zak smiled without showing his teeth. Just a flicker of his lips told of his amusement at his prisoner's reactions.

Colleen swept debris into a pile near the door. Then she leaned the broom against the wall, walked back to a place just behind the stove, pulled a shovel off the wall and carried it to the front door. There, she shoveled the debris up and walked outside. Before she left, she looked at Zak.

"I understand Spanish," she said. "I know what you threatened to do to Pablo."

"Pablo understands Spanish, too, Colleen. He knew I would do what I said I would do to him if he didn't talk."

Colleen went outside. Zak heard her toss the debris onto the ground.

He turned back to Ted O'Hara.

"I'm thinking of letting both Deets and Medina here go," he said. "We're not equipped to handle these prisoners."

"That would be a big mistake, Zak."

"If we take on any more prisoners, we'll be outnumbered," Zak said. "We're already short on guards for these two."

"Still, these men would give Trask valuable information. Information he could use against us when we meet up with him."

"I'm not worried about Trask at this point," Zak said.

"You're not?"

"No. He knows I'm on his trail. He thinks Deets is dead, probably. When Pablo here doesn't show up, he'll figure he's dead, too. That won't worry him any. That's why he left this man behind. He doesn't care, but if there was a chance Pablo could kill me, he'd have one less worry."

"So, you're just going to let these men go back to Trask and blab all they know."

"I could cut out their tongues," Zak said, just as Colleen came back inside.

She stopped, stared at Zak with a look of horror on her face.

"You wouldn't . . ." she said.

"There's probably a pair of pliers or some black-smith's snips in here," he said. "I could either cut off their tongues or jerk them out by the roots."

"You—You're a savage, Zak Cody. A cruel, heart-less savage."

"Yes'm," Zak said.

Medina shrank away from him.

"I know you're joking, Zak," O'Hara said. "But I hope you reconsider about turning these two men loose to run off to join Trask."

"I'll let you know my thinking in a while, Ted. First, I want to question Pablo here a little more. You can call Scofield back in here. Nobody's going to ride up on us tonight."

"You're sure?"

"I'm sure. What's more, we're going to spend the night here. We all need sleep. I'll post guards."

"This place is filthy," Colleen said again.

"You'll welcome the rest," Zak told her. "We'll help you clean this place out."

O'Hara walked to the door, called to Scofield, "Come on, Corporal. You're relieved."

"Yes, sir," Scofield said, and after tying his horse to the hitchrail, he entered the adobe.

"You relieve Rivers guarding the prisoner, Sco-field," Zak said. "Rivers, you help Colleen shovel out what she sweeps up."

"Yes, sir," Rivers said as Scofield walked back to relieve him.

Zak holstered his pistol after easing the hammer back down. He took Medina by the arm, led him over to the wall next to Deets.

"Sit down," he said. "You, too, Deets."

The two men sat down.

"Scofield, shoot them if they try to get up."

"Yes, sir," Scofield said.

Zak walked back to O'Hara.

"Let's go outside and talk, Ted. I'll tell you why I'm going to let these two men go tell all they know to Trask."

"I can't wait."

The two men walked out into the night. The moon was up a few degrees above the horizon and cast a soft silvery light over the adobe and the surrounding countryside. When they were out of earshot of those inside, Zak stopped. O'Hara stood next to him, waiting to hear what he had to say.

"Nice night," Zak said.

"Are you going to tell me your plans, Zak?"

"No, Ted, I'm not. But those two prisoners in there will think I am. By the time they catch up to Trask, they'll each have a different story. And each one will embellish their stories to suit themselves."

"That's taking a long dubious chance, if you ask me. You don't even have a plan, do you, Zak?"

"Oh, I have a plan all right, Ted. And you'll see signs of it as we continue on after a good night's sleep."

"Signs of it?"

"You don't need to know everything just yet. Better if you don't, in fact. You might be recaptured by Trask, you know."

"Not if you don't let those two men—"

"I'll give the orders here, Lieutenant," Zak said. "You just watch and wait."

O'Hara shook his head. He was puzzled and showed it. Zak said nothing. He looked up at the starry sky and breathed deep of the air. Rivers came to the door a few times and threw out shovels of dirt and debris from the adobe. In the distance, a coyote yipped and then a chorus of yowling canines sang their plaintive songs, ribbons of music floating on the night air.

O'Hara shivered at the sound. "Coyotes give me the willies," he said.

"Coyotes," Zak said. "Or maybe Chiricahua, sounding like coyotes."

O'Hara's eyes narrowed as Zak let a shadowy smile ripple through his lips, his dark eyes bright with moonlight.

25

Zak worked out the hours in his head.

After retrieving his hat and slicker from Deets, he ordered Scofield to bind the hands and feet of both Medina and Deets. Zak took the first two-hour watch. He found Medina's horse where the man had said it would be, led it back to the adobe and hitched it to the rail with all the others. Then he took a torch down to the road and examined the tracks left by Trask, Ferguson, and the other men in their bunch.

He figured that by the time he arrived at the adobe, Trask had been gone for at least four hours. He knew the outlaws wouldn't last the night before they'd have to stop and get some sleep. And he figured they'd sleep at least three hours, perhaps four. No more than that.

At that pace, Trask would reach the last stage stop sometime in late afternoon. Certainly while there was plenty of daylight left. Welch should be there waiting for him. If not, he'd surely be there shortly afterward. They would study O'Hara's map, plan their campaign against Cochise and the Chiricahuas that night, leave the next morning.

That was the way Zak figured it, and he knew that his calculations could not be far off.

That gave him plenty of time to do what had to be done.

His own campaign against Trask, Ferguson, Welch, and their war party would begin early in the morning. And by the time he turned Deets and Medina loose, they'd have a long ride to rendezvous with Trask.

He was betting they'd never make it. Trask would be long gone by the time Deets and Medina reached that last adobe shack.

Zak rode a wide circle in the moonlight, picking his way with care, noting the landmarks, crossing and recrossing the road. He marked the moon's progress as it rose in the sky and painted the edges of cactus a dull pewter, daubed silver into wet muddy low spots, and glazed the rocks with a misty gray-black patina that made them shift shapes as he passed. It was cool, but not so much that he'd have to don his light jacket, tucked away in a saddlebag. He chewed on dry hardtack and strips of jerked beef, washed the food down with water from his canteen.

He loved the far lonely places, and as he rode, he felt grateful to the Great Spirit for giving him this peaceful night under a canopy of bright stars, whose clusters seemed at times like the lights of distant cities. The Milky Way, the fabled Star Path of the Lakota and the Cheyenne, blazed a brilliant trail across the heavens, more stars than the sands on all the shores of the world.

When he rode back to the adobe at the end of two hours, he felt rich and alive, his plans set in his mind. And he felt that great peace upon him that he always felt when he was outdoors, all alone, contemplating the vastness of the universe, the complexity of all life and all things.

Hugo Rivers was awake and waiting for him when Zak rode up to the hitchrail and dismounted.

"I hereby relieve you, sir," Rivers said in a soft whisper. "Everybody's asleep. Any orders?"

"Just ride a wide circle, no more than a hundred yards from the shack at any time. Figure two hours, then Scofield will take the next watch."

"Yes sir. And, sir?"

"What is it, Rivers?"

"I believe Miss O'Hara is awake. She was mighty restless and I saw her put more wood on the fire a few minutes ago."

"Why are you telling me this, Private?"

"She, ah . . . she spoke to me, sir. Told me to tell you to wake her if she was asleep when you came in. She wants to talk to you, I think."

"Very good, Rivers. On your way, now."

Rivers mounted up and rode off into the night.

Zak waited until he was well gone and then started walking toward the adobe. Before he got to the door, Colleen stepped out. She had a shawl wrapped around her shoulders, a bandanna covering her hair.

"Take a short walk?" she said. "Before you turn in?"

"Sure, Colleen," he said, offering her his arm.

She slipped her arm through his and they walked out on the plain.

"You smell nice," he said.

"I keep lilac water with me. To freshen up."

"Yes, you smell of lilacs."

"It's nice of you to notice."

"Can't sleep, Colleen?"

"Oh, I lay down. Dozed. But . . ."

"But what?"

She stopped, and so did he.

"I—I keep thinking about you," she said. "I hate myself for judging you. For accusing you of things."

"It's all right."

"No it isn't," she said. "You're such a mystery to me. I—I've never met a man like you, Zak. You're—You're . . . oh, I don't know, a kind of enigma, a puzzle I can't quite figure out."

"Is it necessary to figure everybody out?"

"Not everybody, silly, just you. And, yes, I think it's necessary. I was attracted to you the first moment I saw you. I felt . . . something. I don't know what it was, but I was drawn to you. Like a moth to a flame."

"You were at Fort Bowie. Plenty of male companionship available."

She sighed.

He smelled her faint perfume, and it added a pleasing dimension to the night. She looked lovely in the moonlight, even shrouded up as she was. She could be feminine wearing a burlap sack for a dress, he thought, a ragweed crown for a hat.

"Average men," she said, "with average thoughts. And, by average thoughts, I mean—"

"I know what you mean, Colleen."

"See? You do know what I mean. The men I met at Fort Bowie were mostly obtuse. Do you know the meaning of that word?"

"Yes. You had no feelings for them. They were

just faces and forms. Like blocks of wood, pieces of lumber."

"Straw men, more accurately."

They both laughed.

She touched his arm and they gazed at each other. He felt a longing in her that matched his own. Perhaps it was the night and the quiet, but he felt drawn to her. She was a puzzle herself, he thought. She had strong opinions and she had a tongue as sharp as any fishwife's, but she was also gentle and sweet and very alluring.

"Colleen," he said, catching his senses up from his romantic reverie, "this . . . this attraction, or whatever you want to call it, whatever it is, can't go anywhere. You and I come from two different worlds. You're a schoolteacher, refined, educated, genteel, even. I'm a rough man used to rough living. That bark on me is going to stay on me until I die."

"Don't talk like that, Zak. You're much more than that. You—You would fit in anywhere. You could be an important man. With the right woman. I sense that about you."

"You would have me change to suit you, your idea of me," he said, and knew it was true.

"No, I didn't mean it that way, Zak. I just mean, well, you won't always be doing what you're doing. Chasing bad men. Shooting and killing. There's a better side to you. I know there is."

"I am what I am, Colleen."

"You're stubborn, too," she said.

"Maybe. But I think you may be missing the point. I've chosen this life I lead. I was given life and I cherish it. But one thing I don't want is to fit into somebody else's mold. I would be tempted, with a beautiful woman like you, but I know it would never work. If I was transplanted to a city and a house with a fence around it, little children at my feet, I'd always be looking over the fence, the horizon, and wishing I were back on the Great Plains, hunting buffalo, running with the Lakota, sitting at a Cheyenne campfire, catching trout high in the Rocky Mountains. I'm wild, Colleen, as wild as they come, and I could never settle in one place and assume a respectability I never had, or ever wanted."

"You sound so sure of yourself, Zak. But it seems to me that you are fighting with yourself, deep inside, fighting against who you are, the life you've chosen for yourself."

"No, Colleen. I'm happy with who I am and what I do. You must understand that."

She sighed again.

"I don't think I ever could," she said. "Not after knowing you as I have, even for so brief a time."

"Just live in the moment, Colleen. Don't try and look into the future. All the life we have is just this one single moment. And this moment is forever. That's something I learned from the Lakota. Life is a journey and it's a circle. We follow our paths and when we come to the end it's another beginning."

"I don't know if I understand you," she said.

"No matter. Someday you'll remember what I said tonight and it might even make sense."

"I don't want to quarrel with you anymore."

"Then we won't. This journey we're on now is strange for you. It's as if we're in a different world, both of us, and the rules of civilization and decency have been left by the wayside. We'll finish the journey, and we will have learned something, you and I. But after that, we must say good-bye to each other. You will go your way, and I will go mine."

"You make it sound so final."

"We have the moment," he said. "This moment."

He took her in his arms and kissed her. It was a long, lingering kiss, and she pressed against him until he could feel her warmth, the pulse of her being. He felt dizzy with rapture, and the scent of lilacs wafted to his nostrils and made him feel giddy and aroused.

"Oh," she said, when they broke the kiss. "Oh, my. That—That was wonderful."

"Can you sleep now, Colleen?"

"I—I don't know. Maybe. I wish there was more, though."

"Just this moment, Colleen. No other."

They walked back together, arm in arm. He felt an odd sense of contentment, but he knew that nothing had been resolved. Perhaps nothing ever would be.

But they had had that moment, and for now it was enough for him.

He slept, waking only when the watch changed, and then fell back asleep, dreaming of lilac fields and wild horses, the shining mountains, silver streams that sang as they coursed through steep rocky canyons, and soft snow on the high peaks, a woman dressed in a bearskin and children rolling hoops and chasing after them with sticks that turned into wriggling snakes.

Just before dawn he heard a commotion, and a

man groaned in pain. He sat up and reached for his pistol.

"Get the bastard," Rivers shouted, and Zak saw a dark shape looming over him. One of the prisoners had freed himself and disarmed Rivers.

Colleen screamed in terror.

O'Hara struggled to his feet and was knocked down.

The man, carrying a rifle, hurtled straight toward Zak. The rifle was pointed at him.

He heard the lever work and a shell slide into the firing chamber, the hammer lock in place on full cock.

The horses outside whinnied, and his hand flew to the butt of his pistol.

He wondered if he would have time. He wondered, in that split second of eternity, if he would ever have time to keep his own death at bay.

His arm felt numb from sleeping on it and his fingers were rubbery and nearly lifeless.

Time. Was there enough time to draw and shoot?

All he could do was try.

That was all any man could do.

Time be damned.

26

Zak raised his pistol just far enough to fire at Pablo Medina. He hoped the man would run into his bullet. A moment after pulling the trigger, he ducked and rolled to one side. He heard the explosion from the rifle, so close the sound was deafening. The bullet ripped into his bedroll and plowed a furrow in the dirt floor.

Medina grunted as Zak's pistol bullet smashed into his lower abdomen. He pitched forward, the rifle falling from his hands, as the bullet crushed veins and capillaries, mashed flesh into pulp and nicked his spine before blowing a fist-sized hole in his back.

He cried out in pain, and hit the floor screaming at the top of his lungs.

He kept screaming as Zak raised up, cocked his pistol again and took aim at Medina's head, ready to fire from a distance of three feet.

"Kill him," Rivers shouted.

Scofield drew his pistol, crouched a few feet away from the fallen man.

Colleen put her hands to her ears, shrank against the wall as if trying to escape the hideous screams, the gushing blood that pooled on both sides of Medina.

Zak held his fire, his gaze fixed on Medina, who kept screaming, his back arched as if he were gripped in the vise of a seizure.

Hoofbeats pounded on the ground outside, and a moment later Ted O'Hara burst through the door, slamming it back against the wall. He crouched low, a rifle in his hands, his head moving from side to side.

"What in hell's going on in here?" he said.

"Get out of the doorway, Ted," Zak said. "Medina tried to escape."

O'Hara saw the man on the floor, then looked toward his sister, who was still pinned against the wall, a small fist in her mouth.

He sidled to one side, still in a crouch. He seemed like a coiled spring, ready to pounce.

Medina continued to scream.

"Do something, Zak," Colleen said, taking her fist from her mouth.

"Yeah," Scofield said, "put that poor bastard out of his misery, will you, Colonel?"

Zak considered that suggestion. It would seem the humane thing to do. Under the circumstances. Blood poured out of Medina's back wound, little spurts ejecting with every beat of his heart. The screaming wasn't helping any, either. Pump, bleed, pump, he thought.

He leaned over and clamped a hand over Medina's mouth, shutting off his scream.

"*Callate*," he said.

Medina swallowed his scream, but sweat broke out on his forehead, and the muscles in his face expanded and contracted with the pain he felt all through his body. Zak drew his hand away.

"*Ayudame, por favor. Me duele mucho.*" Help me, please. I am hurting very much. There was an agonized pleading in Medina's voice.

Zak snapped his fingers, looked back at Rivers.

"Bring me a small piece of kindling wood," he said. "Quick."

Rivers, paralyzed until that moment, jumped toward the stove, reached down and picked up a small sliver of wood. He took it to Zak, handed it to him.

Zak stuck the wood inside Medina's mouth.

"Bite on it," he said, in Spanish.

Medina bit down and tears streamed from his eyes.

"Thank God," breathed Colleen.

O'Hara walked over to Zak, stood over Medina, then looked at Rivers.

"How did this man get loose, Private?" he asked.

"Sir, I don't know. He—He untied the ropes around his ankles and managed to free his hands. He did it real quiet. I didn't know he was loose. He jumped me, grabbed the rifle out of my hands."

"You weren't watching him close enough, Rivers."

"No, sir."

Rivers retreated to the back of the adobe shack. Zak got to his feet.

"Can we do anything for him, Zak?" O'Hara asked.

"He's losing blood fast. My bullet must have cut an artery. Not all of the blood is coming out his back."

"He's bleeding to death, then."

"It looks that way."

O'Hara turned his head. He could not look at the dying man. Colleen remained cowering against the wall, her gaze fixed on Zak. Scofield's face was a mask of hatred and contempt as he gazed down at Medina.

Zak eased the hammer down on his pistol but didn't put it back in its holster.

"I think this man's paralyzed," he said. "Bullet probably sheared off part of his backbone."

"He's not moving much, with all that pain," O'Hara said.

Morning light began to seep in through the windows. Medina groaned, but he didn't spit out the stick and scream. Zak felt pity for the man. At the same time, he thought of how often men made mistakes in judgment that cost them their lives, or crippled them for life. Medina was probably bleeding to death, but his last minutes on earth would be agonizing. The man should have known better. What caused someone like him to think he could get away like that? Loyalty to Ferguson, or to Trask? Or was he like some cornered animal, so hungry for freedom that he would risk his life to escape? Well, Medina had lost. The risk had been too great.

Zak saw the light spreading across the landscape, turning the rocks to rust, casting shadows to the west, pulling all the cool from the earth. In the distance he heard the call of a quail, and he saw a pair of doves fly across the barren land, twisting in the air like dancers with wings.

"Scofield, you and Rivers start carrying wood outside. Everything that will burn—tables, chairs, firewood. Pile them up nearby at the highest point of the land. Break the furniture up if you have to. Build me a tall pyramid." Zak turned to Colleen. "If you have any female things to do, Colleen, best get to it. We're leaving."

"What about Pablo there?" she asked.

"What about him?"

"Are you just going to leave him lying there in agony?"

"There's nothing I can do for him," Zak said.

"So, you're just going to watch him die. In agony."

"I'm not going to watch him die."

"But he's going to die," she said.

"Yes."

"Oh, you . . ." She flounced out of the adobe, into the dawn. He heard her rummaging through her saddlebags at the hitchrail. There was a rustle of paper, the ruffle and flap of cloth, footsteps on the hard cool ground.

Medina retched and spat the stick onto the dirt floor. Blood bubbled up out of the hole in his back.

"We better move him," O'Hara said.

"Grab an arm," Zak said.

The two men pulled Medina away from the vomit. Zak turned him over so he lay on his back. His face was wet with tears, his eyes glistening like ebony agates.

"I do not feel my legs," Medina said, in English.

"Do you feel pain?" Zak asked.

"No more." This, in Spanish.

"You're paralyzed, Pablo," Zak said. "If you know any prayers, say them."

"There is no priest."

"No. There's just you and God."

Medina began to weep, without shame. Zak and

O'Hara looked at each other. O'Hara shook his head. Zak nodded.

"You just goin' to leave me back here?" Deets said from the rear of the room.

"Take him outside, Ted," Zak said. "I'll be out soon. Have Rivers and Scofield knock down those hitchrails and stack them with the other wood. There should be a maul or a hammer in here somewhere, a pry bar, maybe."

"Will do," O'Hara said. He walked to the back of the adobe and looked around for something to tear down the hitchrails. He found an old sledgehammer, picked it up. Then he walked over to Deets, untied the rope around his ankles and stood him up.

"You run, Deets," O'Hara said, "I'll shoot you down."

Deets growled low in his throat but said no words.

The two men walked outside.

Zak heard voices as O'Hara gave commands and Scofield answered him. Rivers came in and carried out a table. He came back for a chair.

"You want us to tear apart these bunk beds?" he asked Zak.

"Everything that will burn, Hugh."

"First time you've called me by my first name," Rivers said. "It's Hugo, not Hugh."

"All right, Hugo. What's in a name, anyway?"

"Huh?"

"Never mind," Zak said.

Rivers was outside for some moments. Zak heard Scofield lay into the hitchrails with the sledge. Apparently Rivers spelled him, because Scofield entered the adobe to carry out another chair, a shelf board, and a wooden box.

"Pile's gettin' pretty big," he said to Zak, who still stood over Medina.

"Keep stacking it up, Scofield."

"Yes, sir."

Medina stopped crying. He put a hand to his face and rubbed his cheeks.

"There is pain now," he said, his voice a whispery rasp. This was in Spanish, and Zak spoke to him in Spanish.

"Did you pray, Pablo?"

"Yes. I will die soon, maybe."

"Maybe."

"You do not shoot me? To make it quick?"

"No. You're going to have to die on your own, Pablo."

"I want to die now. Give me a gun."

"You are Catholic, Pablo?"

"Yes."

"Is it not a mortal sin for a man to take his own life?"

"I think so, yes. But the pain . . . it is so much now."

"If there is no priest, to whom do you confess, Pablo?"

"Maybe to God. Maybe to you."

"Better God than me."

"Maybe," he said. "I will confess."

"Ask to be forgiven for your sins," Zak said.

"Yes, I will do that."

"The dying will be your penance."

"What?" The man's eyes glittered behind the tears.

"Does not the priest give you penance? Prayers to say, good deeds to do?"

"Yes, the priest does that. He says to say the Hail Marys, the Our Fathers. So many for so many sins."

"Say those, then. It will take your mind off the pain, perhaps."

Medina closed his eyes. Zak could see his lips quivering, opening slightly and closing again, as if he was murmuring the prayers or confessing. Then he heard the word *peccata* and realized that Pablo was speaking in Latin, that ancient, dead language that was never spoken until the Catholic priests took up the practice.

A Jesuit had told Zak about Latin, how it was always only a written language until the priests spoke the Mass in that tongue. The priest had studied Latin and spoken it for two years before he took his vows. The language was precise, highly inflected, and suited the Church's purposes. Zak believed that the Church made the language sacred and holy to separate themselves from ordinary people, add mystery to their canons. And now Pablo Medina was talking to his God in the Latin. Somehow, it seemed fitting. Zak saw blood streaming from underneath him and the color seemed to drain from his face. His lips paled and stopped moving.

"Good-bye, Pablo," Zak said, in Spanish. "Go with God."

Medina crossed himself with pathetically slow movements and then all the strength seemed to leave him. His arm flopped down and lay across his chest.

But then, when Zak thought he was gone, Medina gasped and a shiver coursed through his torso. He opened his eyes wide and looked up as if seeing a phantasm. He choked, gasped, then let out a last breath. His mouth opened, but he did not breathe anymore.

"*Vaya con Dios*," Zak said again, and turned away.

He walked outside and drew a deep breath. The air was clean and cool. The desert scents wafted to his nostrils and filled him with an odd warmth.

Colleen walked up from where she had been, beyond the road. She was carrying a small towel, a canteen, a bottle of lilac water, and a bundle of sanitaries.

"Can you make us some coffee before we go, Colleen?" Zak asked.

"Yes. The stove is hot, we've water and a pot. Do you have a cup?"

"In my saddlebags."

O'Hara and Deets were up above them on the slight ridge, watching the soldiers break the legs off tables and chairs, pile them atop a pyramid of wood.

"Is Pablo . . ." Colleen's eyes bore into Zak's, searched his face.

"He's gone, Colleen."

"Thank God," she said.

"God had nothing to do with it," he said, a trace of bitterness in his tone.

She started to retort, but saw the look on Zak's face and swept past him, disappeared inside the adobe. Another pair of doves whistled past, and the thin high clouds glistened white and peach in the morning sun. Zak looked to the east, to the land of the Chiricahua, and thought of Cochise.

Now there, he thought, was a man to ride the river with.

And they both had one more river to cross.

— 27 —

Zak carried a flaming faggot out to the pile of wood.

"After this gets going," he said to Rivers and Scofield, "cut down all the cactus, cholla, yucca, and whatever else is green and throw it on the blaze and then we'll get the hell out of here."

He threw the chunk of blazing kindling into the pile of wood, near the bottom of the pyramid, and watched as the flames licked at the fuel. O'Hara, Colleen, and Deets stood by, drinking their coffees, watching the wood catch fire.

"Mind telling me what this is all about, Zak?" O'Hara asked.

"I hope it'll be a signal fire, Ted."

"A signal fire? For whom, if I may ask?"

"For Cochise."

"Cochise? Did I hear you right?"

Ted almost choked on his coffee. Colleen, too, looked surprised. Deets stood there with a dumb look on his face. He'd stopped bleeding and Zak had untied the rope around his wrists. He, too, was drinking coffee. Another of Zak's acts of kindness toward his prisoner.

"You heard me, Ted. We're going to need Cochise."

"What will he make of the fire?"

"I expect one of his scouts will see the smoke when it starts rising. Cochise will want to know what it's about."

"That seems like a pretty long shot to me," O'Hara said.

The first plumes of smoke began to lift off the pyre. They were thin at that point, but as Scofield and Rivers threw green plants on the top, the smoke spread out and thickened. Soon, the fire was blazing and smoke spiraled up to the sky, spreading as the zephyrs caught it.

"Now, go inside the adobe and bring those bunk mattresses out," Zak told the soldiers. "Toss them on the fire and then mount up."

"Yes, sir," Rivers and Scofield chorused.

Zak finished his coffee while the soldiers piled on the damp mattresses. The feathers crackled and fumed, adding bulk to the rising smoke. A tower of black and gray smoke above the blaze, smoke that could be seen for miles around.

He put his cup back in his saddlebags. "Mount up," he ordered.

Colleen and Ted tossed the rest of their coffee onto the ground. In moments they were mounted, along with Rivers, Scofield, and Deets.

"Deets, you can light a shuck," Zak told his prisoner.

"Huh?"

"Go on. Ride up that road and tell Trask anything you want."

"You mean you're just turnin' me loose? I can go?"

"Nobody's going to shoot you in the back, Deets. Go on. I have no further interest in you."

For a moment Deets appeared unsure of himself. He looked at O'Hara, who gave no indication of approval or disapproval. He looked at Rivers and Scofield. Their faces were impassive.

Then he clucked to his horse and turned him toward the road.

He stopped, turned back to look at Zak.

"You really going to sic Cochise on us, Mr. Cody?"

"You bet your boots I am, Deets."

Zak smiled, but there was no warmth in it. It was the kind of smile that would curdle milk, or the blood in a man's veins. Deets turned and rode off slowly toward the road. Everyone around the fire watched him go.

"That was a big mistake, Zak," O'Hara said. "You'll lose the element of surprise."

"I want Trask to know his days are numbered," Zak said.

"You might be numbering our days," O'Hara said.

Zak ticked spurs into Nox's flanks. He rode off to the east, the others following. He could still smell the smoke, and he knew the fire would burn long enough to serve its purpose.

He took an angle, away from the road, straight into the heart of Chiricahua country. He had cleaned his pistol, oiled it, reloaded it with six brass cartridges. His rifle, too, was loaded and ready. He knew that because of his wound, Deets could not travel fast. By the time Deets reached that last old stage station, Zak figured he would be smoking the pipe with Cochise. And, maybe, Jeffords would be there, too. The more the merrier.

Quail piped and he saw a coyote slink toward the shack they had just left, its nose to the ground, its tail drooping. The coyote was a gray shadow on the landscape, a ghost left over from the dark night and the flash flood. A survivor, slat-ribbed, lean, scavenging for scraps, leftovers, and maybe a dead man lying inside the adobe, his scent already rising, like the smoke from the fire, to alert the buzzards that were already circling in the sky.

Cochise would see them, too.

Everything was perfect, Zak thought. Just as he had planned.

28

Lieutenant John Welch needed only one glance at the map Ben Trask had spread out on the table.

"That's Lieutenant O'Hara's map, all right," he said. "That's his writing on it."

Trask smiled with satisfaction. He jabbed a finger down on one of the X's O'Hara had drawn.

"And that's where we'll find Cochise and his whole damned tribe. Think you can find it, Lieutenant?"

"You're damned right I can find it. He's got compass directions, everything we need. I'm ready to go if you are. Looks to be about a two-day ride. Three at most."

"Let's do it," Trask said.

They walked out of the adobe together. Welch's troops were mounted, and Ferguson stood by on horseback with his men and Trask's. He held the reins of Trask's horse. Trask took them and climbed into the saddle.

Ferguson was looking off toward the west, his eyes squinted to narrow slits.

Trask adjusted his boots in the stirrups, looked off in the same direction that Ferguson was gazing.

"What are you looking at?" he asked.

"Smoke," Ferguson said. "Way off."

"I wonder what it means," Trask said.

"I have no idea," Ferguson replied.

Welch barked the orders and his troops moved out in a column of twos. There was no guidon, and all of the troops, including Welch, wore civilian clothes. The only clues that the men were in the army were their rifles and their boots. Otherwise, they looked like any group of ordinary townfolk.

"Did you see all that smoke in the sky over to the west of us, Trask?" Welch said after a few minutes.

"Yeah, I saw it."

"What do you make of it?"

"Something caught fire."

"Looks to be somewhere near the old stage road."

"Could be."

"It doesn't worry you?"

"Why should it? It's miles away. Hell, I've seen smoke all my life. There's always somebody burnin' something, leaves, trash, you name it."

"Not likely anybody's burning leaves in this country," Welch said.

"I've seen 'em burn dead horses and dead cattle, too," Trask said.

"Up north, you see smoke like that, you think one thing. I'm talking about Colorado, Montana, the Dakotas."

"Yeah. Injuns."

"That's right," Welch said.

"So, did you ever see Apaches send smoke signals?" Trask asked.

"No, but I've only been here about a year."

"Don't worry about it, then. I ain't."

Welch looked at him.

Trask had the bark on him, all right. But the smoke gave Welch an uneasy feeling. He looked around at the wide sky, the blueness of it so pretty it could make a man's eyes well up, and the little puffs of clouds. As pretty a day as he'd ever seen.

But there shouldn't have been smoke to smudge that pretty blue sky.

29

They rode past the sunset and through the long night, Zak in the lead. Scofield slept in the saddle, with Rivers making sure he didn't fall from his horse. Ted let his sister sleep as she rode, and he kept close, ready to catch her if she fell. Rivers and Scofield took turns, but neither truly slept. They just kept going.

Zak stopped every four hours so everyone could walk around and stretch. Toward morning he halted to build a fire, make coffee. The coffee kept them going, and when dawn broke they were on horseback once again, riding straight into the rising, blinding sun.

Near noon Zak took out his silver dollar and began flashing it like a signal mirror. An hour later he got an answer. Three flashes. He tipped the dollar and sent back three flashes. A single flash answered him, which he also acknowledged.

They all saw the flashes.

"You know who that is, Zak?" O'Hara asked.

"I think so. Wait."

Zak flashed the coin again. There were answering flashes.

He put the silver dollar back in his pocket.

"Well?" O'Hara said.

"That was Anillo. 'Ring,' in English. He told me a place to meet. Cochise will be there."

"How far? How long?" The news seemed to give O'Hara new energy. He was as bright-eyed as a recruit after his first shave.

"One hour. At an Apache well I know. They know I'm coming with you, your sister, and two bluecoat soldiers."

O'Hara laughed. "I'm glad I made friends with Cochise."

"Yes. He will listen to us. Now, do you know where Trask and Welch might be going?"

"I know exactly where they're going, if they follow the map I marked for Trask. I think Cochise will know it, too. Maybe you, too, know it."

"Tell me about it, Ted."

"I picked this place because of a story an old Apache told me when we passed by it. It is an open area with a narrow entrance. The plain is surrounded by low hills. The chief at the time, a man named Lobo, lured the soldiers there. He made it look like a camp. The soldiers meant to wipe out the Apaches. The Apaches hid behind the little hills, and after the soldiers entered the box canyon, the Chiricahua sealed it off with many braves. When the soldiers started shooting at the lodges, the Apaches rose up all around and fired arrows down at the soldiers. The soldiers who tried to ride back out were met by men with lances and bows and were cut down. I didn't know whether to believe the old man, but I can't forget that place. When Trask asked me where he could find Cochise and his gold, that's the spot I marked on the map."

"That was smart of you, Ted."

"Do you know the place?"

"I do. The Apaches call it the Canyon of Blood."

"Yes, that's it."

"Perfect," Zak said.

An hour later there arose a hush over the land. O'Hara felt it and glanced around, an apprehensive look on his face.

Rivers and Scofield went quiet, too, and began scanning the land all around them.

"It's so quiet," Colleen said. "All of a sudden."

Then she let out a cry as a nearly naked man emerged out of the dust and rock ahead of her, his face painted for war, a rifle in his hands, a pistol hanging from his waist.

"That would be Anillo," Zak said. He raised his right hand in greeting.

"He—He nearly scared me to death," Colleen said in a breathy whisper.

Anillo held up his hand, then turned and ran at a lope up a slight rise.

Zak looked at the sky.

It was not yet noon. The place where Trask was headed, Blood Canyon, was no more than a few hours from where they now were. Time to get there, maybe, before Trask arrived, and set the trap for him, a trap that O'Hara had practically guaranteed.

Time enough for Trask to experience what Zak called an Apache sunset.

As they topped the hill, O'Hara, Colleen, Scofield, and Rivers all gasped at the sight.

There were the Chiricahuas, all mounted on their

ponics, their faces daubed in bright colors, the colors of war.

And greeting Zak with open arms was a most impressive man, the fiercest one of them all.

Cochise.

30

They sat in a circle, on blankets laid down by the Chiricahua. Cochise puffed on the pipe, blew the smoke to the four directions, passed it to Tesoro, who passed it to his son, Anillo. The pipe was passed to O'Hara, then to Scofield, Rivers, and finally to Cody.

Zak presented Pablo Medina's rifle and pistol to Cochise, who took them, hefted them, and grinned in appreciation. Next, Zak gave a rifle and pistol to Anillo, items that had once belonged to Al Deets. He handed them pistol and rifle cartridges. The conversation was in Spanish.

"It is good to see Red Hair again," Cochise said to O'Hara.

"It is my honor to be with the great Cochise," Ted said.

"And, my brother, Shadow Rider, it is good that you are here."

"We come, Cochise, to ask you to help us stop a war with the white men. We wish to go to the Canyon of Blood."

"We will fight there?" Cochise said.

"Yes."

"Who do we fight?"

"We will take the rifles and pistols from many white men. Red Hair will arrest these men and return them to Fort Bowie, where they will stand trial."

"You do not want us to kill these white men?"

"I will give you one white man. You will take this man to an Apache sundown."

"Ah, that is good, Shadow Rider."

"Let us do this now, Cochise. We must be at the Canyon of Blood before the white men come. We must give them a surprise. I do not want blood to be spilled."

"You talk of war without blood, Shadow Rider."

"That is what I want. If we do this, the Chiricahua can live in peace on their own lands."

When the ceremonies were over, Zak rode with O'Hara and Cochise, while the warriors rode single file ahead of them. In the rear, Colleen was flanked by Rivers and Scofield.

They reached the small entrance to the canyon by mid-afternoon.

"This is the place," O'Hara said. "It appears to be deserted."

"Look off to the south," Zak said. "Toward Fort Bowie."

O'Hara shaded his eyes and stared at the land for several seconds.

"I don't see anything," he said. "Just empty land. Not even a bird."

"Just above the land, Ted. It's faint, but it's there."

Cochise was looking in the same direction.

O'Hara stiffened. "I see it," he said. "Is that dust?"

"That's dust. Men are riding this way, and they're in a hurry."

The dust was a faint scrim just above the horizon. The way the sun caught it, the particles shimmered a reddish color, turning a tawny yellow, then back to rose.

"The dust is far," Cochise said.

"Do you remember the battle here, Cochise?" Zak asked the Chiricahua chief. "Do you remember the story?"

"I remember. We will do as my fathers did."

Cochise deployed his braves behind the small hills. Anillo and a small band flanked the entrance to the shallow canyon, covering themselves with dirt and lying flat among the desert plants.

"Put Colleen behind that little hill at the farthest end, Ted," Zak said, "and tell her to stay put. You and I, Scofield and Rivers, will be the gate that closes on Trask and his bunch once they enter the canyon."

"I don't see—"

Zak pointed to a series of small mounds about fifty yards from the entrance. "We'll leave our horses with Colleen and walk there, become like the Apaches.

"You mean lie down in the dirt."

"That's what I mean," Zak said.

In less than fifteen minutes there wasn't an Apache to be seen. Zak and O'Hara, along with Rivers and Scofield, lay behind the mounds, hats off, concealed by bushes and cactus.

The dust cloud in the sky grew larger.

Zak put his ear to the ground. He could hear the pounding hoofbeats. He knew that the Chiricahua were all doing the same. The Apaches would be able to gauge the distance, and they would be ready.

So would he.

In the stillness, a quail piped a warning as the riders approached. Zak saw them and his heart began to pound in his chest. He looked at Ted and put a finger to his lips. Ted nodded.

Trask, Ferguson, and Welch were at the head of the column. Trask had a map in his hands, while Welch studied a compass.

"That's the place," Trask said, his voice loud enough to carry to where Zak waited. Cochise knew what to do. If it worked, it would all be over in a matter of minutes. And no blood would be spilled.

Everything, though, had to work just right.

Zak watched as Trask galloped into the canyon. The riders behind him all filed in, disappeared from Zak's view.

"Now," he said, and got to his feet. O'Hara, Rivers, and Scofield all leaped to their feet and followed Zak as he ran toward the entrance. Anillo and six braves appeared like magic out of nowhere, and close by, Tesoro and his men sprouted out of the ground.

At the same time, as Zak and his group joined up with Tesoro and Anillo, Apaches with rifles appeared on the tops of the small hills, their rifles aimed at the outlaws and soldiers. Trask reined in, and all of the men halted their horses. For a long moment they all seemed to be frozen. They looked like statues or figures in a painting.

Zak strode into the silent arena.

"Throw down your weapons," he said. "You are surrounded. If you don't, the Apaches will kill every one of you, to a man."

His voice seemed to echo as it traveled from one end of the canyon to the other.

"Do it now, Trask," Zak shouted, "or I'll order Cochise and his men to blow you all out of your saddles."

Trask turned to Welch and Ferguson. Zak couldn't hear him, but knew he was talking it over.

"*Now,*" Zak shouted.

The Apaches on the hills leaned toward the men below, rifles at their shoulders. Trask looked at both ends of the canyon and saw the Apaches, O'Hara, Scofield and Rivers.

"Hands up," Zak ordered, and a dozen Spencers fell to the ground. Hands flew up into the air. More rifles clattered to the ground. The last to surrender was Trask, but the Apaches had him cold, and he knew it.

Zak motioned to Anillo and Tesoro to follow him. O'Hara, Rivers, and Scofield trotted to catch up to him.

Apaches streamed down from the hillocks into the bloodless arena.

"You bastard," Trask said when Zak walked up to him.

"Get off your horse, Trask."

In seconds all of the men were surrounded by Apaches. O'Hara and the two soldiers under his command began to take their pistols.

Trask dismounted. "What are you going to do with us?" he asked Zak.

"Some of the Apaches are going to escort Lieutenant O'Hara and his prisoners back to Fort Bowie. You're staying here, with Cochise. You came after the gold, didn't you?"

Trask was speechless.

Some Apaches brought horses, and many began to mount their ponies. Others gathered up the rifles and pistols, exclaiming their pleasure at the trophies that had fallen into their hands.

Colleen rode in, leading their horses. Her eyes were wide with wonder. She sat there, looking down at Zak.

Zak grabbed Trask by the collar and took him over to Cochise.

"You're going to experience an Apache sundown, Trask," he said. "Think of it as my hole card. What you draw next is going to bust your flush."

"Huh?" Trask said. "What's an Apache sundown?"

"You don't know what an Apache sundown is, Trask? That's when a Chiricahua stakes you out on an anthill early in the morning, pours sugar water all over your buck naked body, daubs it in your nose and eyes and ears, in your mouth. Ants go crazy over anything sweet. They'll swarm all over you and start eating you from the inside out. You'll scream until sundown, if you last that long, and beg for an Apache war club to dash your brains to strawberry jam. After sundown you can't scream any more and your light goes out, permanent. It's sundown for you on this life, and old Sol is never going to rise on you again, because by morning the critters will eat you down to bones, and what the coyotes and buzzards miss, the worms will take care of, over time. It's better than you deserve, Trask, and maybe Hell won't be so bad at first."

"You bastard," Trask said as the Apaches led him away.

O'Hara let out a breath.

"Well, Zak," he said, "you pulled it off. I didn't think it was possible, but . . ."

"We'll see to it that these men and Willoughby get a court-martial."

"I didn't see Deets among these men," O'Hara said.

Zak laughed.

"We'll probably find him waiting at that last line shack. He might as well be punished with the rest of them."

Colleen frowned.

"Will you be around to testify?" she said.

"No, I won't be there, Colleen. As soon as I deliver these men to Fort Bowie, I'll be riding on. The judge can read my report in court."

"Just like that? You're riding on?"

"Yes. I'll say good-bye, first, of course."

"It's always good-bye with you, isn't it, Zak?"

Her eyes were misting and there was a catch in her throat. He hated to break her heart, but he could never live in her world.

He didn't answer. He didn't have to.

Yes, with him, he thought, it was always good-bye.

But this one would be the hardest good-bye of them all.